Free Falling

KIRSTY MOSELEY

ISBN -10: 1484079795
ISBN-13: 978 1484079799

Acknowledgements

The gorgeous cover for this book was made by Hilda at Dalliance Designs. Hilda, thank you so much for making it even more beautiful than I could have even dared hope for. You're amazing. Love hearts in eyes. xx

Dedication

This one is for my dad. He'll probably never read this book because it isn't the type of thing he likes (not enough serial killers in it for him) but that doesn't matter. I just wanted to say thank you for being the man that you are, and for making me the girl that I am. Yes, I am like you, everyone says it, but so what? You're pretty freaking awesome so I'm secretly proud that I have some of your traits! I read somewhere once that a dad is a girl's first love. I couldn't agree more.

Forever, a daddy's girl. x

chapter one

I heard the alarm beep behind me but it quickly cancelled so I didn't bother to open my eyes. I was just drifting back into blissful sleep again when I became aware of someone singing quietly in my ear, and fingers trailing up and down my side, tickling my skin. I couldn't help the goofy grin that stretched across my face.

"...to you. Happy birthday, dear Maisie. Happy birthday," a soft kiss was planted on the side of my neck making me draw in a ragged breath, "to you."

I opened my eyes and half rolled over to see Luke lying against my back. His gorgeous face was merely inches away, and his big brown eyes were locked onto mine. His dark brown hair was messy and sticking out at all angles, but it suited him like that, it made him look a little rough and ready. He had a five o'clock shadow across his strong jaw and a big smile on his face that matched my own.

"Hip hip," he mumbled, his lips almost touching mine.

"Hooray?" I asked, giggling.

He laughed too and finally pressed his soft lips to mine. I smiled against his mouth and wrapped my arm around his neck, pulling him closer to me as he sucked my bottom lip into his mouth, nibbling on it gently. I opened my mouth, praying I didn't have morning breath, but knowing Luke he wouldn't even care if I did.

I lost myself in the bliss of Luke's kissing, silently wondering, as I had done hundreds of times, just what it was that he saw in me. Out of all the girls he could have chosen, he chose me, and I'd never understand it. His hand traced up my stomach as he kissed me deeply, making my toes curl as my body got so excited that I could barely think about anything other than his taste and the feel of his fingertips trailing over my body. Finally, he pulled away and kissed the tip of my nose.

"Good morning," I mumbled, my voice barely above a whisper because of just waking up.

"Good morning, birthday girl," he answered. "You know, I'll never get used to how beautiful you look in the morning. The no make-up and messy bed hair really does it for me. So perfect," he whispered, gripping my hip and pulling me closer to him again.

I smiled, tracing my fingers across his broad shoulders. "You're just saying that to get into my pants."

He laughed and brushed his nose against mine. "Been there. Done that. You're wearing my t-shirt," he replied, grinning proudly as he tugged on the bottom of his t-shirt that I'd slept in.

I giggled and bit my lip. I'd had a year and seven months with him, and he still managed to make me feel like a giddy little girl, it was a little crazy really. "Whatever, Luke." I pulled his mouth to mine again as I rolled my eyes playfully.

He pulled back as I tried to deepen the kiss. "How about I give you your present now?" he offered, stroking the side of my face. The way he was looking at me made my face heat up; if I didn't feel exactly the same about him then the soft, tender way he was looking at me would scare me. We were only eighteen, but I knew this was him, this was the guy, the one, and the look on his face told me that he was thinking exactly the same thing about me.

"Does your present involve me moaning your name?" I asked, raking my eyes over his body slowly, drinking in every inch of his sculpted chest, the V line that led down to the waistband of his black boxers that he was wearing.

He laughed wickedly. "The one I bought doesn't, but if you want I'll give you that one after."

I sighed as I thought about it, tracing one finger across his scratchy jaw line, imagining what it would feel like tickling my body. "Definitely," I purred, nodding enthusiastically.

He grinned and immediately jumped out of the bed, and again I was struck by how lucky I was that this boy wanted me. Luke Hannigan was a jock, very popular at our school, and although he could be a jerk when he wanted to, he was the most adorable boyfriend in the world. Why he chose me I still didn't understand. I wasn't beautiful, I wasn't popular, if anything I was a little nerdy. I took my school work seriously; I didn't wear short shirts or slutty tops and jump on the sidelines cheering him on while he played football. I preferred to go without make-up and pull my hair up into a messy topknot, slob around in sweats and a t-shirt, than wear high heels and tank tops. I would rather go camping and wake up early so I could go hiking and watch the sun rise than stay in a spa and get a manicure. On paper Luke and I were total opposites. When we first got together people thought he was crazy for going for a nerdy girl like me. Thankfully he did though and I couldn't be happier about it.

He came sauntering back over to the bed and dropped down next to me, making me giggle as he caught me looking at his body. His eyebrow rose knowingly as he smirked at me. He held out his hand, revealing a little box about the size of his palm. "Happy eighteenth birthday, baby," he whispered.

I gulped and took the box from his hand. "Thanks. I hope you didn't go crazy," I muttered, looking at him gratefully. He smiled and shook his head as I tore at the shiny red paper he'd wrapped it in, eager to see what he'd bought me. When I got to the soft black velvet box, I chewed on my lip. My pulse drummed in my ears now that I knew it was jewellery and something I could keep and treasure. I smiled and pulled open the lid, gasping when I saw what he'd bought. Inside the box was an oval gold locket on a delicate gold chain. There was a swirly pattern on the front, with a little diamond set in the middle. It was beautiful.

"Luke, this is-" I gasped, not having the words to describe the exquisite thing he'd bought me.

He smiled and took the box out of my hand, flipping the locket over and handing it back to me again. I looked down at it and my heart melted into a puddle. He'd had it engraved on the back.

'True love lasts for always,
Yours forever,
Luke x'

My eyes filled with tears. I still couldn't think of anything to say. I had no words to describe how incredible this present was and how special it made me feel that he had gone out and chosen something this beautiful, just for me. "Thank you, it's..." I looked at him in awe, and he kissed me lightly.

"You're welcome," he whispered against my lips. "You like it though, really? If not then I'll buy you something else." He seemed a little worried about his choice.

I shook my head fiercely and clutched the little box to my chest protectively. "I love it, and I love you," I said honestly.

He grinned. "I love you too, Maisie." He pointed at the box I was holding for dear life. "I couldn't find a nice picture of us to put in it that was small enough. We'll have to get one photoshopped or something."

I grinned and gripped the locket, releasing the little catch to open it, only to find a badly cut out photo of us had been placed inside. My heart swelled because of the effort he went to. He must have sorted through hundreds of photos just to find one that semi fitted in there, but the top of his head was cut off, as my was chin.

"I'll sort something out," I confirmed. "Put it on for me?" I requested, holding the box out for him. I watched as he pulled the delicate necklace from the box, I held my hair up over one shoulder and giggled as the cold locket touched my chest. When he was done, I gripped it in my hand and looked back at him, smiling smugly that he was mine. "How about the other present now?" I flirted, raising my eyebrows, smiling seductively.

He grinned and literally pounced on me, making me giggle and fall back into the pillows. Things were getting hot when suddenly there was a knock on the door. I squealed and pushed him off me, at the same time that he jumped back, shocked, and fell on his butt out of the bed, groaning as his head hit the floor.

I bit my lip and looked at him worriedly. "You okay?"

The door opened and I yanked the covers up to my shoulders, covering the fact that Luke had taken his shirt off me seconds before the interruption. In walked my mom with a tray in her hands and a big smile on her face. I flicked my eyes to the floor on the other side of the bed, noticing that Luke had laid back, hiding himself from view as my mom walked in.

"Morning, happy birthday!" she chirped, completely oblivious that I'd snuck my boyfriend into the house while everyone was asleep last night.

"Hi, er... Thanks?" I muttered, trying not to blush.

"Are you getting up anytime soon? I'm making a birthday breakfast," she offered, grinning happily. I smiled and nodded enthusiastically. Birthday breakfasts were the best, my mom made literally anything we wanted. I had the same every year - blueberry pancakes with whipped cream. She made my goofy twin brother a fried meat filled mess, and my dad usually went for chocolate chip pancakes, but Mom had to burn his for some reason, he was a little weird like that.

"Heck yeah! I'm just gonna, er..." I grasped wildly for some excuse that would give me a few minutes in my room so that Luke could get dressed and I could sneak him back out of the front door.

She smirked at me and put the tray down on my dresser. "I made you a coffee. Breakfast will be done in about fifteen minutes so that'll give you time to drink it," she said, shrugging, still grinning. "And Luke, next time you sneak in, make sure you park your car more than two houses away," she teased, smirking at the empty space where he was hiding down beside the bed.

My mouth dropped open in shock as Luke sat up from where he was, looking at her guiltily, rubbing the back of his neck. "Yeah, sorry about that, Riley," he muttered, wincing. I just sat there blushing as my mom shook her head and rolled her eyes.

"Amateurs," she teased. "Don't let Clay or Alex catch you in here, you know they'll hurt you," she joked, laughing to herself.

I giggled, and Luke nodded quickly. That was true, my dad and brother wouldn't take too kindly to the fact that my boyfriend had secretly spent the night here. "I won't, thanks," Luke agreed sheepishly.

She smiled and walked back towards the door again. "I made you a coffee too, Luke." She waved her hand at the tray dismissively.

When she closed the door Luke and I looked at each other and burst out laughing. He pushed me down into the bed and pulled the covers over our heads, pressing his almost naked body against mine as he grinned at me in the semidarkness. "Your mom is so cool," he said, kissing my cheek.

I nodded in agreement. I definitely had the best mom going, she was easy to talk to, supportive and never judged me for anything. She completely understood my decision to sleep with Luke a year ago and took me to go and get on the pill when I was ready to take the next step. She'd made everything easier for me, and I loved her for it. Luke wasn't allowed to stay over, but I usually snuck him in for special occasions like valentine's day or birthdays.

I was definitely lucky when it came to my parents, my dad was awesome too, but so overprotective that it was annoying sometimes. But I guess I could understand that, I was his little girl after all, and it mostly worked out in my favour too considering I was a total daddy's girl and got spoilt rotten most of the time.

"You'd better get dressed and leave before my dad catches you in here though," I suggested, giggling as he flinched. My dad didn't have a particular problem with Luke, he would probably treat any boyfriend I had the same; he liked to test him and tease him to make sure he wasn't going to run away and hurt me. You'd think that after a year and seven months that he'd finally give up and accept that Luke wasn't going anywhere though.

"Yeah, good idea."

He kissed me one more time and then pushed himself out of the bed looking a little reluctant to leave. I smiled and watched as he pulled his jeans on, looking around for his t-shirt that he'd taken off me and thrown somewhere in a fit of passion. I spotted it on the sideboard on the other side of the room and giggled as I nodded to it. He grinned and slipped it on, before reaching for my hand and pulling me out of the bed so I could get dressed too.

While I threw on some pyjamas, I could feel his eyes on me. "You know, I think you look even hotter at eighteen than you did at seventeen," he mused as I pushed my arms into my robe.

I laughed and slapped his chest as he went to wrap his arms around me again. "Come on, let's get you out of here," I suggested, taking his hand and heading towards my bedroom door. Easing the door open, I stuck my head out, looking everywhere to make sure the coast was clear. Lucky for me my bedroom was right at the top of the stairs and the front door was at the bottom. He just had to get down thirteen steps, cross the short entranceway, and then we were home free.

When I saw no one, I grabbed his hand and pulled him out of the room, both of us almost sprinting down the stairs. Just as I got to the bottom step, I saw a blond head appear in the doorway of the kitchen. I held my breath, skidding to a halt and Luke slammed into me from behind because I'd stopped so suddenly. His arm snaked around my waist quickly to stop me from falling on my butt as we both looked up with wide eyes.

Oh no, please be Alex and not Dad!

Of course, I wasn't that lucky, it was my dad - but he hadn't noticed me because he was studying the newspaper as he was walking through the door. My mom walked up behind him, smiling, when suddenly her eyes widened as she must have seen Luke standing behind me. I silently begged her for help with my eyes. Almost immediately she grabbed my dad's hand, giving it a little tug. He turned around to face her, turning his back on us as she wrapped her arms around his neck and kissed him. I gulped, a little grossed out. I should have been used to it by now though, they were always kissing like loved up teenagers when they thought they were alone. Unfortunately, parent kissing didn't get easier to witness no matter how many times you were subjected to it.

I was stuck on the spot, wondering if she was going to take him back into the kitchen so I could get the front door open and get Luke out, or if she meant for me to get him out now while they were kissing.

They broke the kiss and Dad laughed. "What was that for, Riley Bear?" he asked, wrapping his arms around her.

"Just wanted to kiss you, that's all," Mom replied. She pointed her finger forcefully at the front door a couple of times behind my dad's head, signalling for me to move. Luke squeezed my hand and we both crept forward towards the door, counting the steps.

"And you didn't get enough of that this morning?" my dad teased, causing my mom giggle.

"Eww!" I hissed, cringing at the thought of what that meant. Luke's hand clapped over my mouth, pushing me gently, making me walk faster to the door.

More sounds of kissing started from behind me again, and I shuddered. When I made the final step to the door, I opened it slowly, being as quiet as possible. Luke slipped through and I blew him a kiss as he squeezed my hand as a goodbye. He'd be back in a little while anyway to pick me up for school, but he had just really wanted to stay over so he could be the first person I saw when I woke up on my birthday. He'd always been adorable like that. I sighed dreamily and closed the door, forgetting to be as quiet as I should have been.

"Hey, what are you doing?"

I gulped at the sound of my dad's voice. "Er, I was going to, um... get the paper for you?" I offered weakly.

He laughed and held the up newspaper in his hand. "I got it, sweetie, but thanks," he chirped as he came bounding over and pulled me into a bone crushing hug. "Happy birthday! Oh man, my little girl a legal adult." He shook his head, looking at me in awe.

I laughed and nodded. "Yep, so can I get a tattoo?" I asked, only half joking. If he said yes I was definitely getting one today.

He raised one eyebrow at me. "No," was all he said, and I couldn't help but smile. He grinned happily at me as he tugged me towards the kitchen and the smell of deliciousness that wafted through the house. "So, think you'll get anything nice for your eighteenth?"

I grinned, thinking about the locket that was hanging around my neck. "I guess I'll have to wait and see if the birthday fairy has been," I joked, squeezing my arm around his waist. That was something he used to tell me and my twin brother, Alex, when we were younger and were too excited to go to sleep the night before our birthday, that if we didn't go to sleep then the birthday fairy wouldn't come. When we stepped into the kitchen I laughed as I took in the array of pink and blue balloons, the 'happy 18th' banners, and the presents scattered over the dining table. "Well the birthday fairy's been in here!"

My dad grinned, and I chewed on my lip excitedly. Today was going to be a great day, sure I was going to school, but I'd get to hang out with Luke at lunchtime. Tonight we were all going out for family dinner; both sets of my grandparents were coming too. I'd managed to convince my parents that Luke needed to come with us because he was part of my 'extended family'. Then tomorrow was Friday, which meant that Luke was taking me to an all ages night at a club to celebrate my birthday. Saturday night would be even better though, because on Saturday Luke and I were going camping near the lake, just the two of us. I sighed contentedly. My life was just perfect, and eighteen was definitely going to be my year.

chapter two

I dressed in my usual casual attire of jeans and a plain fitted t-shirt, scraping my long brown hair back into a ponytail, the same as every other day. As usual, I didn't bother with any make-up. I wasn't exactly a girlie girl so things like that didn't happen in my normal dressing routine. I skipped back down the stairs and stopped when I heard Luke's voice in the kitchen. He was talking to my dad.

"Clay, it's only camping, we've been before and you didn't mind," he stated.

I heard a heavy sigh. "Yeah, but Alex went then too, and other friends. All I'm saying is that you'd better take care of her. I don't like the idea of you two being alone together all night, but I guess I need to accept that she's an adult now." Dad's voice was a little gruff as he spoke.

"Honestly, you don't have anything to worry about. I'll always take care of her," Luke answered. He sounded extremely exasperated so I wondered how long my dad had been grilling him for. I hadn't heard him arrive so for all I knew he could have been subjected to the inquisition the whole time I was showering and dressing for school. Luke certainly put up with a lot from my dad, but other than the occasional threats and stuff they got on great.

"Look, it's just that you two are moving on so fast, what with the whole applying for the same colleges thing... I just don't want any mistakes to mess up your futures. You understand what I'm saying?"

"Yeah, of course. Maisie and I are always really responsible like that," Luke replied easily, as if talking to my dad about our sex life wasn't anything out of the ordinary. "I know we're young but you knew you were in love at our age, you and Riley were already married by the time you were our age."

"Riley and I are different, I'd known her my whole life," my dad countered defensively.

"And I've known Maisie since we were thirteen."

I decided it was time to put an end to this conversation before my dad started getting annoyed or anything. He honestly did like Luke, but he just hated the thought of his little girl growing up. He never seemed to mind Alex going to parties or hooking up with girls all the time, but a serious boyfriend for his little girl was something entirely different.

I cleared my throat as I walked around the corner, gaining their attention immediately. "I'm ready to go whenever you're done with this little man-to-man chat," I joked, waving my hand between the two of them.

Luke smirked at me and my dad grinned sheepishly, like he'd been caught in the act. "I was just telling Luke about the potential bear threat for Saturday night. Maybe you should just stay home to be on the safe side?" Dad suggested, laughing quietly.

I shrugged. "We'll take anti bear spray," I joked, playing along.

Luke laughed and stood up from the stool he was perched on, coming over and draping his arm across my shoulders. "Happy birthday," he whispered, kissing the side of my head as he held up a bunch of daisies. That was his flower of choice for me. He always bought them because when we first started dating I'd joked and told him they were my favourite because they rhymed with my name. He'd since learned that they weren't my favourites, but it kind of stuck, so daisies were his thing now.

I smiled gratefully and pressed against him, my stomach fluttering because of his presence. Gripping the front of his grey hoodie, I pulled him closer to me and pressed my lips against his. Almost instantly a loud, dramatic throat clearing came from my dad's direction, so I pulled back and shot him a glare. Clearly it was alright for him to make out with my mom all the time, but I wasn't even allowed to kiss my boyfriend hello on my birthday.

"Thanks, Luke." I smiled down at the flowers as I slipped my hand into the back pocket of his jeans.

He smiled and brushed his knuckles across my cheek, his eyes soft and tender as he looked at me. "You ready to go before your dad starts hounding me again?" he joked, grinning slyly at my dad who rolled his eyes but smiled despite himself.

I nodded, chuckling. I stepped away from him and kissed my dad's cheek. "Thanks so much for all my presents, you didn't need to buy me all of that." They'd gone above and beyond this year, buying me a wicked new laptop ready for when I went to college in a couple of months, and a beautiful new watch.

He waved his hand dismissively. "It was your eighteenth. Your mom and I thought you'd rather the laptop than a car of your own..." He trailed off looking at me hopefully, as if he suddenly doubted their decision. They'd bought my brother a car, just a starter car of his own, nothing new or special, but he'd loved it and ran out of the house wearing nothing but a pair of boxers just so he could test drive it. I wasn't even sure he was back yet.

I smiled and nodded. "I love the laptop, it's incredible, and it's way better than a car."

His shoulders loosened as he smiled. "Not sure your brother would agree."

"Yeah but Alex just hates driving around in Mom's cherry red Rover." I held up my flowers to him. "Can you ask Mom to put them in a vase for me?"

"We'd better get going, Maisie," Luke said from behind me, tugging on the end of my ponytail playfully. I smiled and took the hand he was offering, letting him pull me out of the kitchen. I couldn't stop the excited grin that spread across my face. Today I was eighteen, a legal adult; I was the baby of my group of friends so this day had seemed to take forever to get here.

"Have a good day at school. Don't forget we're going for dinner tonight. Your grandparents will be here at six!" my dad called as we walked out of the door.

• • •

AS WE PULLED INTO the parking lot, the car was immediately swamped with people, the same as it was every morning. Luke's friends and teammates all converged around us, wanting his attention about some sport that was on last night that I just wasn't interested in. I put on my polite fake smile and stepped out of the car. I couldn't stand Luke's friends, they were complete and utter jerks, and I genuinely had no idea why Luke hung around with them at all.

"Luuuuuuuuke!" Ricky jeered, playfully punching him in the ribs. I tried my hardest not to groan as I looked longingly at the front door of the school. I didn't want to stand here today and listen to them drone on about football, parties, girls and more girls. I just wanted to get inside and talk to people who actually liked me, instead of people who tolerated me because I was dating the quarterback.

"What up, bud?" Luke greeted him, slinging his arm around my shoulder, stopping my escape. I sighed quietly and sat on the hood of his car, preparing myself to be bored stiff, when surprisingly Luke shook his head. "Can't stop to talk, my lady has a birthday today so I'm guessing she wants to go see her friends?" Luke said, looking at me with a smile.

I kissed him quickly and nodded. "Yeah. You stay here and talk though, I'll see you at lunchtime," I suggested, jumping off the hood of his car, ignoring how the girls sneered at me and looked me over in my choice of outfit. No one thought I was good enough for Luke, no one saw what he saw when he looked at me, but that was okay as far as I was concerned, as long as *he* saw it then that was all I needed. I couldn't resist sending a smug smile to Sandy, the queen bee at our school whom every young and impressionable girl aspired to be. I knew she wanted Luke, but he'd never shown the slightest bit of interest in her. She gave me a fake smile in return and just turned away, bitching about me to her friends, it couldn't have been more obvious if they whispered behind their hands whilst pointing at me.

Luke frowned and shook his head, pulling me closer to him. "No way. If I could, I would spend your whole birthday with you, but I guess that's not possible, so I'll settle for every spare second you have," he cooed, kissing me softly. Immediately his friends started jeering and making cat calls about how we should get a room. I just ignored them the same as I did every other day.

He pulled away laughing and playfully punched the nearest guy to him, before nodding towards the front door, signalling for me to lead the way. I practically skipped up to the building, clinging to him. So far, this was easily the best birthday ever. Last year had been pretty special too though, because that was the night that Luke and I first slept together, but for some reason this one just seemed perfect from the very first second I woke up in his arms.

As we approached my locker, I saw my two best friends, Beth and Charlotte, there waiting for me. They were holding open a homemade banner that said 'happy birthday' on it. I laughed because of how much effort they'd gone to, there was glitter and everything. Both of my friends were adorable, yet so different at the same time. Beth was extremely ditsy and was always off in her own little dream world. Charlotte, on the other hand, was a computer geek. What she could do with computers blew my mind; if something technical needed doing then she was the one to ask. She'd gotten herself into some trouble when she was only fourteen because she had accidentally hacked into the police department network. She hadn't meant to, she was just fooling around trying to break their security for fun, and actually did. Thankfully they realised that she wasn't actually trying to do any harm, but I think she was now on their hacker watch list – a feat she was secretly quite proud of.

"Happy birthday!" they both cheered as I got up to them.

I smiled and they both grabbed me into a bone crushing hug. "Thanks."

"Here, we bought together," Beth chirped, holding out a flat rectangular present that I already knew was a book because of the shape of it.

I smiled and tore off the paper. "You didn't need to get me anything," I gushed as I pulled it open. Inside was a photo album, they'd done a design on the front, both drawing on it and writing 'Senior Year' on the front. "Aww, I love this. Thanks girls!"

"Open it," Charlotte encouraged.

I frowned, confused, but opened the front cover to see three tickets for the midnight preview screening of the second Hunger Games movie that came out in a few weeks. I squealed excitedly as I threw my arms around them both.

"These are great, I can't wait!" I chirped as we all started doing a happy dance in the middle of the hallway. From the corner of my eye, I saw the A-list girls looking at us with disapproval, but I just didn't care, I was happy being a nerd so they could disapprove all they wanted.

Someone cleared their throat next to us, so we stopped and I looked to see it was a freshman. He shifted on his feet nervously, probably a little scared to approach a senior. "You're Maisie Preston, aren't you?" he asked, flicking his eyes to Luke who looked like he was body guarding me because of the glare he was shooting the poor guy.

"Er, yeah?" I confirmed, confused.

"Principal Bennett wants to see you in her office," he muttered, cringing away from Luke as he stepped closer to me possessively.

The Principal wants to see me? "Oh really? Okay, thanks for telling me." I smiled at the guy reassuringly because he looked like he was three seconds from passing out. Without saying anything else, he turned and scuttled off. I turned to Luke and raised one eyebrow, waiting for an explanation for that face. "Death glare for a freshman, really?"

He shrugged casually, not seeming bothered by my stern face. "He was looking at your butt as you were jumping around."

I rolled my eyes. Luke could be a little possessive sometimes, but I could handle that, being with him was worth putting up with a little jealousness every now and then. "So what? People look at you all the time, does that mean I have to start glaring at the girls for looking at something that's mine?" I asked, smirking at him playfully.

He smiled and pulled me closer to him, crushing the photo album and tickets between our bodies. "I love it when you call me yours," he whispered, looking at me hungrily. I smiled and pressed my lips to his, biting on his bottom lip gently, making his fingers dig into the small of my back.

Suddenly his arms were gone from my waist and his body jerked away from mine. I looked up, shocked; Luke was now a foot away from me. My brother, Alex, had hold of the back of his sweater as he frowned angrily. "Five inch gap between you and my sister while I'm around, you know that, Hannigan," he growled, pushing Luke away from me.

I sighed in exasperation. Sometimes my twin was the most annoying thing in the world with his protectiveness. "Grow up, Alex. Just go run along and try and get your fill of some slut's pants before school starts, huh?" I waved my hand dismissively. Alex didn't like Luke much, never had done for some reason.

Alex frowned at my comment but didn't reply. Instead, his blue eyes that were the exact shade of mine turned to Charlotte. He swept one hand through his messy dark blond hair as he turned on the charming smile that most girls in the school swooned over. "Hey, so am I getting a birthday present?" he asked, looking at her suggestively.

I groaned and rolled my eyes because he was starting earlier than usual today. Flirting with Charlotte was usually restricted to lunchtimes or after school when she came over to our place. It was innocent enough; they were friends really too, but he just liked to tease the life out of her because she wasn't very experienced in that department. "I forgot to buy you anything," she answered, shrugging.

He smiled, his eyes glittering wickedly. "That's okay; I'll just take your first kiss." He leant in close, his lips heading towards hers.

She squealed and pulled back, frowning at him, pushing on his chest to get him away from her. "That's not for you to decide!" she retorted, clearly annoyed.

He smiled and kissed her on the cheek quickly. "You know I'll get it sooner or later, Char." He waggled his eyebrows at her before walking off, laughing at her horrified expression.

I sighed and handed my presents to Beth. "I'd better go see what Principal Bennett wants. I'll see you guys in class later."

Luke groaned and kissed me again as I went to walk off. I kissed him back, gripping the front of his hoodie, not wanting to leave either. "I wanted to spend more time with you on your birthday," he whined, pouting.

"You could always sneak in again tonight if you want," I suggested, shrugging.

He grinned and nodded eagerly. "I like that idea!" I laughed at his enthusiasm. Luke was coming to the meal with us tonight, so he'd just have to go home then sneak back in again once everyone else was asleep. "I'll park more than two houses away this time so your ninja mom doesn't know I'm there." He laughed, kissing my forehead softly.

"Good thinking. I'll see you at lunch." I patted him on the backside as I walked past, heading to the office to see what the Principal wanted. I knew I wasn't in trouble, I was never in trouble. As I walked into the reception, I was immediately waved through to Principal Bennett's office.

She looked up as I walked in, pushing her thick rimmed glasses up her nose as she smiled warmly at me. "Maisie, thank you for coming, dear. I have a favour to ask of you," she trailed off looking at me hopefully as she waved at the seat opposite her desk.

I nodded, sitting down. "Okay, sounds intriguing." I was always being asked to do things, I was on a lot of the committees and panels at school, arranging dances and charity events, I was kind of a 'go-to girl' for our Principal.

"We have a new student starting on Monday. His name is Zachary Anderson. He's transferring from another school." A frown lined her forehead. "Anyway, I wondered if you wouldn't mind meeting him in the morning, giving him the tour of the school, helping him find his classes and locker, that kind of thing," she said, looking at me hopefully.

I shrugged and nodded in agreement. "Sure, no problem."

She smiled gratefully. "Thank you, Maisie, I appreciate it." She shuffled some papers on her desk, pushing her glasses up her nose as she read one over. "It looks to me like he was struggling a little in his last school and his aunt has requested a tutor to help him catch up with the new schedule. Would you be interested? She's willing to pay." She looked at me questionably over the rim of her glasses.

I nodded enthusiastically. I loved tutoring and the money always came in handy considering Luke's family had a ton of money. Compared to the Hannigans, my family looked relatively poor even though my dad earned really good money in his engineering job. Extra cash was always good, and then I didn't have to let Luke pay all the time when we went out, even though most of the time he insisted anyway.

"Absolutely. What does he need tutoring in?" I asked, curiously.

She smiled and clicked her tongue, not looking too impressed over whatever she was reading about the new guy. "Looks like just about everything. I would concentrate on the staple subjects though. There's not long left before graduation, so it's more important to pull up his average on those. He's already repeating senior year."

I raised one eyebrow at the repeating a year comment. He obviously didn't make much effort at school. Staple subjects meant English, mathematics, and science, all of my favourites. "Okay sure," I agreed. She handed me a stack of papers. I flicked through them quickly, seeing they contained his locker combination and schedule, everyday things. "I'll just meet him at the front door then, the same as usual?" I'd done a lot of these initiations. Usually I just got the new people settled, ate lunch with them for a couple of days until they found their feet, and then they went off to do their own thing with friends they'd made.

She smiled. "That'd be swell. Thanks again."

I headed out of the office, folding the papers and pushing them into my bag, heading to class quickly.

• • •

THE NEXT COUPLE of days passed quickly; luckily Luke didn't get caught staying over that night. The only ones we really had to worry about catching us were my parents, because his were hardly ever home. He actually had a better relationship with his housekeeper than he did with his parents. The Hannigans had their own pharmaceutical company that they were both CEOs of, so they travelled a lot. Luke was, therefore, very lonely, though he never admitted it. He liked to spend as much time at mine and around my family as possible. If he had the chance, I had the feeling that he would move into mine permanently.

Saturday finally came around, though not soon enough in my opinion. I finished packing up my camping things excitedly. Luke came by just after lunch to pick me up. He had the whole range of camping gear, so it wasn't like we were going to be living in squalor tonight. He had a six man tent with different sections for bedrooms, a little area in the middle for sitting in, and it even had a canopy outside so you could sit under cover if you wanted to. Luke liked to camp. Apparently it was something he did with his dad when he was little, that was, of course, before Mr Hannigan started to get too busy to spend time with his son.

"Hey there, baby, are you all packed?" he asked as I walked down the stairs with my rucksack on my back.

I nodded and smiled, looking him over. He looked extremely handsome today in loose fitted jeans and a plain fitted white t-shirt. Today was going to be a good day, but tonight would be even better because I'd get to lounge around a camp fire eating Luke's perfectly cooked s'mores. "Yeah, you got everything? We'll stop at the store and buy food, right?" I asked, mentally checking off what I was supposed to bring. The only things I had to bring, according to Luke, were my clothes and my flirty smile.

"Yeah, we'll stop on the way. Come on then, let's get going before your brother or dad start to lecture me about looking after you again," he suggested, laughing quietly to himself.

As if on cue, my dad walked out of the lounge and frowned. "You guys all done? Luke, can I have a quick word?"

"Too late for a discreet exit," I whispered, squeezing his hand gently.

He laughed and kissed my forehead before following my dad into the kitchen. I felt so sorry for Luke; he undoubtedly loved me a lot because he put up with the overprotective guys in my family and never once complained. I flopped down next to my mom on the sofa. "Can't you rein dad in a little? Surely he knows Luke well enough by now that he doesn't have to give him the talk every time we're staying out for the night?" I asked, resting my head on her shoulder.

She stroked the side of my head. "You know what your dad's like. Overprotective. Drives me crazy sometimes too, but it's part of his personality, Alex has it too, so I'm afraid you and Luke are done for," she replied, laughing to herself.

I sighed and nodded. "Lucky Luke's so awesome that he doesn't mind."

My mom laughed. "Yeah, Luke's great," she agreed. "And as much as your dad makes a show out of teasing him and stuff, he likes him too."

A few minutes later and they both walked in, laughing together, so whatever talk they had obviously went well. "Are we ready to go now?" I asked, looking at

Luke pleadingly. I really wanted to leave already, it would take us two hours to drive up to the place he wanted to camp near the lake, and we needed to stop for food, then it would take him a little while to set up the tent. I didn't want to be doing that too late; I wanted to start the fun already.

My dad nodded, gripping my hand and pulling me to my feet. "Yep, no wandering off on your own, you stay with Luke. And if you see a bear, as long as you run faster than your quarterback you'll be fine." He leant in conspiratorially as he continued, "Maybe trip him so he gets mauled instead of you."

I laughed and hugged him, wanting to leave before he thought of something else he could lecture us on. "I will do. Say bye to Alex for me." I pulled back and smiled at Luke, discreetly flicking my eyes to the door so he'd not linger a second longer than necessary. He smiled and picked up my bag like a proper gentleman. His actions and sweet nature really didn't match his tough, jock exterior. He was different when he was around his friends, still adorable to me, but he got loud and sometimes quite rude. When he was drunk he could be downright annoying, but thankfully he didn't drink terribly often.

My parents followed us out to Luke's Jeep, relaying instructions about safety in the water, being careful in the woods, and calling home when we arrived so they would know we were safe. When we finally pulled out of the drive I sighed and settled down into my seat. I beamed over at Luke excitedly. Twenty-eight hours of his company with no one to interrupt, this was going to be bliss.

chapter three

The camping trip was incredible, the same as it always was when I went away with Luke. He pulled out all the stops, turning what could have been a boring camping trip, into something romantic and memorable. We'd laid under the stars, eating s'mores, just talking and laughing. The moon had been full and reflected on the lake that we'd set up camp next too. It was so peaceful that it was like paradise. Later, he'd cuddled up next to me in the dark of the night, whispering how much he loved me and how he planned for us to buy a summer place on the lake so that we could visit at weekends. He'd painted a beautiful picture of how we would swim off the jetty and how we'd get a boat so he could teach our kids how to fish like his father had taught him. Everything about the trip had been magical and breathtaking. It was the most special moment of my life, and I would remember it forever.

Unfortunately, time seemed to whizz past, and before I knew it, it was Monday and we were back to reality again. As I stepped out of Luke's car, I didn't get to escape from his friends this time. I sat there on the hood of his car, discreetly checking my watch every few seconds wondering just how long they could actually talk about a football game. When the subject turned to Ricky and the *two* girls he had slept with on Saturday night, I just couldn't take it anymore.

I pushed myself off the car and looked at Luke with a fake smile, pretending that I hadn't just sat there listing all of my favourite music in my head in a bid to block out the ramblings of the imbeciles that he called 'friends'. "I need to go meet this Zachary guy," I said, shrugging at his curious glance.

He frowned but nodded at the same time. "Want me to come?"

Tailor laughed. "I've never seen a guy more pussy whipped than you, Hannigan," he mocked, making all of his friends laugh.

Luke frowned. "Pussy whipped my ass. You know who's boss, right Maisie?" he asked, cocking his head to the side and putting on the big show that he liked to do around his friends. Sometimes I hated this act, most times I could stomach it, but other times it just pissed me off. Today, because I'd had such an incredible weekend with him, I decided to let him run with it and show off to his friends.

I nodded, looking at him through my eyelashes. "You're my boss, Luke," I purred, smiling suggestively. His friends all started muttering things like "sweeeeeet" and "niiiiiiiice" obviously thinking this was some sort of kinky game going on between us. In reality, Luke obviously needed his ego to be stroked a little, I could do that, I was a good girlfriend, and if he needed to feel like the big shot today then that's what I'd make him feel like.

He smiled at me gratefully before gripping my waist and pulling me to him roughly. His lips claimed mine in an almost primal and possessive way. The kiss was so good that it actually made my knees a little weak; he obviously felt this too so he clutched me to him tighter, holding me steady. When he finally released me from the intense kiss, I was a little breathless.

"Don't you ever forget it," he said, smirking at me and then raising an eyebrow at his friends in a 'who's the daddy now' gesture.

I smiled and tried not to roll my eyes. 'Jerk Luke' looked like he wanted to come out to play today. "Well I'll see you at lunch then." I waved over my shoulder as I headed to the front doors to wait for the new guy who was starting today. After about ten minutes I still didn't see anyone that I didn't recognise. I frowned. Had I missed him? Maybe he'd arrived earlier than Luke and I did, and he'd slipped into the office, waiting for me there.

I sighed and headed to the office, finding the receptionist sitting there tapping away on her keyboard. I flicked my eyes around the office, the chairs were empty, no one was in here waiting for me. I rested my arms on the little counter, waiting for her to be done. She smiled sweetly at me. I had a good relationship with her; I was in here often enough doing my duties for the numerous committees I was on.

"Hi, I was waiting outside for the new student, but I can't see him anywhere. He hasn't by any chance got past me or something has he? Maybe he came in here?" I suggested, smiling hopefully. I didn't want to go trudging around the school looking for him.

She shook her head. "Sorry, Maisie, I haven't seen any new students. Have you been out front the whole time?" she asked, looking at me curiously.

I resisted the urge to groan. I hadn't exactly been waiting for him the whole time; I had been getting bored out of my brain listening to Luke and the people he labelled as his friends. Technically there was plenty of time for Zachary to get to the front door without me seeing, slip in, and start wandering the hallways of the school having no clue where to go. *Awesome, I was asked to do one thing and I can't do it right! Stupid Maisie, and stupid Luke too!*

"I was in the parking lot for a bit," I admitted, wincing.

She smiled sympathetically. "Well, maybe you should wait back out front for a little while again. The bell won't ring for another five minutes so maybe he's just cutting it fine. If he comes in here then I'll send him out to you. If not then I guess he must be in the school somewhere."

Great. That means I'll have to go searching the hallways looking for a guy that I've never even met. Mondays suck! I nodded and headed out, sitting on the front step of the school, watching every person who walked past me to make sure I'd seen them before. When the bell rang I looked back slightly panicked. I didn't want to be late or miss my biology class, but I needed to find this guy.

I wrung my hands together, wondering if I should just go to class and leave him and hope that someone else found him wandering the halls and showed him to the office. Then I remembered I had his schedule and locker combination. I groaned and flicked my eyes around, undecided. The thought of being late for class was actually making me feel a little sick. If Alex were here to witness my indecision, he would be laughing his ass off at me and calling me a nerd or a geek.

I took a deep breath and decided it was my responsibility to find him. I shouldered my bag and marched into the school with a frown on my face, though I knew I couldn't actually blame him for getting here before I did and going into the school not knowing I was supposed to meet him here. I walked up and down the hallways; I knocked on boys' bathroom doors before heading in there to double check. I went to his first period class, physics, to see if someone had showed him there already, but the teacher told me he was absent. I resumed my search, but I couldn't find him anywhere.

I completely missed my first period and was still searching the second floor when the second period bell went. *Someone has to have found him by now and taken him to the office, surely!* I pulled out the guy's schedule and looked at it worriedly. He had two classes with me this afternoon, gym and English. I sighed and reluctantly trudged back to the office. There was an awful, uneasy feeling in the pit of my stomach because the poor guy was probably wandering around the school somewhere.

The receptionist smiled up at me as I walked in. "Found him?" she questioned, tucking into her muffin.

I shook my head. "No. I've looked everywhere. He's not in his first class; I've checked the hallways and bathrooms. Has he not been in here?" I asked, wincing and praying she would say yes. I couldn't help but wonder if I was going to get into trouble for not looking after him like I'd promised. I'd never been in trouble at school, ever.

She shook her head. "I haven't seen him or anyone else. You're the only one that's been in today."

I groaned and put my head in my hands. I really needed to get to class, I was already over twenty minutes late for algebra, and I didn't want to miss it, I loved all things math. "I'm gonna get to class. I'll search for him again later. I'm hoping someone's found him and shown him where to go already." I winced, looking at her for her permission to abandon my search.

She nodded. "Okay, well if he comes in I'll send you a note to let you know. You're eating lunch with him, aren't you?" She grabbed a piece of paper, jotting down mine and Zachary's names as a reminder.

"If I can find him, then yeah." I smiled gratefully and pushed myself away from the counter. I practically ran to my algebra class. As I knocked and walked in, all eyes in the room snapped to me. I noticed Sandy smirk in my direction, her eyes raking down my body looking at my simple jeans and tank top with Luke's hoodie combo I was wearing today. "Sorry I'm late." I winced as I walked in, looking at an extremely angry Mr Turner.

"Where on earth have you been, Miss Preston? Class started over twenty minutes ago, and now you're disrupting everyone!" he roared.

I flinched, taken aback by his outburst. "Er, I was looking for a new guy?" I offered weakly.

Some people snickered at my comment but I wasn't sure why. "Aww, is Luke not handling things too well or something? I'm available, Maisie!" Freddie shouted suggestively from the back row, making everyone howl with laughter.

My mouth dropped open in shock. "Of course he is!" I cried.

His smirk grew wider. "So why the need for a new guy?"

I opened my mouth to shout at him for being a jerk, when something slammed down on the desk at the front, almost making me jump out of my skin. I yelped and looked back to Mr Turner, shocked. He'd slammed his textbook down onto the table. His face was beet red as he glared, first at me, and then at Freddie.

"You two have lunchtime detention!" he shouted, pointing at us both.

I gasped. *What the heck? I didn't do anything wrong, why am I getting detention?* "Mr Turner, I was looking for a new student! Principal Bennett asked me to meet him and-" but I was cut off by a wave of his hand.

"I don't care what Principal Bennett asked you to do! You've just waltzed into my class twenty minutes late, with no note I presume?" He looked at me expectantly. I gulped noisily. I didn't have a note, so he was right there. I shook my head and he continued, "Then you two proceed to have an inappropriate conversation in front of the whole class, further disrupting us!"

I felt my heart start to race in my chest. I'd never had a detention before. I actually felt a little shell-shocked; my whole body felt cold. Was this what it felt like every time you got into trouble? I hated the feeling, it was awful. I had an obsessive need to do my best and this detention would be the first black mark I would ever have against my name at school.

I opened my mouth to protest and beg, to tell him that I could get a note from the Principal herself to explain, but he cut me off again before I even uttered one word. "If you speak then it'll be an afterschool detention too," he warned.

I could feel the cold sweat running down my back at that statement. I snapped my mouth closed and shook my head, but Freddie didn't. "A detention? What the hell for? I didn't do anything wrong!" he cried, clearly annoyed.

Mr Turner glared at him. "After school detention then too. For both of you!"

I gasped again. "What? Why?" I asked, trying desperately not to cry.

"Now tomorrow too!" Mr Turner roared, his evil eyes coming to rest on me.

I whimpered. First I lost someone who I was supposed to be looking after, then I completely missed biology and I was pretty sure I had a quiz. And now I had two detentions? Could this day possibly get any worse?

As if answering my question, Freddie jumped out of his seat, glaring back at Mr Turner. "You can't give us detention for nothing! You're just in a freaking foul mood and are taking it out on us. What's up, Turner, did you not get any at the weekend?"

The whole class had gone quiet, mouths hanging open in shock. Mr Turner looked like he was struggling to breathe as he glared at Freddie like he wanted to kill him on the spot. "You," he hissed, pointing at Freddie. He turned and pointed at me making me flinch from the hardness to his eyes. "And you. Lunchtime detentions for the rest of the week, and after school tomorrow. And if I hear one more peep out of either of you two for the rest of the lesson, then it'll be after school detentions for the whole week!" he said, his voice so low that it almost came out as a growl.

Freddie laughed quietly to himself, and I knew what he was going to do before he even did it. He was one of Luke's jerk friends and I knew Luke would do exactly the same thing in this situation. Act the big shot. Freddie was a troublemaker, and was always in detention; this was probably nothing out of the ordinary for him. Me on the other hand...

He sat back down, deliberately slowly, leaning back in his chair, putting his hands behind his head as if he was chilling out. His face was innocent and happy as he said, "Peep."

Mr Turner almost smiled, almost, but then it was gone to be replaced by the hard stern face of a strict teacher. He just as calmly and deliberately walked over to his desk and shuffled his papers there. "Very well, Mr Silverton. You and Miss Preston will now both have detention lunchtimes and after school for the rest of the week." He turned to me and pointed to a seat that was free at the front. "Sit!" he ordered.

I obediently trotted over to the seat and plopped down in it, my mouth hanging open in shock and my eyes prickling with tears. I wanted to protest and plead that it wasn't my fault, but I didn't dare say anything else in case it made it worse. I had an excuse, I had a reason for being late to his class, but he just didn't want to listen.

I turned to glare at Freddie who was laughing quietly to himself; he got a discreet high five from Ricky who was sitting next to him. I wanted to kill him, I really did. But I knew Luke would do that for me once he found out I couldn't eat with him all week because of Freddie's antics. I pulled out my book and tried to concentrate on anything other than the fact that I had just gotten into trouble at school for the first time ever. I scrawled on the top of my notepad, 'Mondays suck', then I quickly scribbled it out before anyone saw it. That statement wasn't right anyway, it wasn't that Monday's sucked, it was that the new guy sucked. If I hadn't been waiting for him then I wouldn't have been late to class in the first place and my academic record would be perfect, the same as always.

The rest of the day was just as bad, I was in a seriously foul mood. I text Luke to tell him that I couldn't meet him for lunch and that I had detention after school too. As he replied, my phone got confiscated so I didn't even get to read his response. Freddie sat next to me in the lunchtime detention, digging his finger into my ribs the whole time, throwing me little notes with pictures that he'd drawn on them of me with my head stuck in a book or some other degrading nerd joke.

I did my best to ignore him, I really did, but I secretly hoped that Luke punched him in the face for this little stunt. I didn't have time to explain to Principal Bennett that I hadn't found Zachary so he would have to eat alone today, I was pretty sure I'd get into trouble for that too. All in all, my morning was disastrous.

Gym class wasn't much better; I fell over and scraped my knees while we were running. Zachary didn't turn up to this class either, and I felt so guilty that I wanted to cry even more. I felt terrible as I thought about him possibly hiding in the bathrooms because he didn't know where he was supposed to go or do.

Over the course of the morning, I figured that all my troubles had originated because I had sat with Luke and his friends this morning instead of going straight to the front doors to wait for Zachary. I didn't want to blame Luke, I really didn't, but the more I thought about it, the more annoyed with him I became. I knew I was being irrational, but *he* was the one that made me sit there and listen to that idiotic conversation this morning. It was one of *his* friends that got me detention. *His* text got my phone confiscated.

The day dragged beyond belief and felt like it lasted a lifetime. After another excruciating hour of detention spent with Freddie at the end of the day, I headed to the office to go and explain to Principal Bennett that I couldn't find Zachary. I just hoped I would be able to convince her to talk to Mr Turner, and I could get out of the detentions for the rest of the week.

As I approached the office, I winced, wondering if I was about to get into more trouble for being irresponsible and not meeting him. I held my breath as I walked up to the receptionist. She looked up and recognition shot across her face. "Oh, Maisie, I meant to send you a note." She smiled apologetically.

"A note? You found him then?" I asked.

She shook her head, leaning in closer to me with a mischievous look on her face. "No. As it turns out, he decided he didn't want to start today. He skipped. Principal Bennett has been talking to his aunt for the last half an hour. I think he's in big trouble, and he hasn't even started here yet. Not really a good start, skipping on your first day." She laughed quietly to herself, looking like we were having a good gossip about the new delinquent.

My hands clenched into fists at her revelations. The stupid guy couldn't even be bothered to show up to his first day? I had sat there waiting for him, searched the school, got detentions, and had my phone confiscated, all because of him. Everything was his fault and I already felt myself hating him for it. I had never taken an instant disliking to someone in my life. I had always believed in giving people chances, forgiving and forgetting, making the best of something and not holding grudges. I hadn't even met Zachary Anderson and it looked like he was the exception to that rule. If he were in front of me in that moment I would probably punch him in the face for tarnishing my academic record.

I frowned. "I don't have to meet him tomorrow, do I?"

She smiled sadly. "Principal Bennett would like you to." She shrugged and looked at me questioningly. "His aunt has promised he'll be here tomorrow."

I closed my eyes and huffed in defeat. "Fine." I stomped out of the office, heading to the parking lot to wait for Luke by his car. His football practice would be finishing soon. I pulled myself up on the hood and settled on my back, closing my eyes, taking calming breaths. After a few minutes I remembered that I hadn't asked to get my detentions quashed. I shook my head at myself in disbelief, I didn't have the mental strength to go back into the school though, I'd just have to sort it out tomorrow.

After another ten minutes, someone grabbed my ankles and pulled me forward, making me slide down the car. I squealed and snapped my eyes open quickly, in a state of panic. I looked up to see Luke smirking at me. Just as my butt crashed into his crotch, he bent forward putting his arms either side of my head, his face inches from mine, his whole body pinning me against the car.

"Now this is a nice way to meet me, sprawled out on the hood of my car. Maybe next time you could do it in a bikini or something?" he suggested, waggling his eyebrows at me.

I laughed and wrapped my legs around his waist, pulling him closer to me. Looking into his big brown eyes made my mood lighten instantly, they made me forget what a crappy day I'd had, and how annoyed I was. His playful smile made an unconscious smile to creep onto my lips too. "Maybe for your nineteenth birthday," I teased, running my hands up his back.

He pouted. "But my birthday's not for another eight months!" he whined.

I grinned and shrugged. "The wait will build the anticipation."

He laughed and kissed the tip of my nose. "Come on then, baby, let's go home, and then you can whine about your day while I try my best to cheer you up." He pulled back, taking my hand and helping me down from the hood of his car. I smiled gratefully, already knowing he'd have me smiling and laughing by the time he left my house tonight.

chapter four

As it turned out, Zachary Anderson obviously didn't feel like starting school at all. He skipped the whole week. I gave up waiting for him after Wednesday. Every day the Principal would call his aunt and apparently she would apologise profusely and promise he would be there the following day, but as of Friday he had officially skipped all week. I was secretly hoping that Principal Bennett would just tell him not to bother starting at all if he couldn't even drag himself here willingly. She didn't strike me as the kind of person to give up that easy though, she liked a challenge, and Zachary was certainly turning out to be that. So far, he was certainly living up to his 'I'm a delinquent and I'm repeating senior year' reputation.

The week passed unbelievably slowly. I had to go to the detentions because Mr Turner refused to let me off them and made a big show to the Principal that it was more about the conversation and lack of respect, rather than me being late for his class. The only good thing about detentions was that I got my homework done quicker than normal, which meant I could spend more time with Luke in the evenings.

Tonight I planned on letting a little lose though and having fun. It was Ricky's eighteenth so he was having a party at his house. I dressed up a little more than usual, going for a blue all in one, strapless playsuit. It looked cute and showed off a lot more leg than I would ever dream of flashing, but I was with Luke all night and I knew he'd appreciate it. I was staying at his place tonight; my parents didn't know, of course, they thought I was staying with Charlotte. Alex had agreed to cover for me, in exchange I had to do all of his chores for a month and make him grilled cheese whenever he asked for it.

I'd just finished packing my overnight bag when there was a knock on my bedroom door. I turned and shouted for them to come in, knowing it would be Luke. As soon as the door opened, his eyes went wide, and his mouth dropped open as he raked his eyes over every single inch of my body. I bit back a smile at his lustful expression.

"Holy shit, Maisie. Damn!" he almost growled.

I laughed and did a little twirl. "Look okay?" I asked, not really needing confirmation, I could see the approval in his eyes.

"Okay? My God, baby… or maybe I should say, my Goddess." He bit his bottom lip, his brow furrowed as his eyes raked over me slowly.

I laughed and grabbed my red sandals that Luke had bought me a couple of weeks ago. I pulled them on then walked over to him. He was still checking me out, obviously thinking of all of the dirty things he wanted to do to my body tonight.

"Let's go get this party over and done with so that you can take me home with you for the night, huh?" I purred, tracing my hand up his chest lightly.

His hands went to my outer thighs, brushing across them teasingly. "These legs blow my mind," he breathed, shaking his head, looking slightly pained. "I think maybe you should change. I'm not sure I'm gonna be able to drive us there without killing us."

I laughed at that. "What?"

"I'm warning you now, I'm not going to be able to keep my eyes on the road on the way there," he admitted, shrugging casually as if this was no big deal.

I slipped my arms around his neck and pulled him closer to me, pressing every inch of my body to his, trying not to shiver as his hands trailed up to cup my butt. "If you kill us then we won't be able to do any of those dirty things that you're thinking right now."

He laughed, smirking at me. "I am thinking a lot of dirty things."

I kissed him lightly, pulling away as he went to deepen the kiss. I purposefully left my lips close to his so they would brush together when I spoke. "And I'll do every single one of them, so long as we live to see the end of the night."

He moaned breathily, taking my hand and tugging me towards the door quickly. "Let's just go to the stupid party so we can leave already." He stooped and picked up my overnight bag, practically dragging me out of the door as I giggled at his eagerness.

• • •

THE PARTY WAS IN full swing by the time we got there; people were already wasted even though it was only just after eight thirty. Luke had his arms securely around my waist, his chest pressed tightly against my back as we headed to the kitchen to find Ricky and wish him happy birthday.

"So we tell Ricky happy birthday, have one drink, one dance, then I take you home with me for some naked private time. Deal?" Luke whispered, tightening his arm across my stomach.

I giggled and nodded in agreement, subtly brushing my body against his teasingly. "Deal."

He groaned in my ear and pushed me against the kitchen island lightly, pressing his whole body to mine possessively. "You're being a bad girl tonight," he breathed seductively in my ear.

I looked over my shoulder at him, trying to appear innocent. "I'm never a bad girl. I'm Maisie Preston, innocent to the core," I protested.

"I took that innocence, Maisie. You can't claim to still have that!" He laughed and kissed me, making my knees tremble slightly, and I was glad I went for flat shoes tonight instead of heels; otherwise I might have fallen over because of the feeling that went into the kiss.

He pulled back and put his forehead to mine. "Let's get a drink, then we're leaving," he whispered.

I nodded, but I knew that wouldn't happen, because just as he finished speaking, his group of friends walked in, all teasing each other and pushing each other around. I sighed as they spotted Luke. His arm stayed around my waist, but his posture changed. The act that he put on for his friends was back again, I just hoped he didn't end up getting into a fight if he got too drunk.

Several hours later, Luke and I were totally wasted. He was supposed to have been driving tonight, but after the drinking competition started he decided we would get a cab to his instead. 'Drunken jerk Luke' was on good form tonight. So far he had already insulted most of the teachers; he'd made digs at the computer club, which had pissed off Charlotte. He'd annoyed my brother by calling him a 'self-obsessed player who only thinks about where to get his dick wet next'. He'd basically made jokes and nasty comments about everyone in the room, except for me. Lucky for him he was popular otherwise he probably would have been thrown out hours ago. I could tell by Alex's expression that he wanted to sucker punch him for his comment.

When my legs were too tired to hold me anymore, I boosted myself up on the counter, sitting and laughing with my girls while Luke sat with his friends and snorted vodka. I had drank a lot more than I normally would, and had somehow been roped into playing 'I never' too which didn't help.

Sandy sashayed her way into the kitchen, her eyes on Luke as she smiled seductively. My jaw tightened as I watched from across the kitchen. Luke was sat on one of the stools because he was a little unsteady on his feet. She pulled herself up onto the counter next to him, her short skirt rising slightly higher as she did it and the hoe didn't bother to pull it down either.

"She's such a slut," I slurred, pointing at Sandy with my cup, slopping Captain Morgan on my leg.

Charlotte and Beth both nodded in agreement. "Are you gonna go stop her hitting on your man?" Beth asked, hiccupping in the middle of her sentence.

I shrugged. The movement made me wobble and almost fall off the counter I was perched on top of. "Nah, he's a big boy he can tell her himself," I rejected, waving my hand dismissively.

I laughed as they talked; Luke kept leaning away from her as she leant in, obviously flirting with him. Suddenly he disappeared behind the kitchen island, a loud crash followed, and hysterical laughter. I frowned, confused for a second until I realised that Luke had just fallen off his stool and landed on his ass. I burst into a fit of giggles, as did everyone else in the room; people were cheering him and shaking their heads.

Ricky grabbed his arm and pulled Luke to his feet where he swayed, rubbing one hand over the back of his head and the other over his lower back, frowning drunkenly. His eyes flicked to me, and he pouted like a child. "I don't think I'll be able perform very well tonight, baby. I think I may have had a little too much to drink, and my ass hurts."

I laughed and rolled my eyes at him. "You can make it up to me in the morning when your killer hangover's gone."

He smirked at me and grabbed the stool, sitting back down again. Sandy smiled and handed him a new cup of drink because he'd spilt his all over the floor with that little stunt. "Bottoms up, Luke," she said, smiling at him suggestively.

He laughed and downed his drink in one before scrunching up the cup and throwing it over his shoulder. "Bottoms in any direction works for me, right Maisie?" he chirped, laughing hysterically at his own non-funny joke. Sandy smiled and jumped down from the counter heading out of the room, throwing one last seductive look over her shoulder at Luke, but he either didn't see it or chose to ignore it because he didn't react to it at all.

After another ten minutes, Luke put his head on the counter and groaned loudly. I pushed myself off the nice little seat I had found next to the alcohol and headed over to him, staggering and walking into people as I did it. My eyes were a little unfocussed, but I obviously wasn't as bad as Luke. I put my hand on his back, rubbing gently.

"Okay?" I asked, leaning heavily on the counter.

He shook his head. "No. I don't feel good. Actually," he swallowed loudly, "I think I need to puke." He pushed himself up from the stool and ran, with surprising stability, towards the stairs.

I cringed at the thought. "Yuck! Rinse your mouth after," I called after him, laughing to myself.

"He alright? You need someone to take you home, Maisie?" Freddie slurred. His eyes raked over my body slowly, making my skin crawl. "I could help you get to bed if you need a hand… or any other body part you might need." He smirked at me, but I was just too drunk to care.

I didn't bother making any comeback as I turned away from him, looking for a bottle of water or something; I was actually thirsty even though I'd been drinking like a fish all night. I felt a hand slide down my back, squeezing my ass.

I frowned and span around, slapping the hand away, glaring at Freddie. "You need to get lost before I tell Luke that happened," I threatened.

"Luke's too wasted to care. Come on, Preston, let's go somewhere private and I'll show you how a real man performs," he suggested, gripping my hip and leaning in.

I put my hands on his chest and shoved as hard as I could, causing him stagger back a step and me to almost fall into the counter behind me. Just then I spotted Alex from the corner of my eye and I felt my heart rate start to return to normal. "Screw you, Freddie. Just go away before I call Alex over here to kick your ass," I warned, nodding towards my twin brother who looked like he was trying to eat the girl he was kissing.

Freddie looked in that direction and I saw his eyes widen. His hand immediately dropped off my hip. It did benefit me sometimes, having a brother that would happily beat the crap out of any guy that even looked in the direction of his sister. He had beat on Luke a couple of times when we first got together, and he certainly wouldn't stand for a jerk like Freddie putting his dirty hands all over me.

Freddie frowned and shook his head; he didn't say anything just walked off through the crowd, obviously heading to find another girl to try out his sexual predator moves on. I leaned against the counter, waiting for Luke to come back, but he didn't. Just as I was starting to get worried about him, a girl walked up to me and smiled.

"Hey, Maisie. Luke asked me to tell you to meet him upstairs in one of the bedrooms," she chirped, giggling to herself. I frowned. Selena wasn't exactly one of my friends, she was in the A list at school and was one of Sandy's little cheerleader minions. I was actually surprised that she would even do a favour for Luke that involved her talking to me in the first place.

"Okay, thanks," I replied, still a little confused. "Did he say which one?" I frowned at the stairs.

She smiled sweetly. "Third door on the left I think. It's Ricky's bedroom."

I smiled and thanked her before waving goodbye to Charlotte and Beth who were just about to leave, and then I headed upstairs to find Luke. I was guessing that he'd either thrown up and needed help to clear up the mess, or he was fine and wanted to start the naked private time earlier than planned. I crossed my fingers for the second one and headed to the back of the house, doing my best to weave through the crowd that were dancing like crazy people. I almost fell when someone bumped me in the side as they did their take on the running man move.

I stumbled up the stairs, bumping into people and apologising, trying not to laugh when they shot me glares. I couldn't help but get excited while thinking about the dirtiness of having sex in someone else's bed while the party raged on downstairs.

Third bedroom on the right Selena had said. I ran my hand along the wall and counted the doors as I went past. When I got to door number three I twisted the handle and literally fell into the room, giggling hysterically as I sat on the floor shaking my head at myself. *That was so incredibly graceful!*

I heard a little squeal and a grunt, and I flicked my eyes up from the floor quickly, only to see something I had never thought I would see in my life. Luke was butt naked, laying on his back on the bed; a girl was riding him, moaning, with her head tipped back in pleasure. He gripped her hips to stop her as I walked in. His face went pale and his mouth dropped open in shock, while the girl - who I now recognised as Sandy - whined and begged him not to stop, desperately tried to grind her hips against him again.

I gulped and blinked, unsure if what I was seeing was actually happening. *Maybe I've drunk so much I've passed out and this is a nightmare. Please let me wake up!*

"Maisie! It's not... no... shit!" Luke cried, shaking his head fiercely as he shoved Sandy off him forcefully, making her squeak and fall onto the bed.

I pushed myself up off the floor quickly, blinking a couple more times to make sure what I thought I was seeing, was actually happening. Unfortunately it was. I could feel my heart breaking at the betrayal. I loved him so much, and he was screwing another girl while I was downstairs? How could he do that to me? I thought I knew him, I would have bet my life on it that he would have never done this to me, ever.

He jumped away from her and literally fell off the bed with a heavy thump. Sandy giggled and shot me a wicked grin. I wanted to punch her face as she stood up, picking up her clothes from the floor and sauntering across the room, stepping over Luke. When she got to the door where I was standing, she smirked at me before turning back to him smiling seductively. "Same time next week, Luke?" she asked, laughing and walking out of the door, still naked, apparently not even caring who could see her outside. I couldn't move. I couldn't even punch her in her evil face. The betrayal and hurt felt as if it was killing me slowly.

Her words seemed to echo in my ears. *Same time next week...*

Had this happened before? Had he cheated on me before? My legs felt weak so I slumped against the wall, using it for support as I gasped for breath. I felt sick. My eyes prickled with tears as everything I thought I knew in life was slowly being washed away like it was nothing. All of our future plans, everything we'd shared, every promise he'd made me, had all been a lie. For so long I'd been on cloud nine with him, blissfully happy, and now I was just free falling, hurtling into oblivion and waiting for the final crash that would kill me. How could I have been so stupid? Of course someone like Luke wouldn't be satisfied dating a nerd, of course he was off sleeping with other girls, how had I not realised until now?

He rolled over, grabbing his jeans, trying to put one leg in but he kept missing the hole as he swore and grunted, unable to do it. "Maisie, I'm sorry. I'm so, so sorry! Please, baby, please?" he begged, looking at me with desperation and panic clear across his face.

My heart was beating way too fast in my chest, my ears were ringing, and my whole body started to sweat. I needed to get out of here; I needed to get some fresh air. The room smelt like sex and it was making me feel worse. I'd never felt so hurt, so low, and so worthless in my life.

"Luke, why?" I whispered, looking at his face, trying to work out why I wasn't enough for him, why I wasn't good enough for him to just love me and want just me like I did him.

"I'm sorry, Maisie. I don't know. It just happened! I was in the bathroom and then she just threw herself at me, the next thing I knew I was naked on the bed and you walked in. I'm so sorry. I love you so much, so much!" His voice was husky and thick with emotion. He pushed himself up and tried to stand but he swayed on his feet and fell into the edge of the bed as he continued to try and put on his jeans. I'd never seen him so drunk, but that was no excuse for this, there was nothing that could make this situation better.

"And you couldn't have said no?" I could feel the anger building now. The hurt and betrayal were still there, but rage was taking over as the dominant emotion in my body. "You couldn't have said no to her? What does she have that I don't have? What is it about her that you wanted, Luke? Her perfect body and blonde hair? Her slutty clothes and too much make-up?" I growled.

He shook his head fiercely but instead of answering he bent over and grabbed the trashcan from the floor, throwing up into it violently. He groaned and sat on the edge of the bed, throwing up again and again. A wave of compassion washed over me. I never liked to see him ill or hurt; my whole body longed to go over and comfort him, to hold him and beg him not to cheat on me again.

"I love you," he croaked, wiping his mouth on the back of his hand, looking at me through watery eyes.

I wanted to tell him I loved him too, because I did, I really loved him, and that was what hurt the most, the fact that I loved him so much. But I couldn't just forget this ever happened and pretend everything was normal. Luke and I had promised that we would never cheat on each other, ever, and up until about four minutes ago I would have bet my life that he would always keep that promise to me. I couldn't have been more wrong.

"I need to go home," I whispered. I couldn't stay here anymore, I needed to go.

He tried to stand up but he just fell straight back down again. "Maisie, come here. Please, I want to come to you but I can't. Please? Can you help me with my clothes and then we'll get a cab to mine," he begged, stretching out his hand towards me. His other hand was on the side of his head; he was wincing as if he had a headache.

"You just slept with another girl. I'm not going home with you," I croaked, shaking my head.

His face fell as he squeezed his eyes shut. "Please?" he begged. "I don't feel right. I... I think someone put something in my drink. I wouldn't have done it otherwise, I swear. Please, I know you're hurting, but please forgive me?"

My feet started to move towards him of their own accord, my body was already forgiving him because that was probably the easier thing to do. I wanted to be with him. I wanted the things we'd planned for our lives. I fell down on my knees in front of him, pushing the trashcan out of the way, not looking at the contents and trying to ignore the smell of it. He grabbed my face pulling me closer to him, looking right into my eyes. His whole face was the picture of sorrow and remorse. I looked into his brown eyes that I had stared into for the last nineteen months. His pupils were enormous, he was unquestionably stoned, yet I hadn't seen him take anything.

"Do you have any idea how much you've hurt me?" I asked. The tears continued to fall down my face uncontrollably.

He nodded and wiped the tears away, looking like he was in pain. "Maisie, that would kill me if I saw you doing that with another guy." He pulled me into a hug, stroking the back of my head softly. "Please forgive me?" he whispered.

I closed my eyes and wrapped my arms around him, pressing my face into the crook of his neck. I wanted so much to say yes. Luke was the only guy I ever wanted; he was my first kiss, my first boyfriend, my first. I thought it would last forever, but I hated cheaters. Once a guy got away with cheating once, then they would do it again and again, and I refused to be treated like that.

I pulled back so I could look at him. Immediately he crashed his lips to mine. I kissed him back because it was just a natural response to; kissing Luke was like breathing, something I didn't even need to think about. When he nibbled on my bottom lip wanting to deepen the kiss, I closed my eyes and the first thought that popped into my head was, *I wonder if he kissed Sandy like this...*

I jerked away from him and swiped angrily at my mouth. Where was my self-respect? I'd just walked in on him screwing another girl and I was about to forgive him and let it go as if it was nothing? I was a stronger person than that, wasn't I?

I jumped to my feet and slapped him hard across the face, ignoring how he winced and hissed through his teeth. I grabbed his jeans from his hand and shoved my hand in his pocket, getting his car keys out before throwing his jeans across the room so he would have to get up and get them.

"You're an asshole, Luke. I can't believe I let you sucker me in for so long," I shouted angrily.

He looked at me stunned, his mouth hung open in shock. I turned on my heel and stormed out, slamming the door behind me, ignoring how he screamed my name over and over. Drunk or high, he shouldn't have cheated on me, I would never do that to him, ever, and I deserved someone who could say the same about me.

I desperately tried to stop crying as I stormed through the house, but I just couldn't. The hurt that I felt inside was making me feel sick and slightly lightheaded, but the shock had sobered me up a lot. As I staggered across the lounge, I saw Ricky dancing with a girl, so I walked up to him and grabbed his arm, pulling him round to face me.

"Luke's upstairs, he needs some help. Go sort him out and make sure he gets home. If he asks, tell him I don't want to speak to him," I instructed, swiping at my face again, wiping the traitor tears away.

Ricky's mouth dropped open in shock. "What? What are you talking about, you don't want to talk to him? Are you kidding?" he asked, shaking his head, looking at me like I'd lost my mind.

Sandy sauntered past me, grinning proudly. Before I knew what I was doing, I grabbed the back of her hair and pulled her to a stop. Obviously I was over the shock of it now, all that I felt was anger and hurt, and I wanted her to hurt too. She screamed and gripped my hands, trying to get me to let go, but I just tightened my grip.

"I left him upstairs for you, why don't you go finish what you started? It's not fair on a guy for you to stop half way through, he'll get blue balls," I growled angrily as I shoved her away from me in the direction of the stairs. She glared at me angrily, one hand on the back of her head, she was obviously in pain. She opened her mouth to say something back so I just held up one hand to silence her. "You need to find some respect for yourself. Seriously, you're a dirty tramp, and that's all these guys see in you, an easy lay, nothing more. Dirty, quick party sex is all sluts like you are good for," I stated, looking her over distastefully before I turned and stormed off towards the front door. I ignored Ricky shouting after me, asking me what had happened and where I was going.

As soon as I was outside the door, I kicked off my sandals. I picked them up and hurled them as far away from me as I could, Luke had bought them for me and I didn't want them touching me. I walked up to his car and pressed the button to unlock it. As I was doing it, I knew it was wrong and dangerous, but I just didn't care. I needed to get as far away from Luke as I could and then maybe that would stop my heartache a little.

I saw the front door open and Ricky came running out of the house, looking around quickly. I jumped in the car and adjusted his seat, starting the engine and peeling out of the space, narrowly avoiding taking the bumper off a parked car as I did so. I didn't look in the mirror as I sped away from the house. I just needed to get home and crawl into my bed and sob myself to sleep.

I could barely see where I was going through the tears that just wouldn't stop coming. I swerved as a car stopped with no warning in front of me, I pulled around it and then realised that, in doing so, I'd run a red light. "Shit!" I shouted, slamming my hand down on the steering wheel. *Oh well, if any cameras caught that then the car is registered to Luke, so he'll get in trouble not me!* That thought made me laugh, so I ran the next stop light on purpose. No one was around anyway; it was after one in the morning.

As I was driving down the street, someone walked out into the road in front of me. I gasped and slammed both feet down on the brake as hard as I could. Instantly the car was sliding and skidding as I gripped the steering wheel for dear life. The tyres were squealing on the road.

I'm about to kill someone. I'm drunk, uninsured, and I'm about to run someone down.

The guy was just standing there watching as the car skidded towards him. I couldn't see his face because he had on a grey hoodie, but I had the feeling he was looking right at me. The last thing he would see before he died would be my hysterical and horrified face - not a pleasant sight I'd bet.

I screamed as the car just went on and on. Everything was moving in slow motion, barely a couple of seconds had probably passed, but I couldn't breathe, my heart had stopped. I wanted to close my eyes so I wouldn't see when his body made impact with the car, but I couldn't, they were stuck open wide, as was my mouth.

chapter five

Just as the car was about to smash into him, he jumped straight up in the air, a two footed jump. The car was still going forward so as he landed his feet hit the hood of the car. What happened next I couldn't be sure of, but it looked to me like he ran up the windscreen. I heard footsteps on the roof and finally the car screeched to a halt.

I twisted in my seat, covering my mouth, stifling the scream that just continued to rip its way out of my throat. I looked out of the back window and saw him do some sort of backflip off the back of the car. He landed gracefully on his feet and then turned back to look at me.

My heart was crashing in my chest; my drunken brain was unable to take in what I had just seen. *He has just jumped onto the car, ran over the top of it and then done a somersault off the back? Am I dreaming right now?* I fumbled with my seatbelt and jumped out, my whole body shaking.

"Are you fucking blind? Did you not see me there?" he shouted angrily, waving his arms to make his point.

I whimpered and slumped against the car for support, still unsure as to what exactly happened. I gulped and gasped for breath. This was definitely the worst night of my life. Luke had cheated on me, and now I almost killed someone and was going to be in so much trouble for driving under the influence. "I'm so sorry," I croaked. "Are you okay?"

He waved his hand dismissively. "Fine. You should watch where you're freaking going though. You could have killed me!" he growled. My legs wouldn't support me anymore; I nodded and slid down the car and onto the floor, pulled my knees up to my chest and sobbed, rocking myself gently. "Er, look it's... don't cry about it… I'm fine," the guy soothed, obviously uncomfortable.

"I'm sorry," I mumbled again, pressing my face against my knees.

"Forget it, it's all good. I kinda wish I had someone to tape that though, I could have added it to my profile," he said, laughing to himself.

Profile? What on earth is that about? I sniffed and turned my head, wiping my face on the back of my hand. "What profile?" I asked. "How did you do that anyway? *What* did you do? I just don't get it. One minute you were in the road and the next you were jumping down from the roof of the car, not a scratch on you." I shook my head in disbelief, my voice breaking as I spoke. Maybe this really was a dream like I thought earlier. Maybe this was an alcohol induced nightmare. Or maybe this was something out of a fantasy movie and he was a vampire or werewolf or some other dark and dangerous mythical creature.

"Parkour," he replied, shrugging.

Par-what? "Huh?"

He smiled and pushed the hood of his sweater down so I could see him properly. He was a good looking guy, brown eyes, shaven dark hair, and a strong jaw. If I wasn't in love with Luke I would have said this guy was hot, but I never looked at other guys like that really.

"Parkour. Freerunning. Not heard of it?" he asked sarcastically, looking at me like I was stupid.

I gulped. I'd heard of freerunning but not the word parkour, was that what that was? The whole jumping onto a moving car and running over the top of it to avoid being crushed to death? "Oh, yeah I've heard off it. I've just never seen it. That was just," I trailed off, not having the right word to complete the sentence.

"Amazing?" he offered, smirking at me as he ran a hand over the back of his head, obviously proud of himself.

I shook my head. Amazing wasn't exactly what I was going for. "Weird and scary more like," I admitted.

He laughed. "Yeah well, it saved me from a few weeks in a cast, so I'll take weird and scary."

I winced as I thought about how badly I could have hurt him. I was so stupid to have driven Luke's car. What was I even thinking? My parents were going to go crazy when they found out about this. "I'm really sorry."

"Should you even be driving? You smell like a damn brewery," he stated, waving his hand in front of his face, looking at me disgusted.

I shook my head. "No. I was at a party and I stole my boyfriend's keys because I wanted to go home," I admitted, crying again at the thought of Luke.

He frowned. "He wouldn't take you or something?" he asked, shifting on his feet as if he was uncomfortable having a conversation with me. Maybe he didn't like crying girls, but then again, what guy did?

I gulped, not wanting to get into this with a stranger. "We should get you to the hospital or something," I replied, changing the subject.

He snorted. "I'm fine. Not hurt at all, just chill. Next time don't drive drunk." He turned on his heel and started to walk off, leaving me there sitting on the floor against the car, crying helplessly. He stopped after a few steps, his shoulders stiff; he turned back to me and frowned. "Do you have someone that can come and get you?"

I sniffed and shook my head. I couldn't call my parents about this; I'd be in so much trouble. Alex was at the party. And Luke, well, even if I could call Luke, he wouldn't be able to help me because he couldn't even get his jeans on.

The guy sighed. "How about I drive you home?" He looked slightly bored, as if this happened to him every day and was nothing out of the ordinary.

Is he seriously offering to drive me home? I almost kill him, and he's offering me a ride? He doesn't even know me; shouldn't he be reporting me to the police for DUI or something? "Really?" I asked, my voice croaky from all the crying.

"Yeah. Unless you want me to leave you here on your own, this isn't a nice area though so I wouldn't recommend it," he answered, shrugging as if it was no big deal. He got out a pack of cigarettes from his pocket, pulling one out with his teeth before offering me the packet, one eyebrow raised. I shook my head quickly and frowned. I hated smoking. "Well, do you want a ride or not? I'm not waiting around all night," he barked, his tone clearly annoyed that I hadn't answered him.

I nodded quickly and tried to push myself up using the car as leverage. My hand slipped and just as I was about to fall on my face, he gripped my elbow and righted me, pulling me to my feet. I smiled gratefully. "Thanks," I mumbled, sniffing and noticing that my voice barely even worked because of all of the crying.

"How much did you drink anyway?" he asked, wincing as he turned his face away as if he smelt something distasteful.

I discreetly sniffed to see if I really smelt that strongly of alcohol, but I couldn't smell anything at all. "I don't know. A lot I think."

He nodded and let go of my arm. "My ride's over here. You should lock your car otherwise it'll get stolen. I'm already a little worried about what state it'll be in if you leave it here all night," he said, looking over Luke's BMW M6 appreciatively.

I shrugged. "I don't care; it's my ex-boyfriend's."

He raised one eyebrow, looking at me curiously. "I thought you said your boyfriend wouldn't take you home, now you have your ex's car?"

I shook my head. "Same guy. He's now my ex because he couldn't keep his dick in his pants tonight," I stated, feeling my lip tremble as I said the words. I didn't want to think about it again, I didn't want to think about the fact that the guy I was totally and utterly in love with had just cheated on me and thrown everything we had down the toilet for a one night stand.

He frowned. “Stupid guy,” he mumbled so quietly I was barely even sure if I heard him right. Then he grinned at me, tossing his half smoked cigarette on the floor and stubbing it out with his toe. He had a wicked glint to his eye as he bent down and picked up a rock the size of a baseball, holding it out to me. “Want a little payback?” he offered, nodding at the car when I didn’t quite understand what he was getting at.

“Payback? What’s that supposed to mean?” I asked, shaking my head in confusion.

He laughed. “Don’t you want to hit him in the worst place imaginable? Well, after a kick to the balls anyway.” When I still didn’t get it he sighed and stepped closer to me, taking my hand and putting the rock in my palm. “A guy’s car is important to him, if someone were to come along and smash his windscreen during the night... well, that would be very unfortunate, wouldn’t it?” he asked, smirking at me.

I gulped, watching his face to see if he was serious. He wanted me to smash Luke’s windshield and then pretend it wasn’t me? I looked back at Luke’s car. It was his baby, but I didn’t think he would be that bothered if it got bashed up, his family had too much money to be concerned over a piece of glass that needed replacing. Besides, he had two cars, so this was really no big deal if it got a little damaged; he wouldn’t care so there was no point.

“Don’t you want to pay him back for cheating on you? Don’t you want to hurt him like he hurt you?” he purred, his voice so seductive and encouraging that I actually shivered. It felt like he was the little devil that was sitting on my shoulder telling me to do bad things. “Cheating on you, while you were at the same party no less. The guy deserves something, doesn’t he?” he teased. I could hear the amusement in his voice.

I turned to frown at him. I wasn’t smashing Luke’s windshield, it wouldn’t accomplish anything and would just leave his car open to thieves during the night. “I don’t want payback; I just want to go home.” I sniffed and wiped at my face again, noticing that the tears had finally stopped; maybe I’d finally ran out, who knows.

He rolled his eyes as I dropped the rock down onto the floor. “Girls like you want to be walked all over. I wonder how many times he’s screwed some tramp and then done you straight after,” he mused as he turned to walk off.

I felt the anger boiling in my system. His words hit me hard. *Just how many times has Luke been with another girl and then had sex with me in the same night?* Before I knew what I was doing I’d picked up the rock and thrown it as hard as I could at Luke’s car. I wasn’t standing very far away from it so the shot hit the middle of the glass, leaving a huge indented crack and the rest of the windshield crumbled and cracked too. Immediately the car alarm started wailing and the lights started flashing, lighting up my feet and legs. The sound was deafening in the silence of the deserted street and I couldn't help the little scream that escaped out of my mouth.

"Holy shit!" the guy cried next to me, then he burst out laughing, picked up the stone from the hood of the car, and grabbed my hand, starting to run down the street, dragging me along with him. As I ran, for some reason I started to laugh too. I felt a little good for doing that. Hopefully the car alarm would sound for so long that it would kill his battery too.

We ran, holding hands, laughing. I enjoyed the sensation of my hair whipping back, and the wind blowing in my face. I liked the adrenalin and the fear of being caught. For some reason all of those things made my heart thrum in my chest and a smile stretch across my face. I felt kind of free, more alive somehow. We ran until I couldn't do it anymore. When my lungs felt like they were on fire, I pulled him to a stop and put my hands on my knees, gasping for breath, and swaying a little on my feet from the alcohol. I looked up at him to see him leaning against the wall, his arms crossed casually. He looked the picture of ease as he smirked at me, not even a little out of breath even though we'd been running flat out for a good three minutes.

"You need to get fitter, little rebel. If you're going to be a good criminal then you need to be able to make a quicker getaway than that," he teased, raising one eyebrow at me.

I laughed and stood up, clutching at my ribs as they burned from the effort of breathing. I honestly did need to get fitter, he wasn't even breathing hard yet I was sweating like a turkey just before thanksgiving. "I think I'll stick to that one act. I've never done anything even remotely bad in my life," I replied, grinning like a mad woman. I was actually still on a high that I had done that to Luke's car; payback certainly was going to be a bitch on this occasion.

He grinned and shook his head, obviously amused. "Well then I'm glad I was there to witness your demise," he teased, winking at me. "Come on then, let's get you home so you can puke then sober up." Before I could even answer, he turned and started walking back the way we came, not even bothering to wait for me.

"I'm Maisie," I said, trying to keep up with him as he walked quickly down the road. I stumbled every other step because I had no shoes on and was still feeling the effects of the alcohol. It was harder to keep in a straight line at this slower pace, with him not holding my hand and dragging me along.

He turned his head and looked at me over his shoulder, as if he was deciding if he wanted to tell me his name or not. After a couple of seconds he obviously decided he did want to. "Zach," he muttered, shrugging.

I followed him down the road, wondering if I was about to be killed. This was a classic thing you should never do, go off with a stranger for a ride; this was what my parents had drummed into me since I could remember. 'Never accept a ride from a stranger, no matter what they promise you' but here I was, following a guy I had only just met to some unknown place. I really was stupid.

chapter six

As we walked down the street he tossed the rock I'd thrown at Luke's car into the shrubs. "Why did you bring that?" I asked curiously as I jogged to catch him up.

He smirked at me. "You wanted me to leave your fingerprints all over the rock that smashed his window? If you want we can just go back and slip a confession on there with your name and address, telling the cops where to find you," he suggested, laughing quietly to himself.

"I didn't think about fingerprints. Oh my God, am I going to get into trouble for doing that?" My eyes widened as I started to feel nauseous. I'd just broken the law and vandalised someone else's property and that fact was only just sinking in. My heart was racing in my chest as I stopped walking and started to panic.

Zach laughed and grabbed my elbow, shaking his head. "Nah, no one was around, there's no CCTV on that street, and I removed the evidence. As far as you're concerned, the car was in perfect condition when you got out and left it." He looked at me sternly as he started to drag me along again.

I thought about what he said. No one else but him saw me do it, and after tonight I wouldn't even see him again anyway, so there was no chance I was getting into trouble for this, at least, I hoped not anyway. The worry was starting to kill the buzz a little but deep down I was still glad I did it. That small payback did make me feel marginally better.

He stopped after another couple of minutes and smiled at me. "Ever ridden on a bike before?" His voice held an amused twang to it.

A *bike?* I looked at what he was standing next to, a huge black motorbike.

Holy crap, is this his 'ride'? Is he seriously expecting me to get on this death-trap? It didn't even look like it was roadworthy, it was rusted and scratched up, the seat was a little torn and the stuffing was leaking out.

"No way," I whispered, shaking my head. There was no way I was getting on this bike with him at all. I had been in a car accident a couple of years ago with Alex, I knew how much it hurt, and that crash had been fully protected and encased in metal, this, this was pure exposure to the road if you fell off. There was not a chance in hell I was getting on this thing.

"Yes way," he countered, laughing at me as he swung his leg over it and fumbled in his pockets for his keys.

I stood there with my mouth agape, just watching as he started the engine, well *attempted* to start the engine anyway because it took at least five tries before it roared to life. Even the sound of the engine screamed danger. It didn't sound at all healthy; it was loud and whiney and threatened to give out at any minute.

"I'm not getting on that thing. I'll just, um," I trailed off, thinking and weighing my options. I could call Alex and see if anyone at the party was sober enough to come and get me. Or maybe I could call a cab - but if I did that I wasn't sure how I would pay for it because I didn't have my purse. I could call my parents, but then how would I explain everything to them? I could walk home, but it was well over half an hour to walk to my house from here and I had no shoes...

He grinned and shook his head. "Pussy," he teased, cocking his head to the side, looking at me mockingly.

I scowled at him. I didn't like him calling me that, for some reason I felt like I wanted to prove myself to this stranger that I'd met less than twenty minutes ago. "I'm not, it's just that thing doesn't even look like it could hold my weight as well as yours, its wheels would probably fall off!" I answered. Then I flinched when I realised that I'd just made a bitchy comment about his bike when he was being nice and offering me a lift home. I opened my mouth to apologise, but he spoke first.

"We can't all ride around in our cheating boyfriend's sports car!" He frowned and looked away from me, obviously annoyed.

I chewed on my lip and felt a wave of guilt wash over me. I was being so horrible to him, and all he was doing was being nice to me. This wasn't me, I wasn't like this usually, I was Maisie Preston, sweet and kind to everyone, but Luke had turned me into this bitter, nasty person. This was another thing that was his fault.

"Sorry, Zach. I was out of order saying that. I'd like a ride if you're still offering it, but I understand if you want to tell me to jog on," I said, looking at him apologetically.

He chuckled quietly. "I've never said the words 'jog on' in my life, I'd usually go for something stronger," he said, a grin stretching across his face. I smiled apologetically and he rolled his eyes, "Come on then, little miss DUI, let's get you home, huh?" He patted the seat behind him for me to get on.

I winced and looked longingly back up the road, contemplating my options again.

"Get on, Maisie!" he ordered, grabbing the front of my playsuit and pulling me towards him. I squealed as my clothes moved. Where he pulled me, the top came away from my body, so I quickly clutched it to my chest again so he didn't get an eyeful. He laughed and let go. "Almost got a flash then. Maybe next time." He winked at me and I gasped. *Maybe I really should walk home.* "Get on the bike before I run out of gas from sitting here idle for so freaking long. I do have places to get to you know, I don't just hang out on the streets waiting for random drunken girls to run me down!" I winced thinking about almost killing him and stepped closer, gripping his shoulders for support as I climbed, in an exceptionally unladylike fashion, onto the seat behind him. He laughed and stood up with his legs either side of the bike, and pulled off his hoodie, passing it to me. "It'll be cold when we get going and you're only in that slutty little outfit," he said, nodding down at the flimsy clothes I was wearing.

"I'm not a slut." I frowned in protest but pulled on the offered sweater at the same time.

He smirked at me and shrugged. "Tell that to your legs that are exposed almost to the pleasure zone which, coincidently, is pressed against a stranger's ass," he commented, laughing as I slapped his back.

"Are you gonna drive me home or stand there making assumptions about me all night?" I asked, trying to sound stern but failing miserably, he was actually pretty funny.

"Sure. Where to?" he asked, looking at me curiously over his shoulder. I told him my address, giving a few directions when he didn't quite know where it was. "Yeah, I think I know it. If I go past it or miss a turn then just tell me and I'll turn around." He took my hands and put them on his sides, signalling for me to hold on.

I nodded and gripped his t-shirt. I could feel his toned muscles under my hands; I knew he would be in good shape because of the whole freerunning and jumping over a moving car thing. "Where's my helmet anyway?" I asked, looking around for it hanging somewhere.

"Don't have one," he answered as he pulled out. I jerked back in the seat from the take-off and screamed, throwing my arms around his waist and pressing my face into his back. My heart was beating out of my chest from the fear of it. *This is such a stupid idea; I'm so going to die. Hopefully it'll be quick and painless!*

When we didn't immediately die, I pulled my face away from his back and looked over his shoulder. Then, before I knew what was happening, it started to feel nice. The wind was blowing across my face again like when we were running from Luke's car. It was almost like flying. My heart slowed down as my stomach got a little fluttery as the adrenalin started to flow through my veins.

I grinned and pressed my mouth and nose into his shoulder to make it easier to breathe, but I kept my eyes firmly forward as I wrapped my arms tighter around his waist. This was my first time on a motorbike, and I had to admit, I loved it. The fluid way that he mastered the bike and leant into the corners, it was almost sexual, and for some reason I felt a little weird to be doing this with him. This innocent ride home was actually sexy as hell.

Way too soon, he pulled into my street, slowing down and eventually came to a stop outside of my house. I took a couple of deep breaths as I pushed myself off the bike. My legs were a little wobbly from the vibrations of the journey, but even that was a gratifying feeling. I smiled and pulled off his hoodie, handing it back to him, trying not to grin like an idiot because the feeling riding on the bike caused in me. I didn't want him to know how much I enjoyed it because then he'd be smirking at me again.

"Thanks for the ride. Sorry again for almost killing you earlier," I said, wincing sheepishly.

He laughed and shook his head dismissively. "What's a little car accident between friends?" he joked. "You got keys, right?" He nodded towards the house in prompt.

I nodded, knowing there was a spare key hidden under a rock around the back of the house. "Yeah, thanks." I looked at him, unsure what else to say to this stranger than had just shown me an act of kindness and saved me from a whole heap of trouble.

"No problem. Maybe I'll see you around." He gunned the engine and his bike took off, roaring off up the road, leaving me standing there in the cold, watching him ride off in a puff of black exhaust fumes.

As soon as I was on my own I started to think about Luke again. Zach had taken my mind off it for a little while, but as soon as he rode off all I could think about was the betrayal that I felt in the pit of my stomach and how my heart felt like it was physically aching. The thing that got to me the most was the fact that I was actually worried about Luke. I'd left him at the party, unable to stand, throwing up and alone. I hated myself for still caring, but I did.

I gulped and forced myself to walk inside the house before I broke down on the front lawn. Once in the solitude of my bedroom I closed my door silently behind me. I didn't want my parents to know I was home; I just didn't want to see anyone right now. I slumped down onto my bed, ignoring how my bare feet put dirt smudges over the sheets. I pulled the covers up over my head to muffle the sound, and then I sobbed my heart out for the guy who I thought would love me forever. I sobbed for my lost future with him, I sobbed for the time that

I'd already wasted with him, I sobbed for the special things that I gave him of myself, things I could never give anyone else: my first kiss, my virginity. I just sobbed until the tears dried up and my chest hurt from the effort.

I wanted sleep to come and take me so I could stop thinking about it, but that didn't happen. Instead, I laid there awake all night, replaying everything good that happened between us, our plans, our memories. I just laid there wondering when the exact moment was that I ceased to be enough for him.

By the time morning came I felt a little dead inside. I didn't know what to think or feel. I'd had to turn my cell phone off during the night because the constant ringing and buzzing had driven me crazy. I reached over and grabbed it, turning it on again. The texts started coming through immediately. Twenty-six in total, all from Luke. I deleted them all without reading them, I didn't want to know what he said, I didn't want to hear his apologies, they weren't enough.

I unclasped my hand, stretching out my stiff fingers from where they had been in the same position all night - wrapped tightly around my locket that Luke had bought me. I couldn't let go of it. During the night I'd just laid there reading the inscription on the back over and over again. 'True love lasts for always. Yours forever, Luke'. *Yours forever.* The words brought a sad smile to my face every time I read them. Obviously his idea of forever and my idea of it were miles apart.

At just after ten in the morning there was a loud knocking on the front door. I already knew it would be him. I looked around my room for some sort of escape or somewhere to hide. I didn't want to see him, not yet, I couldn't face it. Voices drifted up the stairs, belonging to my dad and Luke. My dad was telling him that I wasn't here, that I stayed at Charlotte's, so obviously I was quiet enough that they didn't hear me come in last night.

I pushed myself out of the bed and crept to the door, opening it quietly and peeking down the stairs, but staying back so I wouldn't be seen.

"Clay, she's here! Please just let me go check her room," Luke begged desperately.

"What is going on? You look like crap, Luke," Dad questioned.

"Please can I just go check her room? I need to speak to her," Luke begged. His voice sounded so weak and sad that it made my knees tremble. He was upset too, but I refused to feel guilty about it, this wasn't my fault.

My dad sighed in frustration. "Fine. Go see for yourself."

I quickly pulled open my door and stepped out; I didn't want Luke in my room. "I don't want to talk to him," I said to my dad's shocked face. Immediately he put his arm across the bottom of the stairs, stopping Luke from getting to me, even though he didn't know why he was doing it or what was going on. I really had the best dad in the world.

"Maisie, please! I'm sorry, please I'm so sorry, baby," Luke cried, his eyes full of anguish and pain.

I sniffed and shook my head, walking down the stairs to see him better. My dad's arm was now across Luke's chest as Luke shoved and thrashed trying to get to me. "It's too late," I whispered, stopping when I was about three steps from the bottom.

His whole face fell. "No! It's not too late, don't say that. I didn't know what I was doing; someone put something in my drink last night. You know I would never cheat on you! You know me!" He looked at me desperately, his whole posture just looked crushed, and I wanted to wrap my arms around his neck and comfort him, but I just couldn't move my feet from the step I was on. I needed to stay strong; the relationship obviously wasn't what I thought it was if it meant that little to him that he would forget me for a quickie at a party. Drunk or stoned, you just didn't do that to someone who you love.

My dad was looking between the two of us, a shocked and confused expression on his face. "You broke up?" he asked incredulously.

Both Luke and I ignored him, our gazes locked on each other; he was begging me with his eyes. "It's not too late; please tell me that, Maisie. Please tell me I get another chance," he croaked, still trying to push my dad's arm off him so he could get to me.

I could feel the tears rolling down my cheeks again. "I'm sorry, I can't," I whispered, not trusting my voice to speak properly.

"No! I won't give up on us, Maisie. I won't!" Luke shouted wildly. I flinched, and my dad shoved Luke back a step towards the door. "Someone put something in my drink! I swear to you, I didn't even really know what I was doing, I swear!" He continued to thrash as my dad pushed him towards the door. "I love you, baby."

My breath caught in my throat at those words coming out of his mouth, every time he said them to me they melted my heart, and this was no exception, I still relished the sound of every single syllable.

"Just go," I whispered. He was breaking my heart all over again, seeing him just made everything came back, and the worst part was, the thing that I could see in my head the clearest right now, was him naked on the bed with another girl.

He dropped to his knees. "Please don't do this." His face showed his heartbreak. For a split second I reconsidered. "You and I are meant to be together, Maisie, you're my everything. Please? Just please don't give up on us, because I never will," he pleaded, not even bothering to wipe the tears from his face.

A stair creaked behind me. "What's happening? What's with all the shouting, some of us are sleeping off a hangover you know," Alex grumbled, slinging his arm around my shoulder, yawning in my ear. I turned to face him and his whole posture stiffened, his jaw tightened. "What the fuck have you done to my sister, Hannigan?" he shouted, letting his arm drop from my shoulders as he stepped in front of me protectively.

"Just stay out of it, Alex!" Luke snapped, getting to his feet again, trying to look around Alex, who was standing there like he was guarding the crown jewels. "Maisie, let's just go somewhere, let me explain," he suggested.

I shook my head in rejection. I just needed this meeting to be over, I couldn't see him anymore. I dug my fingers into Alex's back. "I don't want to talk to you, Luke. Please just go," I begged, nodding to the door.

"Explain what? What have you done?" Alex asked, looking at Luke angrily, his whole posture agitated and alert. He was going to go crazy when he found out that Luke had cheated on me.

"Alex, it's fine, just leave it," I whispered, trying to push him away from the protective stance he was in so that he'd look at me.

"My sister is standing here crying, it's not freaking fine!" he growled, shaking his head angrily. I had to smile at how overprotective he was of me; Luke had some real guts to still be standing there in the hallway because my dad looked like he was trying not to kill him too.

"Leave, Luke," I ordered sternly. I didn't want to see him get hurt; I still loved him and I didn't want to see him in pain.

His eyes tightened as they met mine. "Will you talk to me later? If I give you some time, will you answer your phone later?" he asked, looking at me pleadingly.

I needed to get him out of here before Alex found out what happened. It surprised me that he hadn't already heard considering we were at the same party last night. Then again, he was probably too busy sleeping with some girl to notice what was going on around him.

I nodded. "I just can't deal with this right now. Please just leave," I said quietly. Luke opened his mouth to protest, but I shook my head, cutting him off. "For me, just leave?" I begged. I just couldn't deal with anymore right now, I needed to go back to bed and try to sleep, because my head was pounding, a migraine was building up behind my eyes that was making me feel dizzy.

He nodded and looked at the floor, his shoulders slumped. He was literally the picture of sorrow. "I love you, baby," he whispered as he turned and walked out of the door.

As soon as he was gone my dad slammed the door. "What the hell happened? You two broke up? I always just thought you would end up together," he mumbled, looking at me slightly confused.

"Yeah we broke up; I don't want to talk about it." I turned towards my brother. "And you, you leave him alone, you hear me? If you hurt him I swear, Alex, I'm hurting you right back, get it?" I said looking at him sternly.

He frowned at me as his jaw tightened. "Just answer me this, did he cheat or something? He was wasted at the party last night, I left fairly early and someone said that you'd already left. I just assumed you went home with Luke," his eyes flicked to my dad quickly as he carried on speaking, "I meant Charlotte, that you went home with Charlotte," he amended.

I sighed, knowing that I needed to tell him the truth; my humiliation would be all around the school Monday anyway. "Yeah, he did. I just don't want to talk about it right now. Just leave him alone though, okay?" He sighed deeply. He clearly didn't like the idea of it, but he nodded somewhat reluctantly. "Thanks. I'm going back to bed, I didn't sleep well last night and I have a killer headache." I smiled weakly, trying to get them to stop worrying about me as much.

"Want me to send Mom up?" Dad offered, rubbing my back lightly.

I shook my head. "No, I just want to be on my own for a little while."

• • •

AS IT TURNS OUT, the 'little while' that I wanted to be on my own for, turned into a fairly long while. I didn't leave my bedroom for the rest of the weekend. I just sat there at my desk or on my bed, crying or thinking about Luke and what I wanted. He tried to call me again, but I still couldn't speak to him. I answered and spoke to him for just long enough to tell him where I left his car and that I may have ran a couple of red lights. I didn't mention the windshield.

I didn't leave my room, didn't get dressed, didn't want to speak to my friends, I didn't even eat. I was the definition of sad. If you looked up sad, pathetic, and heartbroken in the dictionary, there would be a picture of me next to all three of them.

I laid awake all of Sunday night, just dreading Monday. At home I had Alex and my dad to tell Luke to leave when he came to the door - which he did on more than one occasion - but at school I knew I would have to speak to him. Even just getting to school was going to be different, Luke always picked me up, and now I was going to be arriving with Alex. It was kind of like the end of an era.

As I stepped out of the door on Monday morning with Alex, I didn't expect to see Luke's Jeep parked there, and him to be leaning on the side of it, holding a bunch of daisies and a bag of Hershey's Kisses. He smiled weakly at me as I walked up the drive.

"Alex, will you wait for me in your car?" I requested, looking at him pleadingly as he immediately tensed up and started glaring at Luke. He sighed and nodded, walking off and getting in his car, turning in his seat to watch me. He really was so overprotective it was plain ridiculous.

I walked up to Luke slowly; not quite knowing what words could start this conversation. "What are you doing here?" I asked, trying not to meet his sad eyes. He looked terrible, like he hadn't slept either. Dark circles resided under his eyes, and his skin and hair had lost some of the shine and glow. He was even wearing rumpled clothes, which was very unlike him considering he had enough clothes to wear a new outfit every day and throw it in the trash instead of in the laundry. He looked like death warmed up.

He smiled weakly. "I thought I might get to speak to you this morning. I haven't been able to get past your brother and dad all weekend, so I thought I'd try now considering this is the first time you've left the house in two days," he answered. His eyes locked onto mine as he stepped closer to me.

"How do you know I haven't been out for two days?" I asked, trying not to let the sad tone of his voice affect me.

"I slept in the car. Stalkerish I know, but I just wanted to see you," he admitted, wincing.

I laughed humourlessly. "Comfortable?"

He shook his head and laughed quietly too. "Not in the slightest. But I just needed to be here in case you changed your mind and were ready to talk to me." He handed me the flowers and candy. "I got you these yesterday, they're a little wilted now though. I guess they didn't enjoy being in the car overnight either."

The situation felt like it was crushing me. This was the Luke that I fell in love with, the one that always put me first and made me feel like I was the most special girl in the world. I couldn't help but wonder if he'd made *her* feel like that too. This was just too much. I had no idea what I wanted to say to him, I had no idea where we went from here or if there was any way I could get past this.

"Luke, I just can't do this. Please can you just give me some space?" I asked, chewing on my lip, willing myself not to cry anymore.

"Maisie, you know I would never cheat on you," he said, bending his head and looking directly into my eyes, tracing one finger across my cheek.

I snorted and batted his hand away from my face angrily. "Well you did a pretty good impression of someone faking sex."

He groaned and gripped his hands into his hair. "Someone put something in my drink! I didn't take anything but I felt like shit, like I wasn't in control or something. After you left I just couldn't stop throwing up. I spent the rest of the night in hospital attached to a drip trying to get my fluids back into my system!" he cried, looking at me desperately. "You know I'd never do anything like this to you. You're my life, Maisie, the only good thing I have going. It's me and you, that's how it's supposed to work." He took my free hand, rubbing circles in the back of it with his thumb.

"I can still see it, Luke. Every time I look at you all I see is her on top of you! How can I forget that? How?" If he had the answer, if he could make me forget, then I'd take it like a shot. If I could go back in time and never go to the party then I would give anything for it. I believed him when he said he wouldn't have cheated on me if he hadn't been high, I could tell by his face how much he meant it and how hurt he was. This was a one-time thing. He had never done it before, no matter what Sandy said, that was the first time he'd cheated. That thought brought me a little comfort, but it didn't mean that I could forget it.

"I don't know," he whispered, his lip trembling as he spoke. "I want to forget it too. I wish with everything inside me that it never happened; I hate myself for hurting you. I love you so much." His hand brushed my face again and I couldn't help but close my eyes and turn into his hand so he cupped my cheek. We just stood there, neither of us moving, I just enjoyed the closeness of him and the heat that spread through my body from his hand. I loved him too, but I had the strong feeling that everything was ruined, whether he meant to cheat or not, he still did it. I felt bad that he was hurting, but I could still feel the betrayal and the pain in the bottom of my stomach, my heart was still broken.

"I just need some time, Luke. I love you too, but I just don't know how this can get any better," I admitted.

"I'll give you some time, if that's what you need. I'll wait forever, because you and me, Maisie, we're supposed to be together. You're the only person I've ever truly loved, the only one it would kill me to lose. I can't lose you. I'll do anything to make this up to you, anything," he said, kissing my cheek softly.

His lips were only on my skin for a split second, but I could feel the ghost of them the whole drive to school. Alex tried to talk to me, but I just looked out of the window, watching the streets pass by in a blur.

When we pulled into the parking lot Alex jumped out, jogging around to my side and wrapping a protective arm around me as people started to stare and whisper. Obviously news had already spread. I let him lead me into the school as I pretended not to notice how everyone gossiped and pointed at me as I walked past. Alex waved off his friends and girls that wanted to talk to him; instead he walked me directly to my locker where Charlotte and Beth were already waiting for me.

"There you go, girls, twin sister delivered. Now it's up to you to look after her until the end of school," Alex stated. He bent and kissed the top of my head softly. "If you need me today then call me." I nodded weakly, forcing a smile.

As soon as he left I was immediately pulled into a hug by both of my friends. They both started fussing over me and saying soothing things like Luke 'wasn't good enough for me' and that 'I was better off without him'. All three of us knew that it wasn't true, but I appreciated the solidarity from my girls. I sighed and grabbed my books from my locker knowing that life didn't stop just because I felt like I'd lost a huge piece of me. From the corner of my eye I saw Luke walk in; he stopped at the end of the corridor and smiled weakly at me before turning and walking off in the other direction. I looked up at the ceiling and willed the tears that were building up, not to fall. That was nice that he did that, I knew he wanted to talk to me, but I appreciated that he respected my request for some space.

Once I had everything that I needed, I decided I should to go to the office and see if the new guy had decided to grace us with his presence. I secretly hoped he'd skipped again today because I didn't have the energy or the will power to be courteous to someone today. I probably wouldn't be a very good welcome to the school; the state I was in would probably scare him away from here altogether.

"Guys, I'm going to the office to see if the new guy is coming in today," I said, smiling and trying to pretend like I wasn't close to bursting into tears.

Charlotte clicked her tongue and waved her hand dismissively. "Let someone else do it. You don't need to be doing that today," she scolded, shaking her head.

I sighed. "I have to, I was asked to. You know what I'm like, I have to do things to please people," I joked, shrugging. She rolled her eyes and I blew them both air kisses, promising to meet them in third period because that was the only lesson I had with them both. I headed to the office, praying that he wasn't here. As I walked in the receptionist smiled at me, her face lighting up and I could see she was waiting to gossip with me.

"Skipped again?" I inquired. "Is he getting excluded and he's not even started? That must be a record."

She shook her head, leaning over the counter to talk to me. "He's here! He's in the office; I think he's in a lot of trouble though. His aunt drove him here personally; she practically dragged him in here." She nodded towards the closed office door, and I groaned. *Great, that means I have to show around the new guy and eat with him. Now I can't just escape into the bathrooms at lunch and hide!*

"Great," I lied, smiling. "I'll just sit and wait then shall I? I assume I'm still showing him around?"

She nodded. "Yeah, thanks Maisie." She pointed to the chairs off to one side so I went to sit down and wait for him to come out.

A few minutes later and the Principal's door opened a couple of inches. "Oh he'll behave and come every day even if I have to drive him here myself," a lady said sternly from inside the office.

"Can we stop talking about me like I'm not here? You have any idea how patronising that is?" a guy asked sarcastically.

"Zachary!" the same lady scolded.

I groaned. I really didn't want to be showing this guy around at all.

"What? You're pretending like I'm not even in the room, like I'm freaking five years old! Anyway, whatever, are we done? I need a smoke," he said, sounding bored.

"You cannot smoke on school grounds!" Principal Bennett chimed in quickly, her voice firm and full of authority.

"Fine, I'll leave the grounds then," he answered; I could hear the amusement in his tone. I caught the eye of the receptionist who was listening too. Her mouth was agape and her eyes sparkled like this was the most exciting thing that happened to her for weeks. "Am I dismissed? Shall I send in the next delinquent for punishment?" Without waiting for an answer, the door opened and I watched as he walked out.

My stomach dropped as I laid eyes on him. He had a huge smirk on his face that was exactly as I remembered it from Friday night. He scanned the room, winking at the receptionist before his gaze fell on me and his predatory smile got even bigger.

"Well, well, well. Little miss DUI, come for a second shot at killing me?" he mused, looking almost happy to see me.

chapter seven

My mouth dropped open in shock as my eyes widened in horror. Zach walked over and plopped in the seat next to me, looking chilled and relaxed as his aunt was in there apologising for his behaviour and promising that he would be good and make a real effort at the school. His posture didn't look like he was going to be making much of an effort though.

"The Principal will scold you now," he teased, nodding towards the office door. "What did you do anyway? Smash something?" he asked, leaning over to talk to me in private, putting emphasis around the word smash.

I gasped. *I knew that freaking windshield thing would come back to bite me in the ass!* Luke hadn't said anything about it to me and he probably wouldn't even mention it, he'd be annoyed if he found out it was me though. "Shh!" I hissed, glaring at him.

He laughed and ran a hand over his shaven hair. He looked like he'd just been dragged out of bed, literally. He was wearing grey sweatpants, with black boxers underneath – I could tell the colour because the sweats hung so low on his body that you could probably see the crack of his butt if it weren't for the waistband of his boxers. His white t-shirt clung to his body showing off his muscles underneath, and he wore the same grey hoodie that I had borrowed Friday night.

I couldn't speak; I had no idea what to say. Do I beg him to not say anything? Was he going to hold this against me forever? I was supposed to be tutoring this guy too; I certainly didn't want to do that now. Not him, he was a cocky jerk and he would drive me crazy if I spent more than ten minutes in his company.

"You look like shit," he commented.

Make that three minutes in his company.

I looked down at what I was wearing, my usual type of thing that consisted of plain t-shirt and jeans, ponytail, no make-up, the same as a usual school day. "Wow, that's so sweet, thanks," I muttered sarcastically.

The door to the office opened and an extremely harassed looking lady with blonde hair walked out of the office, scowling at Zach. Principal Bennett followed close behind her, she too was harassed looking. I had a feeling Zach could piss off more than just me in three minutes.

"Oh, Maisie dear, thank you for coming. I assume you've already met Zachary," she said, looking at me almost apologetically.

"Zach," he corrected acidly.

I stood up, smiling politely. "Yeah, we've already met." I nodded, wincing at the double meaning to those words.

Principal Bennett motioned towards the blonde lady who was obviously Zach's Aunt. "This is Mrs Kingston. Mrs Kingston, this is Maisie, the girl I spoke to you about, the tutor," she introduced. Zach chuckled darkly behind me, but I ignored him, he was obviously amused that I was supposed to be tutoring him.

The lady smiled and nodded. "It's lovely to meet you, Maisie. I'm sure I'll be seeing more of you around the house then," she said, smiling sweetly.

I smiled apologetically. "Actually, Mrs Kingston, something's come up and I won't be able to tutor Zachary anymore." I flicked my eyes to him as I said his full name, knowing that would obviously annoy him. "I can happily recommend someone else that will be willing to do it though." There were always plenty of people wanting extra cash around here.

Zach jumped out of his chair. "Oh no, I don't want anyone else. I want you," he protested, looking me right in the eyes, bending slightly so our faces were on the same level. "You can sort out this thing that's come up. Right, little rebel?" he asked, raising one eyebrow at me.

Did he just call me little rebel as some kind of threat? Oh my freaking goodness, I hate this guy! "I have a lot going on right now, I don't think I'm in the right frame of mind to take on a tutoring job," I answered through my teeth, trying desperately to keep my tone light and friendly.

He smirked at me. "A lot going on? Like getting fitter so you can run further without having to stop?" he offered, laughing quietly to himself.

Oh yeah, he's definitely blackmailing me!

His aunt cleared her throat. "Well if you can't do it and know of someone who can, then give them my number, okay?" she requested, holding out a card to me.

Zach snatched it out of her hand and stuffed it in his pocket as he looked at me challengingly. "Maisie's going to do it. Aren't you?"

I could feel my fists clenching in anger. I really wanted to punch him in his smirking face. "I guess it would be alright. We could see how it goes," I offered, looking him right in the eye, showing him that I wasn't going to be intimidated by his badass attitude.

"Great," his aunt chirped. "Right well then I'd best be off to work. Zach, please behave." She looked at him pleadingly, and his face softened as he rolled his eyes and nodded. She turned back to Principal Bennett. "Thank you for your time, and we really are both very sorry." They shook hands and she left, leaving us standing there with the Principal.

"Well, you'd best get on with the tour then. The bell rings in five minutes, would you like a note to get you both out of first period so you can do a thorough tour?" she asked, already reaching for the yellow pad behind the desk and scribbling two of them.

No, I want to get rid of this jerk as fast as possible! "No, it's fine; I'll just go with a quick tour. I'm sure Zach can find his way around on his own."

She waved her hand dismissively and handed me the two slips. "Don't worry. Take the longer tour and show him the way to all of his classes, it'll be easier once the hallways are empty."

I frowned and nodded, storing my pass into my bag and handing Zach his one. He semi screwed it up and pushed it into his pocket, then turned and smiled sweetly, motioning for me to go first out of the door. "Ladies first."

I took a deep calming breath. I needed to remember he seemed like a nice guy when I met him Friday night. He could have got me into a lot of trouble and left me stranded by the side of the road – but he didn't. Therefore I needed to give him a chance today. Maybe he was just behaving like this because he was scared and was putting on a front. Starting a new school was undoubtedly a little daunting.

I headed out of the door and turned back to smile at him, only to find his eyes were glued to my derrière. I gasped and shoved on his chest. "Stop staring at my ass!" I growled angrily.

He laughed and rolled his eyes. "Pur-leaze, that thing could barely even be classed as an ass! Besides, it's hidden under the t-shirt, I couldn't perv on it even if I wanted to," he retorted, looking at me distastefully.

I frowned and suddenly felt self-conscious. 'Barely be classed as an ass', what was that supposed to mean? "Just shut up," I scolded, turning and walking off up the hallway, pulling his schedule and locker information from my bag. I headed up to his locker and handed him the combination. "That's your locker there if you want to store anything."

He laughed and held up his empty hands. "Don't have anything to store."

I frowned. "Well where are your books and stuff?"

He laughed, shrugging noncommittally. "Lost them?"

Wow, this guy is stupid! "No wonder you're repeating senior year," I scoffed as

I turned to walk off up the hallway to show him where his classes were. The rest of the tour was quiet, neither of us spoke apart from me telling him where things were, pointing out the fire exits and the gym, bathrooms, and the cafeteria.

When we were done there was still a little while left until second period started. "Want to go to the last fifteen minutes of class, or get a drink instead?" I asked, shrugging.

"Whatever," he grunted, folding his arms across his chest.

I smiled and decided to be the bigger person and make some small talk. Instead of heading to classes, we stopped at the vending machines; I bought two bottles of water and led him out onto the benches at the side of the school. I sat down and handed him one.

"So, how long have you been doing partor?" I asked, smiling, trying to be friendly.

He laughed and rolled his eyes. "It's parkour, sweetheart," he corrected sarcastically. I sighed and closed my eyes. He was making this so difficult. Why did this have to happen to me today? I had to meet him at lunchtime today too. He was going to drive me crazy by the end of the day if he kept being this sarcastic and snappy. He sighed too and surprised me when he started talking again; I was expecting him to just ignore me for a while or something, just to prove that he was the jerk I thought he was. "I've been doing it for the last three years I guess. I train a lot, it takes a lot of time to master."

I opened my eyes and smiled at him gratefully. *Hmm, maybe he is going to go easy on me after all.* "Yeah? How many classes does it take before they teach you how to avoid getting flattened by a drunken girl driving a stolen sports car?" I joked.

He smiled causing a little dimple to appear in his right cheek. "That one's a basic requirement, survival guide number one. You'd be surprised how often that comes in handy."

"So, how come you're transferring mid-semester?" I asked curiously. My best guess was that he'd moved house or something. He was obviously living with his aunt, but I didn't want to pry and ask why he didn't live with his parents.

He laughed. "I'm not transferring. I was excluded from my last school," he said, shrugging as if it was no big deal as he pulled his hood up and then pulled out a packet of cigarettes from his pocket.

I eyed him warily. He wouldn't smoke on school grounds, would he? Surely he was just after a reaction from me. "What were you excluded for?" I asked curiously.

He grinned. "The final straw was smoking, but I was hanging by a thread for fighting and skipping class before that," he muttered, pulling out a cigarette and offering me the packet.

I shook my head and frowned at him. "You got excluded for smoking? That kind of seems a little harsh," I admitted.

He shrugged. "Yeah, it didn't help that I forgot to stub out my butt properly and the carpet in the English block caught fire," he replied indifferently. I gulped at his words. As I opened my mouth to speak, he pulled a silver lighter from his pocket, flicked the flame on and cupped his hand around it as he brought the tip of his cigarette to it. I gasped in shock that he was seriously lighting up in the school, especially after what happened in his last one.

I ripped the freshly lit cigarette from between his lips and stubbed it out onto the bench, looking around to make sure no one saw. "What the hell are you doing?" I hissed, glaring at him.

He frowned at me angrily, but didn't say anything, just pulled out another one and lit it. I snatched it out of his mouth and stubbed that one out too. He was really angry now, his jaw tight as his eyes seemed to hold a burning passion in them that actually made me flinch. I glared back at him. Neither of us spoke as he calmly got another from the packet. Before he could even flick the flame on his lighter I grabbed the packet and his unlit one from his hand, put it on the table and poured the rest of my drink onto them.

He jumped up in shock and dived for the packet, flicking the water from it. "What the hell are you doing? Are you stupid or something?" he shouted, his whole body tensing up as he scowled at me.

I calmly stood up and nodded. "Yeah, I'm the stupid one. I'm the one who set fire to my old school and got kicked out. I'm the one who's repeating senior year because I couldn't be bothered to turn up and go to class. I'm the one that actually pays to put poison inside my body because I think it looks cool. Absolutely I'm stupid," I stated sarcastically.

He stared at me for a couple of seconds before a smile twitched at the corner of his mouth, then he broke out into a full smile. I frowned, a little confused at the sudden change in mood. "There was me having you pegged for a little pushover girl who wouldn't say boo to a goose and wouldn't in a million years stand up for herself. I guess I was wrong, huh?" He regarded me almost proudly.

I frowned. I'd never met anyone as confusing as this guy. One minute he behaved like a jackass, and the next he was being nice, I literally couldn't keep up with him. I had a feeling that most of this was an act to get a reaction from people, maybe he liked the attention.

"I guess you did," I muttered, my voice a little weaker now. "Anyway, the bell's about to ring so maybe we should think about getting you to your next class. I assume you are going to class?" I asked, raising one eyebrow at him curiously. It wouldn't have surprised me if he'd walked out of school as soon as the tour finished.

He cocked his head to the side. "Do I have any classes with you?"

I nodded and pulled out his schedule. "Two. Both after lunch."

A wicked smile crossed his face. "Then I guess I'm sticking around, wouldn't miss the opportunity to piss you off for the world," he stated, laughing quietly as I glared at him. I grabbed my bag and walked off without waiting for him, I headed in the direction of his history class. He caught me up easily. "So, does the cheating ex go to this school?" he asked.

I frowned and looked him from the corner of my eye. Why did he have to bring up Luke again? I was getting along fine not thinking about him, Zach and his 'look at me I'm a badass' personality were keeping my mind off the betrayal for a while.

"Yes, and so does the slut he cleated with," I muttered, hugging my bag to me, wishing that everything would just go back to normal or that I would stop feeling this pain every time I thought of Luke and what he'd done.

"Today's gonna be fun for you then I bet," he teased, laughing quietly.

I stopped walking and closed my eyes. "Do you have to be such an asshole? Look, I'm sorry I almost ran you over. I'm sorry I ruined your cigarettes. I'm sorry that you have to come to this school when you would probably rather be somewhere else, screwing slutty girls, or jumping over cars, or whatever the hell is it that you find interesting. Just don't take it out on me, okay?" I hated the way my voice shook when I said it, I hated the way I felt so broken and vulnerable, I just hated everything about myself at that moment.

He laughed. "Wow, you're definitely getting better at the bitchy comebacks. You need a little more practice though so I'll let you keep working on them. Come on, little miss DUI, I don't want to be late for my first official class," he chirped, clearly having a great time at my expense.

I gritted my teeth. This torture would only last for a couple of days, by then he would know his way around and meet a couple of friends. Then I'd be free to pretend like I didn't even know him. "Right well, I'll show you where your class is and then you're on your own until this afternoon when I'll see you in gym," I muttered, just wanting to be away from him. I scribbled my name and number at the top on a piece of scrap paper and then handed it to him along with the stack of paperwork Principal Bennett had given me the other day. "There's a map of the school and a list of your classes. If you get lost or anything then that's my number. Or you could just ask someone, I'm pretty sure the girls will help you," I stated, turning my nose up at the thought of the girls that were going to be swooning over the new badass.

Zach shoved my number in his pocket and followed along at my side as we walked through the deserted hallways. I made the most of the quiet because I knew that in a few minutes they would be teeming with people and everyone would stare at me, whispering about how Luke had cheated. I swallowed the lump in my throat. All I wanted to do was go home. During the night I'd actually considered finishing my senior year by correspondence. That idea was getting more appealing by the second.

"The Principal said I'd be eating with you today," Zach said casually at my shoulder.

I frowned and shrugged. "You don't have to. I have things to do so if you wouldn't mind braving it on your own," I suggested hopefully.

He smiled that dimpled smile again. "What you gonna do at lunchtime? Cry in the bathrooms about the prick that thought with the little head at the party?" he joked.

"Do you have to be such an ass?" I snapped, shoving on his shoulder.

His smile faded instantly. "Sorry, I was just joking around." An apologetic expression crossed his face before he frowned and looked at the door of his next class. "Thanks for showing me the way; I'll see you at lunchtime. No crying over the dickwad, okay? He's obviously stupid to have done that to a girl like you," he stated, crossing his arms over his chest, clearly uncomfortable.

I raised one eyebrow. That was the first nice thing he'd said to me. He looked like a fish out of water, like he wasn't used to being nice or something. His eyes were looking anywhere but me, and I couldn't help but smile a little.

"Right, well, okay, yeah," I muttered weakly, not knowing what else to say. "I'll see you in the lunchroom then." I turned and headed off towards my class, wanting to get there before the hallways filled with people. Today was going to be hard; thank goodness I didn't have any classes with Luke though so I got out of that one. The same couldn't be said for Sandy though; she was in my gym class, as was Zach. That class was going to be a nightmare no doubt.

I stopped outside of my class and pulled out my textbook as the bell rang, pretending to be engrossed in it as people streamed out of the classroom. I gulped, my eyes filling with tears as people were already having whisper conversations about me. All I could hear were people telling the story over and over, how I had walked in on my long term boyfriend in bed with another girl.

I just kept my head down and willed the tears not to fall. The worst part of all of this was: the one person that had caused me all of this pain and sadness, was the one I really wanted to hug me and comfort me. My body longed for Luke; I wanted to bury my face into the side of his neck and wrap my arms around his broad shoulders, clamping myself to him. I hated myself for wanting that, it made me feel like a worthless pushover. How was I supposed to make myself stop loving the guy? Could I? I wasn't sure of the answer to that question at all.

• • •

I KEPT MY HEAD down during class, not making eye contact with anyone, pretending to be engrossed in the lesson. The time passed, slowly, but it passed.

As soon as the bell sounded I made a quick exit, not wanting to linger and talk to anyone. As I stepped out of the door I was engulfed in a hug by Charlotte who quite often met me from class so we could walk to third period together.

"Okay?" she asked, pulling back, looking at me sympathetically. I sighed deeply and shook my head, willing myself not to cry again. "You know, I could hack the FBI and put a warrant out for Luke's arrest if it'll make you feel better," she suggested, grinning at me hopefully.

I laughed and rolled my eyes. *She probably can too.* "It's fine, it'll settle down."

A wicked smile crept onto her lips. "I already gave Sandy some payback this morning during my computer science class."

I chewed on my lip and giggled. "What did you do?"

She shrugged casually. "Hacked her Facebook and changed all of her settings, sending out a status that said and I quote, 'I'm a dirty whore who likes to watch midget porn instead of doing my school assignments'," she said laughing to herself. "I might have also sent out a few hundred friend requests to some people who she wouldn't really want to be friends with."

I wrapped my arm around her waist as we walked down the hallway. I felt ten times better now that I had someone with me; the looks that I got off people weren't as bad when I had someone distracting me. "What kind of people?" I asked, shifting my heavy bag on my shoulder.

She grinned. "Freshman, nerds, faculty, strippers, everyone I could find."

I laughed. Sandy was going to be furious when she realised, but she'd never know it was Charlotte, she was too good at things like that. "Thanks, Char." We stepped into class then and headed for the back, still talking back and forth about other computer things Charlotte could do to her as payback.

When the lunch bell rang at the end of class I smiled at Charlotte and Beth. Half the day was done, I just needed to get through lunch and then three more lessons then I could go home and hide in my room, listening to Boyz II men. When I got to the lunchroom entrance I stopped as I saw Zach leaning casually against the wall. Girls and boys were milling around talking to him, looking at him, seeming to hang on his every word. I was right earlier, he was undoubtedly going to be popular with the girls here, they were already adjusting their shirts and skirts, trying to get his attention.

I sighed and rolled my eyes. One good thing about him being accepted by the popular crowd was that I didn't have to eat with him today. Charlotte nodded in his direction, cocking her head to the side looking at him curiously. "Is that the new guy, Zachary something or other?"

I nodded. "He prefers Zach."

"You gotta eat with him?" she asked, pouting at me.

I waved it off and shook my head. "He looks like he's all set. Come on, I'm starving." I nodded towards the canteen and got about three steps before someone shouted my name, making everyone stop talking and look at me.

I groaned. *As if I'm not centre of attention enough already!* I turned and looked at him as he pushed himself off the wall, smirking at me. "Yes, Zach?" I smiled politely.

"I've been waiting for you. You ditching me? Now that's not very nice is it?" he teased, narrowing his eyes at me.

"I thought you were alright," I replied, nodding at the fangirls he'd already accumulated that were waiting for his attention again. "Looks like you have people to sit with already."

He laughed and rolled his eyes. "So, how was your morning? I heard you told a guy to shove a note up his ass and then stormed out of class telling the teacher to eff off," he said, looking at me with an almost hopeful expression on his face.

I sighed dramatically. The rumour mill in this school were working overtime today! "Yeah, my day happened just like that. How was your day, Zachary?" I turned and walked towards the lunch line, not caring if he followed me or not. Charlotte looked at me with one eyebrow raised as her gaze flicked to Zach, raking down his body with an appreciative bite of her lip.

He laughed and kept up with me easily. "My day's going great. So far I've got four girls' numbers." His eyes flicked to Charlotte, a smirk on his face. "Care to make it five, sweetness?"

She snorted, and I knew any thoughts she had about him, were now gone. She hated being called pet names. If she was crushing on him at all, that was now gone. "In your dreams," she replied, waving a hand dismissively.

He laughed and pulled a burger and fries onto his tray. "Probably actually."

I turned to him and looked him dead in the eye. "Zach, I don't want to do this today, okay? I've had a really long day already and I'm only half way through. If you could just cut the annoying comments down slightly, otherwise please go find someone else to eat with."

He grinned and started munching on his fries. "The comebacks are definitely getting better." He winked at me. "So, about this tutoring thing. We don't really need to do that, do we? I'll just say I'm meeting you at the library and stuff, you'll get paid, and everyone's a winner."

I scowled at him distastefully. "I'm not doing that. If you want an easy ride then you find another tutor," I stated confidently. I smirked at him. At least now I'd get out of the whole tutoring thing.

He cocked his head to the side, studying me, as if he were assessing how serious I was. After another minute he frowned and nodded. "Fine. But I don't do libraries," he grumbled.

I sighed and grabbed a sandwich, not even hungry in the slightest, but I needed to get something otherwise Charlotte and Beth would be looking at me worriedly and fussing over me. I didn't say anything, just ignored him for the rest of the line, watching Charlotte's back as she chatted with a girl in front of her about fundraising for the IT department. I was dimly aware of Zach following behind me as we walked to the table where a couple of our other friends were already sitting. He plopped himself down right next to me.

I looked up just as Ricky and Luke walked into the canteen. My back stiffened automatically. Was Luke going to approach me? I always ate lunch with him, every day for the last nineteen months. I shifted on my seat awkwardly.

Zach elbowed me in the side as Luke's eyes flicked up and met mine. I saw hurt and sadness on his face that just broke my heart all over again. "Who's that? Please tell me you weren't dating a jock! The nerd with the jock, how cliché," Zach mocked sarcastically from beside me.

My mouth dropped open. I wanted to make an angry retort, but nothing was coming out. I felt my eyes prickling with tears and I willed them not to fall. Luke raised one hand slightly in acknowledgement and mouthed the word hi to me.

"Wow, you sure can pick 'em, huh? Let me guess, quarterback? Maybe the running back? Hmm, this is probably going to hurt," Zach muttered, nudging me again to get my attention. I dragged my eyes away from Luke and looked at Zach, still not seeming to remember how to speak. *What's going to hurt? What is this guy even talking about?* He smirked at me and slipped his arm around my shoulder. I frowned and shifted so it would drop off, but he just adjusted his position and moved it back there again.

Before I knew what happened, something slammed down onto my table making me jump and yelp as I glanced up to see a furious looking Luke had slammed his fist on the table. He was glaring, not at me, but at Zach.

He leant over, his eyes fixed on Zach. "Don't touch her!" he growled, knocking Zach's hand off my shoulder.

I frowned at Luke. I hated it when he got all possessive, and it wasn't even as if he had a right to anymore anyway. Zach just laughed. "Luke, don't start," I warned, looking at him sternly.

Zach stood up next to me, smirking at Luke. "So, you're the one I need to thank? I've been trying to catch you all day just to say thanks for screwing up with Maisie. If you hadn't fucked that little cheerleader on Friday night then I wouldn't have had the most amazing rebound sex with your girl," he said, running his hand up my back again to grip my shoulder tightly.

I gasped and jumped out of my seat, but before I could even open my mouth and tell Luke it wasn't true, Luke lunged for him. Zach shoved me backwards at the same time as he stepped forward in front of me protectively. I stumbled but managed to catch myself before I fell on my ass. I watched with wide eyes as the two of them started fighting in the middle of the lunchroom. Both reining blow after blow on each other as people gasped and started heckling and clapping along, just like in a bad teen movie.

chapter eight

I could see Luke's lip bleeding, as was Zach's nose. I screamed at them to stop, and stepped forward, grabbing Zach's arm because he was closer to me, but before I could do anything I was immediately pulled back again. Two strong arms wrapped around my waist and literally lifted me off my feet, turning me and carrying me a couple of feet away.

When the arms disappeared I glanced up to see a furious looking Alex. He stepped in front of me protectively as he watched the two boys fight it out. Zach launched himself at Luke, throwing them both onto the table, knocking peoples' lunches everywhere; he straddled Luke and punched him over and over in the face and chest. He was a serious badass, and I was pretty sure that Luke hadn't landed more than a couple of punches on Zach, and one of those was probably because he'd taken the time to shove me out of the way.

I dug my fingers into Alex's side as my tears started to fall. "Alex, stop them for goodness sake. Please?" I hated seeing Luke get hurt.

"Let the new guy kill him, it'll save me doing it," he growled, shaking his head.

"Alex, please?" I begged, pressing my face into his shoulder blades, trying to block out the sight of it, but the sounds of the fight were rebounding off the walls, making each crash and blow echo and seem even more horrifying.

Alex sighed and nodded. "Fine, but just stay out of the way. You don't *ever* step into the middle of a fight, have I taught you nothing?" he scolded, shaking his head at me in disapproval.

I flicked my eyes to the fighting pair in time to see Luke throw Zach off him, both of them crashing to the floor, Luke now on top. "Can we leave the safety lecture until later?" I cried, pointing at them, shaking my head at my twin who was more concerned about me getting hurt than breaking up the fight.

He sighed and nodded again, turning on his heel. He wrapped his arms around Luke from behind and pulled him up to his feet. He was still thrashing, trying to kick Zach as he was dragged away a few steps. I could see Alex talking into Luke's ear, his face hard and angry, I had no idea what he was saying but by the distasteful look on Alex's face he didn't like touching Luke at all.

Zach pushed himself up off the floor; he smirked at Luke who immediately started thrashing in my brother's arms again. Zach brushed off his clothes. He didn't look too bad at all; judging by the way he acted, he was probably used to getting in fights. "Thanks again for screwing up, Luke. She's the best lay I've had in ages," he teased, grinning and winking at me.

I scowled at him and Luke threw off my brother's hold, jumping for Zach again, but Alex grabbed him in time and stopped it, putting his body between the two boys. "Back off, Hannigan!" Alex shouted, shoving on Luke's chest hard, making him stumble back a couple of steps.

Zach smirked again over Alex's shoulder. "Yeah, back off, Hannigan," he teased, winking at Luke.

"Son of a bitch!" Luke shouted.

Before I knew what happened, Luke was on the floor and my brother was shaking out his hand so he'd obviously punched him. "Calm down, fucktard!" Alex growled, sneering at Luke who was looking a little dazed as he sat on the floor.

Zach smiled and patted Alex on the back. "Nice punch," he congratulated.

Alex turned and punched Zach in the face too, making him crash back into the table. My mouth dropped open in shock as Alex stepped closer to him. "Don't make up shit about sleeping with my sister!" he shouted angrily.

Zach smiled and rubbed his jaw, looking at Alex appreciatively. "Ouch, dude. You seriously fight great. You train?" he asked, not seeming to be bothered about the fact that my brother had just punched him in the face.

Alex frowned, looking a little taken aback by Zach's comment too. "Yeah, amateur kickboxing league," he muttered, shaking his head.

"Break it up! What on earth is going on in here? Hannigan, Preston!" a male voice bellowed. I looked up to see a couple of teachers running over to us. Mr O'Conner, the gym teacher, was at the front, looking murderously angry as his eyes took in the situation. Food was all over the floor, there were broken plates everywhere, students all in a crowd looking at the three boys in the centre.

Zach held out his hand to Alex, smiling happily as if this whole scene hadn't just happened. Alex frowned but took his hand anyway, pulling him to his feet, his body still tense as if waiting for a sly attack or something.

"And who are you?" Mr O'Conner growled, looking at Zach when he was on his feet again.

Zach did a little bow. "Zach Anderson, new pain in your ass." The watching crowd laughed at his comment.

"Principal, all three of you!" Mr O'Conner barked, pointing at the door.

Alex frowned but didn't protest; Luke winced as he rubbed his hand over his bruising cheek but headed out without another word. Zach just laughed.

I watched the three boys go, hoping that Alex didn't get into too much trouble. I would owe him for that, I asked him to break it up and get involved, so if he got detention then it'd be my fault. The crowd dispersed quickly now that the teachers were here. I saw a blonde head step in front of me. I gulped when I looked up at Sandy's smug face.

"You're not worth all that," she stated, sneering at me.

I wanted nothing more than to push her to the floor and rub the spilt spaghetti over every inch of her face, making her look like an Oompa-Loompa. "And you think you are?" I asked, shaking my head at her.

She grinned at me, flashing her straight white teeth. "Luke thinks I am. He told me that I was the best night of his life," she stated, picking at her manicured nails.

I couldn't help but laugh at her comment. That couldn't be true, they didn't even get to finish, he was throwing up all night and spent the night in hospital. That was clearly not the best night of his life! She was obviously lying, trying to upset me. I knew she wanted Luke; she had done for a long time. *It wouldn't surprise me if I find out that she was the one that drugged him just so she could have her way with him.*

Then it occurred to me what I'd just thought. Had she been the one to spike his drink? She gave him a drink after he fell off the stool, then one of her friends came and told me where to find Luke. Did she plan to have me walk in on them like that? Had she set this whole thing up?

I felt my eyes widen with shock. Would she really go that far though? To drug someone to get them into bed? Did she want him that much, and hate me that much? "Did you-" I started, but the warning bell sounded, signalling there was five minutes until afternoon classes. Without another word, she turned and walked off. She shot me a smug smile as she let the door slam shut behind her.

My heart was racing in my chest. If she'd planned the whole thing then I kind of felt sorry for Luke; she'd used him, and taken advantage of him in a way. But he would still have been able to say no, he certainly wasn't fighting her off and telling her no when I walked in the room, he was clearly enjoying himself. Did it make a difference if someone spiked his drink or not? He was in full control of himself; he pushed her off when I walked into the room so he could have stopped it at any time if he wanted to. She wasn't exactly forcing herself on him, or was she? Maybe I needed to speak to Luke about it again.

I felt the bile rise in my throat as I immediately started to picture it again. I closed my eyes and tried to shake the images away. All I wanted was to erase it from my mind, if I could do that then I would be able to forgive Luke, I would be able to have the future that I planned, the happy one with the adorable guy. Instead, I get to see that smug witch walk around, knowing that she slept with my boyfriend.

I hung my head and tried to ignore the whispers of people around me. Charlotte and Beth ran up to me immediately, Charlotte gripping my arm tightly as she looked at me worriedly. "You alright?"

I nodded and shrugged, not really knowing what to say. Maybe I was going into shock or something, I kind of felt a little numb, like this was all happening to someone else. It was quite nice to feel numb and not feel the heartbreak; I secretly hoped it lasted for a little while. "I'm fine. Come on, let's get to class," I suggested, trying to keep my voice stronger than I felt.

Beth looked at me sympathetically. "Everything will get better, Maisie."

Charlotte frowned, looking like she was trying to think of something to say that would help. "Your brother is seriously hot when he fights. If he didn't ruin it as soon as he opened his mouth, then I would definitely tap that," she stated, waggling her eyebrows.

I burst out laughing and she smiled proudly. It was obviously her intention to take my mind off what had just happened. "Yuck," I replied, pretending to gag.

She grinned and linked her arm through mine. Beth took my other, and we talked about Alex being a badass as we walked to our lockers to get our books before the next bell rang for the start of class.

I grabbed my gym bag and headed there, feeling the dread sink in with each step. Both Sandy and Zach were in this class. People were staring at me even more after the whole fight scene that took place a few minutes ago. Instead of changing in the locker rooms, I headed to the bathrooms next door and changed into my black shorts and white t-shirt, pulling on my sneakers and then reluctantly headed out to the gym to see what we were doing today.

Sandy and her little followers were all milling around in their little circle of perfection, bitching obviously about some of the other girls in the class. I stood at the back, chewing on my lip, wishing this day was over with already. I found myself wishing Alex was here with me. The boy drove me crazy most of the time, but his presence was calming to me, like he was my rock or something. I wished I could just shrink into his side and hear his annoying voice just to keep me company.

Sandy smirked at me and her friends all turned to look at me, making me shift uncomfortably on my feet. The girl that had told me that Luke wanted to speak to me at the party, smiled at me almost apologetically, but I just looked away as Mr O'Conner walked in.

"Right then guys and girls, we're running laps today so get those behinds in gear and no slacking," he barked, waving his hand at the door.

The gym door opened again just as Mr O'Conner was telling us about how many laps to run, how to warm up and cool down. Everyone turned to see who dared enter class late; Mr O'Conner was a seriously harsh teacher when it came to punctuality.

Zach entered, smirking at the class, his nose slightly red, his lip split, and his knuckles red raw. "Sorry I'm late, some jackass teacher sent me to the Principal," he chirped. I looked at him warningly and shook my head, nodding towards the front where Mr O'Conner was standing. Zach's eyes settled and me and his smirk grew bigger as he looked me over in my clothes. "You rock that gym kit," he teased, winking at me.

"ENOUGH! OUTSIDE EVERYONE!" Mr O'Conner bellowed.

Everyone jumped and practically ran for the door; Zach grinned and crossed his arms over his chest, looking at the teacher challengingly. I gulped and headed out of the room not wanting to witness another showdown.

I walked slowly to the field, and stretched out my muscles, getting ready to run. Sandy stopped next to me, stretching out her long toned legs as she tied her long immaculate hair into a perfect twist. "The new guy's hot," she stated, raising one eyebrow. I looked at her with as much hate as I could muster as I imagined ramming her face into the mud and standing on the back of her head. "I think maybe he's even hotter than your ex-boyfriend. Maybe I'll give him a try and see which one screws the best before I decide which one I want."

I opened my mouth to speak but I was cut off by a male voice behind me, "Trust me, I screw better. Thing is though, sweetheart, you just don't do it for me. I like a girl to have a little more up top, and I'm not talking about bra size."

I laughed and turned back to see that Zach was looking at Sandy distastefully. She huffed and turned to walk off to her group of waiting clones. "Nice knock-back," I congratulated.

He laughed and stepped to my side. "Thanks. So that's her, huh?" he asked, looking Sandy over in her short shorts and tank top. I frowned and nodded. "Don't see the appeal myself. I like a little mystery, something that you have to work for. With her, you see what you get before you even unwrap, where's the fun in that?" he asked, turning his nose up slightly.

I grinned and rolled my eyes, trying to look like I disapproved but I just couldn't, I loved that he wasn't interested in her, it reminded me of how Luke used to be before everything got ruined.

"So how much trouble did you guys get in for fighting?" I inquired as we started to jog around the track.

He shrugged. "Two days lunchtime detention. No biggie."

"Why did you do that anyway?" I asked curiously. He must want to get expelled from here too or something.

He grinned. "Just thought your dickwad of an ex deserved a little payback. He was seriously pissed with me," he explained, laughing happily.

I raised one eyebrow at him in disbelief. "You like to make a good impression, huh?"

He shrugged. "People think of me what they want. I don't need other people's opinions to validate who I am. If they don't like me then that's tough luck for them. I call it like I see it. I thought your boy needed to hurt, obviously the thing that's hurting him the most is losing you. He's got it bad, so I decided to rub his nose in it a little more," he said, shrugging as we continued to run.

I gulped and dropped my eyes to the floor, not wanting to talk about Luke and his feelings for me. "I don't like fighting," I said sternly.

"Duly noted, but sometimes it's necessary. For example, you need to punch that hoe in the face," he stated, nodding at Sandy who was running about a hundred yards in front of us.

I snorted at his comment. "I'm not punching anyone in the face; nothing can be solved with violence."

He laughed and bumped his shoulder against mine. "Maybe you're right, punching her won't actually solve anything, but it'll make you feel better."

I laughed. It probably would too, but I still wasn't doing it, that wasn't who I was. The rest of the lesson we just jogged with him teasing me about how unfit I was. The boy wouldn't leave me alone, no matter how many times I told him to just run ahead and not wait for me. He stayed firmly planted at my side the whole time and even walked me to the locker-room to change after.

"Walk me to English after?" he asked, cocking his head to the side.

I shrugged, pulling my sweaty t-shirt away from my body distastefully. "Whatever. Meet me here then, okay? I need to shower."

He grinned wickedly. "I could come and help if you want, wash your back for you," he suggested, raising one eyebrow.

I rolled my eyes and didn't bother to comment on his slutty remark. Now that I'd gotten to know him a little better I realised that he was actually a pretty nice guy. He was unquestionably cocky and opinionated, but he reminded me a little of Alex in some ways.

I showered and changed as quickly as I could, heading out, only to find him pressed up against a girl who I recognised as one of Sandy's little minions. She was giggling while he leant in, one palm pressed against the wall near her head; he was obviously flirting his ass off with her, and doing well too by the look of it.

I didn't bother to interrupt their little session, I just turned on my heel and headed to English class on my own, choosing a seat near the front so people wouldn't be able to talk to me too easily. He came in five minutes after class had started, earning him a warning from the teacher. He frowned at me angrily and plopped down in the seat a couple of rows from me, tapping his hand on his desk, looking out of the window, not paying attention to anything the teacher said for the whole lesson.

When the bell rang he walked over to my desk and kicked the leg of my chair to get my attention as I packed my books. "What was that? I thought you were meeting me?" he growled angrily.

I shrugged. "I didn't want to interrupt you, you obviously have a need to flirt with as many girls as possible in one day, who am I to ruin that for you? You're probably going for some sort of record by getting as many phone numbers as possible on a first day," I teased, smirking at him as I shouldered my bag.

He frowned and sighed, shaking his head and strutting off without answering. I watched his back as he walked away. Guilt washed over me. I should have waited for him earlier; we had agreed it after all. I'd have to try and catch him tomorrow to apologise or something.

I headed to my locker, pulling out my books for the last lesson of the day. I did it deliberately slowly, just wanting a couple of minutes peace. People started filing out to their respective classes, so I closed my eyes and took a couple of deep breaths. There was only one more lesson left now, but I wasn't sure I could make it through anymore. I chewed on my lip and considered skipping my last class, I could easily catch up, and it wasn't like I ever usually did it so no one would suspect anything foul if I missed one class.

Movement at my side caught my attention. I opened my eyes and looked up just as Luke stopped next to me. He looked bad; Zach had certainly done a number on his face. His cheek and jaw were red, his lip split and swollen. I daren't even think what his body looked like. He looked incredibly sorry for himself, his head hung and his shoulders slumped. His deep brown eyes met mine, and I felt my heart break all over for him. He was so sad, so rejected, so low, but I just didn't know what to do, I didn't know if I could forgive him. I just knew deep down that everything was ruined, I didn't think there was any way we could come back from this.

chapter nine

"Can I talk to you, just for a minute?" he asked quietly as he frowned at the floor.

I still wasn't ready to talk to him at all, but I couldn't exactly say no with him looking like that. I nodded, swallowing the sadness that seemed to make my throat swell up. I closed my locker and leant against it, waiting for him to speak, unsure what he was going to say.

He swallowed loudly and kicked his toes at the floor absentmindedly. "I just wanted to apologise for what happened in the lunchroom. I was totally out of order doing that, and I'm sorry if I embarrassed you even more than I already did. I'm such a prick, and I'm so sorry," he said quietly, not looking at me.

"You are a prick," I confirmed. He grinned at me then and nodded, looking a little amused, like he was trying not to laugh. "What's funny?" I asked.

His smile grew bigger. "I just still find it funny when you cuss. It's just so random that a bad word would come out of a pretty mouth like yours, it just shocks me still," he said, laughing quietly and shoving his hands into his pockets, rocking on his heels.

I laughed weakly. Luke had always found me cussing strange, he liked it a lot. "I forgot about that," I muttered, rolling my eyes at him.

His smile slowly faded. "So, am I forgiven?" he asked, looking at me hopefully.

I frowned. "For starting a fight, yes. For cheating, no."

He frowned too, but he didn't look shocked. Maybe he expected me to say something along those lines. "Okay, that's fair enough. Can I just ask one thing?" he whispered, looking at me curiously. I nodded, giving him the go ahead. "You didn't really sleep with that guy, did you?" he asked, his voice breaking slightly as his eyes burned into mine, a pleading, almost begging expression on his face.

"Do I really have to answer that?" I asked incredulously. *Does he really think that little of me that I would cheat on him the same as he did to me?* I pushed away from the lockers and glared at him, my anger flaring up again. *How dare he ask me that! Stupid jerk!* "I'm done. This conversation is over," I stated confidently as I started marching down the hallway towards the exit, deciding that I would actually skip my last class after all.

"Maisie, I'm sorry!" he called. "Wait, where are you going?" he asked, jogging to catch me up.

"Home. I've had enough for today."

He grabbed my hand, making me stop. "Home? You want a ride? I could drive you so you don't have to walk."

I sighed and closed my eyes at his sweet offer. That was Luke all over, and one of the reasons why I fell deeply in love with the guy. "Luke, please just let me have some time. Please? I just can't be around you right now," I whispered, begging him with my eyes to just drop it and leave.

Suddenly someone shouted something that sounded like 'catch it' and then people were laughing, running towards us down the hallway, coming from the direction of the science lab. I looked up at them, confused, until I spotted a frog hopping down the hallway with about four people chasing after it, laughing, trying to catch it. Bile rose in my throat as my heart seemed to stop and then take off in overdrive. I had a terrible phobia of frogs. I knew it was irrational, but when I was younger Alex had found a dead toad and rubbed it on my face before he pushed it down the back of my top. I was a little scarred from that experience.

I squealed and threw myself at Luke, literally climbing up his body until I was wrapped around him like a baby monkey. I could hear screaming but quickly realised that it was me, so I bit my tongue and buried my face into the side of his neck, squeezing my eyes shut. I didn't even care that I was probably embarrassing myself in front of people, or that I was behaving like a child right now. I just needed Luke. He was like a safety blanket, and it was a natural response for me to throw myself on him.

"Baby, it's fine. Shh, it's fine," Luke cooed, rubbing my back softly, one arm hooked under my ass, supporting my weight. "It's okay. I won't let it over here. Loosen the fingers a little, can you?"

I gulped and suddenly realised I was digging my fingers into his back, my nails probably hurting him, but I couldn't move my hands an inch. "I want to go!" I practically shouted.

"Okay, I'll take you outside," he suggested. I could feel that we were moving, but I couldn't think about anything else other than the irregular beating of my heart and the squirming horror that was building in my stomach. I squeezed myself to Luke tighter, clamping my body to his and pressing my face harder into the side of his neck. He patted my behind lightly and I risked pulling my face away so I could take a quick glance around. We were in the parking lot, safely out of the school, no frogs in sight.

"Thank you," I mumbled, finally loosening the death grip that I had on his back and shoulders. He seemed to breathe a sigh of relief when I did that so I knew I'd been hurting him.

"No problem. Though one day I think you need to see someone about this fear, baby, it's getting a little out of hand," he joked, laughing quietly. "Not that I'm complaining about having you wrap yourself around me like that, of course," he added.

I pulled back slightly to see he was smirking at me. I laughed and rolled my eyes at him. "Of course you wouldn't."

He smiled and set me down on my feet, stepping closer to me, pressing his body to mine, and cupping the side of my face. "See, Maisie, you do need me, we both know it," he whispered, his brown eyes locked onto mine as if he could see down into my soul.

I gulped noisily. I knew that statement was true but I didn't want to admit it to him. "You were just the unlucky one that was closest to me in my moment of panic," I lied, shaking my head.

He laughed and kissed my forehead. "If that's what you want to be believe, then sure."

I smiled and rolled my eyes. "Get out of here, you're supposed to be in class," I ordered jokingly, nodding my head in the direction of the field where he had his next period.

His smile faded, to be replaced by a serious expression. He brushed his hand down the side of my face. "I love you," he said, his voice full of promise and emotion. He kissed my forehead again making me close my eyes at the soft feel of it, and then he was gone. I opened my eyes to see him jogging away towards the field, not looking over his shoulder at me at all.

I couldn't make sense of my feelings. What was I supposed to do when I couldn't even figure out what was going on in my own head? Sighing, I pulled out my cell phone, sending a quick text to Alex that I was skipping class and going home early so I didn't need a ride today.

The wind whipped around me, so I hugged myself against the cool air and trudged out of the school gate, not once looking back. My mind was a mess, I just wanted to switch it all off and stop thinking and feeling. Everything was so overwhelming that my eyes prickled with tears again. My thoughts flicked to Luke and what had just happened. The reality of events hit me with a huge wave of humiliation. I'd just screamed over a frog, then been carried out of the school like a baby. *Wow, that's so impressive, Maisie.* My face flamed with embarrassment because people had probably seen what happened, Luke, of course, wouldn't care in the slightest, but other students would have heard me scream and seen me throw myself at him like a small child. They were probably going to be talking about me even more tomorrow.

My feet seemed to be moving of their own accord; I wasn't thinking about where I was walking, I was lost in thought and on autopilot, so when I looked up my surroundings surprised me. I was at the children's play park not far from my house. Luke and I hung out here a lot before he got his car and could drive us places. My eyes settled on the roundabout where we would sit and talk for hours on end. This place held bittersweet memories for me. I chewed on my lip as I looked around, thinking of all the fun and smiles that I'd shared here with Luke. My heart ached. I missed him.

I headed over to the roundabout and sat down, using my foot to push it gently around while I closed my eyes and enjoyed the sensation. My stomach fluttered as a memory washed over me - the first time Luke kissed me. We'd been sat right here, it was our third date and he'd said that there was something he needed to do because he just couldn't stop thinking about it. When I'd asked him what it was, he'd smiled that beautiful cheeky smile and leant in, pressing his lips against mine just for a second before he pulled back and beamed over at me.

I smiled to myself, tracing my lip with my fingertip; I could almost still feel his mouth against mine. But then another thought hit me. Luke with her. A whimper left my lips as I laid back against the cold plastic and gave the roundabout another push with my foot. I stared up at the clouds, my mind running rampant as I thought about that night and what I'd witnessed. My concerns from earlier were haunting me again. He'd said that someone put something in his drink - would she do that? And if she did, was he trying to tell me that he was raped? He looked like he was in control, but what if he wasn't? What if she put something in his drink for the sole purpose of seducing him? I knew I needed to speak to Luke about this possibility. If he felt like he'd been taken advantage of then I had no right to be shutting him out like I was. If he felt like he had been attacked then I should be supporting him wholeheartedly, not pushing him away from me. If the situation were reversed and someone had put something in my drink then I would need him to support me, not break up with me.

My phone beeping in my pocket caught my attention. Shifting awkwardly so I could shove my hand into my pocket, I pulled it out. I had a new message from Alex.

'Where R U? Why R U not home if U left early?'

I frowned and looked at the time. It was after half past four. My eyes widened in shock. Had I really been laying here, just thinking, for that long? I jumped up, sending a text that I was on my way and then headed home quickly.

When I got to my house I spotted a motorbike in the drive, parked behind Alex's car. I frowned at it wondering who it belonged to. As I pushed open my front door the smell of food wafted out, making my mouth water and my tummy rumble because I hadn't really eaten all day - my lunch had been scattered across the floor when Luke and Zach had been fighting.

"Maisie, that you sweetheart?" my mom called from the kitchen.

"Yep," I confirmed. As I walked up the hall, I was almost bowled over by my dog, Chester. He was a little black cocker spaniel and he was adorable. But he was getting on in years now; he was almost twelve years old. "Hey, boy." I bent and scratched behind his ears while he wagged his tail like crazy at me. He followed behind me as I walked to the kitchen where I could hear my mom cooking. "Hi," I greeted, seeing both of my parents standing there.

My dad smiled, cocking his head to the side quizzically. His green eyes regarded me with concern, so I forced a smile. "Hey. How come you're so late?" he asked.

I sighed, knowing they would hound the answer out of me later anyway, so I might as well just tell them now. "I had a little run in with Luke at school, I was just walking and thinking, that's all. I didn't realise the time."

I saw my dad's fist clench at the mention of Luke's name. He was doing well restraining himself actually; I was surprised that my dad didn't punch Luke when he first found out.

"What did that little punk do now?" he growled.

I sighed. "Nothing. Can we just..." I trailed off, wincing; I really didn't want to talk about anything today.

My dad sighed too. "I heard your brother got detention for fighting at school today. Care to elaborate on that? He wouldn't," he said, raising one eyebrow in question.

A wave of love washed over me for my twin. He hadn't explained anything about the whole lunchroom scene to my parents, I was extremely grateful to him. *Yet another thing I owe him for.*

"Seriously? You can't figure out what happened all by yourself?" I asked sarcastically.

My dad grinned. "I can actually; I just wanted someone to give me a play by play of Alex smashing Luke's face in. I'm sorry I missed it," he answered, shrugging casually.

"Clay," my mom hissed, her tone warning. I smiled gratefully at her. Movement behind me made me turn, and in walked my brother.

He smiled sadly at me, wrapping his arm around my shoulders and pulling me into a hug. "You okay there, Maze-daze? Hard day?" he asked, looking at me worriedly.

I sighed and relaxed into his embrace. "I'm fine. Thanks, Alex, I owe you," I admitted, smiling weakly.

He shrugged. "Let me tap your friend's ass and we'll call it quits."

"Alex!" my mom scolded, throwing a dishcloth at him.

"Charlotte wouldn't even go there anyway," I dismissed, shaking my head confidently. I heard Alex grumbling something under his breath, but I didn't even try to understand what he said because at that moment, the toilet flushed in the downstairs bathroom. I looked around the kitchen, a little confused. *We're all here, so who on earth is in the bathroom?*

When the toilet flushing perpetrator stepped into the kitchen, I groaned. How had I not put two and two together when I saw the bike out the front? Zach didn't look at me though as he went to stand next to my brother, crossing his arms over his chest defensively.

I smiled weakly. *Is he still annoyed with me for walking off and leaving him after gym class?* "Hey there, Zachary. How's the face? You look like shit," I teased, smirking at him, using the words that he'd said to me this morning.

A smile twitched at the corners of his mouth but he was obviously fighting it. "Still getting better with the bitchy comments, if we keep going you'll be able to hold your own in an argument by the time you graduate," he replied, his voice cool and aloof. He didn't even bother looking at me.

I laughed at that comment. "What you doing here anyway? Got nothing you need to be jumping over?"

He sighed and frowned. "I came to hang with your brother. Also, I thought maybe I'd get to talk to you about tutoring and stuff. Maybe we should make up a schedule?" he offered, finally looking at me.

I groaned quietly. I'd forgotten about that. "You sure you wouldn't rather just let someone else do it?" I asked, putting maybe a little too much hope in my voice because he frowned and shook his head forcefully. "Fine," I grumbled. "I'm going to wash up before dinner." I headed into the bathroom, closing the door behind me before leaning against it and sighing deeply. I already knew this was going to be a rough evening. On top of having to plan out a tutoring schedule with Zach, I knew I needed to speak to Luke about Friday night. I needed to know how he felt about what happened with Sandy, how he saw everything. That was going to be an extremely painful conversation. This was going to be a long night, I could feel it. I already knew I'd be crying myself to sleep tonight.

chapter ten

After washing my hands, I stepped tentatively out of the bathroom. Hushed whispers caught my attention, so I stopped just outside the door and listened to what they were saying. "So, she said there was a run in with Luke. What happened?" my mom asked.

"Ask her. I'm not getting involved. I have the twin loyalty thing that I was born with," Alex answered in his cool and aloof tone. I smiled gratefully. Sometimes, just sometimes, I loved having a brother.

"Alex, be serious. We're trying to help," my mom whispered back. "She looks so sad and she hasn't really opened up to anyone about it. It can't be good to keep it all bottled up inside like that."

This time it was Zach who came to my defence – just maybe not the way I would like him to have done it. "I told her she should punch that Sandy girl in the face. But apparently violence solves nothing," he joked, laughing to himself.

Having heard enough and not wanting to get caught listening, I pulled out my phone and snuck up to my room, needing to get one of the things cleared up, or at least set the ball in motion. I text Luke, asking him to come over at about eight o'clock so we could talk. He replied immediately with a yes, as I knew he would. I sighed and headed downstairs and was grateful that the conversation seemed to have turned to something other than me.

They were talking about Zach's freerunning and the disciplines of it. Zach was trying to convince my dad that it was, in fact, a sport even though it wasn't classed as it. That it was basically gymnastics, mixed with martial arts and a lot of other things thrown in.

I stood in the doorway, just listening to him talk. He was so passionate about it, the way he waved his hands as he spoke, the way his mouth pulled up into a smile or his forehead creased with a frown. If I could just get him to apply the same passion to his schoolwork he'd probably be an A-student. He had already proved with a couple of things that he said to me today that he wasn't a brainless moron. There just had to be some reason why he wasn't connecting with classes. Maybe he liked the attention of being a delinquent; I'd heard that a lot of people did. Maybe he was starved for attention at home or something – though that wasn't true from what I'd seen this morning with his aunt. She certainly had a fond smile for him, but then again, maybe he hadn't been living with her that long. Maybe the lack of attention was a by-product of why he lived with his aunt in the first place. I guess only he knew for sure.

He turned to look at me then; he'd caught me staring at him, trying to work him out. He smiled his cocky little smile and raised one eyebrow. *Wait, does he think I'm checking him out?* The knowing smirk that slipped onto his face clearly indicated that he thought he'd caught me looking at him for a reason other than the truth. Even though that kind of thing had never even entered my head, I felt my cheeks heat up and my eyes dropped to the floor. Both of those reactions probably confirmed his theory that I was lusting after him. *Damn it, what is wrong with me? Can't I just make it through one hour without embarrassing myself?*

I sighed and stepped into the room, stubbing my foot on the doorframe and tumbling into the room, catching myself on the table. *Huh, apparently I'm struggling to make it through a minute without embarrassing myself, not an hour.* Zach's smirk grew bigger as Alex laughed and chirped, "Epic fail, Maze-Daze!"

I righted myself as my mom passed steaming plates of pasta to the three laughing males in my house. Even my dad was having a little chuckle at my expense. Perfect.

Sitting down and looking only at my plate, I silently hoped that talk wouldn't turn to me and Luke again. I tried my hardest not to think about him coming over later and how that painful conversation was going to go down. Luckily for me though, Zach steered the conversation to sports, and the whole meal was spent with the three males talking about freerunning, kickboxing and football.

When we were finally done eating I looked at Zach expectantly. "Want to work out a schedule now or something?" I offered, hoping he'd say no. Then again, maybe tutoring him would keep my mind from wandering to other things; he seemed to be able to keep my mind off Luke pretty easily.

He nodded but then offered to help clear the table. My mom waved him off, smiling. "I got it; you go do your tutoring thing. I assume that's what this is about?" she asked, smiling kindly.

He nodded and rolled his eyes. "Yep. Apparently your daughter is one of the smartest students at school so I have to be humiliated by being tutored by someone younger than me," he replied, shrugging.

I laughed at that statement. He was repeating a year; therefore, everyone was younger than him. "Come on then, let's hurry this up, I have something to do tonight," I suggested, eyeing the clock worriedly. It was almost six thirty already, and Luke would be here at eight. I turned and headed out of the door, knowing he would follow me. I stalked up to my room, rummaging through my schoolbag for a binder or notepad or something that we could work with.

When I found everything, including coloured pens to make it easier to make him up a studying schedule, I turned to find him stretched out on my bed looking the picture of ease. I frowned and he raised one eyebrow, putting his hands behind his head, kicking off his shoes.

"So, shall we get down to the really gritty stuff?" he offered, smirking at me suggestively.

I sighed and stomped over to my bed, gripping his legs and shoving them out of the way so I could sit down at the foot of my bed, glaring at him. "If you're not going to take this seriously then you can just find someone else to tutor you, Zachary," I stated, dumping all of the books and pens on his legs.

A frown slipped onto his face. "Stop calling me that, I hate that!" he snapped.

I'd definitely hit a nerve there with the name thing. "Fine, I'll stop calling you that, seeing as you asked me so nicely," I replied, rolling my eyes at him. "Are you going to work hard at this or not, because I'm not wasting my time if you're not going to bother."

He sat up and pushed all of the stuff off his legs. I thought he was going to get up and walk out, but he didn't. Instead, he nodded and rubbed the back of his neck. "Yeah, I need to graduate this year otherwise I'm screwed."

"Screwed, how?" I asked, frowning and trying to work him out. He was such a complicated person at times. Sometimes he came across with his devil may care attitude, but just now he actually looked a little vulnerable, worried even.

He blew out a big breath and closed his eyes. "I've been offered an opportunity, an awesome opportunity, but the offer is only good if I graduate." I raised one eyebrow, prompting him with my silence to continue. He chewed on his lip and seemed to be weighing his options before he spoke, "I got offered a job, my perfect, dream job actually. Stuntman for an upcoming action movie," he explained.

My mouth popped open in shock at that little bit of information. "Holy crap, really?" I gasped.

He nodded, smiling proudly. "Yeah, but because of certain things that I really don't want to talk about, I need to finish high school to prove to them that I can stay focussed. So far, I don't seem to be able to stay focussed enough to stick to anything. So, if I can't graduate in a couple of months then I'm screwed like I said."

Wow. Am I sitting on the bed with a future movie star? That thought was a little weird actually. "Well I guess you'd better work hard this time then, huh?" I teased, picking up a pen and throwing it in his direction. He caught it effortlessly and smiled, rolling his eyes.

For the next hour he actually took me seriously. There were no cocky jokes, no snide remarks, and no slutty comments. I was more than a little proud of his effort. We'd talked through his weak points, discussed action plans, and finally drew up a schedule so we could get together and study. We also made up a homework planner for him too, so that he could do that on his own. I was really hoping he'd stick to it, but I guess only time would tell. When we'd done all the hard work and had a planner for both of us, he grinned.

"You're such a nerd. Why did we have to colour it in? This isn't art class," he teased, laughing at his sheet that was all boxed in and coloured to make it easier to understand.

I snatched it out of his hands and flopped down onto my stomach. "The red ones are the most important staple subjects that take priority. The blue ones are second, and the green-" I started to explain, but he jumped in and cut me off.

"Third, I get it. I think I can see where this is going," he joked, nudging me over on the bed as he laid down next to me.

"Exactly. The white bits are where you have free time. Yellow is for less important things that you don't actually require to graduate. With this like this then you can see where you are and if you have a spare half an hour then you can work on the yellow or something," I suggested, shrugging and smiling at his schedule proudly.

It had taken a long time to work out when we would meet up. His freerunning training took a lot of his spare time, also the fact that he didn't want to go to the library was a bit of a pain, but we'd gotten there eventually. We both had free periods at the same time on Tuesdays and Wednesdays for an hour so we would do it then at school. On Mondays and Thursdays it was to be afterschool, either at my place or his. The only thing I didn't like about those two days was that he said he'd drive. I didn't have a car, so it was the back of the bike for me for two days a week so that we could get home to study.

Fridays were the biggest pain to sort out. He went freerunning with his training group on Fridays afterschool for at least an hour where they would plan out their weekend activities and what they would jump over. So that left us with two options on Fridays, I either waited at school and let him pick me up - which he freely admitted that he'd probably be late for, or, I went with him to his training session and I could get on with my own schoolwork while he was doing his thing. We agreed to see how it went each week, to stay a little more flexible on Fridays. I actually could have just waited at school and had Alex drive me home, but he normally had some desperate girl hanging all over him ready for the weekend. I didn't really want to sit in the car with him getting pawed by some hoe he would drop by the time morning bell rang on Monday.

"If I get free time it won't be spent on the yellow sectioned crap," he stated, shaking his head fiercely.

I laughed and looked over at him. He was grinning happily and actually looked pretty cute, not like a badass at all. "So what will you be spending it on? Hooking up with easy girls or smoking your life away?" I joked, propping my head up on my elbow and waiting for a little more information about him. So far he'd been fairly secretive.

He shrugged. "I don't hook up with easy girls."

I snorted at that, remembering him leaning in and flirting with the girl outside of gym earlier, also the *'I've got four girls' numbers already'* comment at lunch. "Uh-huh, and I like to smother myself in whipped cream and run naked in the street," I said sarcastically.

He raised one eyebrow. "Now that I could watch in my free time." I laughed and slapped his shoulder which made him laugh too. "Honestly though, I don't hook up with easy girls," he repeated.

"So you like the harder to get ones then?" I joked; picking up that he'd said the word easy twice now.

He smiled. "Think what you want. Your opinion makes no difference to me, little rebel."

I frowned. "If I have to stop calling you Zachary, then you have to stop calling me names that link in with what happened on Friday night," I instructed.

He pouted at me. "But I like calling you that. I like the fact that I'm the only one that's seen you do something naughty."

I laughed because of how dirty the word naughty sounded just because it came out of his mouth. I smirked at him. I wasn't a totally innocent girl, Luke and I had gotten a little naughty at times. But he was right in one way; I'd never broken the law before Friday. "I've done plenty of naughty things," I corrected.

He smiled and leant in closer to me, his breath blowing across my lips, his eyes doing a kind of smouldering thing as his gaze held mine. "Oh yeah? What kind of things, and would I be able to either get a full description or maybe join in next time?" he purred seductively.

I gulped. *Oh wow, is he flirting with me? Am I flirting with him? What on earth am I doing right now?* I laughed nervously and sat up on the bed, crossing my legs and trying to think of something to say to that.

"Just because I'm not easy doesn't mean that I'm interested in you," I stated indifferently.

He laughed. "And who said I was interested in you anyway? Getting a little ahead of yourself there, Maisie? I never took you for a big ego type chick," he countered. I gulped and blushed like crazy because I'd just assumed that he was hitting on me, and apparently had made a fool out of myself. He smiled at my unease and patted the bed for me to lay down next to him again. "I'm kidding.

You don't have to worry though; I wasn't hitting on you, I promise. I don't date, so you're safe," he vowed, looking away and fiddling with the highlighter pen he was holding.

I settled myself back down on the bed next to him but made sure that we had a gap between us just in case he was messing around. "You don't date? Why's that then?" I asked, not believing a word of it. He was a good looking guy, he had to date. He had girls throwing themselves at him, that much was obvious from today at school.

He shrugged. "I don't date because I don't want to fall in love with anyone."

I frowned, trying to work out if he was just messing around with me right now. He looked so serious though. "Why, are you afraid of heartbreak?" I teased, growing more and more curious with each passing second.

He smiled sadly and shook his head. "No. But what's the point in falling for someone when it won't go anywhere? I would hate to tie a girl in with me for life, that would suck for her. So I just stay away from girls altogether," he explained, his brown eyes locking onto mine. I studied his face trying to think of what that actually meant. Tying a girl to him for life, why would that suck for her?

"What?" I asked, confused.

He laughed and picked up my schedule, holding it out to me. "So yeah, you're safe. Let's just stick to the tutoring thing, okay? Personal stuff stays out of it," he suggested. "Plus, your butt doesn't do anything for me."

I laughed and slapped his shoulder, trying to fake hurt. "Don't keep insulting my butt, I'll get a complex about it," I scolded playfully.

He winked at me. "I guess I'd better get home soon. My aunt will be worried about me, I didn't tell her that I was coming here after school, so she's probably wondering where I am."

"And what will she think when you walk in with a smashed up face?" I asked, wincing as I looked at his split lip and bruising jaw.

He waved his hand dismissively. "She'll just be pleased that I stayed the full day at school." I laughed, and he moved on the bed, scooping together all of his things that we'd made. "I'll see you tomorrow, Maze-Daze."

I groaned. "Please don't call me that either."

He opened his mouth to answer but was interrupted by a commotion coming from downstairs. I could hear Alex growling something, there was a slight crash as something banged against the wall. Then I heard Luke's voice too, shouting that he was invited and that I wanted to talk to him. I gasped. *He's early! I didn't tell anyone that he was coming over. Crap!*

I sprang off the bed and ran for the door as fast as I could before Alex got too angry and they started fighting again. As I burst out of my room, I looked down to see Alex was practically pinning Luke against the wall as they shouted at each other. Alex looked ready to kill.

"Alex! I did invite him!" I shouted, running down the stairs as fast as I could without breaking my neck.

My brother looked up at me and frowned, his grip not loosening on Luke for a second. "What the hell? Why?" he cried angrily.

I reached his side then and looked at him pleadingly, trying to keep my eyes away from Luke's for as long as possible; his eyes always were my favourite part about him. "Because I need to talk to him," I explained, frowning at Alex because he hadn't let go yet. He looked like he was having trouble not beating my ex-boyfriend to a pulp. My dad was there too, I didn't see him at first but my mom was standing in front of him trying to calm him down. He looked like he wanted to kill Luke too. I sighed dramatically and grabbed Alex's wrist, pulling to get him to let go of Luke's hoodie. "Alex, just leave it. I said I invited him over, so just go already will you?" I requested, trying to look stern even though I actually loved him for doing that for me. I loved how protective he was of me, it was adorable - it's just that it was infuriating at times.

He made a kind of growling sound as he shoved Luke away from him, making him hit the wall again that he was already being pinned against. "I swear to God, Hannigan, if you hurt my sister again I'm going to kill you," he promised, his voice full of menace.

Luke nodded, signalling that he'd understood, so Alex walked off. He mumbled something to my dad before they both stomped off into the lounge together, still grumbling cuss words under their breath. My dad was worse than my brother at times. I turned back to Luke and smiled apologetically, but he wasn't looking at me, he was looking over my shoulder with an angry expression on his face.

I frowned and turned, expecting Alex to be watching us or something, instead, Zach was walking down the stairs, a cocky smile on his face as he held Luke's gaze.

"Wow, you should see someone about that face, it looks bad," Zach suggested, grinning.

Luke seemed to tense as he stepped closer to me, his eyes not leaving Zach's. "What are you doing here?" he spat.

Zach's eyes flicked to me as he shrugged. "Just screwing your ex again," he replied coolly.

"Goodbye, Zach!" I interjected before they could get into an argument about it again.

Zach laughed and winked at me as I practically pushed him out of the front door. "Tell your brother I said bye, and thank your mom for dinner." I nodded in acknowledgement and practically shut the door in his face which made him laugh again outside.

I chewed on my lip and looked back to see Luke looking at me expectantly, obviously waiting for an explanation. Well screw him, I didn't owe him anything, he should know me better. "Let's go upstairs and talk then," I suggested, ignoring the tense atmosphere. He was so jealous that his jaw was twitching where he was grinding his teeth together.

I walked off without waiting for him, heading to my bedroom, dreading this whole conversation. It was necessary though, I needed to find out if he felt like he'd been taken advantage of, because this whole situation would change if he did.

When we got in my room I sat on my desk chair because I didn't want to sit too close to him. He trotted over and sat on my bed, looking at his hands, his shoulders slumped. I took a deep breath and tried to come up with words that would actually make sense, but my mind was too jumbled to form a coherent sentence.

"So, I just... about Friday... and..." I closed my eyes and willed my mouth to work.

"Maisie, baby, I'm so sorry," he whispered.

I nodded; I knew he was sorry, his whole posture and attitude was showing me how much he regretted it. "I know. I just figured I should talk to you about it and find out what happened."

He sighed and closed his eyes letting his head drop down so he was looking at his lap.

"Luke, just tell me what happened on Friday night. In your words. I don't want you to tell me what I want to hear, I want you to tell me what you felt happened, okay?" I suggested, just needing to get this done already so I would know one way or the other.

He ran a hand through his hair, not looking at me as he spoke, "I was drunk, really drunk. I don't remember much of it, but I started to feel sick and managed to get upstairs to Ricky's bathroom before I puked. When I turned around she was there, leaning on the door frame, smiling." He looked up at me then with a pained expression on his face. "I just remember thinking that I wanted to go home. I was washing my hands and I was going to come and get you to see if we could leave. But she started taking her shirt off and I was a little too shocked to do anything. Then she kind of threw herself at me I guess, I don't really know, it was all happening so fast. I didn't think about anything else, my head was swimming, and nothing seemed to matter and she was so insistent and was undressing me. I just," he winced and shook his head, "I'm sorry."

My heart was hurting so much as I started to imagine how that happened. I imagined her lips on his, her tongue in his mouth. My lungs felt like they were constricting, so my breathing was a little shallow. "Luke, you said that you were at the hospital, and that someone put something in your drink," I said, trying to get the information out of him without saying the words.

He nodded. "I wouldn't have done it otherwise. I would never cheat on you, baby. You're my life. I love you more than anything," he promised, looking at me pleadingly.

"So, you didn't know what you were doing? You were drugged and didn't know what you were doing?" I asked, bracing myself for his answer.

He frowned. "Maisie, I don't know what you're getting at. What is it that you're asking? If you want to know if I regret it, then the answer is yes. If you want to know if I'll ever cheat on you again, then the answer is never. I promise this was a onetime thing. I can't lose you, please?"

I took a deep breath and looked at him as I asked the thing that I couldn't stop thinking about since lunchtime. "Luke, did she take advantage of you? You said you wouldn't have done it if you weren't drugged. Do you feel like she," I took a deep breath, "raped you?"

He recoiled, seeming a little taken aback by my question. He didn't speak for a minute or two, and I felt like the silence was killing me slowly. He was obviously thinking about his answer, a thoughtful expression covered his face as he looked at his hands. Finally, he shook his head. "Not really," he admitted.

Part of me was glad for him. The emotional turmoil he would feel if he'd answered yes would have been hard for him to deal with, so I was glad that he didn't feel like that. The extremely selfish part of me, the part that was hoping for my boyfriend back, was a little disappointed. I hated myself for being so nasty, but if he'd answered differently then I would have thrown my arms around his neck and given him my full support. I would have Luke, sure it would be hard to work past, he would have had a lot to deal with, but we would have gotten through it together.

"You felt like you were in control and you could have stopped it if you wanted to?" I questioned, just needing to make sure he was okay.

He nodded. "I have the strong feeling that if I'd said that she'd taken advantage that I wouldn't be facing losing you right now," he muttered. Luke always was smart with things like that.

I frowned and shrugged. "You didn't answer differently, so," I trailed off not knowing what else to say.

"Maisie, is there anything I can do? Anything?" he asked, looking at me pleadingly.

"I love you, I really do," I replied. "But you did that knowing I was downstairs, knowing that she wasn't me, knowing that I would never do that to you. Yet you still did it. That hurts so much, Luke." I willed the tears not to fall in front of him, there was no doubt I would be crying myself to sleep later, but for right now I was trying to be strong. "I just don't know if I can forget this. I want to hate you, I want to punch you in the face and scream at you. I want to hurt you like you've hurt me."

He moved off the bed then and knelt in front of me. "Do it then. Hit me, scream at me, do whatever you need. Please, just give me one more chance. Just please don't let this be it," he begged.

His beautiful brown eyes that I loved so much locked on mine and I didn't want to say this was it; I didn't want to completely cut it off with him. I actually didn't know if I could forgive him, but I couldn't rule it out. "I don't know. I'm so confused. I love you; I honestly still love you, but..."

"But you don't want to be with me," he whispered. A pained expression crossed his face; it was like devastation, like I'd just taken everything important away from him. I knew I was probably the only person that knew Luke properly. He had no one else really, his family were hardly ever around, and his friends only got to see the showy side of him. I was probably the only one he had ever opened up to. I was probably the only one that knew the real Luke Hannigan. The thought of him being alone if I cut him off, was actually painful to me. I hated the thought of him being sad. I really loved him too much for my own good.

"Maybe we could be friends? See what happens?" I suggested, wanting to take the hopeless and hurt look off his face. Didn't everyone deserve a second chance? If I had made that mistake then I knew I would be begging him for another shot, just like he was right now.

His head snapped up, his eyes wide and hopeful. "Really? I'd love that, baby." He put his hands on my knees, gripping tightly as he pushed himself up so our faces were on the same level. I gulped at his words, the familiar pet name sounded like melted chocolate coming out of his mouth. It shouldn't make the hairs on the back of my neck stand up, it shouldn't make my heart race in my chest, and it shouldn't make my stomach flutter. But it did. "I'd love the chance to win you back. As much as you don't want to admit it, you and I are perfect for each other. You need me just as much as I need you," he whispered.

My arms acted without my permission and wrapped around his neck, pulling him closer to me as I buried my face in the side of his neck, breathing in his smell that made my skin prickle and my stomach flutter. I knew I couldn't just cut it off with him because my body's reactions to him were involuntary. He was right, I did need him.

"Let's just take it slow and be friends," I repeated, putting emphasis around the word friends. He nodded, pressing his face into my hair as he wrapped his arms around me too, crushing me against his chest. I have no idea how long we stayed like that, unmoving, unspeaking, but it didn't feel like long enough.

He pulled back and smiled his heart stopping smile. "I'd better go; your brother and dad are probably waiting to jump me outside or something. I can't deny them the satisfaction of beating me to a pulp again. Your dad hasn't even taken a swing yet, so I guess I need to allow that to make him feel better," he said, laughing quietly.

I smiled at that, he was probably right there. "Okay, well I'll see you tomorrow at school."

A small frown crossed his face. "Think I could pick you up in the morning? Drive you to school?" he asked hopefully. "As friends of course," he added the last part quickly.

I gulped; I wasn't ready for that kind of thing yet. It was hard enough being at school with everyone knowing and gossiping about me and him; I couldn't show up with him and spark more rumours about us. People would already be wondering why it was that we were being friends; I couldn't show up with him too.

"I think I should ride with Alex."

He sighed and nodded. "Okay. I'll see you at school then." Before I could protest, he leant in and pressed his lips against mine. The familiar sparks and little bursts of heat rushed through my body because of how perfectly his lips fitted mine. Then it was over. He pulled back and smiled at me sadly before he stood up and stroked his hand down the side of my face. "I'll wait as long as you need. I love you."

I didn't know what to say to that, so I said nothing. He took that as his cue to leave and walked off; leaving me watching the place that I last saw his body. I touched my lips; I could still feel the ghost of his kiss there. Running my tongue over my bottom lip, I could still taste him.

I forced myself to go downstairs to spend some time with my family. It was obvious they were worried about me. It took longer than I thought to assure my ape of a brother that I wasn't forgiving Luke too fast, and that we weren't back together. It took even longer to get him to agree not to shove his fist down Luke's throat.

I made small talk with my parents about Zach's tutoring schedule. Finally, after faking that I was okay for another half an hour, I excused myself to bed. As I curled in the sheets I could feel the sadness trying to creep over me again. As soon as I was in the darkness my mind drifted to Luke again. I willed myself to fall asleep quickly, but that didn't happen. Instead, I cried for another half an hour before drifting into a shallow and uneasy slumber.

chapter eleven

When morning finally came I felt terrible because of barely sleeping. I was on auto-pilot as I dressed and trudged to Alex's car. As we pulled into the parking lot of the school I spotted Luke sitting on the hood of his car, three spaces down. His friends were all hanging around him, talking, but he seemed a little distracted. When we pulled into the space he sprung away from his car and headed over, a smile stretching across his face. I watched the way his unbuttoned black shirt blew in the light wind, the white t-shirt stuck to his body showing off how sculpted he was from all the football he played. I watched the way the smile showed off his pearly white teeth and strong jaw. I sighed sadly. He still had an effect on my body; I was still incredibly attracted to him. The trouble was I also noticed how the other girls looked at him too. They had always looked, but before I'd been confident in his affections so them looking had never bothered me; I didn't get jealous because I trusted him. Now though I felt a little sick with jealousy.

Alex said his goodbyes as he eyed up a group of girls who were standing off to one side. He was obviously choosing his weekly target. What with all the excitement yesterday and fighting with Zach, I guess he didn't get to make a move on many girls.

Luke reached the car just as I closed my door. "Hey, baby," he greeted. His hand moved to take mine so I shied away slightly which made his face fall. "Sorry," he muttered, letting his hand drop to his side as he kicked his shoes on the ground.

"Morning," I replied, trying to ignore the way he looked so sad.

"Morning."

I laughed uncomfortably, and flicked my eyes around to see that everyone was watching us. Some people were discreetly watching but pretending to do something else, some people looked away quickly as I glanced in their direction, others were outright staring with their mouths open. "Well, this is awkward," I muttered, chewing on my lip.

Luke smiled at me apologetically. "Shall I walk you in, or...?" he trailed off, looking at me hopefully.

I took a deep breath and forced a smile even though I felt like crying. "Sure. Oh, did you get your assignment done for English?" I asked, trying to change the subject. I was pretty sure he had an essay to hand in today.

He smiled at me gratefully, probably because I was making an effort to be friends. We talked a little awkwardly as he walked me into the building. I kept my hands firmly gripped onto the straps of my schoolbag because his hands were swinging dangerously close to mine. People were watching as we walked past and I tried my best not to see them - well, I tried to pretend like I didn't see them anyway.

Whispers were starting as we walked down the hallway and all I wanted to do was curl up in bed and cry. I looked up the hallway and frowned. People were crowding near my locker; an excited murmur was rippling through the crowd. *What on earth is that about?*

Out of nowhere Charlotte grabbed my arm and yanked me to a stop. "Maisie! Oh my God. I've reported it to the janitor; they said they'll get it sorted once everyone goes to class. It's disgusting. I bet it was the witch that did it," she hissed, her jaw tightening in anger.

"Huh?" *The janitor will get what sorted?*

Her eyes widened as her grip on my arm tightened to the point of pain. "You haven't seen it?"

Luke stepped forward and looked at her curiously. "Seen what, Charlotte?" he asked, rolling his eyes.

Charlotte didn't reply, just dragged me forward, shoving people out of the way. "Move it or lose it. Come on, people, get out of the way!" she ordered.

I followed behind her helplessly, weaving through the gathered students, wondering what was going on. The crowd parted, people turned to look at me, and the murmur got even more excited as people regarded me with wide eyes, obviously waiting for my reaction to whatever it was. Sandy smirked at me and my hand clenched into a fist as Zach's words from yesterday echoed in my head, 'You need to punch that hoe in the face'. I wanted to, I really did, but I forced myself to look away from her taunting smile.

Charlotte stopped and I looked up at whatever was so urgent, only to see that someone had vandalised my locker. One big bold word had been spray painted on the yellow door of it, large red letters, the paint thick and angry looking.

BITCH

"What the heck?" I cried, frowning at it angrily. *Why on earth would someone write that on my locker? That's just stupid because I'm not a bitch at all!*

"I know, it's disgusting!" Charlotte growled, shaking her head angrily. "It should be gone by lunchtime apparently."

I felt my face flush with embarrassment because everyone was staring at me. I hated to be the centre of attention, and it looked like every gaze in the hallway was locked onto me in that second. Why would someone even write that, who wrote it?

"What the hell is that?"

I turned to see Luke had pushed his way through the crowd and had stopped at my back. His eyes were glued to my locker as his jaw twitched angrily. My mind was whirling, trying to think of someone that would want to write that on my locker. I got along with everyone; I was well liked - just not popular. I guess the popular girls had never really liked me because I was dating the quarterback, but none of them would resent me that much, would they? Maybe Sandy...

In the back of my mind I could hear Luke ranting loudly, asking who did it, if anyone saw anything. He was incredibly angry by the sound of it. My eyes flicked to Sandy again. She was giggling behind her hand, whispering conspiratorially to her friend.

"Did you do that?" I asked her, pointing at it angrily. I couldn't think of a single other person in the school that would have a problem with me like she did.

She raised one eyebrow looking at me incredulously. "No. But the person who wrote it obviously has your number though huh? You certainly are a bitch," she replied, straightening her shoulders as people turned to watch the exchange.

Anger made my stomach shake as I glared at her. "Sandy, what's your problem? What have I ever done to you? So I went out with someone that you wanted, so what? Does that mean that you have to hate me forever and make snide remarks about me all the time?" I growled.

She snorted and looked at me distastefully. "Well you're not dating him now though, are you? He saw how ridiculous he was being and came to me eventually," she replied, shrugging and smiling at me wickedly.

I stepped forward to make an angry comment back, but Luke was quicker and pulled me behind him as he glared at her. "You don't talk shit about her. She's worth a million of you; for one thing she's not a nasty skank. There's a reason I fell in love with her and not you, she's not a fake bimbo whore who's up herself. You were a drunken mistake, nothing more than that, so don't flatter yourself," he hissed angrily.

Her mouth dropped open in shock as her cheeks flushed pink with embarrassment. "Well you weren't exactly that good in bed, Luke Hannigan! Total waste of a condom if you ask me!" she retorted.

Luke's body stiffened but he didn't reply. She turned on her heel, flicking her perfectly straightened, natural blonde hair over her shoulder as she stomped off, with her girls following behind her like little lapdogs following their master. Luke turned back to me and shook his head, frowning. I could feel my eyes filling with tears and I willed them not to fall. People were still staring at me and I didn't want anyone to see me cry.

Why was this all happening to me? I had a great life before this all happened. Everything was perfect, I had the perfect boyfriend, great friends, everything was planned out and exciting. But then everything fell to pieces around me.

Luke frowned and turned to the side. "Everyone just get lost. Just go to class or something, seriously, just leave!" he ordered. Because he was still Luke Hannigan, most popular jock in school, everyone seemed to move as one as they whispered and dispersed quickly.

I glanced up to see Zach leaning against the wall opposite me, his arms folded over his chest, he was watching me intently. His eyes locked onto mine. I gulped at the intensity I saw there before he tightened his jaw and walked off too.

"Baby, you okay?"

I snapped out of the little haze I seemed to be trapped in, and looked up at Luke. He was watching me with a concerned look on his face. I nodded and stepped forward into his body, just needing a little comfort. Instantly, his arms wrapped around me, enveloping me in his beautiful smell. I pressed my face against his chest and tried my hardest not to cry as I wrapped my arms around his waist, clamping myself to him.

"This will all get easier. I'm sorry," he whispered, kissing the side of my head softly as he stroked my back.

I sniffed and pulled away. "I know." I turned back to my locker and the awful red writing again. "I better get my books and stuff and get to class." I smiled at Charlotte who was just looking at me sympathetically. "Someone's gonna clean this off, right? I don't need to do anything?"

She nodded. "They'll sort it out, don't worry."

Sighing, I forced myself to punch in my combination and open it, grabbing my books for the morning class. Inside I was dreading Alex seeing this, I hoped they got it removed before he did because he would be crazy mad about it. I wouldn't be able to stop him hearing about it, but seeing it would make his 'protective big brother' instincts even worse. When I had everything, Luke walked me to class and Charlotte headed off in the other direction for hers.

"Want to eat lunch together?" Luke asked, cocking his head to the side, smiling hopefully.

I shrugged but nodded at the same time. "Sure."

• • •

MY MORNING WAS spent with people asking me constantly about my locker. I had repeated myself over and over again so much that even I was bored of the sound of my own answers. Sandy had ignored me completely in first period. We sat at opposite ends of the classroom and as soon as the bell sounded, I packed up and practically ran out of the room. I hated this attention; it was like everyone was watching me, waiting for me to blow a gasket or something.

At lunchtime I headed back to my locker, only to see that the ugly writing had gone. In its place was a freshly scrubbed clean patch of silver. I cringed because the rest of the locker was yellow apart from that patch. It was glaringly obvious that something had been written there and scrubbed off. People were watching me discreetly, so I forced myself to put on a brave face and store my books, grab my purse and slam the door shut. I was going for the unconcerned approach, but I was pretty sure I didn't pull it off very well.

"Hi." I jumped and turned to see Zach leaning against the locker next to mine. One of his jeaned legs was crossed over the other, his arms folded over his chest. A small smile tugged at the corners of his mouth. He nodded towards my locker. "So, who did that?"

I shrugged, but again my mind flicked to that blonde witch. I couldn't think of anyone else. "My best guess is the man stealing cheerleader," I replied, leaning against my locker next to him.

"Maybe." He nodded, pursing his lips as if he was thinking about something really hard. "Anyway, change of subject. Want to get food? I'm starving," he said, rubbing his flat stomach in little circles.

I winced. "Um, I agreed to eat with Luke."

He frowned looking at me like I was stupid. "You two got back together last night?"

I shook my head quickly. "No. We're just being friends. We're seeing how it goes," I corrected.

He smiled then. "Good, because you deserve better than him. I can't see your story ending up like that, you won't end up with a cheating jerk," he commented.

I laughed quietly. "Oh yeah? And how will my story end? Who will I end up with?" I asked, rolling my eyes at how silly he was.

His arm slung around my shoulder as he winked at me. "You'll end up with the bad boy," he replied, grinning wickedly.

I snorted and slapped my hand into his stomach which made him laugh and his arm drop off my shoulder as we walked down the hallway towards the lunchroom. "Bad boys don't do it for me." I shrugged teasingly. *Wait, am I flirting with him again?* I didn't even know if this could be classed as flirting, if it was classed as that then I had no idea I was doing it at all. I didn't mean to if I was.

"Everyone loves a bad boy," he countered, winking at me teasingly.

"Nah, the bad boy will be expelled before the end of the year anyway, so that's not how it'll happen." I smirked at him and he just laughed.

"Let's hope that's not true or I'll need to find myself a real job in a few months," he said, frowning distastefully. We talked easily for the rest of the short journey to the lunchroom.

As we stepped in, Luke pushed himself away from the wall where he usually met me. He frowned at Zach hatefully before looking at me. "Ready?" he asked, seeming to completely ignore Zach's presence.

"Maisie said I could eat with you guys. That's alright with you, right, quarterback?" Zach said, smiling politely.

Luke's hands tightened into fists as he seemed to struggle with his jealousy. I shot Zach a warning look. He obviously couldn't resist pushing Luke's buttons.

I sighed as they seemed to have some kind of unspoken conversation. "I'm going to eat with Char and Beth," I muttered, walking off and heading to the line to get my food. I grabbed a sandwich and drink and paid before they had even moved from the spot where I left them. Their conversation wasn't a silent one now. I couldn't make out what they were saying, but judging by the angry looks on their faces and the gesturing hands, it didn't look like friendly chat about sports.

As soon as I sat down, Alex came bounding over. His hand gripped my shoulder as he looked at me angrily. "Why didn't you call me and tell me about your locker?" he asked, shaking his head forcefully.

I brushed his hand off and smiled reassuringly. "It was no big deal. It's gone now so don't worry about it," I suggested. I had enough to deal with already; I didn't really need him going all protective caveman on me.

He raked a hand through his hair as he spoke, "You still should have called me, Maze-daze."

"Just leave it, Alex. Everything's fine," I assured him.

He sighed and nodded. "Fine. But call me in future," he instructed. He turned and walked off. Luke was coming in the other direction, carrying a tray of food towards my table. As they passed each other, Alex purposefully slammed his shoulder into Luke's. I closed my eyes as the tray clattered to the floor and Alex laughed. "Sorry, Hannigan. Didn't see you there."

"Alex!" I warned, shaking my head as I opened my eyes. Luke was obviously trying not to react; his teeth were grinding together while my twin just smirked challengingly in his direction.

Luke wouldn't start a fight with my brother; for one thing he knew that Alex was doing it on my behalf so he probably felt he deserved it. Another reason he wouldn't start a fight with my brother was that Alex would kick Luke's butt, and they both knew it. He was a serious badass at things like that; he actually wanted to be a professional kickboxer and was already champion of the junior league.

"I'll go buy something else," Luke muttered, turning and walking off without even acknowledging what had happened. I shot Alex a dark look, but he just shrugged unashamedly as he walked off.

"Your brother is hot when he's all rough like that," Charlotte whispered, giggling.

I laughed and shook my head. Zach was walking up the aisle then, heading in my direction. I cringed inwardly at how awkward this lunch was going to be if both him and Luke were going to sit with us, but thankfully he caught my eye and nodded towards my where my brother was sitting. I smiled gratefully and he did a cheesy handshake-bump thing with Alex before setting his tray down and sitting with him.

When I looked away from Zach, Charlotte and Beth were still talking about how fine my twin was. I just started on my sandwich and let them get on with it; I was used to talk about my 'hottie brother'.

Luke plopped down next to me, but the girls didn't even acknowledge his presence as they carried on talking amongst themselves. "Hey. Sorry about that," I muttered, smiling apologetically at him.

He shrugged easily. "No worries. It's not like I don't deserve it, so don't apologise." He put a blueberry muffin down in front of me. "Got you this."

I sighed and felt my heart stutter because he was always sweet like that. "Thanks."

The rest of lunch was fairly quiet. I just ate my food, trying to pretend that everyone wasn't watching mine and Luke's every move. The rumour mill seemed to be waiting with baited breath for the gossip.

My next two classes were fun. I had them both with Zach, and he really was a funny guy. I did a little more unintentional flirting, but it was harmless really because he knew I was still hung up on Luke, and he'd already said he didn't date. Both of us knew it wouldn't go anywhere, so I just let myself be myself and have fun for a change. I even enjoyed my gym class because he chose me to partner him and we were practicing kicking a football. I was terrible as I expected, but much to his obvious efforts, it turned out that Zach couldn't kick to save his life either. Both of us were in hysterics as we missed the goal posts time and time again. It was nice to laugh and I didn't once think about Luke or my locker.

After braving my last class on my own, Zach was waiting by my locker at the end of the day. I groaned because this was going to be our first tutoring session. That part was okay, it was the getting home part that I was dreading. He was driving, and that therefore meant another ride on his bike.

"Ready?" he asked, grinning. We'd agreed to go to his place to study today because his aunt wanted reassurance that he was actually working. Apparently she hadn't been too impressed with the state of his face when he went home last night, so to make her feel better we were studying at his house so she could keep her eye on him. I'd already text Alex and my mom to tell them.

I nodded, grabbing the rest of my books from my locker. "Lead the way then, bad boy," I teased, laughing.

I followed him out to the parking lot and over to his motorbike. He stopped beside it and dug around in his rucksack, pulling something out. I smiled when he held it out to me. "I thought you didn't like to wear one," I mused as I looked down at the black helmet.

He shrugged. "I brought it for you to use, you wanted one last time."

"You brought me a helmet?" I smiled gratefully at him because that was thoughtful. He opened his mouth to answer but was cut off by someone shouting my name behind us. I turned to see Luke striding over; he looked murderously angry. "What?" I asked, wondering why he looked so mad.

"You're not going anywhere with him," Luke barked, glaring at Zach as he pulled me into his body, clamping me to him possessively.

I shoved on his chest, pushing myself away from him as I glared at him with as much hate as I could muster, which probably wasn't that much considering I was still in love with him. "Just grow up will you? What the hell is your problem?" I cried, throwing my hands up in exasperation.

Luke pointed over my shoulder, his eyes angry and his jaw tight as he glared at Zach. "Him! He's my problem. The way he looks at you is my problem. Him taking my girlfriend home is my problem!" he shouted angrily.

Movement at my side told me that Zach had stepped closer to me. My mouth had gone dry; I had no idea what to say. Luke was delusional, what on earth was he thinking?

"Why don't you just leave her alone already?" Zach growled, his voice angry and full of force. He stood the same height as Luke, but the way he held himself was more confident and assured, so he somehow looked taller.

Luke sneered at him. "So you can worm your way into my girlfriend's pants? I don't think so!" he countered, reaching for my hand again.

I felt my cheeks flame with embarrassment at this conversation. *Seriously, this is just plain ridiculous!* "Luke, for goodness sake, get a grip of yourself, you're being irrationally jealous!" I scolded, shaking my head firmly.

"There is no freaking way you're going home with him on that pile of scrap metal. I'll drive you home," he growled.

I frowned and shook my head. "Luke. I'm going to Zach's place to tutor him."

He snorted and shook his head, gripping my hand and pulling me closer to him again. "Not on that thing you're not. No way!" he stated, looking at me sternly.

I looked at him incredulously. Was he seriously going to tell me what I could and couldn't do? He had no rights to that anymore - not that he had the right in the first place, but he lost his say when he bedded that tramp at the party.

"Don't tell me what I can do. You don't own me!" I hissed, slapping his hand off my arm angrily. "Go to practice and stop being such a jealous idiot," I instructed. I turned to Zach and took the helmet out of his hand. He was grinning at Luke triumphantly. "And you, stop smirking and start the damn bike!" I stated.

He laughed and threw his leg over the bike, kick starting it. I tried not to flinch as it roared to life; the loud growl of the engine made my stomach tremble with fear. I gulped and pulled the helmet down on my head, noticing how it fitted nicely. I turned to glare at Luke who was just standing there with a scowl on his face and his whole posture tight and angry. I swung my leg over the bike, scooting up close behind Zach and wrapped my arms tightly around his waist, praying I didn't die before we got to our desired destination. I bit back my little scream as we lurched forward and left a seething Luke behind us.

chapter twelve

I'd actually forgotten how much I enjoyed being on his bike. By the time we pulled up at his house, I was in a state of euphoria and didn't want it to end. My fingers were aching where I was holding on so tightly, but the adrenalin of driving so fast, leaning into the corners, and the wind whipping my clothes around, all of it made the biggest smile stretch across my face. When he cut the engine I was actually a little disappointed, but at least I had the ride home to look forward to.

When we stopped, he kicked on the stand and I just sat there, listening to my heart race in my ears as I smiled like an idiot. Zach talking snapped me back to reality. "As much as I enjoy having you wrap yourself around me, are you planning on letting go anytime soon?" he asked sarcastically, smirking at me over his shoulder as his hands brushed over my arms that were clamped around his waist.

I laughed sheepishly and unwound my arms from the bear hug that I had him trapped in. "Sorry. They should put handles on these things," I muttered, feeling my face flame with embarrassment.

"They do." He nodded towards the rear of the bike and I spotted a little handle there, welded just behind me.

I frowned. "So how am I supposed to hold onto that? Ride backwards?" I asked incredulously.

He laughed, shaking his head as he stood up, climbing off the bike. "Are we really sure that you're the right person to be tutoring me?" he joked, raising one eyebrow playfully.

"Oh ha ha, you're very funny today," I muttered, rolling my eyes as I climbed awkwardly off the bike. When I pulled the helmet off my head, he burst out laughing. "What?"

"You have helmet hair," he chuckled. I groaned and shoved the helmet in his chest, freeing my hands so I could smooth back my ponytail again while he just laughed quietly at me and stowed the helmet in his bag. "Come on, I'm hungry." He walked off towards his house without waiting for me. As I followed behind him, I looked at the place he lived; it was a sweet little detached house with a white front door. The front yard looked well-kept and everything had a little cute feel about it.

"This is a nice place," I commented as I followed him inside and into the hallway. It was just as cute inside as it was outside; everything had that homey feel about it.

He nodded. "It's alright I guess. It's not as nice as your house. Your parents must earn a bundle, huh?" he replied, nodding up the short hallway, motioning for me to go first.

"I guess, I don't really know. My dad works hard at what he does." I shrugged. At the end of the hallway I stepped into an adorable little rustic kitchen. His aunt was sitting at the table with her laptop out, chewing on her pen thoughtfully. She looked up and smiled as we walked in together.

"Hey, guys. Good day at school?" She raised one eyebrow at Zach. "You did go, didn't you? I didn't get a call so you must have done."

He nodded, sighing. "Yes, Olivia, I went. I stayed there all day like a good little boy, and I didn't even get in any fights today. Aren't you proud of me?" he asked sarcastically.

A fond smile twitched at the corner of her mouth as she nodded. "I'm so proud of you, Zach," she replied with fake enthusiasm, holding her hand over her heart. "I think you deserve a reward for attending a whole day at school. How about I buy you the GI Joe that you've been bugging me to get you for ages? You know, the one with the interchangeable accessories?" she suggested teasingly.

I laughed, liking her already.

"Actually, it was the Ken doll I wanted," he shot back, playing along. She laughed and reached into her purse, pulling out something and tossing it to Zach who caught it effortlessly. "Sweet!" he chirped happily. I looked over curiously to see he was smiling lovingly at a cell phone; obviously it had been confiscated pending him going to school today.

His aunt looked at me and smiled. "Nice to see you again. It's Maisie, isn't it?"

I nodded, smiling politely. "It's nice to see you again too, Mrs Kingston."

She waved her hand dismissively, making a scoffing sound. "Don't call me that, it makes me feel old. Olivia is fine." Zach pulled open the fridge; grabbing the orange juice and chugging it straight from the carton which made his aunt gasp and throw her pen at him. "How many times do I have to tell you not to drink from the carton?" she cried.

He shrugged, swallowing and putting the juice back in the fridge. "At least a couple more times," he replied casually as he wiped his mouth with the back of one hand. I made a mental note never to drink juice in his house. He turned to me and smiled. "Want a soda or something?" he asked, pulling a can of Pepsi from the fridge and passing it to me without waiting for me to answer.

"You're a pig," I scolded, shaking my head at him. He was so much like Alex that it was unreal; maybe it was a teenage boy thing, though Zach was nineteen so he wouldn't even be a teenager for much longer.

He just grinned in response.

"Zach, I bought chicken but they didn't have breasts like you wanted, so I had to get strips, that okay?" Olivia asked, looking at him hopefully.

He shrugged. "Sure, that'll work," he answered. He nodded back to the door we came in through. "Let's go study then before your colour coded tutoring schedule becomes irrelevant. We don't want to run out of time and have to skip the red section, do we?" he teased, looking at me with mock horror. He grabbed a pack of cookies and two apples, then ushered me out of the kitchen.

"What do you want chicken for?" I asked curiously, following him up the stairs.

"Dinner. Olivia can't cook, and if she ever does cook, eat it at your own risk because that crud is toxic," he replied, shuddering.

I laughed and looked at him to see if he was joking. "You cook?" That had to be a joke; he couldn't really cook, surely.

"Yep, pretty freaking awesomely actually," he boasted. He shoved open a door at the end of the corridor, exposing the messiest bedroom I'd ever seen in my life. I stopped, looking at the clothes all over the floor, the unmade bed, the empty packets and soda cans, the screwed up paper scattered everywhere. The place was disgusting, and I couldn't even identify the colour of his carpet because it was barely visible.

"Seriously? You expect me to tutor you," I motioned around the room in disgust, "in here?"

He grinned. "Sure. The crap won't bite ya," he joked, pressing on the small of my back, forcing me step to into the room.

I cringed as my foot collided with what looked like a half-eaten pie. "Are you positive about that?" I closed my eyes, wishing I was home already. "New rules, tutoring is always at my place," I added as an afterthought.

"Don't be such a princess," he scolded, laughing as he pressed on my back again, making me step deeper into the hazard he called a bedroom.

I groaned, glancing around again at the room and wincing. It really was gross. "Do you even have a desk under all that clutter?"

He laughed. "Nope. We'll have to do it on the bed," he replied, and then a smile tugged at the corners of his mouth so I knew he was thinking about how dirty that sounded in his mind.

"Awesome," I muttered, tiptoeing over his clothes and magazines that littered the floor, heading towards his bed. I plopped my bag down on it as he grabbed the sheets, tugging on them and making it a little flatter to sit on rather than a bulky quilt pile in the middle where he'd obviously just gotten up and left it this morning. My eyes raked over his walls, looking at the posters and clippings he had stuck up. They all seemed to be of the same guy. "Who's that?" I asked, squinting at the brown haired guy that was probably in his late thirties. He looked a little familiar, but I couldn't place him.

"Cyril Raffaelli," he answered as if that made perfect sense.

I raised one eyebrow in question. "And he would be?"

"The best traceur that ever graced God's green earth," he replied, looking at the poster in awe.

"Tracer? Like detective type thing?" I asked, looking at the poster again. He didn't look much like a detective.

Zach burst out laughing and shook his head at me as if I was stupid. "Traceur," he corrected as if that slight difference in pronunciation made all the difference. "It's someone who practices parkour. He's a stuntman and my personal hero," he explained, plopping down on the bed, watching me.

I blushed, feeling stupid for not knowing that, though why I would know that in the first place was beyond me. "Oh, the jumping over stuff," I replied, nodding, playing dumb.

He grinned and rolled his eyes. "Yeah, the jumping over stuff."

"So where do I know him from?" I asked curiously. I knew nothing of parkour, so it wasn't from that.

"Movies?" he suggested. "You ever seen District 13?"

"Nope." I studied the guy again and suddenly it hit me. "Oh I know! The guy that dives out of the helicopter in Die Hard 4!" I said excitedly. "I loved that movie. Mostly I loved it when Bruce Willis kicked his butt."

He laughed. "That's him," he confirmed. "Hey, we should watch District 13, you'll love it. It's French subtitles though, but I bet you like foreign movies being super brainy and all."

I frowned as he stood up, heading over to his cupboard and pulling it open to reveal a shelf jam packed full of DVDs. "Zach, we're supposed to be studying," I reminded him, unzipping my bag and pulling out my notebook. He sighed, frowning, looking like he would rather be doing anything other than this. I sat down on his bed and kicked off my shoes, crossing my legs. "English first?" I suggested.

He groaned and flopped down on his bed face first, burying his face in the pillow. I ignored his obvious unwillingness and flicked open my notebook. Big black writing on the first page caught my eye. My mouth dropped open in shock at the word that was written there, the same word that desecrated my locker this morning. *'Bitch'*. I frowned at it, not knowing how on earth it had got there. How the heck had someone got hold of my notebook and written that across my Spanish essay without me even knowing? Why would someone even do it in the first place? My mind flicked to Sandy again, it had to be her, I'd humiliated her at the party in front of everyone when I called her a dirty tramp, and this was probably her revenge so I had to rewrite my assignment.

My jaw clenched tightly as an acrid taste filled my mouth. *I really should have taken Zach's advice before and punched her.* I flicked through my book to see that almost every page had the same ugly black scrawl on it, ruining all of my work that I'd done for classes. I spotted my Algebra notes that I'd made this morning, they'd been ruined too, so that meant that this had to have been done today, either lunchtime or this afternoon.

Something hit me in the arm, snapping me out of my angry state. I slammed the book shut, trying not to cry from anger. I wasn't very good with emotions; I cried easily, I guess I was a bit of a weakling of sorts. I looked back at Zach to see he'd hit me in the arm with his book, one eyebrow raised curiously. "We starting then or what?" he asked.

I gulped, nodding. "Yeah, I guess, sorry," I muttered.

He cocked his head to the side, looking at me like a curious puppy. "What's up?"

I smiled, appreciating the concern in his tone. "Nothing," I lied. "Right, so have you read The Crucible?" I asked, motioning towards his book that was in perfect condition and looked like it hadn't even been opened.

He smiled sheepishly. *I'll take that as a no then!* "Sure I have. It was awesome."

I laughed and rolled my eyes at him. "So there's no need for me to go over the general plot with you, right?" I asked, smirking in his direction.

He pursed his lips. "Well, I'd actually like to hear your take on the plot, just so I can be sure that you appreciated it to its full potential like I did," he answered smugly.

I had to laugh; he was actually a pretty funny guy. He smiled and scooted up next to me, biting into an apple and handing me the other one as we started going through book step by step.

• • •

AFTER AN HOUR LATER we were doing really well. He was actually a pretty quick learner, well, when I could keep his mind on task anyway. His thoughts seemed to wander off a lot and start veering off onto other things so I had to rein him back in again. I could see why he would have such a problem with studying on his own, with no one to keep him on track he was probably doodling in his notebook within ten minutes. But he did seem willing to learn, which was a good thing.

He threw down his pen suddenly and stood up. "I'm hungry and I need to start dinner. Want to come and help me?" he asked, looking at me hopefully.

I shook my head. "No, but I'll sit there and read to you while you cook dinner, how about that?" I offered.

He groaned, rolling his eyes. "Isn't there a movie of this I could watch instead of reading it?"

I laughed and grabbed my shoes, putting them back on before I stood up so that my feet didn't touch anything rancid that was on his floor. "Two movies actually, but they both sucked, so read the book," I instructed.

As it turns out, I didn't get much reading done while he cooked, because his aunt was still sitting up the table, and she could probably talk the hind legs off a donkey. My head was spinning as she talked on and on, but she was an extremely nice person. Her and Zach seemed to get on really well, the conversation bounced back and forth while he prepared a homemade chicken pot pie. When the front door opened, Olivia bounced out of her seat and headed into the other room eagerly, talking to someone.

Zach frowned and shoved a large ceramic dish into the stove, then washed his hands. "That'll be done in an hour. You want to stay for dinner?" he offered.

"Er..."

"You might as well stay; you'll be here still anyway. I'll just drive you home after," he suggested, shrugging casually.

I chewed on my lip. "Okay, sure. I guess I can put your cooking skills to the test then, huh?"

He nodded, seeming pretty proud of himself. "You'll love it." He nodded to the hallway, signalling for me to go first as usual.

"How do you know how to cook then?" Not many guys knew how to cook; especially not things like a pot pie. Alex wouldn't have a clue where to start with that - then again, Alex burned grilled cheese.

"My dad taught me, he liked to cook," he replied shrugging. My ear picked up on the past tense of that statement. My mind was whirling, wondering again why he was living with his aunt and not his parents. "You going or what?" he asked, motioning towards the hallway again because I hadn't started walking because I was trying to work out his past.

I nodded and headed into the hallway, seeing Olivia standing with a blond stocky guy who was probably in his late forties. Olivia smiled warmly. "Maisie, this is my husband, Alan. Alan, this is Zach's tutor, Maisie." She waved a hand between us in introduction.

He nodded in acknowledgement, looking a little bored as he threw his keys onto the sideboard. "Tutor, like that's worth it," he muttered under his breath.

I felt the frown pull at my forehead. "It's nice to meet you, Mr Kingston." I forced my tone to be polite like I was always taught, but the hard expression on his face wasn't very welcoming at all.

"Alright, Uncle Alan?" Zach chirped sarcastically from behind me.

The guy's eyes flicked to Zach, a scowl slipping onto his face. "Go to school today or did you make your aunt cry again?" he barked.

I flinched from his hard tone, shifting on my feet as Zach pushed me towards the stairs, his face mirroring the hard expression of his uncle's. "I went," he spat. "We're going to study." Alan made a scoffing sound in the back of his throat as Zach forced me to walk up the stairs, his whole body tense.

I tried to pretend like I couldn't hear Alan talking to Olivia as we walked away. "Waste of freaking money. A tutor, really? Like that kid will ever graduate, he's a fucking waster," Alan growled.

"He is not a waster! He just needs some extra help, that's all," Olivia hissed.

I cringed at how uncomfortable this situation was as they then started having a full blown argument at the bottom of the stairs about how Zach was a useless sponger and was ruining everything, that Alan didn't want him here, and that he made everything hard, that they were already struggling with money and Zach was just a deadbeat kid who'd never amount to anything. Olivia was arguing back that he was family and that she'd never abandon him. By the time we got into Zach's room, they were practically screaming at each other.

Zach slammed the door behind him, making it rattle on its hinges as he gripped his hands in his hair, his whole body tight with anger as he leant against the door, kicking it with the back of his heel. I didn't know what to say or do. What was there to say? He obviously didn't get on with his uncle, that much was glaringly obvious. The whole situation was really sad.

"You okay?" I asked quietly, touching his elbow tentatively.

"Just grab your stuff, I'm taking you home now," he snapped, shoving himself away from the wall and grabbing my schoolbag, throwing my books and pens in there angrily.

"But we haven't finished," I protested.

"I don't give a rat's ass!" he growled. "I'm done. We're done."

I frowned, stepping in front of the door, blocking it as he stalked over to it again, obviously ready to leave. "Zach, look, I'm sorry that happened, but we should finish studying. You were doing so well," I encouraged.

His jaw tightened, his hard brown glare locked on me. "What's the point? He's right, I'll never graduate anyway. I'm just wasting their money and your time."

I gulped at his words. He sounded like he really believed them; there was a defeated, resigned tone to his voice that was actually painful. "Zach, of course you'll graduate. I'll help you. If they're struggling with money then I'll just help you for free, how about that?" I suggested. I didn't really need the money anyway, extra cash was nice, but it wasn't necessary, I got an allowance from my parents anyway.

He snorted. "Oh yeah, way to make me feel more like a freaking sponger!" he growled, reaching around me and grabbing the door handle.

I pressed my back against the door so he couldn't open it. "Stop snapping at me, I've done nothing wrong!" I cried, shoving on his chest angrily, but he didn't even move, it didn't even make him step back because he was obviously too strong for me to have any effect on. "I'm offering to help you because you said you really wanted to try this time. You said that you want to get this stuntman job, then go get it. Giving up is just going to confirm everything he's thinking; so graduate and prove him wrong!" I challenged, glaring at him the same way he was glaring at me.

Silence lapsed over us as he obviously thought it through. I could see the indecision on his face, I could also see a desire, he definitely wanted that job, but the desire was almost entirely masked by anger. After an uncomfortable minute of him just scowling at me, his shoulders seemed to loosen, and he swallowed loudly. "You're more of a fighter than I gave you credit for," he muttered.

A smile twitched at the corner of my mouth because I knew I'd won. "Yeah, I guess practicing my bitchy comebacks on you is helping with my confidence. I should thank you for that," I joked.

He laughed, his eyes dropping to the floor as he chewed on his bottom lip.

I reached down and took my schoolbag from his hand. "We should finish up with that English assignment, and then maybe work on some biology?" I suggested hopefully.

A frown lined his forehead but he nodded at the same time. "Okay, but I don't want you to do it for free. I have a job, I can pay you," he agreed.

I smiled because he was still willing to try, and headed back over to the bed, not caring this time that I stood on all of his crap as I marched across the room. "Whatever. Come on," I replied, deciding that I would get this boy to graduate if it was the last thing I did. I would love to see the look on his uncle's face when that happened. Zach trotted over to me, plopping down, still looking sad and angry, but he picked up his book again, flicking to the right page so we could finish up.

• • •

DINNER HAD TO HAVE been the most awkward time of my life, ever. Olivia tried to lighten the mood by talking to me, and then would try to bring Zach into the conversation too, but every time he opened his mouth and said something, his uncle would grumble something incoherent or make a scoffing sound. Even I wanted to punch him. I had no idea how Zach kept his temper the whole dinner. The only good thing about it was the food. Zach was right, he did cook pretty damn awesomely, I was definitely impressed.

After dinner we headed back to his room to get my things. Zach grabbed a bottle of drink, a towel, a pair of shorts and a t-shirt. "What you up to?" I asked, eyeing him curiously, wondering why he was packing a bag.

"Going to the training hall for a couple of hours. I go every night, gets me out of here," he replied, shrugging casually.

"Gonna do your traceur stuff?" I asked, proud of myself that I got the word right.

He grinned and nodded. "Yeah."

I debated asking if I could go and watch him. I'd never really seen it properly, and that one move I did see of his was pretty crazy; I'd like to see more of it. But I didn't ask because he probably needed some time on his own after the whole disastrous family meal thing we'd just endured. Besides, I was going to watch on Friday anyway, because after school I was going with him to meet with his team before we went to study. I was actually pretty excited about that for some reason.

The drive home was just as thrilling as I expected it to be. When he pulled up outside my house, he didn't cut the engine. I gripped his shoulders and climbed off; pulling off the helmet that he'd given me to wear again. He smiled wickedly, so I quickly smoothed down my hair and rolled my eyes.

"How come you brought me one of those to use anyway?" I asked, handing the helmet back to him.

He shrugged. "You wanted one, so I got you one. I'm just chivalrous like that," he stated, smirking at me.

I rolled my eyes and shouldered my bag. "Well have fun doing your Spider-Man thing," I joked.

He grinned. "I will. And I'll see you at school tomorrow, little rebel," he teased.

I frowned and slapped him in the arm. "We agreed to drop that!"

He smirked at me and gunned the engine loudly, making a cloud of black exhaust fumes billow around us. I stepped back, waving my hand in front of my face and coughed dramatically for emphasis, which made him laugh as he pulled out, speeding off down the street.

I smiled as I watched him drive away. When he was out of sight, I headed into the house to find my mom in the kitchen just finishing up washing the dishes after dinner. "Hey," I greeted, dropping my bag onto the side. She jumped and turned to smile at me warmly as I headed over to her side and grabbed the dishtowel, drying up the stuff that was on the draining board.

"Hi. So how'd it go?" she asked, looking at me curiously. I'd told her that I didn't really want to tutor Zach, that he was annoying and cocky. She'd told me to give him a chance; apparently she quite liked him from the meeting yesterday.

I shrugged. "Okay I guess. We got a lot done."

"That's good," she commented, passing me the last plate before pulling out the plug and flicking the bubbles off her hands. "You got a delivery today. They came tonight. They're calla lilies," she said, nodding behind me.

I frowned, turning to see a beautiful bunch of lilies sitting on the side. My mom had already put them into one of her glass vases for me, arranging them neatly. They were beautiful - but not the usual flowers that Luke gave me. "Luke came here?" I asked. My stomach fluttered because he'd gone to so much effort for me, I loved that he was trying so hard to win me back. I still didn't know how I felt about the whole thing, but him wanting me so much made me feel special and needed. Maybe there was a chance for us after all. Maybe I could try and move past this and remember how great it always felt when we were together. I missed him dearly and I wished he was here right now so I could throw my arms around his waist and clamp myself to him tightly, never letting go. I really missed just knowing that he'd always be there when I needed him.

She shook her head. "A delivery guy brought them," she answered. "They're lovely, though I'm not really struck with his choice of flower. White lilies are usually given at funerals and stuff," Mom continued, drying her hands on the towel I was holding.

"They are?" I headed over, smelling them, instantly smiling because of their sweet aroma.

"Yep. Doesn't he usually buy you daisies?" I nodded in confirmation. "Well, maybe he wanted to spend a bit more to try and impress you," she suggested, shrugging.

I frowned, picking up the card that my mom had put on the side next to the vase. "Maybe," I agreed. "I'm gonna go put these in my room and then I think I'm gonna soak in the tub for a while." I really had some thinking to do; my mind was already racing, planning out whether I should call him and thank him, and what I should say. I picked up the heavy vase in one hand, trying not to spill the water as I grabbed the card and my schoolbag and headed up to my room, sniffing the blooms again as I walked, smiling to myself.

Once I was in my room I sat them on my dresser and turned my attention to the card, wondering what he'd said in it. Secretly I was hoping for some heartfelt apology, some beautiful words that would make the broken, betrayed part of me just melt away so I could forgive him. This was probably his apology for getting jealous and telling me what to do at the end of school today.

I ripped open the envelope and pulled out the little card, only to realise that they weren't from Luke at all. My first thought was disappointment, because I'd obviously assumed wrong and he wasn't making a huge effort to win me back. My second thought was anger. Tears of indignation stung my eyes as I growled in frustration, throwing the card on the side. I ripped the flowers from their vase and dropped them into the trashcan roughly, shoving them down and breaking the stems on them, no longer finding them beautiful.

I was going to seriously murder Sandy. I picked up the card from the side, not reading the single printed word on there that I'd already seen scrawled several times in my notebook tonight. I ripped it into tiny pieces and dropped it on top of the flowers, my jaw aching where I was clenching my teeth so tightly together. Not only had she possibly drugged my boyfriend, had sex with him, humiliated me in front of the whole school, defiled my locker and notebook, but now the witch had sent me funeral flowers? She really had gone too far, and tomorrow I was confronting her about it. All thoughts of 'violence solving nothing' were gone from my mind now.

chapter thirteen

I'd woken in the morning all prepared to do this. The anger was still boiling in the pit of my stomach; I'd been spurred on by the sight of the broken flowers that now decorated the inside of the trashcan in my room. But now that I was here though, now that I could see her laughing with her little posse at the end of the hallway; my courage was fading fast, as was my nerve.

I didn't really like to make a scene, and confronting her in front of the whole school, calling her out for being a vindictive little slut, was definitely going to be a scene. I'd waved off my friends this morning, making excuses of needing to speak to a teacher because I'd wanted this moment. And now it was here, I was chickening out.

People lingered in the hallway like usual, leaning up against the lockers, chatting about the events of the previous evening or swapping tales of essays gone wrong. I couldn't focus on it though; all I could see was her with her blonde hair, shining like golden strands because of the sun streaming in through the window behind her, lighting her up like she was wearing a delicate sparkly halo. Why did everything about her have to be so annoyingly perfect? Life was unfair.

Her tinkering little laugh rang out down the hallway as people looked at her in awe as she stood there all high and mighty in her tiny little shorts and shirt that left virtually nothing to the imagination. I tried to force my feet to move, to close the thirty or so feet to her side so I could plant my foot firmly on her ass. But nothing was happening, I wasn't moving. Self-loathing trickled down my spine as instead of walking to her side and doing what I'd been planning on doing all night, I walked to my locker instead.

I punched in my combination, ignoring the clean patch from the janitor scrubbing the word off that she'd scrawled there. Angrily, I shoved my books in, taking out the ones I would need for my morning classes instead. As I picked up my history book, a piece of red paper fell to the floor, landing on my foot. I bent and grabbed it, frowning at it curiously. It was a red envelope; a capital M was written on the side in elegant cursive, like it had been traced from some old fashioned calligraphy set or something. Someone had obviously pushed it through the slots of my locker.

I glanced around, but no one was paying the slightest bit of attention to me as I ripped it open and pulled out the folded sheet of red paper. Out fell a long white silky petal. I watched, entranced, as it floated to the floor elegantly. I looked back at the note in my hand, not having a clue who it was from. Words had been typed there using some sort of old fashioned typewriter. The words made the hair on the back of my neck stand up on end.

Hope you enjoyed my flowers last night.
You'll pay soon.

I stared at it, confused. You'll pay soon? What the heck was that about? Pay for what? Suddenly it hit me like a truck. I'd pay... this was from Sandy again! I'd pay for embarrassing her at the party like I did last weekend! My anger spiked immediately as I dropped my schoolbag at my feet, not even bothering to shut my locker as I half marched, half ran up the hallway towards her. When I got to her side I shoved her shoulder, making her squeal and stumble forward a few steps into one of her friends, before she turned and glared at me.

"What the hell do you think you're doing?" she cried, looking at me with wide eyes.

I slapped the note against her chest harder than was necessary. "You stay the hell away from me, you hear?" I growled. People had turned to watch now, I could feel all eyes on me, but I wasn't letting that affect me. She needed to know to back the heck off. "Just leave me alone you vindictive little witch!"

Her jaw tightened as her shoulders seemed to stiffen. "Me? What the hell would I want to go anywhere near you for?" she asked, looking me over distastefully.

Oh yeah, of course she's denying it! "I mean it, Sandy, you just back off! Is it not enough that you've already split me and Luke up?" I ranted, throwing my hands up in exasperation.

A small, nasty smile twitched at the corners of her mouth as she raised one eyebrow. "It's not even nearly enough," she replied coldly. "I'm just glad you're finally in your place, which is nowhere near Luke!"

My jaw ached where I was clenching it so tightly. Her sky blue eyes were alight with happiness as she stood there, taunting me with her perfect looks. "Oh just get over it. Even though we're split up he still wants nothing to do with you, so have some pride and stop acting like a desperate skank!" I countered.

She gasped, looking a little taken aback before a wild ferocity crossed her face. "You! You're the little skank! You muscled in on the quarterback thinking his popularity would drag you into a good social standing, well I've got news for you, princess, you're nothing, and you never will be. You were never good enough for him. A little nerd like you could never satisfy a guy like Luke. Of course he was begging me for it, of course he was all over me last week, he finally wanted someone who could fulfil his needs! And that wasn't the first time it'd happened either!" she screamed, her cheeks flaming with anger.

Her words felt like she'd stabbed me in the heart. *Begging her for it? Wasn't the first time?* For about two seconds I actually believed her, and then I remembered Luke's distraught and horrified expression on the day following the party. I believed him, he had never cheated before, she was just trying to hurt me.

"You lying little-" I started, but she was still on full flow and cut me off.

"Now that you're out of the way he'll be running to me as soon as he realises that he's better off without you. Give it a couple of days and he'll be begging me for it again. He'll be hanging all over me, and you'll have to watch it all. That boy's as good as mine already," she interjected, smirking confidently.

The last of my control slipped as a red haze of rage seemed to cloud my vision. I launched myself at her, ignoring the gasps and squeals of delight that came from the enthralled spectators. We slammed into the wall as one of my hands tangled in her hair, pulling roughly as she let out some sort of primal scream, trying to throw me off. A hand connected with my face but I was too wired to even feel it. The adrenalin was making it hard to focus as we both fell to the floor, screaming abuse at each other as we clumsily slapped and clawed at each other. As we rolled over, both of us trying to gain the upper hand, my elbow collided with the floor making me let out a little yelp, but I didn't release my hold on her. It didn't hurt too much; besides, I was too focussed on trying to kill her to actually have time to feel the pain I was sure to feel in a few minutes.

The rage built as her nails dug into my forearm, scratching and drawing blood. I had no idea how long we were rolling around on the hard floor for. In the back of my mind I could hear people excitedly cheering us on, chanting 'fight' like they did when Luke and Zach had been fighting a couple of days ago.

Arms wrapped around my waist, tightening and lifting me off her, pulling me backwards. But I didn't stop. I thrashed against their hold as I continued trying to rip her head off.

"You little bitch!" Sandy screamed, reaching for me too. But one of the football team had grabbed her too and were turning her away from me as her face contorted with rage, her eyes flashing as her teeth clenched.

I couldn't really see clearly through the fog of anger that had settled over me, but I was vaguely aware of moving. Either I was moving or someone was moving me, I wasn't sure which as I continued to thrash to no avail.

My eyes flicked around quickly, noticing that Sandy was getting further and further away from me as someone was practically dragging her down the hallway. There was a huge crowd of people all milling around, watching with wide eyes and open mouths. The expression was the same on every face, excitement and shock - every face except one. A solitary figure stood off to one side, leaning casually against the wall, one leg crossed over the other, hands in his pockets, and a small smile on his face. Zach. As his eyes met mine I realised that he was fixing me with a proud stare. I frowned at him as he pulled his hands from his pockets and gave me a fake round of applause before winking at me.

Suddenly a door slammed in my face and the death grip that someone had me in, loosened marginally. "Calm down, baby."

I swallowed and blinked a couple of times, trying to figure out what had happened. A door. A door had closed in front of me and now I was in a classroom, being restrained by...

"Calm down, baby," Luke cooed again.

I threw off his hold angrily, turning to glare at him because he'd stopped me from tearing her fake blonde extensions out like I'd wanted to. "Calm down? She just slapped me!" I cried, only now registering that my cheek was stinging from the blow. I could still taste the metallic tang of my own blood where my cheek had mashed into my teeth. My arm hurt too and was definitely going to bruise.

Luke's teeth ground together angrily as he nodded, his eyes settled on the side of my face. "I can see that. But you hit her first," he stated rationally. "Now, what was that about?"

I frowned and crossed my arms over my chest defensively, trying to gain some self-control because my emotions were frayed and any second now I was going to burst into tears, I could feel it building. "She's a witch. She said some stuff about you and I got angry," I finally replied, not really wanting to get into the whole accusation thing again. We'd gotten off track and the fight wasn't actually specifically about that, it was more about her making moves on my ex-boyfriend. What I had hit her for was her remarks about Luke, so that wasn't a lie I'd just told.

His head cocked to the side, an apologetic look on his face. "Maisie, I'm so sorry about what happened, but fighting with her in the middle of the school isn't going to take back what I did. You'll get yourself in trouble, in fact, that's probably what she wants to happen," he explained. I scowled as his hand reached out and smoothed my hair back from my face, tucking some loose bits behind my ear. "Another couple of seconds and teachers would have been all over that fight. That's not you, baby. My Maisie doesn't get into trouble at school." *That's true. Maybe I should have waited and jumped her in a dark alleyway when no one was around.* "Just please don't start anything else with her, okay?" he pleaded.

Somewhere in my angry state of mind, I registered that he was defending her. The witch that he had cheated on me with, the girl that was now starting up some sort of hate campaign against me, he was defending her.

Anger built again as my hands clenched into fists. "Oh I'm sorry, did I just ruin your chances of getting laid tonight? Will she take out my indiscretion on you and not let you tap that tonight?" I spat acidly.

His mouth dropped open as his eyes went wide. He literally gaped at me like I'd just said the most ridiculous and shocking thing in the world. "My chances of getting laid? With her? Are you crazy?" he choked out, his voice strangled as he shook his head and looked at me like I'd actually lost my mind.

Her words were ringing in my ears. *'He'll be begging me for it. He'll be hanging all over me and you'll have to watch it all.'*

Before I could stop myself, I slapped his chest as hard as I could, making my hand sting and him flinch. "Well she was good enough for you last weekend!" I screeched. I could feel the angry and insanely jealous tears rolling down my face now as I lost my battle to stay composed. I looked away from his handsome face. *Why do I have to love him so much still? It's just unfair.*

"That was a mistake and won't ever happen again!" Luke growled fiercely, bending so his face was level with mine.

"Yeah, until she throws herself at you again and you can't say no." My heart hurt. I'd gotten up this morning fully prepared and ready to confront her, and then I'd just fallen to pieces and had made myself come across as a jealous and bitchy girl. Why couldn't I have some of my brother's courage? He wouldn't have let her say all those things to him. "She said you were as good as hers already." A sob made my voice crack and my chin wobble as I thought about Luke not actually being mine anymore. What if she was right? What if he did need something more fulfilling, what if I wasn't enough for him? What if he did realise that he was more suited to the school cheerleader, rather than a nerdy student? What if he did start chasing her around like I frequently imagined happening lately? How would I cope with that?

I watched as anger crossed his face. His teeth ground together as he cupped my face in his hands, titling my head up so that my eyes met his. "I don't want her. I don't want anyone other than you. I'll never cheat again, baby, never. I'm yours forever," he practically growled. The intensity in his brown eyes was a little overwhelming as he gazed at me.

The 'yours forever' part made my hand touch the material of my shirt in the centre of my chest, my fingers tracing the outline of his locket that I had hidden under my shirt because I couldn't bring myself to part with it. My pulse seemed to drum in my ears, and before I knew what I was doing, I'd gone up on tiptoes and crashed my lips to his possessively.

He responded immediately, crushing his body against mine, kissing me back fiercely. The kiss was hot, sizzling, scramble your brains hot. It was different from any kiss we'd ever shared before. This one was filled with jealousy, passion, lust, and a lot of pure neediness. Every cell in my body seemed to come alive as our tongues tangled together. I couldn't get close enough as everything seemed to fade away, the graffiti, the party, the cheating; all of it just disappeared as I lost myself in the beautiful familiarity of Luke's kiss.

My hands twisted into the back of his hair, making him moan into my mouth and clutch me closer to him. Everything was so incredible, just like it used to be, but filled with more passion where it hadn't happened for a while.

But as he broke the kiss and pressed his forehead to mine, his eyes still closed and his mouth pulled into a dazzling grin, I realised that nothing had changed. He'd still cheated, and everyone knew it - that wouldn't go away just because of one kiss, and neither would the hurt that accompanied the knowledge that things would never be the same again. It was easy to pretend that everything was fine while his lips were pressed against mine; it was easy to forgive, but the forgetting part, that was the hardest.

He sighed contentedly, his hand stroking my back as he kissed my nose, my cheeks, and my forehead, before hugging me so tightly that I could barely breathe.

I reluctantly pulled out of his arms and looked at him apologetically. I knew I shouldn't have done that. I'd accidentally just built up his hopes that everything was fine when, in reality, I felt far from fine. I still wasn't ready to move on yet. I couldn't let him go, but at the moment I wasn't ready to get back with him, and I wasn't sure I ever would be. I loved him, that much I knew for certain, but I still didn't know if I could get over seeing him screwing another girl. The image was still engrained in my memory every time I saw her smug face.

Instantly Luke's face fell. A small line formed between his eyebrows as his arms dropped from my waist down to his sides. A wave of guilt washed over me, making me feel like the one that had done wrong instead of him. "Sorry, I shouldn't have kissed you. I was just caught in the moment and upset," I whispered, swiping at the tears that were now drying on my face.

He smiled, but it didn't reach his sorrowful eyes. "Don't apologise," he replied, shrugging, obviously trying to go for casual indifference.

I gulped at the pain I could see behind his fake smile. "I'm trying to forget it, it's just hard. I need time," I explained, taking his hand and rubbing my fingers over his knuckles. His hands felt so soft and my mind wandered to memories of them in mine, or his fingertips caressing my cheek. Another lump formed in my throat.

He nodded, stepping closer to me again and wrapping his free arm around my waist. "Time is something that I have a lot of," he whispered. "I'll wait until you've cleared your head. We both know we're made for each other."

The sincerity of those words made my eyes prickle with tears again. Deep down I knew he was right. When it was just us, like now, I could see my future with Luke, my happy future with the house and the kids. But my stubborn pride and my self-worth were trying to force me to move on and let him go. My head was telling me to be a stronger person, one who didn't need a man to complete her, but my heart was still stuck in the moment with Luke. My whole being was revelling in the feel of being in his arms again and being surrounded by his smell. I was torn. With his warmth and protectiveness wrapped around me I knew I needed him, even if I didn't want to admit it.

While I was still figuring out what my next words should be, he pulled back and smiled at me. "Let's get you to class, huh?"

I nodded, thankful for the reprieve. His hand tightened in mine as he stepped away and opened the door, leading us out into the now deserted hallway.

chapter fourteen

Being the centre of attention really wasn't my strong suit. The staring and curious glances that were directed at me made my head ache and my shoulders stiff. Whispering erupted everywhere I went that morning, excited gossiping as I walked past people. *'That's the girl that I was fighting with Sandy,'* or *'Apparently her boyfriend cheated and now she's lost the plot'*. I tried to ignore it, I really did, but it followed me around like a grey thundercloud, dampening my mood with a wave of depression and humiliation.

By lunchtime I just wanted to go home and cry. Luke and I had eaten together again, which was slightly weird after the fact that I'd kissed him in the morning, but thankfully he didn't mention it. The rest of the day was much the same. People weren't getting bored of staring at me in the slightest. Gym was especially hard because Sandy was there too. I noticed with some measure of satisfaction that she looked a little weary of me, and didn't really make eye contact with me at all. That, coupled with the fact that she had a subtle bruise forming across her cheekbone, made me feel marginally better. Of course Zach was there, making jokes, fooling around, being sarcastic to the teacher and generally not doing anything he was told to do. As usual he made the class more bearable for me. I even managed to laugh a couple of times, despite Sandy, the boyfriend stealing hoe, being within a hundred yards of me.

By the end of school I was well and truly ready to go home and crawl into bed, maybe get a huge hug from my dad and curl into his side when we watched TV like I used to when I was a little girl. I didn't want to wait for Alex to finish his football practice, so I decided to walk home instead. Lucky for me it was a fairly pleasant day, so I enjoyed the sunshine as I walked. After a couple of minutes my cell phone vibrated in my pocket.

I pulled it out and answered it without looking at the caller ID. "Hello?" I was met by nothing but silence. "Hello?" I tried again, frowning. "Hello?" When no one answered I sighed and disconnected the call.

I barely managed to get the phone back in my pocket before it vibrated with another call. Glancing at the screen I saw it was an unknown number. "Hello?" I answered. This time it wasn't dead silence. No one spoke, but I could hear quiet breathing. Someone was on the other end of the call, they just weren't talking.

"Alex, is that you fooling around? Because it's not funny!" I snapped, glancing around the deserted road as I shifted my bag on my shoulder.

The breathing continued on the line.

"Who is this?" I asked, pulling the phone away from my ear and looking down at it again as if the answer would magically appear. "I think you have the wrong number." I disconnected the call again and suddenly the phone buzzed in my hand - unknown number calling again. *What the hell?* I decided to just leave it this time. It was obviously someone playing a joke on me and I wasn't rising to it this time. I rejected the call and turned the phone off, shoving it in my jeans pocket.

Anger built up inside me. Had I not been through enough recently? Now someone had decided to heavy breathe on a call? People sucked! My mind suddenly wandered to Sandy again. But she wouldn't call me, would she? Not after this morning, surely.

I huffed and lifted my chin, pulling back my shoulders, trying to appear unaffected. Whoever was calling me - probably Sandy - was obviously trying to upset me and was probably watching my reaction. Well she wasn't getting the satisfaction of upsetting me, not this time! I marched home angrily, my thoughts only on her and how much she'd screwed up my life. I'd never hated anyone more.

• • •

THE FOLLOWING DAY was better in the sense that someone had broken into the school overnight and vandalised the Principal's office with wet toilet paper and silly string. Talk was therefore no longer on me, it was more guided towards speculating who had pranked the principal. For that I was grateful at least.

My day passed quicker than the previous one. At lunchtime I did however get another of those silent calls from the unknown number. I had been sat with Charlotte and Beth at the time; I'd passed it off as nothing, just a wrong number, when in the back of my head I was wondering when this was going to end. I'd noted at the time that Sandy wasn't in the lunchroom; she was probably holed up in the bathrooms, giggling with her friends as she tried to torment me into making another scene. I was convinced that Luke was right in what he'd said the previous morning - the hag was trying to get me into trouble. Therefore I just wouldn't rise to it, I'd pretend as if it weren't happening and hope that she got bored before it started to play on my mind.

Today was Friday, so thankfully I had a whole weekend of relaxing to look forward to. I just had to get through tutoring Zach first though, and then I could relax, but even before that I had to go with him to watch his parkour training that he did on a Friday night with his group. I really had no idea what to expect.

We pulled up in the parking lot of what looked like an old abandoned building instead of a gym like I was anticipating. I was still clinging to him like my life depended on it, grinning with unbridled excitement because of the ride on his bike. He smiled over his shoulder at me as I unwound my arms from his waist and scrambled off, pulling the helmet off and ignoring his chuckle as I smoothed my hair back into place.

Apparently Zach met up with a group of likeminded friends on a Friday evening, and they spent an hour or two going through new stunts, or plans that they had to jump over certain stuff the following week. I had no idea that people actually paid for traceurs to put on performances at shows and stuff. Apparently Zach and his group of fellow freerunners had a show coming up in a couple of weeks, so they needed to build up a routine that looked polished, but at the same time, looked like it was made up on the spot. It all sounded intriguing, but I still just didn't get it or its appeal.

"Ready?" Zach asked, shoving his hands in his pockets and nodding off to my left.

I shrugged. "Yep."

He grinned as we started walking across the parking lot, skirting along the edge of the building that looked like it was extremely close to falling down. The windows were either missing panes, broken or boarded up. Graffiti covered almost every inch of the walls as we walked along. I looked at it all in awe, it wasn't just people tagging stuff and scribbling crudities like usual graffiti, someone had made a kind of mural on the wall. It was incredible, and I looked at it in awe as we walked, taking in all the colours and noticing how perfectly they blended together. It was all segmented off, different scenes in each little section. My eyes stopped on a perfectly spray-painted picture of a geisha in full costume, her little umbrella shielding her from a bright sun overhead. It was beautiful and took my breath away. I stopped, wondering how someone actually created that with paint cans.

Zach smiled, watching me as I looked over the wall slowly, taking in each segment, shocked by the intricacy of each one. "Like it?" he asked.

I nodded, swallowing loudly. "It's incredible. I had no idea people could do this." I'd never seen graffiti like this in my life, usually it was limited to scribbled words that someone had done in a rush, but this, this looked like someone had spent hours, days, even weeks creating it.

Zach took hold of my elbow. "Reggie did that. You can tell him you like it when we meet him," he replied.

"Reggie?"

He nodded, guiding me along again as we walked along the edge of the building to some unknown place. "Yeah. He's one of my group. He's in art school." He led me around the corner where four other guys were all standing, talking and stretching their muscles as they laughed easily. They were all dressed the same as Zach, sweatpants hung low on their hips, t-shirts or vest, and a hoodie. I barely had time to notice that all of the exposed walls around were also covered in Reggie's art - I couldn't bring myself to call it graffiti because that would take away from the beauty of it. They all turned to see who approached; an easy, friendly smile broke out on each face. I let my eyes wander over them all quickly. They were varying in ages, skin tones and builds, but at the same time they all had that mischievous glint to their eye that Zach had.

I smiled timidly as curious glances fell on me. They obviously wondered who I was, that was clear on every single face. Zach's hand released my elbow as he grunted a greeting to everyone, slapping people on the back or shoulder in a friendly way. He turned back to me when he was done saying hi to everyone. "Guys, this Maisie," he announced.

I gave a weak wave; slightly unnerved by the way they were all looking at me, like hunters assessing an injured deer. Before I knew what I was doing I'd stepped closer to Zach, my insides fluttering with nerves. I'd never liked meeting new people at the best of times, but these guys were certainly intimidating and looked like they wanted to eat me or something.

"Hi," I greeted shyly.

One of the guys looked back to Zach with one eyebrow raised curiously. "Girlfriend?" he grunted.

Zach nodded; a hand was placed possessively on the small of my back, pressing and making me step even closer to him. "Yep," he replied. I felt the frown line my forehead because of his lie. *What the heck is that about?*

The four guys' postures seemed to change immediately at Zach's word. Shoulders loosened, eyes that seemed to blaze with fire merely seconds before, now regarded me with just casual interest. The change in attitude was startling.

"Maisie, this is Jase, Stu, Reggie, and Newt," Zach introduced, waving a hand at each of them in turn. *Newt? Nice name...*

"Nice to meet you." I smiled politely.

"Ready to watch your man blow your panties off with his talent?" Jase asked me, smiling a friendly smile now. He was fairly young, probably about seventeen I would guesstimate. His eyes glittered with amusement as he raked a hand through his short blond hair.

I laughed uncomfortably, not knowing how to answer that. "I guess," I replied.

He grinned. "What's up, sweetness, you not wearing any panties? Why so hesitant?" he asked, nudging Zach in the ribs with a proud grin.

Zach rolled his eyes, his thumb stroking a lazy circle against the small of my back. It was strangely soothing. "Ignore these assholes, they're not used to talking to girls, so they forget how to be civilised," he said to me, shooting them a warning glare. "Leave her alone and let's get this session done so I can take her home."

A grin split Jase's face. "Eager to get her home, huh? Don't blame you there," he stated, winking at me playfully.

Oh God, is he flirting with me? I wasn't used to this at all.

Zach's hand left my back and he lunged at the guy quickly. I gasped, panicking, until I realised they were both laughing as they seemed to asses each other, both lunging and striking out at the other, but neither of them landing any blows. I watched as Zach sunk into an attacking posture, his legs bent, his arms out ready like some kind of silent ninja. The other guy did the same, both of them grinning like kids at a pro wrestling match. It was surprisingly sexy, and I couldn't help the little thrill that went through me as they seemed to dive into some kind of kung fu stunt routine that they were obviously making up on the spot.

After a couple of minutes of them aiming kicks and punches, and dodging the blows with apparent ease, the other guy stood up and held his hands up innocently, laughing breathlessly. "Fine, I won't wink at your woman again," he stated.

Zach grinned, wrapping his arm around the other guy's neck, playfully rubbing his hair. "Good, because she's not interested. Right, little rebel?" He looked back and me and laughed as I shot him a scathing look because of the name. Before I could either answer or protest, he leant in and planted a soft kiss on my cheek. I felt the blush heat my face and neck as his lips lingered on my skin for mere seconds before he pulled back and smiled his lazy, playful smile. "Go sit over there and watch your man blow your panties off with his talent," he teased using Jase's words, nodding at a little wall that was behind me.

I gave him a sarcastic smile, rolling my eyes as I trudged over to the wall and hoisted myself up to perch on the edge. My feet dangled inches from the floor as I looked up at them expectantly. Zach grinned and pulled off his black hooded sweatshirt, tossing it at me without warning so I almost fell off the wall as I jerked to catch it.

He grinned wickedly. "Put that on, it's cold," he instructed. It wasn't a question, so he didn't wait for an answer as he turned and walked a few yards away with the other boys, chatting animatedly with them as they pointed at stuff intermittently, waved their hands around or drew on the concrete floor with a piece of chalk. I shrugged his sweater on, grateful of the warmth that it still held from his body. I pulled the sleeves over my hands, cocking my head to the side, preparing to watch what he called 'fun'.

• • •

I'D NEVER SEEN ANYTHING like it; it both frightened and exhilarated me at the same time. It was beautiful in an odd, thrilling kind of way. I watched with an open mouth and wide eyes as Zach and his group fooled around, back flipping off walls, jumping from the top of the building to the smaller building off to one side, literally running up walls and throwing themselves off, seeming to know something that gravity itself didn't know.

I watched with my heart in my throat as Zack literally ran from the top of the building, side jumped a wall as if it was no more than a foot high, hit the ground in a forward roll and then stood gracefully on his feet. It was like gymnastics on steroids. I never expected to like it, in fact, I thought I would hate it, but I couldn't have been more wrong. There was so much going on around me, people calling for my attention, trying to show off, offering to do more and more to impress me, but I couldn't drag my gaze off Zachary Anderson.

At some point over the last hour and a half he'd taken off his t-shirt and thrown it down on the wall next to me. The muscles rippled in his arms and back as he ran up a wall that was easily eight foot high, he then boosted himself up so he was doing a handstand on the wall, before bending in half, lowering his legs so that he was at a perfect right angle, all his weight held on just his arms, suspended eight foot in the air. The balance and strength that it took stole my breath as my heart hammered in my ears. Fear gripped my stomach. The danger of everything they were doing wasn't lost on me, my brain was still envisioning him falling on his face and how much that would hurt, but strangely, I knew he'd be fine. I somehow trusted him to know his limits and keep himself safe.

I learned two things while I watched him and his group prepare for the upcoming festival. One, Zach Anderson was an incredible freerunner. And two, I had never appreciated the male form more than I did when I watched him do it. It was beauty personified.

By the time they were finished my mouth was dry where it had been open, gasping in shock and excitement every few seconds, my eyes stung where I probably hadn't blinked as much as I should because I didn't want to miss a single second of it. They all stood, talking and laughing, congratulating each other before Jase sent me a little wave, grabbed his bag and skateboard and disappeared off in the opposite direction. The others followed, waving to me before heading off.

Zach smiled as he walked over to me. In the early evening sunshine that was just starting to fade, I could see the sweat glistening on his toned chest. He looked older like that for some reason. The mastery that he exuded during his training had kind of made me see him in a new light. When I looked at him now I didn't see the cheeky bad boy that backchat the teachers and fought with Luke, I saw a guy that was so good at something that it made my stomach quiver, I saw a person that loved doing parkour more than anything in the world, I saw a person struggling and wanting something so badly that he would give anything for it. It was simple, Zach wanted to do this professionally, it was easy to read from his demeanour and how seriously he took it all. And I could help him by making sure he graduated.

He grinned, reaching for his bag and pulling out a drink bottle. "Like it or not?" he asked, before chugging on the bottle like he hadn't drunk in years.

Did I like it? Did I even have the words to express how much I enjoyed that? I opened my mouth and then closed it again before laughing because I could barely remember how to speak. He'd literally boggled my mind. I nodded, swallowing, trying to form a coherent sentence.

He smiled and tossed the empty bottle in his bag, pulling out a small towel and rubbing it over his face and neck before moving down to his chest.

And by then I'd forgotten how to speak for a completely different reason as I watched his hand, seeming entranced by the movement of the towel stroking his chest, soaking up the beads of sweat. I suddenly had visions of me doing that for him, my hand gliding over his skin, feeling the grooves of his chest, tracing the muscles.

Oh dear lord I need help!

I sat up straighter, forcing my eyes back to his face as I grabbed his t-shirt, holding it out to him. Maybe if he put the shirt on I'd be able to remember how to speak words other than complete fan-girl gibberish.

"That... Zach... It..." *Snap out of it, Maisie!*

He tossed the towel carelessly into the bag, obviously having no idea that in that moment the pure maleness, the rugged power he was emitting was making my teeth ache with longing. "You got bored I bet," he stated casually as he shrugged on the t-shirt, finally seeming to let me out of the trance I had been in for the last hour. As soon as the t-shirt was over his head, his face disappearing for a few seconds as he pulled it down, I finally got a grip of myself.

I felt the grin stretch across my face as I sprang from the wall I was perched on, practically jumping on the spot as I gushed about how much I loved it, how good he was at it, how it blew my mind on a level I wasn't expecting.

He looked a little taken aback as he listened to my excited chirping with sceptical eyes. "You really liked it? I thought you'd be bored stiff," he replied, shaking his head as he picked up his bag, swinging it over his shoulder.

"Bored? No way! I loved it. The beauty of it, the freeness, the angles, the impossibility of what you were doing, and the bravery. Just, wow," I gushed, gripping his arm excitedly. He raised one eyebrow as he slung a heavy arm around my shoulder and nodded back the way we came. This time as we walked I didn't pay any attention to the art that was sprayed on the walls. The art that I'd found inspiring less than two hours ago, was now in the far recesses of my mind as I asked him question after question about how he got into it, how long he trained for and any other thing I could think of to ask about parkour. He answered everything, smiling, seeming bemused, as if he was expecting my reaction to be the complete opposite of what it was.

By the time we got back to his bike, it was starting to get dark. He grinned that boyish, teasing little smile and held out the helmet to me as he threw his leg over the bike and scooted forward so I could slide up behind him. I gripped the bottom of his hoodie that I was still wearing; about to pull it off, but his hand gripped mine as he shook his head.

"Just leave it on, it's cold on the bike and I'm still sweating anyway," he stated.

I gulped, my eyes flicking to chest as I mentally screamed at myself to not think about him shirtless again. I had no idea what had come over me earlier, but I still felt the residual ebb of it now, flitting through my bloodstream. I definitely needed help from a professional. "Yeah, the Spider-Man stuff looked exhausting," I replied, pulling the sweater down again before taking the offered helmet.

He grinned, gripping my hand tightly, holding me steady as I climbed on behind him, looping my arms around his waist. I tried extremely hard not to spread my fingers wide across his stomach in a bid to cop a sly feel of his muscles, but I just didn't have control of my stupid hand. I palmed his stomach with both hands, my fingers stretching out in what I hoped passed as an innocent move. I could feel the heat of his skin through the thin t-shirt he was wearing; I gulped and pressed myself to him tighter. His shoulders stiffened as he moved his head, seeming like he was going to look over his shoulder at me, before deciding better of it. Suddenly he stood up; kick started the bike, and then sat back down again. I smiled and pressed my helmeted head against his shoulder, closing my eyes, clinging to him as he twisted the throttle, making us burst from the parking lot in a puff of black smoke.

I was still on a high from what I'd just witnessed, so the bike ride was just the cherry on the top of the already very frosted cake. By the time we pulled up outside my house I was almost giddy with glee. I slid off the bike, grinning like an idiot as I looked up at him. He smiled as his hands went to the strap under my chin. I tilted my head as he fumbled, unclasping it before pulling it off and hanging it over his handlebars.

"Come on then, let's get inside and you can make me food, I'm starving," he instructed, motioning for me to walk.

"Maybe you should cook, you're the master chef after all," I replied as I fumbled in my pocket for my keys.

He laughed, following me up the path to the front door. "Your mom can cook then, that pasta was awesome. I assume I'm invited to dinner again..." he trailed off, looking at me hopefully.

I laughed and dug in my other pocket, searching out my keys but I couldn't find them so I swung my bag off my shoulder, crouching down and rummaging in there instead. "My parents are going out straight from work tonight," I informed him. "Either you cook, or I reheat you something that's left over, your choice," I offered, frowning into my bag. *Where the heck are my stupid keys? Did I pick them up this morning?*

Zach sighed, leaning against the door and crossing his arms over his chest. "Neither will be happening if we can't get in," he mocked. "Where's Alex, can't you just knock?"

I shook my head. "He'll be out with friends, drinking before whatever party he's attending tonight."

Zach pursed his lips, watching me curiously. "Want me to smash a window?" he joked. At least I hoped it was a joke.

I huffed and stood back up, shaking my head. "Nah, there's a spare key around back." I headed off with him following me close behind. Using the wall at the side, I leant up and unbolted the back gate, letting us into the back yard before stepping into the shrubbery and searching out the third rock from the left, lifting it to find the spare backdoor key that we hid under there for emergencies.

Zach made a scoffing noise in his throat. "Oh yeah, that's so very safe," he muttered sarcastically, shaking his head in disapproval.

I slapped his stomach with the back of my hand as I walked past to the door with my newly acquired key. "Stop complaining, you sound like a grouchy old man," I scolded, sticking out my tongue at him.

Before I knew what had happened I was knocked off my feet, the world turned upside down and I now faced the floor. "What the hell?" I screeched, giggling at the same time as he tightened his grip on my legs, pinning me over his shoulder, laughing wickedly.

"Shut up and open the door, we're wasting valuable eating time, and I'm starting to digest my own stomach here. In five minutes all that'll be left of me will be a pile of skin and bones," he stated, turning his body so that I now faced the door.

"Wasting valuable studying time you mean," I corrected, still giggling hysterically. Awkwardly I slipped the key into the lock, pressing my hand on the small of his back so I could steady myself. I'd never appreciated just how hard it was to unlock a door until I was trapped in a fireman's lift by a hot freerunner.

"Study comes after food." Even in the delicate position I was in, I could somehow tell he was smiling just by the warm tone of his voice.

chapter fifteen

It seemed that nothing in my life was going to go right at the moment. The whole house had been woken by the phone ringing at just after three in the morning. It transpired that my mom's dad had been taken into hospital with suspected pneumonia. He'd been battling a cough last time he came down to visit us for mine and Alex's birthday. My parents had instantly packed a bag and headed there for a couple of days to help my nanna out. Though Alex and I both asked to go with them, they refused because we had school and insisted that they would only be gone a couple of days. I hadn't really gone back to sleep after my nanna had phoned, so by the time morning came around my eyes were stinging with tiredness.

What made it worse was that I didn't know what to do with myself all day. Usually my weekends were filled by Luke, Luke, and more Luke. But this weekend I would have to amuse myself for a change. I wallowed all morning, sitting around, watching TV, and picking at junk food just to have something to distract myself from the fact that I missed Luke so much it was actually painful.

When I could stand the boredom no longer, I decided to go for a nice long walk. I pulled on a pair of boots and one of Luke's hooded sweatshirts, grabbed a tennis ball, and then Chester and I headed off for a stroll in the field near my house.

By the time I got home I was exhausted and covered in mud but at least I had killed an hour and a half from my weekend. Just as I raised my key to the lock to open the door, it sprang open and Alex almost walked into me as he was about to step out. He had a gym bag slung over his shoulder so I didn't bother asking where he was going.

"Jeez, Maisie, you scared me," he scolded, shaking his head in disapproval. "Were you waiting outside the door until I came along, just so you could frighten the shit out of me?"

I nodded, rolling my eyes. "Of course I was. Scaring you is the highlight of my day."

"Whatever." He smiled before stepping to the side and waving me into the house. "Moving on to more pleasant matters, I'm going to Katherine's after I've been to the gym so don't wait up for me." His voice was almost bragging as he strutted up the driveway and unlocked his car. "Oh, and you got a FedEx delivery while you were out. I put it in your room," he called, before climbing in and starting the engine a second later.

I glanced sceptically over my shoulder, wondering who had sent it and what it was. It was probably a belated gift for my birthday from my surrogate aunt Rachel, my mom's best friend; her and her husband Tom were always late with the gifts. "Okay, see ya," I called, watching as Alex pulled out of the drive. Once I was alone I headed to the kitchen, grabbing a soda and a packet of chips, before trudging up to my room. A rectangular white FedEx box sat on my bed, about the side of a shoe box. I frowned, but decided to go for a shower and change clothes first because of I was covered in mud and grass.

After a refreshing shower, I pulled my wet hair up into a ponytail and slipped on some fresh sweatpants and a tank top. I sat next to the box and picked it up curiously. There was no return label on it. It was light in weight, and something rolled inside as I moved it and set it on my lap, grabbed the tab and tore it open.

As I opened it and lifted the lid I recoiled at the contents. Inside was a stuffed brown bear, but someone had hacked off its head so that the white fluffy stuffing was all over the bottom of the box. The head rolled around as I jerked in shock. The disembodied object rolled over to me and I cringed when I saw that the eyes were missing so more stuffing leaked out of the holes making it look menacing. "What the hell?" I hissed, dropping the box on my bed, not wanting to touch it anymore. I could see two other objects in the box too, a white lily that was withered, the petals were crinkled and browning at the edges. The other item in there I wasn't even sure I wanted to see. It was a red envelope with the letter M written on it in big black pen.

I gulped. My heart was starting to beat too fast in my chest as my fingers hesitantly reached out for it. Being careful not to touch any of the stuffing that lined the inside of the box, I picked up the note. I slowly lifted the flap on the envelope and pulled out the folded up sheet of red paper. I winced because there was that old fashioned typewriter writing again inside it again. Different words this time though:

You're next

My eyes flicked back to the box again, seeing the mutilated bear. *Next? What the heck does that mean?* My eyes widened as my hand flew up to cover my mouth as the penny dropped. Before I knew what I was doing I was on my feet and across the other side of the room as my pulse quickened and fear gripped my stomach. *You're next...*

Whoever had sent this knew where I lived. My mouth went dry as my chest tightened. I suddenly became aware of every single sound outside my window as my imagination started to run away with me. The creak of branches of the old tree in our front yard made me jump a mile into the air. Why would someone start this hate campaign against me? Why would someone send me this? Did someone seriously want to hurt me? First my locker, then notebook, then the flowers, and the note with the petal that was pushed into my locker, and now they were sending me a decapitated stuffed bear? The only person I could think of was Sandy, but she wasn't this unhinged, surely. And if it wasn't her, then who did send it? I had no idea.

Suddenly the door to my room creaked open and I literally screamed like a three year old girl, clutching above my heart as my eyes widened in horror, expecting to see some knife wielding maniac come to pull my eyes out. *You're next...* The words of the old fashioned typed writing swam before my eyes as I just stood there, frozen against the wall, easy pickens for whatever psycho wanted to hurt me.

But it wasn't a psycho that strutted into my room. Chester, my dog, froze when I screamed, looking up at me with wide eyes as he stepped through the door. I blew out a big breath, not even realising that I was holding it in. I closed my eyes as he came over, licking my clenched fist in greeting.

"Oh God, get a grip of yourself, Maisie," I scolded, shaking my head at myself. But I couldn't calm my breathing as my eyes settled on the package on the bed. Someone was trying to scare me - that was all. No one was really going to hurt me. It was just Sandy or someone that found it amusing to frighten me to death. I was being stupid, I knew that, but at the same time I couldn't shake the fear that nestled in the pit of my stomach. All I kept thinking was that I was alone in the house. I needed to rectify that situation quickly.

I took a couple of hesitant steps towards the box again and grabbed my cell phone from the bed where I'd tossed it before going into the shower. Hitting speed dial one, I put it to my ear and waited.

"Hey, baby," Luke greeted, sounding ridiculously eager to hear from me.

At the sound of his voice, my fear loosened marginally. His voice wrapped around me like silk, covering me and seeming to take away some of the anguish I felt inside. "Hi. Luke, please can you come round and hang out?" I asked, noticing that my voice shook as I spoke.

"Come round? Is everything okay?"

I nodded, not wanting to tell him about the parcel or the hate campaign that someone seemed intent on keeping up. I didn't want to talk about it with him, he would go crazy and get all mad because someone was upsetting me, but the thing is I had no clue who was sending it. My only suspect was Sandy, but I wasn't convinced she had the gall to go as far as sending me something like that in the mail. Whoever was doing it was trying to get a huge reaction, to frighten me and make me upset. Well, I wasn't giving anyone the satisfaction of seeing me upset. I'd talk to Charlotte and Beth about it tomorrow, but Luke would just wade in with his temper and make everything worse in the long run, so I decided to keep it from him for now. If something else came then I'd tell him and just let him go all protective caveman on me, but for now I wanted to put that off as long as possible.

"Everything's fine," I lied. "I just want to hang out, that's all. Maybe watch a movie?"

I could already hear him moving around in the background, probably getting ready to come over. "Movie sounds great. I'll be there in five."

I smiled weakly, closing my eyes because I knew I would feel better with Luke in the house. He always made me feel better and took care of me. "See you then." I disconnected the call and looked down at the box on my bed, knowing I needed to hide it from Luke. I couldn't just throw it away though like I did with the flowers, Charlotte would probably want to see it once I told her about it. So I'd have to hide it somewhere for now.

Not wanting to touch it again, I used my cell phone and carefully closed the lid of the box with it before lifting it distastefully and heading over to my closet and pushing it onto the shelf at the top. Once it was in I slammed the closet door and leant against it, feeling my eyes prickle with tears.

Just what had I done to make someone do that? I was a nice person, I was kind to everyone, I never bitched about anyone behind their backs or anything like that. So just what had made someone send me a murdered teddy bear with a note saying I was next?

A knocking on the door downstairs made me practically jump out of my skin as I whimpered and held my breath. I didn't move. They knocked again, and I chewed on my lip. How long had I been standing there musing over why someone would send me something? Would that be Luke, or was it the person who sent it to me in the first place? My cell phone suddenly started vibrating in my hand. I gasped in shock and looked down to see Luke's smiling face on my screen with his number glowing underneath.

I answered it quickly, not moving from the spot. "Hi."

"Hey, you gonna answer your door or what?" he asked, laughing quietly.

I felt the tension leave my body because he was here. I must have been thinking about it longer than I thought and time had passed by without me realising it. I practically ran to the door, throwing it open to see him standing there, smiling the beautiful smile that I loved so much.

"Were you in the shower or something? What took you so-" Before he had a chance to finish his sentence, I threw myself at him, wrapping my arms around him tightly as I pressed my face into the side of his neck, breathing him in. His body stiffened as he wrapped his arms around me in return. "Maisie, what the?" he asked breathlessly.

I sighed contentedly and stepped impossibly closer. Everything about Luke was comforting, from the way his arms fitted around me, to his warmth, right down to his familiar scent that filled my lungs. It felt so nice just being held by him that I didn't ever want to move. There was no denying the fact that I just needed Luke right now, what with everything going on he felt like some sort of safety blanket. My feelings for Luke hadn't diminished at all I realised.

I fought back tears as I pressed myself even closer to him, squeezing him and letting his smell surround me. "I just missed you, that's all," I whispered. That was only half of the truth, I *had* missed him, but the relief that he was here was what made me lose my composure and hug him like he was the only thing keeping me on this earth.

His lips pressed to my temple. "I missed you too. I'm not used to not seeing you at the weekend." He grinned that dazzling smile, flashing me a row of perfectly white straight teeth. His hand moved up to the back of my neck, stroking at my hairline lightly with his thumb. My skin prickled as I unconsciously whimpered because I'd always loved it when he did that. Luke just fitted me so perfectly; everything he did made me melt inside, even just the way his arms wrapped around me made my whole body sag in contentment. I needed him whether I wanted to admit it or not.

I reluctantly pulled back, looking up at him gratefully because he made everything better. All the panic and fear that I'd felt moments before were gone as soon as I looked into his big brown eyes. He smiled down at me, his expression hopeful and purely happy. I felt a smile pull at the corners of my mouth too just because I always had to return his smiles, it was just something in me that reacted without my permission. Even after what he'd done with Sandy, I still had to smile at the boy, it was crazy really. They say that you never really fall out of love. Looking at Luke I knew that saying was true, I would always love him.

"Thanks for coming over," I muttered, not pulling out of his embrace yet because I was enjoying his closeness too much.

He bent his head, his nose tracing up the side of mine, making my breathing falter at the intimacy of the move. But he didn't kiss me like I was expecting; instead he pulled his head away and smiled at me tenderly. "Of course I'd come over. I just hope you're not gonna make me watch some crappy chick flick," he replied, laughing quietly. I laughed too, letting the last of the tension leave my body as my hand slipped into his before giving him a little tug towards the lounge, just eager to cuddle up against him on the sofa like we always used to on a Saturday afternoon. Hopefully he'd stay until Alex got home from hanging out with his newest bed buddy, and then I wouldn't have to be on my own in the house with that box.

chapter sixteen

On Sunday morning I decided to call Charlotte and Beth and see if they wanted to come over. I needed to tell someone about the package I was sent. I couldn't keep bottling it up inside, it would fester and eventually drive me crazy. I couldn't tell my parents, brother, or Luke because I knew they would go mad, insist on calling the police, and would make such a huge deal out of it that Sandy would end up winning. No, instead I was going to pretend like nothing had happened, hold my head up high and smile as if she wasn't important enough to me to bother me. I figured that would have more of an effect than anything else, she obviously wanted a reaction, and there was no way I was giving her another one.

They both arrived together just after eleven, giggling about something as they let themselves into my house as usual. Luckily for Charlotte, my brother wasn't awake yet because usually as soon as she stepped foot in the house he'd be showing off and trying to get into her pants. It was sickening really.

Charlotte grinned, flopping onto the sofa next to me as we exchanged greetings.

I stood up and nodded towards the door. "Let's go to my room and listen to some music or something."

They both instantly stood and followed me out and up the stairs. With each step that I took I felt my apprehension build. I was a little nervous telling them about the box. What if they thought it was more than a joke too? That would kind of make it more real for me. When we got to my room I stepped to the side and let them both pass me as I chewed on my lip wondering if I should just keep it to myself and pretend that it never even got sent in the first place.

They both flopped down on my bed; Beth immediately grabbed my book from the nightstand, flicking through it absentmindedly. I took a deep breath and decided to get it out there and see what they thought about it.

"Um, so there's actually a reason I called you both to come over," I started, wincing as I looked at my closed closet door, not really wanting to touch the box again but knowing I was going to have to. That caught their attention immediately.

Charlotte narrowed her eyes at me. "Please tell me you're not getting back with Luke."

I smiled weakly. Clearly they had no idea what I was about to say. "It's not about Luke, well, actually it kind of is, but it isn't," I mumbled.

Beth's forehead creased with a frown. "You're making even less sense than usual."

I laughed humourlessly and closed the door, leaning against it and closing my eyes. "I know. It's a long story." They both sat there watching me intently as I spoke and told them all about the deep breathing phone calls, the note that I found in my locker, the scribbling on my notebook, and the flowers. Charlotte's body was tensing up like a snake ready to pounce on its victim. Beth's mouth was wide, as were her eyes. I swallowed the lump that was forming in my throat as I knew it was time to tell them about the last thing, the weirdest thing, the box that I'd been sent yesterday.

"And then I got this sent to me yesterday," I muttered, pulling open the closet and grabbing the box that I'd stored there. I plopped it on the bed between the two girls, chewing on my lip, waiting for them to open it and look.

Charlotte's hand shot out, flipping the lid. "What the hell?" she cried, frowning down at the contents distastefully. "Someone FedEx'd you a murdered teddy bear and a dead flower? That's twisted!"

I nodded as Beth immediately pulled the box to her, closing it and examining the packaging that I'd stored with it in my cupboard. "Who sent it? There's no return address," she observed, looking over the front of it again.

I ground my teeth in frustration. "Sandy." She was the only one that would have a grudge against me.

Beth frowned. "How do you know that? It could be anyone." Charlotte flipped open the box again, reaching in and pulling out the note, reading it with wide eyes before she passed it to Beth. "Wow."

I shrugged and slumped down to the floor, sitting cross-legged and watching them. "It has to be her, who else could it be? She's just trying to scare me; she's trying to get a reaction as payback for me calling her a dirty tramp at the party. She's a freak."

Suddenly Beth put the box down and shook her head. "We shouldn't be touching this. It'll be contaminated with our fingerprints now." She set it on the side, looking at it worriedly. "You have called the police, haven't you?"

Okay, I knew this was coming. "Er, no. I'm not going to, and I don't want anyone else to know either. She's just doing it to make me look like an idiot, so I'm not giving her the satisfaction." I lifted my chin confidently. I wasn't going to the police, not over a beheaded teddy bear and a couple of prank phone calls, I'd get laughed right out of there.

Beth's lips pressed into a hard, disapproving line. "Maisie, this is serious, what if it's not her sending it? What if it's not a joke? You have to tell the police."

I flinched; I refused to think about that scenario. "It is her," I assured them. "I don't want a load of people to know about it, but I needed to tell someone. I definitely don't want Alex or Luke to know about this, they'll go all caveman on me and insist that I don't go anywhere alone, you know what they're both like."

Charlotte sat forward, leaning her elbows on her knees as her blue eyes locked onto mine. "But why would she go that far though? Sure, she's minion of the devil, but why would she even bother with you now anyway? She's got what she wanted, you and Luke have split up, she's free to make her move on him if she wanted. So why would she start sending you stuff like this? She's already won, it doesn't make sense."

I groaned in frustration, wishing I hadn't told them. The fact that they were making a big deal out of this was making it worse, I was hoping they'd both just agree with me, and we'd laugh about how stupid Sandy was and then burn the teddy in some kind of voodoo ritual or something. "When has she ever made sense? She already told me that us breaking up wasn't enough for her," I countered. "Look, I only wanted to get it off my chest. I don't want to go to the police; I don't want a big deal made out of it. That's what she wants to happen."

Charlotte nodded slowly. Beth still looked like she disapproved of the whole thing. "You should call the FedEx people and see who sent it, they have records and stuff. Or maybe I could find out another way," Charlotte suggested. There was a mischievous little glint to her eye and a smile pulled at the corners of her mouth which signalled that she was up to no good.

I raised one eyebrow. "How would you do that?"

She sat back and clasped her hands together, smiling in full now which only meant one thing - she was going to do her computer thing again and hack FedEx to see who sent it. "I need my laptop," was all she answered. I rolled my eyes. Beth looked at Charlotte with apprehension clear across her face, she didn't approve of anything illegal and usually shied away from Charlotte once the laptop came out. "I'll look as soon as I get home, shouldn't be too hard to crack their security. We have the tracking number on the box, so it should be a breeze." She looked almost excited as she said it. Computers were her thing so she relished anything that posed a slight challenge to her.

I sighed and nodded. "Okay, but it won't make a difference, that'll just show that it was sent from her, I still don't want to do anything about it. She'll get bored soon enough and she'll move on to someone else."

Beth still didn't look convinced. "All right, but if anything else happens then you should report it, or at least tell your parents. Prank calls and stuff like this is no joke, even if it's only meant to scare someone."

I nodded in agreement. I already decided I'd do that anyway, if something else came along then I'd tell people, but for now I was happy just sweeping it under the carpet. I had too much other stuff going on at the moment; I was still struggling to deal with the fact that Luke had shattered my heart. I didn't want to have to acknowledge that yes, for a few minutes, I was actually scared when I opened that box, and that yes it had actually crossed my mind that someone was, in fact, threatening me. It was easier to pretend like it wasn't happening.

"Once I get the proof that she sent it, we should all jump her or something," Charlotte suggested thoughtfully.

I laughed and rolled my eyes. "I don't like violence."

She raised one eyebrow. "The girl sent you a mutilated teddy bear; I think violence is justified in this situation."

I chuckled at the hopeful glint in her eye. "You sound just like Zach."

"Ooh, and that's another thing I wanted to talk to you about," Charlotte said, eyeing me curiously. "What's going on with you two? Personally I don't think he's a good fit for you, he's too... badass, for you. But you seem to be getting on well," she mused.

I laughed incredulously. "Nothing's going on. I'm tutoring him, and for some reason he seems to like hanging out with me. Nothing more than that. He's a nice guy actually. I don't think he's as badass as he likes to make out he is. He's a pretty complicated person." I frowned, thinking about some of the things he'd said to me, he was definitely complicated and had a lot more going on than he liked to show people. Cocky and arrogant seemed to be an image he liked to portray to people so that they'd stay at a distance. Underneath it all I would bet that he was more sensitive than he let on.

Charlotte pursed her lips and nodded. "I'd sure like to work him out. If only he hadn't called me sweetness, I'd be all over him like a rash." We all burst out laughing and talk turned onto boys and school rather than Sandy and police, for that I was immensely grateful.

• • •

AS SOON AS I STEPPED out of Alex's car on Monday morning, I was instantly met by Charlotte who looped her arm through mine, leaning in conspiratorially. "So I tried everything to find out who sent that package, but I couldn't find anything at all. The records for it seem to be a mystery; the ID of the sender was never logged. I did find out that the office that sent it was in the next town over though. I tried to look through their security footage to see if Sandy was caught on camera sending it, but there was nothing. Either they don't have security cameras, or it was deleted," she told me, raising one eyebrow.

I frowned at that. "The ID wasn't logged?"

She shook her head and shrugged. "Nope. Trust me, if it had been logged and then deleted, I would have seen it, but there was nothing there at all, not even ghost record entries. The sender was left blank," she confirmed. "I reckon she slipped them a few bucks to keep her name off it so no one could prove it was her if you did decide to go to the police."

I sighed dramatically. She'd gone to so much freaking effort just to send me that package. It was a little scary really. "Let's just forget about it. I'm not giving her the satisfaction of a reaction about it." I lifted my chin confidently as we walked towards the school building together. As we got to my locker I spotted Sandy. She was further up the hallway, chatting and laughing animatedly with her little group of likeminded airheads. She didn't even look in my direction. *She's obviously intent in not giving herself away and pretending like she doesn't know anything is going on. Witch.*

Beth marched up a minute later, talking about how she was going to flunk algebra because she hadn't done her assignment for class. I smiled and tried my best to get into the conversation, but my mind kept wandering back to the note and the box. *You're next.* I suddenly doubted my plan to ignore it. As I glanced up at Sandy again the anger built in my stomach. What I really wanted to do was strut over there and finish what I'd started the other day. She looked up at exactly the same time, her eyes met mine and a small smug smile tugged at the corners of her mouth. I frowned, barely holding in my anger because she'd ruined everything and she seemed to be enjoying it so much.

A tap on my shoulder made me turn my attention away from Sandy. Zach smiled down at me, though his eyes seemed concerned. "Hey. You okay? You look tired," he asked, raising one eyebrow.

I sighed and shrugged. "I'm fine. Didn't sleep too well over the weekend that's all." Last night I hadn't managed to get much sleep either. Alex was in the house so I wasn't worried about being on my own, but the box, Sandy, my ill grandad, and Luke were running through my mind practically all night long. Sleep had unfortunately eluded me again.

"How come?"

I waved my hand dismissively, not wanting to get into it all. "My grandad's not well. My parents went to make sure he's alright, so that was stressing me out a little. He's okay though. He's got pneumonia apparently but he'll be fine. My parents are staying down there to help my nanna out for a couple of days." I reached into my locker and pulled out my books for the morning classes.

"Wow, that sucks. Hopefully he'll get better quickly," he replied, leaning against my locker and watching me curiously.

"Hopefully. So, are we studying at my place or yours tonight?" I asked, wanting to change the subject.

"Mine if that's alright, Olivia's still keeping tabs on me." He chuckled darkly as he stood up straighter. "I actually have something I need to do straight after school though so I'll have to pick you up after I'm done. Maybe you could just hang out here at school and I'll pick you up when I'm done, I'll be about half an hour I guess."

I shrugged and nodded in agreement. Alex was going straight to the gym after school to train for his upcoming kickboxing match. I'd already told him I was going home with Zach and wouldn't need a ride. "Sure, I'll just hang in the library for a while until you get back. I need some new books to read anyway."

"You're such a nerd," he joked, bumping his shoulder with mine. I rolled my eyes, about to make a sarcastic comment back, but the bell rang before I could speak. He smiled, nodding over my shoulder. "I'd better go get to class, don't want to be late and earn myself a reputation for being a delinquent."

I laughed at that and waved as he strutted off down the corridor confidently, not seeming to notice the girls looking at him and smiling as they tried to get his attention.

• • •

MY DAY PASSED WITHOUT a hitch. I'd had none of those weird silenced phone calls, no typed notes with petals inside, and nothing was scrawled on my locker. Sandy didn't even look in my direction all day. During gym I silently wondered if maybe the box with the teddy inside was the anticlimactic climax. Maybe she was bored of me not reacting the way that she wanted me to. Hopefully my choice of ignoring it all had the right effect and now she was abandoning her vicious façade against me. One could only hope.

Even tutoring went well. Maybe my luck was finally turning around again and life would get back to normal. After Zach had finally graced me with his presence and picked me up after school, we'd gone to his place to study. We worked for almost two hours, getting a lot done, before stopping to have dinner with his aunt and uncle again. After, he drove me home.

It was cold as I pulled off Zach's jacket and passed it back to him. "Thanks for the loan. I really should remember to bring a sweater or something when we're going to be on the bike," I said, holding it out to him gingerly.

He grinned teasingly. "Just admit it; you'd rather wear my clothes, that's why you always wear silly little flimsy shirts when you know we're studying. You like cloaking yourself in my smell."

I rolled my eyes, shouldering my bag. "Whatever you want to believe, Zach," I replied sarcastically. "Thanks for dinner. See you tomorrow." I turned for the house, hugging myself against the cold. Now that I'd taken off his jacket I was instantly covered in goosebumps.

"See ya."

I waved over my shoulder as his bike roared loudly, then started disappearing down the street. I fumbled with my keys, slipping them into the lock and pushing the door open. As I stepped through the front door of the house I dropped my bag on the floor and frowned at the unusual quiet of the place. Normally the smell of food would hit me as soon as I walked through the door; chatter and the sound of a TV would fill the house. But today I was the only one here because Alex was training until late, and my parents were with my nanna. Even Chester, my dog, wasn't whining and skipping excitedly down the hallway towards me. I didn't like coming in to an empty house, it felt a little eerie.

I decided to go and make a snack before I started on my own homework. The quiet was a little weird as I walked down the hallway. "Chester? You'd better not be asleep on the beds again!" I called, chuckling to myself. He had a fondness for Alex's bed and took any opportunity to sneak in there if his door was left open. I stood at the bottom of the stairs and peered up. "Chester!" I scolded, rolling my eyes. "Come on, dinner time."

I headed into the kitchen, flicking on the lights as I went, knowing that the word dinner would have him scuttling down the stairs within seconds. After scooping out half a tin of dog food into his bowl and changing his water, I stood back against the counter, watching the door. "Chester!" I called again when he didn't appear. I groaned in frustration and marched out, up the stairs towards Alex's room. By the time I got to the top of the stairs though I realised that he wouldn't be in there. The door was shut - unless maybe Alex had shut him in there by accident. As I opened the door though I saw that the room was empty, no indent on the bed, no tell-tale black dog fur on the pillow, nothing.

"Chester, where are you?" I called loudly. I cast my eyes around seeing that all of the doors upstairs were closed so he wouldn't be up here. I sighed and marched back down the stairs. We had a large cat flap in our back door that was actually big enough for him to fit through. We usually kept it locked while we weren't home because Chester could get out through it fine but could never seem to apply the same logic to get back in again. We only unlocked it when someone was home so that they could let him in again.

I strutted to the back door, grabbing my keys on the way past and unlocking it quickly, assuming that Alex had forgotten to lock the cat flap this morning. *Poor little thing. If he's been outside all day he's probably freezing!* As I pulled the door open I saw him. He was lying in the middle of the grass, not moving.

"Chester?" I whimpered and stepped out quickly, rushing to his side.

I gasped when I noticed his shallow breathing. His eyes were closed as if he was sleeping, but he seemed to be struggling to breathe. White foamy spittle coloured the corners of his black lips. "Oh no," I muttered, quickly stroking him to see if he was hurt or anything. My eyes prickled with tears as he let out a low whimper and his eyes fluttered open before closing again. I didn't know what to do; he was just lying there completely still. I needed to call a vet or something.

My eyes landed on something a couple of feet away from where I was crouched. It was a grease proof wrap, white paper, like what butchers wrap meat in. I frowned at it then looked back at Chester. "Did you eat something?" I muttered, shaking my head in confusion. When my gaze landed on something else that was laying on the grass, I felt my body jerk in shock. A white calla lily, exactly like the ones that I kept being sent, laid there as if it was the most natural thing in the world.

A sob rose in my throat. I looked back at my dog, horrified as realisation washed over me. Someone had poisoned my dog, and they'd done it because of me. "No, no, please no."

My hand flew straight to my pocket, pulling out my cell phone and dialling the one person that I knew would be round here in an instant. He answered almost immediately. "Luke! Oh God, it's Chester," I croaked as I buried my face against the scruff of his neck and broke down into hysterical sobs.

chapter seventeen

Mere minutes later, Luke's car screeched to a halt outside the front of my house. He burst through the back gate seconds after cutting the engine. I looked up at him pleadingly, silently begging him with my eyes to help my dog.

Luke's face fell as he looked from me to Chester who was still lying motionless, struggling to breathe. "Shit. He looks bad," he mumbled, dropping down next to me.

I nodded, sniffing loudly. "He's been poisoned. We have to get him to the vets," I croaked, swiping at my endless tears.

Luke frowned and looked at me with doubtful, yet sympathetic eyes. "He hasn't been poisoned, baby, he's just old."

I shook my head adamantly. "He has, look!" I pointed at the lily and felt my chin wobble as guilt washed over me. "See? They left that!"

Luke raised one eyebrow as he looked at the flower. "Left what? Maisie, what are you talking about?" He slipped his arms under Chester's body, lifting him gently. "Look, let's just get him to the vet and see what they say. But, baby, dogs don't last forever; maybe it's just his time."

I groaned in frustration because he wasn't really listening to me. The rational part of me understood because he didn't know about the flowers or notes so of course he wouldn't think anything of it, but the grief-stricken part of me was annoyed with him for dismissing what I was saying. Chester whined quietly and my heart throbbed as I looked down at him apologetically. This was my fault; he was hurt because of me.

Luke strutted towards the gate without waiting for me. "You need to lock your house," he instructed as I stumbled along behind him in a state of panic. I nodded weakly, not thinking clearly. I ran into the house, locking the back door behind me and then running through the house and out the front door, locking that too. By the time I got to Luke's car I saw that he'd already settled Chester in the back seat, laying him out carefully. The car started as I jumped into the back with him and stroked his ears softly.

I cried the whole way to the veterinary clinic while Luke tried to soothe me, telling me that they'd take care of him, that I should think positive, that maybe he'd just eaten something that had upset his stomach. Deep down I knew his words were true, he had definitely eaten something - Sandy the witch had given him something that had been wrapped in grease proof paper and had left me a lily so she could gloat about it.

By the time we got to the clinic Chester was worse. His breathing was so shallow and rapid that it broke my heart. The muscles in his legs were twitching and his nose was bleeding. As soon as the nurse saw Luke carrying Chester in, and me crying hysterically, we were immediately rushed through into a treatment room where two men in green scrubs fussed over my dog, checking in his mouth and eyes, taking blood samples, trying to rouse him to no avail. The nurse stood there asking me question after question about how I found him, what he'd eaten, if he was fit and well this morning. I answered everything to the best of my ability, telling them about the grease proof paper that lay there and my suspicions that someone had poisoned him on purpose. They too looked sceptical but took extra blood samples too so they could do a toxicology report.

"Maybe it's best if you wait in the waiting room?" the nurse suggested when they started trying to make Chester vomit by squirting clear liquid down his throat. Luke nodded, wrapping his arm around my shoulders, pulling me from the room quickly. My legs barely worked as Luke guided me across the waiting room to the seating area. From the corner of my eye I saw the other pet owners looking at me sympathetically as they clutched their pets closer to them unconsciously, obviously now thinking the worst for their ill animals.

I sat down, struggling to breathe as I buried my face into the side of Luke's neck, clinging to him helplessly as I imagined Chester dying, how awful it would be to never see him wag his tail again, or bark excitedly when I came home from school. We'd had him since a puppy and I couldn't bear to lose him.

Time seemed endless as we sat there waiting for news. Finally, one of the vets that were working on Chester opened the door and called us through. I studied his face, trying to guess what the news was. He looked grave, and my heart gave another painful thump in my chest as I imagined the worst. Luke's hand closed over mine as we walked into the room. My eyes flitted to the table, the last place I'd seen Chester before I was ushered out, but the table was now empty apart from some handheld equipment, tape, and a pair of used gloves.

I swallowed the lump in my throat as I waited for him to say the words and tell me the bad news, so it surprised me when he smiled softly.

"He's stable at the moment. We're running a full toxicology report, but preliminary tests suggest that he's ingested some sort of rat poison. We've cleared as much as we can, and given him some activated charcoal. That will hopefully stop most of the poison being absorbed in his stomach and intestines. We've also started a course of vitamin K which will help too. You did the right thing by bringing him in here so quickly," he said, smiling kindly.

I sniffed, closing my eyes as the fear that gripped my stomach loosened marginally. "So he's going to be alright?" I croaked.

"The first twenty-four hours are crucial. Rat poison can be fatal if not treated in a timely manner because it causes internal bleeding. I think we caught it in time, but due to his age I can't be sure. We'll keep him in the emergency room overnight and keep a constant vigil over him. We'll do everything we can," he answered.

Luke's hand tightened on mine as the vet spoke. I nodded helplessly, knowing there was nothing else I could do but wait and see and trust them to do the best for my dog. "Can I see him?" I asked weakly.

The vet nodded, waving his hand at a door at the back of the room. Silently, I followed behind him, down the corridors and into a larger room full of medical equipment. Everything was white and green and looked sterile and clean. Chester lay on a table, a nurse sat next to him, scribbling on a clipboard. She smiled when we walked in.

A little whimper left my lips as I stumbled over to his side, looking down at him through teary eyes. He looked peaceful now, not twitching anymore. His breathing had evened out a little though it still wasn't back to normal. I didn't know what to say so instead I just bent my head and kissed the side of his face.

"He's sedated now. I'm working all night so I'll keep a close eye on him, don't worry," the nurse said kindly as she placed her hand on my back in a comforting gesture.

I smiled gratefully and nodded. Luke was talking to the vet on the other side of the room, looking over a piece of paper before he shook his hand and came to my side. "We should go now, baby. We can call for an update first thing in the morning," he said softly as he wiped one of my stray tears away. With his other hand he stoked Chester's head.

"Okay," I agreed. Luke led me out of the place while I followed numbly behind, unable to think of anything other than my poor little dog and how ill he was. As we got to the front door I stopped as a thought occurred to me. "Wait, don't I need to give them my details and pay or something?" I croaked, glancing back at the reception desk.

Luke shook his head. "I've sorted everything, they've got your details, and mine, so don't worry." He pulled me against his side, wrapping a protective arm around me as he guided me out of the building and over to his car. As he opened my door I pressed myself against him, closing my eyes, grateful that he was here with me and taking care of everything so that I didn't have to. He hugged me tightly as I silently wondered what on earth I would do without him in my life. Luke was my rock, and while I was in his arms, I knew he always would be.

By the time I climbed in the car my legs were weak and my tears had dried up. I sat there almost numb because the horror of what I'd just been through had crushed me inside. Luke got into the driver's side, starting the engine. "Are you alright?" he whispered. I shook my head and turned in my chair to look at him. He smiled sympathetically and reached out, stroking the side of my face with one finger. "He'll be okay," he cooed, leaning over and planting a soft kiss on my forehead.

I smiled weakly and closed my eyes. "Thanks for sorting everything," I mumbled. "You were so great. Thank you."

He pulled back and waved his hand dismissively. "You don't need to thank me," he replied, shaking his head. "I would like to know why you think someone would have poisoned him on purpose though." He raised one eyebrow, his brown eyes locking onto mine as he cocked his head to the side curiously.

My thoughts instantly flicked to Sandy again. I clenched my jaw tightly as anger built up because she'd definitely gone too far this time. Chester was an innocent dog; he didn't deserve anything like this to happen. Hate wasn't a strong enough word for what I felt for her in that moment. "It was her," I spat, shaking my head as my hands tightened into fists. I wanted to go around to her house and kill her, force her to eat poisoned meat so she would suffer like Chester just had. I wanted to watch her struggle for breath as her organs started bleeding like his had.

"Her?" Luke questioned, taking my hand and squeezing gently.

I nodded, sniffing and swiping at my face roughly. I needed to stop crying, I silently wished I wasn't such an emotionally week person. "Can we just go home and then I'll tell you everything," I mumbled, not really wanting to have this discussion in the car. He frowned but nodded, immediately putting the car into drive and pulling out of the parking lot.

The ride home was silent. He held my hand the whole time, tracing soothing circles on the back of it while he drove. I sat there stewing inside, plotting and planning on what I was going to do to her tomorrow. If I knew where she lived I would go there tonight, but I would have to settle for tomorrow instead. When we pulled up outside my house I noticed that Alex wasn't back yet. That was a good thing though because I wasn't ready to say the words about Chester yet, it was still too raw. Luke opened my car door for me and led me towards the house, taking my keys out of my hand and opening the front door. I chewed on my lip as I stepped inside. Even though I knew he wasn't there, I still looked up the hallway, waiting for Chester to skip around the corner yipping excitedly. I wasn't used to coming home to him not being there.

Luke sighed as he flicked on the lights and slipped his arm around my shoulder. "Let's go sit down and then I'll make some coffee or something. What time is Alex due home?" he asked, kissing the side of my head as he guided me to walk into the lounge.

I shrugged. "I don't know. He won't be too late," I mumbled, sitting down on the sofa.

Luke sat next to me, pulling me close to his side as his hand stroked across my hip softly. "So, will you tell me what you were talking about earlier?" he asked quietly.

I nodded and pressed into him as I told him about the hate campaign that someone had started against me recently. The silent phone calls, the scribbling on my notebook, the letters typed on red paper, and the flowers that I initially thought were from him. His body stiffened when I told him that the flowers were the same type as what someone had left next to Chester in the back yard. His jaw was tight; his fingers were digging into my waist as he seemed to be struggling not to let his anger show. I knew he would be angry, he was almost as protective over me as my dad and brother were.

I looked up at him and shrugged sadly. "See, he *was* poisoned. How else can you explain that he ate something and that there was a flower there?"

He gulped loudly, looking a little lost for words as he shook his head slowly.

I sniffed, knowing I needed to tell him everything now, I couldn't keep anything back. "I got a box on Saturday too. It had a flower in there and a teddy bear that had been mutilated. The note in with it said I was next," I whispered. "Obviously she decided to hurt Chester instead and punish me that way."

Luke's mouth dropped open as he jerked in his seat. "Someone sent you a mutilated teddy bear and a death threat? Did you call the police? Christ, Maisie! What the hell did your dad say?" he ranted, standing up and looking down at me, clearly outraged.

I shook my head, shrinking down into my seat because of the annoyance I could see on his face. It was then that I realised that I'd been incredibly stupid. If I'd called the police when I got the box, maybe then the police would have dealt with it and then Chester wouldn't be fighting for his life. I'd buried my head in the sand and made everything worse.

"I-I didn't tell my dad," I stuttered, wincing as he let rip a string of expletives, gripping his hands into his hair. "At the time I didn't think it was a big deal," I continued, trying to explain my actions.

He made a scoffing noise in his throat. "You didn't think it was a big deal? Someone heavy breathing down a phone and sending you notes and stuff *is* a big freaking deal, Maisie!" he chastised.

I nodded, my chin trembling. I didn't know what to say. There was no way I could make this better.

He sighed and plopped down next to me, wrapping his arm around my shoulders. "Look, sorry, I shouldn't have shouted at you, but you should have told someone. You could have at least told me. Why didn't you tell me someone was sending you stuff?" he asked. His eyes searched mine and I could almost see the hurt there that I'd not confided in him.

I smiled apologetically. "I should have, I'm sorry. I thought she was just trying to scare me, I thought she was trying to get a reaction from me so she could laugh about it with her friends."

His frown deepened. "Why do you keep saying she? Who exactly do you think is sending you stuff?"

"Sandy!" I almost spat the word because I was so angry.

Luke burst out laughing as he looked at me like I'd lost the plot. "Sandy? Seriously?" he scoffed, shaking his head in amusement.

I frowned and pushed his arm off me. "Yes her! This all started after the party, when you two..." I swallowed loudly, unable to say the words. He squeezed his eyes shut and sighed sadly; obviously thinking about what he'd done again. "It's her. She's a witch, and she's doing this now because I embarrassed her at the party after," I added for good measure. I crossed my arms over my chest defensively as I glared at him, daring him to challenge what I was saying and defend her again like he did after I'd fought with her at school.

He didn't say anything, just looked at me as if he was choosing his words carefully. "Show me the box," he finally ordered.

I nodded, standing up and motioning towards the lounge door. "It's in my room." Taking a deep breath I walked out, trying not to think about anything else as I marched up the stairs to my bedroom. Luke was following close behind me; a comforting hand rested on the small of my back. As I stepped into my room we both headed over to the closet where I pulled down the box and handed it to him, frowning distastefully.

He opened it, his teeth clenching as he looked at the contents and pulled out the note. He hissed a cuss word under his breath as he read it. "We need to call the police," he muttered through gritted teeth.

I didn't answer. I knew the time had passed for me to brush this under the carpet now; I was going to have to face it and tell the police everything. My eyes wandered over my room as Luke put the box down on my dresser and pulled out his cell phone, dialling 911. Something white caught my attention on my bed, resting up against my pillows. I frowned and walked over to it, seeing that it was an envelope. There was no writing on the front of it. I picked it up quickly, ripping it open curiously. As my fingers closed around what was inside I let out a little whimper. Pulling out the card of the envelope I read the two words on the cover, 'With Sympathy'. It was one of those cards you sent when someone had lost a loved one. I gulped and opened it, expecting to see a typed message in there like from the notes. But other than the standard poem that was printed inside, there was no writing on it at all. Instead, something small and silver slid out and clattered to the floor. My eyes followed it, and I whimpered when I saw that it was Chester's tag from his collar.

"Oh God," I croaked as I looked up at Luke and burst into a fresh round of sobs. The person who had poisoned Chester had obviously concluded that he would die from it.

Luke's eyes widened in shock, his gaze going from the tags to the card in my hand. "How did that... how did that get in here?" He still had the phone pressed to his ear as I threw myself at him and cried into his chest. He cleared his throat suddenly, his arm wrapping around my shoulders as I gripped fistfuls of his shirt. "Yeah, police please." He gulped. "Someone's been in my girlfriend's house," Luke said into the phone, his voice a little shaky as he spoke.

chapter eighteen

It took over and hour for the police to arrive. Our complaint wasn't deemed urgent because no one was in immediate danger.

Luke had finally managed to calm me down, and he'd also managed to get hold of Alex and tell him to come home from the gym. To say that Alex had been shocked would be a severe understatement. He'd looked from me to Luke several times, asking stupid questions over and over before the penny finally dropped and he switched into overprotective, angry brother mode. He didn't seem to believe my suspicions over Sandy either.

When the police finally did arrive we all sat down in the lounge while I relayed my tale over and over again, everything that had happened recently, from the silent phone calls, right down to the sympathy card that I'd found on my bed.

"So the card was on your bed?" Detective Inspector Neeson, the kind faced police lady asked, scribbling on her notepad.

I nodded, clutching at the Kleenex I had in my hand. "Yeah."

A frown lined her forehead as she pursed her lips. "When you came home from tutoring you say that the front door was locked, and that you had to unlock the backdoor to go into your yard?"

I thought back, just double checking in my own mind. I'd definitely unlocked both doors, I remembered it fairly clearly. "Yeah, both doors were locked," I confirmed.

"And you didn't go into your room at that time," she clarified.

I shook my head in answer. "I went upstairs, but only into Alex's room to see if Chester was in there." From the corner of my eye I saw Alex's jaw tighten when I mentioned Chester.

She made a few more notes then before speaking, "When you went to the back yard did you leave your front door unlocked?"

I frowned, thinking hard, unsure as why that would even matter. "I guess. But what does that have to do with anything?"

She smiled kindly, her eyes soft and sympathetic. "I'm just trying to ascertain when the card was placed on your bed. There was no forced entry to the house, so it's possible that someone snuck into the house and placed the card while you to tending to your dog outside," she suggested.

I swallowed my anger. Did that mean that Sandy had been waiting for me to arrive home so that she could sneak in behind me and put the card there?

Alex leant forward, cocking his head to the side. "But then how did Chester get outside if there was no forced entry? I didn't open the cat door, and Maisie said that she didn't either. My parents aren't here so they couldn't have unlocked it."

DI Neeson nodded along, not seeming shocked so she'd obviously already thought along those lines too. "That's another thing that I was about to ask," she answered. "Does anyone have access to the house? A spare key with a neighbour or anything?"

I shook my head in answer, pressing myself into Luke's side, enjoying the solid firmness of his body. Alex answered before I could. "We do leave a spare back door key in the yard for emergencies," he muttered.

A disapproving look crossed the police lady's face as she scribbled on her pad again. "Could you go with Officer Tatum and show him where it's kept?" she asked Alex, before turning to the male cop who had been sitting there silently at her side the whole time. "Greg, bag it up and we can check it for prints," she ordered, raising an eyebrow knowingly, as if everything now made perfect sense to her.

Suddenly her thinking became clear to me too. She thought someone used the spare key to let Chester out, fed him poisoned meat, left a card on my bed, and then relocked the door again after themselves so it wouldn't be obvious. When you thought of it that way, it did make sense.

Alex stood up quickly and marched out of the room, followed by the silent cop.

Luke's arm slipped around my shoulders as the lady turned back to me with inquiring eyes. "Who knows about the key in the back yard?"

I was a little taken aback by her question. I thought about it now and my mind flicked to Sandy. As far as I was aware she had never been to my house before, so how would she know where the key was? "Um, I don't know. Just a few friends that have been with me or Alex when we've forgotten our keys. It's not common knowledge," I answered, still wondering how Sandy knew about it.

Maybe she'd been watching me and saw me use it last week.

DI Neeson took a deep breath, seeming to be contemplating everything. "We'll interview your neighbours and see if any of them saw anyone hanging around your house today," she stated. "Can you think of anyone that may have a grudge against you? Anyone that would want to hurt you?"

Luke stiffened at my side, his arm tightening on me as he shook his head subtly, as if he was unconsciously dismissing my idea all over again.

"I know who it is," I replied confidently. DI Neeson's eyebrow rose in question, her pen hovered over her paper. "Sandy Watson." Luke let his breath out in a slow sigh, his hand stroking the side of my hip.

DI Neeson scribbled down the name on the paper as she spoke, "And what makes you sure that it is Sandy Watson?" she questioned, studying me carefully. I sighed deeply and launched into telling her everything – Luke cheating, me calling Sandy a dirty tramp at the party, us arguing in the school hallway, her wanting Luke for herself and her admitting that us breaking up wasn't nearly enough for her. Throughout the whole thing the inspector looked from me to Luke. She didn't look overly convinced, and I grew more frustrated with every passing second. It seemed that no one was going to take my suspicions seriously.

"So you didn't see her write on your locker or post the note through?" she asked. I shook my head in answer. "And when you confronted her about the note, she didn't confirm that it was her that sent it?"

I frowned. "Well no, but she's the only one that has an obvious problem with me. You asked if anyone has a grudge against me and she's the only one," I countered defensively. Somehow I felt now that she was thinking I had some sort of grudge against Sandy instead and was trying to get her into trouble. I hated that no one was taking it seriously just because she was a silly teenage girl. Yes, it did seem a little farfetched that the head cheerleader would be starting this hate campaign against me, but there was no one else, so it *had* to be her.

DI Neeson nodded thoughtfully, seeming to be choosing her words. "We'll look into it. At this stage there is nothing but guessing involved so we have to tread carefully. I'll look into everything, you can rest assured on that." She motioned to the box and contents that sat at her side having already been placed in clear plastic bags when they arrived. "We're going to take the notes, box, card and flowers in for evidence. I'd like you to have a think about who may have touched the items. We'll have to take fingerprints from anyone that has come into contact with the items so we can rule them out of any evidence we collect from the box." She stood up and ripped out a piece of paper from her notebook, holding it out to me with a pen. "I'm going to bag the rest up and also take prints from the front and back door handles, and also your bedroom. While I'm doing that I'd appreciate it if you could compile the list of names that have had contact with each item."

"Okay." I looked down at the paper, my mind a blank as to where to start.

Luke was obviously more on the ball than I was because he took the pen and paper off me, immediately sectioning it off into columns and then looking up at me expectantly. "So, other than me and you, who touched the box? You said that Alex signed for it, so obviously he touched the outer wrapper. Did you show the box to anyone else?"

I smiled gratefully because, yet again, he was being my rock and making everything easier for me. I sat back against the soft cushions of the sofa, and together we drew up a list of anyone that had touched any of the offending items.

Alex came back with the male cop a few minutes later, announcing that the spare key was actually missing. The perpetrator had obviously used it and then kept it after. That knowledge made a little shiver tickle down my spine. Sandy was obviously unhinged at the moment to have taken it this far, who knows how far she would take this and what else she would do. Her having the key meant that she could come back at any time. Maybe this time she'd hurt my brother, parents, or me. I'd never felt so vulnerable and exposed as I did when that thought occurred to me.

When the police lady was told about the key being missing she immediately put in a call to have the locks in our house changed. After they finished dusting the doors for prints and bagging everything up in clear plastic bags, Alex, Luke and I had our fingerprints done to rule them out of whatever they found on the items.

Finally, after almost an hour of going over everything, I was physically and emotionally exhausted.

DI Neeson smiled softly, raising one eyebrow. "Is there somewhere else you two could stay tonight? The locksmith can't come until morning. Maybe it's best if you make alternative arrangements." She finally clicked the lid of her pen so I knew that they had everything they needed. "Stay with relatives perhaps?" she continued.

Luke smiled at me sadly, squeezing my hand gently. "They can both stay at mine."

Alex seemed to stiffen at Luke's words, a frown covered his forehead as he grunted what I assumed was an agreement.

I let out a deep sigh as a wave of gratitude and love crashed over me for Luke. "Thanks," I mumbled, stroking his knuckle with my thumb.

The police lady stood up and shoved her notebook into her pocket. "I'll put in a call to the veterinary clinic and put a rush on the toxicology report for your dog." She shifted on her feet as Alex stood up, holding out a hand for her to shake. "I'll be in touch tomorrow. If you or your parents have any concerns then call me. You have my number. Call me any time if you think of anything else."

I nodded in agreement and Alex showed them out, leaving me with Luke in the lounge. I sighed. My eyes were already getting heavy. The emotions of the day were weighing down on my and all I wanted to do was sleep.

"You want to pack a bag to bring to mine?" Luke asked softly.

I forced a smile and nodded, but in reality I didn't want to. Packing a bag meant going into my room, and I didn't really want to do that. Knowing that someone had been in there was a little unnerving and I didn't really want to have to face that again. I knew I was just being silly, I knew that no one was in the house because Luke and the police had searched every nook and cranny of it, but just the knowledge that someone had been in my room kind of made the space seem a little sinister to me.

I gulped, hoping Luke wouldn't think I was being stupid. "Will you come with me? I don't really want to go in there on my own," I mumbled, glancing towards the stairs as dread settled into the pit of my stomach.

Luke didn't say anything, just stood up and took my hand, pulling me gently to my feet. Sighing deeply, I let him lead me out of the room. Alex was just closing the front door as we stepped into the hallway. "We're gonna go pack an overnight bag of Maisie's stuff; maybe you could do the same with your things?" Luke suggested.

Alex nodded, his shoulders stiff, obviously not liking the fact that he had to accept help from my cheating ex-boyfriend. I had a feeling that if there were any other choice that Alex would insist we take it so that he didn't have to play nice with Luke.

As my weary legs carried me up the stairs, I purposefully kept my mind preoccupied with what I would need to pack so that I wouldn't think about the sound that Chester's dog tag had made when it slid out of the card and hit the floor, or the fact that the intruder had kept the key – possibly with the sole purpose of coming back at a later date.

When I stepped in my room my eyes darted to my bed as if I was expecting the card to still be there or something. My breathing faltered as my heart seemed to stutter in my chest. It was all a little overwhelming. The emotions and fear were all bubbling up to the point where I wasn't sure if I wanted to smash my room into pieces out of anger, or curl into a ball and cry until I had no tears left.

I gulped, my eyes prickling again as my chin wobbled. Luke's hand tightened on mine as his other hand slipped under my chin, pulling gently and forcing my face round to meet his. His soft brown eyes were kind and caring as he looked at me. "Everything will be fine, baby. Let's just grab your things and leave. You'll feel better once you've had some sleep, you're exhausted," he cooed, bending and planting a soft, tender kiss on my forehead.

I closed my eyes and nodded, knowing he was right. I was dead on my feet and just longed for this day to be over with. I forced myself into action, grabbing my pyjamas and a change of clothes for the following day, while Luke went into my bathroom and collected my wash things. We were done within a couple of minutes. Alex was done a little while after, and so we locked the house and headed to Luke's house for the night with Alex following behind in his own car.

As the automatic wrought iron gates of Luke's house rolled open, I hugged myself against the cold night. "Your parents home?" I asked, frowning up at the dark house, not seeing any signs of life there.

He shook his head. "Nope. They're in Germany. They won't be back for another two weeks." He shrugged, not seeming bothered by the fact that he spent weeks and weeks alone with only his housekeeper to keep him company.

He pulled his car up in front of the expansive house and cut the engine. Alex's car rolled up behind us and stopped too. My body was so tired that I didn't really want to move, but I had to. I forced myself out of the car, smiling at Alex's awed expression. He had never been to Luke's house before and was clearly impressed at the sheer size of it.

"This is where you live?" Alex asked as we made our way up to the front door.

"Yeah. It's a little small, huh?" Luke joked, pulling out his keys and letting us into his house.

Alex chuckled quietly. "Not small, more... poky," Alex replied. His eyes went wide as we stepped into the house and he caught his first glimpse of the high ceilings, the expensive wood floors, and the original art on the walls. No doubt I'd had the same shocked and awed expression when I first stepped in here a couple of years ago too. At first this house impressed me, but the more I came here, seeing it empty and devoid of any life and loving memories, the more it felt like just bricks and mortar. I could easily understand why Luke preferred to spend time at my house that was always filled with people, chatter and laughter.

I stifled a huge yawn, looking longingly at the stairs, desperately needing to lie down because my legs were going to give out any minute. Luke noticed my yawn and placed his hand on the small of my back. "You can take my room. I'll sleep in the green room next door, and Alex can have the blue room," he suggested, raising one eyebrow as if asking if that was alright.

"I don't want to kick you out of your room," I muttered. In reality, actually, I did want to kick him out of his room. His room was familiar to me, it was comforting, I needed that comfort and reassurance right now.

He smiled and leant in, planting a kiss on my forehead. "Just go to bed, baby."

I nodded, not having it in me to argue with him about it. My weary legs carried me up the familiar stairs and down the hallway until I got to Luke's bedroom door. Behind me and down the stairs, I could hear Luke showing Alex where the kitchen was obviously giving him a little tour so he could get his bearings.

I didn't hesitate before twisting the handle and stepping into the bedroom. It was just as I remembered it. The pictures of us together were still dotted around every surface, the chair in the corner of his room was still covered in books and magazines, like usual. The deep red throw and plush cushions that I had helped him pick out, still lined his bed. With everything crazy that was going on around me, I loved that the room was practically the same as when I'd last stepped into it. It seemed to be one of the only things that hadn't been changed recently. I loved his room.

After switching the lights so that his bedside lamp was on instead of the ceiling lights, I slipped out of my clothes and pulled on my pyjamas. Exhausted, I climbed into his bed, carefully folding his throw back to the foot of the bed. Settling back into the pillows, my hand hesitated as it reached out to turn off the lamp. I hadn't shut his drapes so it wouldn't be completely pitch black in here, but I still wasn't sure if I wanted to turn off the light. I had a feeling that I would start to imagine things, not nice things, about Chester, and about Sandy sneaking into my house, touching my things, leaving me that horrible card.

I gulped, deciding to leave the light on for the night. I rolled over, seeing a photo frame holding a picture of me and Luke from a school dance last year. The smiles in the photo made my heart ache. The way he was looking at me in the photo was pure adoration, happiness and love. A smile crept onto my face as memories of us dancing, kissing, talking and laughing came back to mind. I missed the way his arms were wrapped around me in that photo.

Sighing, I forced myself to close my eyes and tried to sleep. It was after midnight already and today had felt mind-numbingly long. Unfortunately, I couldn't switch my mind off. Memories started to haunt me. Chester as a puppy, Chester yapping excitedly as he ran up the hallway, him chewing up my socks and chasing a ball. When my thoughts turned to someone sneaking into my house, a shiver ran down my spine that made me clutch the sheets tightly in my fists and grit my teeth. Although I didn't want it to, my overactive imagination was already playing out scenarios of someone, either Sandy or some other deranged person, wanting to hurt me and my family. I started to wonder if the person who had snuck into my house, had maybe stayed, hidden in the shadows while the police were there. Had they followed us to Luke's house? Were they outside watching the house right now, maybe plotting to hurt Luke in some way too?

Before I knew what I was doing, I'd thrown back the sheets and climbed out of the bed. The thoughts were making my head spin, and I needed a distraction from it. Being on my own wasn't helping at all. I'd barely managed to make it an hour on my own before I was slipping out of the room and creeping towards the green bedroom that was right next door.

Luke sat up in bed as I opened the door and stepped into the room he was occupying for the night. A worried expression crossed his face. I didn't speak as I closed the door and made my way across to the bed, slipping in next to him and pulling the sheets up around my shoulders.

His eyes were tight as his hand reached out to caress the side of my face. "You okay?"

I shook my head, fighting against the tears that pooled in the corners of my eyes. "No," I muttered. "Can I sleep in with you tonight?"

A sad smile crossed his face as he laid back down, spreading out his arm so that I could cuddle up against him. I smiled gratefully because he wasn't asking me to explain anything; it was like he understood how I was feeling, deeming words unnecessary.

I snuggled against his side, letting his warmth cover me in a cloak of safety and protectiveness. His familiar smell made my skin prickle as I pressed myself against him, hiding my face in the crook of his neck. His arm wrapped around me, clamping me tightly at his side as I closed my eyes, already feeling sleep pulling at the edges of my system.

I focussed on his breathing and the feel of his fingers as they ran through the back of my hair. Just as sleep was about to take over, he spoke, "Baby, do you really think it was Sandy?" he asked quietly.

I frowned and tilted my head back so that I could look at him. I didn't really know how to answer that question. On the one hand, yes I thought it was her. She was the only one that I could think of with a grudge against me. But something was nagging at me, some part of me that doubted that she would take it that far. Would she seriously be this unhinged just because she wanted my boyfriend? The police had seemed to think my concerns were nothing much to go on either, which didn't help with the certainty I felt earlier in the day. Maybe it was finally time for me to admit that this may be more serious than just a silly little girl who was jealous of the fact that I was dating someone that she wanted. The more I thought about it, the more I started to doubt that it would be her. But somehow it made it easier for me to cope with if I had a face to put with the anger and fear. It made it a little more bearable to think that it was just a jealous schoolgirl that was doing all of these things. A silly, jealous schoolgirl was far less frightening than admitting that a faceless, nameless, *someone* was trying to hurt me, and possibly my family.

I nodded awkwardly, not liking that I was suddenly starting to doubt my instincts. "Yeah."

Luke chewed on his lip, seeming to be choosing his words carefully. "But she wouldn't though, surely," he mumbled. I shrugged, not wanting to talk about it anymore. I was eager for sleep so this day would be over with already. "I was thinking earlier... what about that Zach guy?" Luke asked, raising one eyebrow.

I snorted and chuckled at the absurdity of his suggestion. "Zach?"

He nodded, his nose crinkling with distaste. "Yeah, I don't like that guy. There's something majorly wrong about him," he muttered.

I grinned and rolled my eyes, already knowing what this was about. "You're just being jealous."

"No I'm not," he scoffed, shaking his head in rejection.

I snuggled up against him again, laying my arm across his chest. "Yes you are," I mused.

It was quiet again for a few seconds as he obviously pondered on that thought. Finally, he sighed. "Okay, I'm jealous," he admitted. "I don't like him. I don't like the way he's just waltzed in here and carved out a place in your life. I don't like you spending time with him."

I sighed deeply, knowing he was being honest and that I should appreciate that rather than scolding him for it. "You don't need to be jealous," I assured him truthfully. There was nothing romantic between me and Zach at all.

He frowned, wrapping a lock of my hair around his finger. "This isn't just about me being jealous though, I was being serious. I mean, how much do you even know about him? He came out of nowhere, and everything was fine before he showed up. This all started after he arrived. That can't just be a coincidence," he countered. His brown eyes bore into mine, reasoning with me silently. I gulped, swallowing the lump that was rapidly forming in my throat as Luke carried on speaking. "You told the police that you didn't go to Zach's place until four and that you were in the library before that. Well, what was he doing while you were there? He could have," he swallowed loudly, "poisoned Chester, and then came back to pick you up after. He had time to do that," he explained. "Did he know about your spare key?" he asked, raising an inquisitive eyebrow.

My mind was racing. Luke was right, Zach had said that there was something he needed to do straight after school and that our tutoring would have to wait. What was so important? Was it poisoning my dog? And the key question... he *did* know about the key because I'd used it while I was with him on Friday night. Luke's question was ringing in my ears – how much did I know about Zach? The answer was not much. He was an incredibly mysterious person; he was sometimes a little weird and evasive. And yes, he did have the time and the knowhow to get into my house...

But even as I was thinking about it and reasoning it out, I was already dismissing it. Zach wasn't like that. Sure he was a bit of a badass, but he was a good guy at heart, I was sure of it. I wasn't going to let Luke's jealousy and bias judgement alter my opinion of someone.

"Well, did he know about the key or not?" Luke repeated.

I shrugged, not wanting to add fuel to the fire by confirming his theory. "I don't know," I muttered, hoping that would suffice. Apparently it did. Luke nodded thoughtfully, his arm tightening on me. I decided I needed to quash his suspicions before he got all caught up trying to link Zach to something just because he didn't like the guy. "Look, it's not Zach. I know you don't like him, but he's an alright guy. He wouldn't do that," I said confidently. "You're just assuming things because you don't like him hanging out with me," I teased, hoping to lighten the mood.

He grinned sheepishly. "Maybe," he admitted. "Because of everything going on though, until the police catch whoever is sending you this stuff, I don't want you going anywhere on your own. Make sure you always have me or Alex with you."

"Yes, Dad," I joked, wriggling to get closer.

He chuckled. "I'm not quite that bad."

"Yeah you are," I countered.

He grinned, bending forward and putting his forehead against mine. His breath blew across my lips as he spoke, "Okay, yeah, maybe I am that bad. But it's only because I love you so much."

My heart melted at his words as the hair on the nape of my neck prickled. "I love you too."

His finger brushed across my cheek as his lips touched mine, so softly I could barely feel it. The kiss was so soft and chaste, sweet and tender, yet held a passion that made my heart rate spike. He pulled back and smiled sadly. "Let's get some sleep, huh?"

I nodded in agreement, not knowing what to say. When I was alone with Luke like this, cuddled up in his arms, it seemed so silly that we weren't together. When we were alone everything just seemed so right and perfect. It was a shame that the outside world just made everything more difficult. When other people were around it just served as a reminder that everything wasn't, in fact, as perfect as it seemed when it was just the two of us.

He guided my head back against his neck, and his body relaxed as he pulled the covers up around us.

Just asleep was about to pull me under, I realised that I needed to say something. "Luke?"

"Hmm?"

"Thank you for tonight. You were amazing. I don't know what I would have done without you there," I admitted. He just made everything easier for me. He took over with Chester, and also was incredible with the police questions. He really was my rock tonight.

A soft kiss was planted on the top of my head. "You don't need to thank me, baby. I'll always be here when you need me. Always."

I smiled at his words and drifted off into a dreamless sleep.

chapter nineteen

Without needing to open my eyes I already knew where I was. I was in Luke's arms, his warm breath blew across the top of my head, and his heart beat steadily under my ear. It was nice waking up to this again. At one point I was convinced that I'd wake up like this for the rest of my life, but after the Sandy indiscretion I wasn't so sure. I wanted to forgive and forget, I really did, but there was still a small part of my brain that was fighting it. That small part of my mind seemed to think that breaking my heart was unforgivable, and that I didn't need him. That small part of my brain was wrong though. I *did* need him. Everything that had happened recently, all of it, just served to prove that I needed him. I probably wouldn't have gotten through it all without Luke. I just had to take another chance on him and admit it.

I frowned, squeezing my eyes shut as my thoughts turned to last night. I silently prayed that Chester was doing okay. I hadn't been called by the vets, so I took that as a good sign. After all, they do say that no news is good news. I tried desperately not to think of Sandy, or some other faceless person, sneaking into my house and up to my bedroom. I didn't want to think about it at all because I could already feel the anger and fear gripping my stomach.

I snuggled closer to Luke while he slept, finally opening my eyes and looking up at his handsome face. What I saw made my heart stutter, it always did, and I wasn't sure anything would change that. He looked so peaceful while he slept, his muscles relaxed, his lips slightly parted as he breathed heavily. There was no denying it, I just loved being in Luke's arms.

After a few minutes of my just lying there, enjoying the closeness, his cell phone quietly started playing some bird chirping melody, gradually getting louder. He shifted slightly, gently holding my head to his chest with one hand while he reached out and silenced his phone with the other. He groaned quietly, obviously not pleased with having to wake up.

"Baby?" he crooned in his sleepy voice that never failed to make me smile.

"Mmm?"

"Time for school," he answered, gently running his fingers through my tangled hair.

School. I really didn't want to go to school today. "Actually I might skip school and go and see Chester," I muttered, chewing on my lip with anticipation. Would he be better today? Would his breathing have returned to normal instead of that raspy, shallow panting? Will he still be lying motionless, with just his limbs twitching? All of those thoughts shot through my mind instantly making me almost not want to go because I was frightened of what I could see there.

Luke's forehead creased with a frown. "They don't allow visitors until the afternoons. Plus they said you should call and see how he is first. Look, why don't we give them a call and see what they say, if they say that he's up to visitors then I'll come with you," he suggested, smiling sadly.

I shook my head in rejection. "No. You'll get into trouble for skipping classes, you know you will. Besides, I can just borrow Alex's car or something." Or maybe I could ask Luke to drop me back home and I'd use my mom's car for the day, she wouldn't mind, she wasn't even here anyway.

Luke raised one eyebrow at that. "You're not going on your own. Not after last night. Not until the police have caught whoever sent you that card and those flowers and stuff." His voice was stern, so I knew there was no arguing with him. Luke was just as overprotective of me as the other two males in my life were.

I sighed in defeat. "Fine. I'll call them now and maybe leave it until lunchtime or something so we don't have to skip classes," I reluctantly agreed.

A sad smile pulled at the corners of his lips as he reached out and brushed the back of his knuckles against my cheek. "You okay today? You slept fine. I was expecting nightmares," he said softly.

I shrugged in answer. "I'm okay. Hopefully the police will find some evidence or something and then this will all be over in a few hours." I didn't feel particularly hopeful of that happening though. Somehow I knew, deep down, that whoever had left the card in my room wouldn't have been stupid enough to leave fingerprints. Again my thoughts turned to Sandy. Hopefully the police would question her and she'd slip up and admit it. They hadn't seemed too convinced last night when I mentioned her, but they were duty bound to look into her. Maybe she'd left some DNA in my house or something, a hair, a fingerprint, anything to prove that she was the one behind this hate campaign. Or maybe she'd be bragging about it to her friends today – how she snuck into my house and poisoned my dog. Part of me hoped that it would be that easy, that she wouldn't be able to contain her delight at having gotten one over on me.

"Hopefully," Luke agreed, bending forward and planting a tender kiss on the tip of my nose. "Let's get dressed and then I'll make you some breakfast."

• • •

THANKFULLY, ALEX WAS blissfully unaware that I'd snuck into Luke's bed last night. I knew he wouldn't be happy about it, even if it was innocent. By the time we got to school, I'd already called the veterinary clinic and was told that Chester had had a stable night. There were still monitoring him closely, but agreed Alex and I could visit after school.

It was hard to leave the warmth and comfort of Alex's car as he cut the engine in the parking lot. My eyes wandered over the front of the building, settling on Charlotte and Beth who were sat on the grass outside, chatting animatedly. I hadn't spoken to them since school finished yesterday, so they didn't know about the dramatic twist of events from last night.

Today was going to be hard. Not only was I going to have to rake it all up again and tell my friends what had happened, I was also going to see *her*. I wasn't sure how I was going to handle the last part at all. I was sure it was her, but the police where the ones that needed to do something about it now, I couldn't get involved. How was I going to just ignore her though? I didn't think I could.

Just as I gripped the handle of the car, Alex touched my arm. "Maisie, I know you said you think this is Sandy doing all of this, but you can't know that for sure. You can't just go accusing her in the middle of school, you know that, right?" he said softly.

I nodded slowly. "I know. The police will sort everything. I'm just going to stay out of her way and ignore her completely."

His eyes studied my face, as if he was trying to see if I was telling the truth or if I was going to go in there all guns blazing. "That's good because if you go shouting accusations at her then you'll probably be in trouble for harassment or something." He raised one eyebrow in warning, his stern expression telling me exactly how much he meant his words. "I don't think it's her. For one thing she's too much of an airhead to think through all of this stuff. Just let the police do their jobs and investigate it."

I sighed, rolling my eyes. No one believed me about what a vindictive little witch she really was. She had everyone fooled with her butter-wouldn't-melt-in-the-head-cheerleader's-mouth act. "Fine," I grunted, shoving open the door and swinging my legs out. *Today is going to be hard enough without starting my morning off with a brotherly lecture!*

I marched up to my friends, ignoring the way that Alex and Luke both followed closely behind me. It was almost as if I had gained two bodyguards or something. Both girls smiled as I got up to them. "Morning," Beth chirped before her smile faded and her head cocked to the side. "You okay?"

I sighed. Obviously my frustration was showing on my face clear as day. I sank down next to them, shook my head and then proceeded to tell them everything that had happened last night – leaving out the fact that I had snuck into Luke's bed for comfort. I had a feeling they wouldn't like that too much either, especially Charlotte who still wanted to seek revenge on him for hurting me. By the time I finished telling them about Chester, the card on my bed and the police visit, Charlotte was frowning angrily, and Beth looked a little confused.

"That's sick, who poisons a dog?" Charlotte cried.

"Shh!" I hissed, shaking my head quickly and looking around to make sure no one had heard. I didn't want everyone talking about it today and gossiping about me all over again. I had enough of that because people were still entertained with stories of mine and Luke's break up.

Beth shook her head, her eyes glistening with tears. "But Chester's going to be okay, isn't he?" she squeaked.

I nodded, patting her knee. Beth was an animal lover at the best of times but she adored Chester. "The vet said he was doing well," I confirmed.

Charlotte cleared her throat to get my attention. "You don't still think it was Sandy, do you?"

I groaned and closed my eyes. "Yes. But apparently no one else does," I snapped, pushing myself to my feet. I didn't want another person telling me I was wrong about her, I didn't want to hear it anymore. I turned and marched into the school, leaving my two friends in stunned silence behind me, still sitting on the grass. I was vaguely aware that Alex and Luke were still trudging along behind me. I looked over my shoulder and frowned. "I don't need a babysitter," I barked, waving my hand dismissively.

"I just want to check your locker and make sure there's nothing in there," Alex replied, not seeming bothered by my harsh tone. He was probably used to it, growing up with me and all.

I groaned in frustration because they were treating me like a child. "Well, it doesn't take everyone to look into my locker," I grunted.

Luke frowned and nodded. "I actually need to go and speak to Mrs White about my history essay that I haven't done," he said, wincing a little. "I'll meet you outside your last class of the morning, and then we can get lunch together, okay baby?" I nodded in agreement, knowing that I would have probably eaten with him anyway had all of this not happened, so I couldn't exactly be annoyed with him for wanting to babysit me. I guess I was just going to have to put up with being babied until the police arrested Sandy. Luke smiled and touched the back of my hand softly, his eyes doing that melting my heart thing that they usually do, so I felt a reluctant smile tugging at the corners of my mouth too.

I watched him walk off up the hallway and then I trudged over to my locker. As I approached it, worry started to cloud my mind. Would there be something in there? Some typed note or a flower? Was some reference to Chester going to fall out and land at my feet? Unlike seconds earlier, I was silently grateful that I felt Alex's presence at my side. As I raised a tentative hand I tried not to notice that it was shaking a little. I held my breath as I twisted my locker combination in and slowly pulled open the door. But nothing happened. Nothing fluttered out, nothing was in there that wasn't supposed to be, my locker was just as I left it the day before.

I breathed a sigh of relief and looked over at Alex who was busy peering in, shoving my books to the side and checking every square inch of it. I let him route around in there, obviously satisfying his brotherly instincts while I leant against the locker and looked up the hallway. Zach was walking towards me, a smile on his face as he sauntered through the crowd, not having a clue about what had happened either.

Luke's words suddenly rang in my ears. 'What about that Zach guy? How much do you know about him anyway?' My eyes searched Zach's face, his lazy grin, and his laidback attitude as he walked towards me. *It couldn't be him that was doing this, could it? No. No, Maisie, you're being stupid! Zach wouldn't do that, he's a nice guy.*

"Hey," he greeted, stopping at my side. "All ready for another boring school day?"

I laughed humourlessly and shrugged. I was already wishing today was over with. "I guess."

"Everything okay?" he inquired.

Thankfully Alex had obviously had his fill of checking my locker so he turned and pushed the door to. "All fine here, Maze-Daze. I'm gonna leave you with Zach, and I'll catch you later. You have your cell, right?" Alex asked, patting his pocket, checking that he had his with him. I nodded, knowing that it was in my pocket from this morning when I called the vet's. "Okay good. If you need me today then call me. Luke's eating with you at lunch time, and then you're with Zach this afternoon. I'll meet you here at the end of school and we'll go visit Chester." His arm looped around my shoulder, giving me a quick, reassuring squeeze before he turned and walked up to his friends.

"What was that about?" Zach asked, stepping closer to me and leaning against the locker next to mine as I pulled out the books I would need for my morning classes.

I sighed, wondering how much I should tell him. Probably everything. Alex was obviously entrusting my safety to him too today so he'd need to know why. I opened my mouth to answer, but a flash of brilliant blonde hair caught my attention seconds before a tinkering little laugh filled the air. My breath caught in my throat as I turned in that direction. Sandy was sashaying her way towards me, flanked by two of her little cheerleader minions.

The anger tasted vile in my mouth as I watched her and the way she moved so fluidly, the way each step was like she was gliding in her four inch high heels. I hated every single thing about her. I bit the inside of my cheek, hoping beyond hope that she wouldn't stop near me. My restraint was fading fast. All I wanted to do was scream at her that she was a psychotic bitch and that the police were going to be busting down her door for what she did.

Unfortunately for me, or maybe unfortunately for her, I wasn't quite sure yet, she stopped in front of me. A smug, sarcastic smile stretched across her perfectly painted pink lips. As if expecting a confrontation, the people around us seemed to hush and turn in our direction, eager to watch another showdown. Anger heated my face as she twisted a perfectly straightened lock of her hair around one expertly manicured fingernail.

"Well you look like shit today. Bad night?" she asked, chuckling to herself quietly as her eyes raked over my body with obvious distaste.

"You know I did," I spat. My voice barely even sounded like mine where I was so angry. I tried desperately to hold on to the thought that I wasn't allowed to start a fight and that the police had told me to stay away from her while they investigated everything. But it was hard. My hand was itching to smack the satisfied grin off her face.

She smiled sweetly. "What's up, princess, didn't sleep too well or something?"

She was taunting me, trying to get me to crack. I knew her game plan, but I couldn't help but go along with it. The words burst from my mouth before I could stop them. "Why did you do that? You're sick in the head, Sandy! Who does that to an innocent dog?" The tears were building, making my vision swim as I struggled to maintain my composure.

Her mouth snapped shut as she frowned at me, seeming taken aback by what I'd said. "What dog?" she asked. Her confusion was clear across her face as she said it, and for a second my conviction wavered. *Maybe she really didn't do it like the boys were saying, and I have it wrong...*

But then I remembered seeing her in the school play a couple of months ago. She was a damn good actor. "Don't play stupid, I know it was you!" I hissed, righting myself to my full height as I glared at her confidently.

She took a half step back, shaking her head, her eyes questioning as she looked at me. "What are you talking about?"

"You snuck into my house last night and poisoned my dog." I pointed at her accusingly, jabbing my finger into her chest for emphasis. The spectators gasped, looking between the two of us with wide eyes. I saw Zach stiffen and stand up straighter next to me.

Sandy laughed incredulously, batting my hand away as her eyes turned hard. "I've never even been to your house. Get a grip of yourself." She sneered at me hatefully, looking down her nose at me as if I was something nasty she'd just stepped in.

"It was you! The police will be able to prove it's you somehow. Your fingerprints will be on the meat wrapper or something," I said confidently, lifting my chin confidently.

"Someone gave your dog poisoned meat?" she questioned. Some sort of emotion flicked across her eyes, but it was gone before I could work out what it was. She shook her head incredulously. "You seriously think it was me? You're crazy. *Crazy-Maisie*," she mocked in a sing song voice, smugly looking around at the people that were gathered to watch. When some of them gave a little half chuckle, obviously appreciating her stupid rhyme of my name, I ground my teeth from anger. "I think that should be your new name. Crazy-Maisie. It fits you even more perfectly than Can't-keep-a-boyfriend-Maisie," she teased, pursing her lips as she folded her arms across her chest.

A sob was fighting to break out of my throat but I swallowed it down, not letting it escape. "You just stay the hell away from me and my family, you hear me? Or... or..." I gritted my teeth, still trying to maintain some degree of control over myself.

She raised one perfectly shaped eyebrow as a smile twitched at the corners of her mouth. "Or what?"

I growled in frustration. I'd never wanted to hurt anyone in my life, but for her I was willing to make an exception. Chester's face came to mind as my eyes burned with tears. I knew I should walk away. I knew I shouldn't have even said anything in the first place, and that I should have just left it to the police, but my feet seemed to be rooted to the floor as the last of my restraint slipped. I couldn't stop myself. It was like someone else was controlling my limbs. That smug smile of hers was my undoing. My hand collided with the middle of her chest, hard. She stumbled backwards a couple of steps, gasping from shock, before righting herself and looking up at me with disbelief clear across her face.

"You little slut!" she hissed as she launched herself at me.

One of her hands went straight to the back of my head as she gripped my ponytail, pulling roughly. Rage boiled in the pit of my stomach as every single bad thing that had happened in the last couple of weeks seemed to taunt me. I pushed forward against her, using my bodyweight as leverage. We both slammed into the lockers beside us making a resounding crash that seemed to echo in the hallway. Gasps erupted around us immediately, just like last time as everyone watched with excited eyes. Her hand connected with the side of my head making me grit my teeth so I didn't squeal from the pain of it. My hand shot to the back of my head, gripping her hand that held my hair. My scalp was starting to burn where she was pulling so hard, so I dug my nails into the back of her hand as hard as I could, feeling her blood wet my fingertips as she gasped and jerked her hand away. Taking advantage of her momentary shock, I lifted my hand and slapped her as hard as I could across the face making her head whip to the side.

The name calling started then as she threw herself at me again, wrapping her arms around my waist and tackling me to the floor. Pain coursed up my back as she landed on top of me, straddling me quickly and slapping and scratching at my shoulders as face as I struggled to grip her wrists and fight her off.

The fight probably lasted just over a minute before hands came down and lifted Sandy off me, just like last time. I sat up quickly, preparing myself to go after her again. I wasn't exactly doing well, but I wasn't ready to give up yet. Unfortunately, a pair of hands grabbed me too and lifted me to my feet.

"Let go of me!" Sandy screeched, struggling and wriggling, trying to get out of the arms of the person holding her. In the back of my mind I vaguely recognised that it was Zach that had pulled her off me and now had her in a vice like grip opposite me.

"Calm down, Maisie," a voice I recognised as Alex, hissed in my ear as the hands tightened on my waist.

"I hope your stupid dog died!" Sandy screamed, still thrashing wildly.

Rage built again inside me. "I'll kill you! You stay away from me or I swear you'll regret it!" I shouted, swinging wildly, hoping that one of my blows would come into contact with her face. Unfortunately, she was too far away from me, also swinging blindly in an attempt to reach me. "You spiteful little bitch! I'll kill you!"

"Maisie, stop it!" Alex growled, pulling me back a step or two just as Sandy's foot came up about to hit me in the stomach. "Get her out of here, Zach," Alex ordered.

Zach nodded; turning a red faced Sandy away from me and giving her a little shove up the hallway. "Just go to class," he instructed, stepping to the left so that he blocked her path to me in case she attempted to make a dive for me again. He gripped her upper arm, nodding up the hallway, motioning for her to walk.

The shock of what had just happened and the pain of her blows were only now starting to register. My scalp burned, and my shoulder and back hurt where I had hit the floor.

Sandy then seemed to turn her frustration on Zach. "Get your filthy hands off me! I don't want your scumbag hands on me!" She twisted, slamming the palms of her hands on his chest. Her voice was full of acid as she sneered at him, her eyes hard and calculating. "I know all about you. My cousin goes to the school you used to go to. He told me all about you and what you used to get up to at school. I know all sorts of things that you probably don't want common knowledge here. Now get the hell off me!" Sandy spat, shoving on his chest again.

Zach's eyes widened as he let go of her this time. "You shut your mouth," he growled through his teeth as his hands balled into fists.

"Why? You gonna make me? I'd heard that about you. Fists first, brain second," Sandy taunted, raising one eyebrow in invitation.

Zach's hand tightened even more. "Screw you," he snorted. "You think I give a shit what you've heard? You're some slutty little girl who takes pleasure in seeing others miserable. Maybe it makes your pathetic little life more interesting or something. Just go to class and stop embarrassing yourself." He didn't move as she glared at him for a couple of seconds. Then all at once she huffed and span on her heel, marching up the hallway with her gaggle of followers trotting along behind her.

I stood there with my mouth wide, trying to take in what Sandy had said about Zach in his old school. Just what was it that he didn't want common knowledge here? Zach turned, his eyes meeting mine for a second before he pulled back his shoulders and marched off through the crowd without another word.

Alex's grip loosened on me so I turned and looked up into his angry face. I winced, rubbing at my shoulder as the crowd started to dissipate. He shook his head dejectedly. "Oh yeah, you did so well with the *'I'm going to ignore her completely'* plan that we agreed on," he stated, raising one eyebrow.

I swallowed loudly. "I thought so too," I muttered.

He sighed dramatically. "Looks like my self-defence lessons were a waste of time too, huh? She kicked your ass big time." He shook his head, picking up my schoolbag and holding it out to me. "You fight like a girl."

I laughed despite myself. "I am a girl."

chapter twenty

Everywhere I went, whispering erupted around me. People were speculating about my dog, who it was that had done it, was it Sandy, if it wasn't Sandy then who was it... I heard Zach's name mentioned in connection to it too after what Sandy had said about him in his last school. I even heard a couple of people suggest that I'd poisoned my own dog in order to gain sympathy and blame Sandy because I was jealous that my boyfriend was in love with her. One person even questioned if I even had a dog in the first place. They weren't even bothering to be discreet in their gossiping. It was disgraceful.

At lunchtime, I was surrounded by friends who were all trying their best to cheer me up and keep my mind off the fact that I was centre of attention for the whole school. I'd apologised to Charlotte and Beth for snapping at them earlier in the morning, and of course was forgiven straight away. Luke and Alex were sat with us too, both of them seeming quieter than usual. Although it was nice to be surrounded by people, they did nothing to block out the stares and gossiping of my fellow students. Everything was just too much for me to deal with. Too much noise, too little air, too many bodies around me. I felt a little trapped.

"I'm just going to the bathroom," I muttered, standing up and quickly waving a dismissive hand at Charlotte as she went to stand too. "I'm fine on my own. I'll just be a minute." She nodded, sitting back down again and continuing with her sandwich. Before either of the boys could protest and insist that one of them should come with me, I scurried away from the table and out of the lunchroom. Once I was out of the hustle and bustle of it all I started to feel a little better, but I still craved fresh air and solitude.

Instead of going to the bathroom like I'd said, I headed down the corridor and out of the side door. The warm midday air hit me in the face and made me sigh in contentment as I let the door swing closed behind me. After a few seconds of just standing there I decided to go the full hog and go and sit in the sunshine of the school field. As I rounded the corner, however, I noticed that I wasn't the only one that looked like they wanted fresh air and alone time. Zach was jogging slow, lazy laps around the field. I hadn't seen him all morning. My guess was that he was hiding and keeping out of the way of the gossip after Sandy's comments this morning.

I watched him running for a few minutes before thinking that he was probably hot. There was a vending machine back inside the door where I came out of, so I headed back inside, buying a bottle of water for him. Once I had it I walked out across the field. He noticed me almost immediately, slowing down his pace before changing direction and jogging towards me. The frown on his face told me that he didn't really want to see me as he stopped in front of me.

"Hey," I greeted, forcing cheerfulness to make up for the fact that he was scowling and kicking at the grass with his foot.

"Hey," he grunted in response.

I held out the bottle. "Bought you this."

His brows rose in apparent surprise as he hesitantly took the bottle out of my hand. "Yeah? Thanks."

I smiled, nodding at the track. "Why are you out here on your own? You could have eaten with me, you know."

He sighed deeply, shrugging. "Figured you might not want to speak to me much today. You've already got enough attention on you without fraternising with a scumbag." His tone was sad as he spoke and I instantly hated Sandy just that little bit more.

I snorted at his explanation. "Don't be silly. Besides, people are gossiping about me whether I fraternise with you or not, so it makes no difference if I talk to a scumbag," I joked, nudging his arm with mine. He laughed quietly, his eyes coming up to meet mine as he chugged down some of the water.

"I'm sorry to hear about your dog. Is he okay?" he asked, cocking his head to the side as he looked at me quizzically.

I nodded, feeling a little pang in my heart at the mention of Chester. "He's okay. He's at the animal hospital right now," I replied. "They said we can probably take him home tomorrow."

"That's good. Glad he's okay, he's cute," he muttered. "So when did all this happen then?"

I sighed and sat down, crossing my legs and picking at the grass. "Last night. When you dropped me home from tutoring I found him in the garden. Someone had fed him some meat, and he was barely breathing." My voice broke as the memories of it surfaced again.

Zach groaned and sat down next to me, placing his hand on my knee and squeezing supportively. "I'm sorry. I should have come in with you and made sure everything was alright before I left you. I shouldn't have just dropped you outside your house when I knew you were gonna be going in to an empty house," he said, shaking his head and frowning.

I forced a smile and used the sleeve of my sweater to dry the tear that leaked out. "It's fine, you weren't to know that someone had snuck into my house and poisoned my dog." I tried to keep my tone light, but a sob made my voice hitch in the middle of my sentence.

"I guess. I still feel like crap about it though. I'm sorry," he muttered. His gaze met mine. I could see little worry lines in between his eyebrows as he seemed to be silently scolding himself for not walking me in to my house last night.

His hand came up, touching my cheek, just at the side of my nose. I winced and cringed away from his hand as a small stinging pain followed his touch. "Looks like you got a couple of scratches when you were fighting," he muttered, letting his hand drop back down to my knee again.

I nodded, shrugging dismissively, not wanting to talk about me getting into a fight in the middle of the hallway. "Yeah, Alex told me off because I fought like a girl and let her kick my ass," I replied.

He chuckled. "You are a girl."

A grin crept onto my face. "That's exactly what I said."

He nodded but didn't answer. He just looked at me, searching my face for something, but I didn't know what. His eyes were so intense as he looked at me that I had to look away from them because it felt like he was trying to read all of my secrets. We lapsed into silence. Zach's thumb stroked the side of my knee in small circles as I played with a blade of grass. It was nice actually, calming even. After everything that had happened in the last couple of days, it was nice just to sit there quietly in the sun and not feel the need to make conversation.

Unfortunately, all good things have to come to an end. The ringing of my phone made us both jump and Zach to snatch his hand back into his lap as he turned his head and looked out over the field. I sighed and pulled out my phone, expecting it to be one of my friends or Alex, asking where I was.

Instead, the name DI Neeson flashed on my screen. I frowned at her name, wondering what this was going to be about. For some reason my mind flicked to Sandy. Did she somehow know that I'd been in a fight with her and now she was calling to scold me for it? I squirmed uncomfortably as I answered the call.

DI Neeson's voice greeted me. "Good afternoon, Miss Preston. I just wanted to let you know that the locksmith completed the work on your house this morning."

"Oh, oh right. That's good," I muttered, feeling my shoulders relax slightly.

"I have your new keys. What time will you be home? I can meet you there," she offered helpfully.

"Um, I'm not sure. Alex and I are going to go and visit Chester straight after school. So maybe four thirty?" I replied, thinking everything through. That would give us almost an hour with Chester which should be plenty of time because apparently we weren't allowed to take him home today anyway.

"Four thirty is good for me. I'll see you at your house then." The line went dead before I could even ask if they had found anything or had progressed with the investigation. Thankfully she hadn't mentioned my altercation with the blonde witch.

Pushing my cell phone back into my pocket, I stood up. I needed to get back before everyone really did start calling me and asking where I was. "I should go back inside. I only said I was going to the bathroom." Zach looked up at me and nodded. "I'm going to have to cancel tutoring for tonight. I'm going to see Chester straight after school."

A grin crossed Zach's face as he nodded. "Tutoring's cancelled? Whatever will I do with myself?" he joked.

"Jump over stuff no doubt," I replied, rolling my eyes playfully.

His deep laugh filled the air as he nodded in agreement. "Probably. Thanks for the water," he said, holding up the now empty bottle.

"No problem. Are you coming in with me?" I asked, nodding back to the building. "Have you eaten?"

He pushed himself up in one fluid motion and shook his head. "I'm just gonna run some more. I get kind of antsy when I get stressed. Sometimes running helps with it, and I can keep myself focussed," he replied, twisting the bottle around in his hands before tossing it towards the trashcan that was off to my right.

"Hmm, maybe I should take up running then," I joked.

A smirk broke out across his face as his eyes twinkled with mischief. "You could probably do with getting a little fitter from what I remember of your running skills."

I gasped and slapped his shoulder, chuckling because I knew he was talking about the night we met and how I had drunkenly ran away from Luke's broken windshield. "Shut it, you," I giggled, which made him laugh too. "Go back to your running and I'll see you in class this afternoon."

"See ya, little rebel," he called as he turned and jogged off towards the open field again.

I chuckled, shaking my head in amusement before turning back to face the firing squad, knowing I was going to be in trouble for sneaking off like I had.

• • •

THE VISIT TO SEE Chester after school left my throat hoarse, my eyes stinging and my heart aching. Although he was a lot better than last time I saw him, he was still weak and just laying around. His little tail wagging as we walked in was the only thing that made him seem more like his old self. The vet had said that he was still on medication and that he was extremely lucky. They were keeping him in for another night as a precaution, but that we could pick him up after school the following day. Leaving him in there had almost broken my heart, but he was better off with the experts for now.

Alex hadn't really said much since we arrived at the animal hospital. When he was upset he was more the strong, silent type; he would be hurting inside and not showing it no doubt. I sat in the car on the way home, chewing on my lip, silently wondering if he blamed me like I blamed myself. After all, the person hurt Chester because of me. It *was* my fault he almost died. The guilt of that was slowly eating me up inside.

As we pulled up into our driveway, the door opened on the brown Sedan that was parked on the street outside our house. DI Neeson smiled over at us, taking off her sunglasses and tossing them into the car. "Good afternoon," she greeted warmly as I climbed out and crossed the front yard to her car.

"Hi. Have you been waiting long?" I asked, nodding at the newspaper that was strewn across her front seat where she'd obviously been sat for a while.

She waved her hand dismissively. "Not long." She nodded towards the house, digging in her pocket and bringing out three bunches of keys. "Let's go inside and put the kettle on, I have some information for you."

Alex stiffened, his hand going up to grip my shoulder supportively. "Do you know who this guy is? Have you arrested him?"

DI Neeson shook her head in rejection, waving her hand towards the house again. "Let's talk inside."

I gulped. For some reason this seemed like it was going to be bad news. I lagged behind as the police lady and Alex both headed to the house, using the new keys to open the door. I hesitated at the door, for some reason not wanting to go in. The house was too quiet. After seeing Chester in the veterinary hospital, still so weak, I couldn't help but miss him greeting me at the door.

Alex and DI Neeson headed straight to the kitchen, so I stopped in the hallway, steeling myself for whatever I was going to hear. Was she going to confirm that it was Sandy? Was she going to tell me that they were arresting her right now and that it was all over? Or was that grim expression on her face for some other reason?

"Maisie, want coffee?" Alex shouted from the kitchen.

I gulped, knowing I needed to get it over with. Taking a couple of deep breaths, I forced myself to move again and walked into the kitchen, seeing them both standing there. "Yeah, thanks." I nodded, smiling gratefully. I took a lot of sugar in my coffee so the boost would probably be a good thing right now.

DI Neeson looked between the two of us slowly. "I've had your dog's toxicology reports come through today. It has confirmed their suspicions that Chester had ingested rat poison."

I groaned and closed my eyes, nodding slowly. In a way, that was a good thing. It meant that their course of treatment that they'd started based on it being rat poison had been the right course of action. Now we just had to hope that he got better and suffered no ill effects from it as a result.

"I've been to the clinic today, and apparently the type that he ingested is the most common brand, a powder, bought at any garden centre or supermarket. So that leaves us with nothing new to go on really. Lab tests on the grease proof paper that we found in your yard show that it contained some sort of raw beef and also showed traces of the same substance. From that we can conclude that this definitely wasn't just an accident and that your dog somehow found the poison himself. Someone definitely put it on the meat before feeding it to him."

I tightened my jaw as a little whimper left my lips. I didn't want to think about it, about someone sprinkling it on the meat and poor little unsuspecting Chester eating it.

"So, do you have leads and stuff? Do you know who this person is?" I asked, echoing Alex's words from earlier, but purposefully not saying the word 'guy' because I was convinced it was a girl that was behind it all.

DI Neeson shook her head, frowning disappointedly. "At this time we don't have any extra evidence. The tech guys in our recognition department are still running the prints that we lifted from your bedroom door so we're waiting for those to come back. Our first priority was the prints that we lifted from the items we collected from your house. Those are being analysed, but it appears that some of them belonged to you two and Mr Hannigan. There are also a couple of other prints on the items from the box, but from the list you gave me of who had touched what, it's a strong possibility that the prints we found belong to your two friends. I've dispatched officers to their houses to obtain prints from them so that we can rule them out, but the sizes of the prints we found are most likely female."

I frowned. *So they have nothing to go on at all?* "What about Sandy, did you look into her?" I asked.

DI Neeson nodded. "I've just come back from meeting with Miss Watson. She was with her mother from the end of school until the time when she went to bed. They went shopping and then went for dinner. Their story checks out. I'm sorry, Maisie, I know you thought it was her, but it looks like you were wrong."

That news felt like someone had punched me in the gut. It really wasn't Sandy? I was so sure, so absolutely sure that it was her. A cold shiver trickled down my spine like ice water. Somehow, not knowing who was doing this, not having a face to the person, made it seem even worse. A stranger had stolen the key to my house and poisoned my dog; a stranger had gotten my phone number and had sent me those notes and flowers. It was definitely easier when I had a face to the person. Now, it could have been anyone, anyone at all. I gulped as Luke's words about Zach came back to mind again. I tried to dismiss it quickly, assuring myself that Zach was a nice guy, but the hair on my arms seemed to stand up as I realised that I actually knew nothing about him at all. Sandy had said today that she knew things about him that he wouldn't want common knowledge. What exactly was that about?

Alex frowned thoughtfully. "What about the phone calls she was getting? Surely you can trace the number?"

DI Neeson leant back against the counter, smiling sadly. "We've tried, but it appears that the calls are from an unregistered number, it's untraceable. We know what network the calls are coming from, but the number is just a throw away sim, pay as you talk, no contract."

Alex's frown deepened. "Have you tried calling it? Give me the number, I'll call him," he snapped.

DI Neeson shook her head, seeming amused by Alex's outburst. "We've tried calling it, each time it's been switched off."

"Well can't you find the location from the signal of the phone or something? I've seen enough episodes of 24 to know they can pinpoint the location of a cell phone signal down to a few meters," he stated, folding his arms defensively.

DI Neeson chuckled quietly. "I'm afraid that we don't have access to Jack Bauer's technology," she replied, her eyes twinkling with amusement. "Though it would make my job a lot easier if we did."

"So you have nothing?" Alex asked, slamming the kitchen drawer and frowning angrily.

DI Neeson didn't even flinch at my brother's anger. "At this time we're still waiting for the Intel. Once we have the partial print recognition reports then we'll have more to go on. We're looking into the paper that the notes were written on, and also looking into the type of typewriter that was used. Hopefully there will be something there. If not then it'll only be a matter of time before we catch the perpetrator. Don't worry, we *will* catch them," she replied, her voice confident. I sighed and nodded, taking the cup that Alex offered to me. DI Neeson's attention turned back to me then as one of her eyebrows rose. "Miss Watson said there was an altercation at school with you today. Care to tell me about that?"

Not really. "Um," I shifted on my feet, dropping my eyes to the floor.

"I told you to leave the investigation to us, not start fights in the middle of school," she said, her voice clearly disapproving.

"She provoked me," I huffed defensively.

DI Neeson cleared her throat. "Maisie, I know you thought it was her that hurt your dog, but she was elsewhere when the incident happened. You have no need to carry around these ill feelings towards her."

I scoffed at her words. *No need to carry around ill feelings for her, apart from the fact that she slept with my boyfriend!*

"Please just leave the investigation to us," she requested. Her tone held a warning so I nodded in acknowledgement. I smiled gratefully at Alex as he skilfully steered the conversation away from Sandy and asked more questions about the investigation.

DI Neeson stayed just long enough to drink her coffee, warn me against getting into another argument with Sandy, and question me again about anyone else that would have a grudge against me. She seemed disappointed when I said I couldn't think of anyone. As she left she promised to be in touch as soon as she had any leads, but for now I was to ensure I contacted her if anything strange or untoward happened.

After she left I snuck up to my room, knowing that Alex was about to call our parents and tell them about the things that had happened and Chester. I didn't really want to be there while he explained everything so I left him to it and went to make a start on my homework assignments.

Stepping into my room alone for the first time since I had found the card was a little hard. The room felt cold and a little alien as I looked around it slowly, checking that nothing was out of place. I wrapped my arms around my torso, hugging myself to try and gain some sort of comfort, but it was no use. A feeling of loneliness settled over me and I suddenly longed for Luke to be here with me. To wrap his arms around me, to pull me onto his lap and rock me like a child. I missed him so much it was almost scary.

Huffing out a big breath, I forced myself to get a grip of this worry and fear before it ate me up. I dropped my schoolbag down onto the bed and flopped down next to it, pulling out the first book that I came across and started to make a start on my work in a bid to keep my mind off everything.

Half an hour later there was a knock at my door. Alex let himself in, a phone clamped between his ear and his shoulder as he put down a sandwich and a glass of apple juice. "Yeah, she's here right now," he said into the phone.

My stomach dropped as I shook my head quickly, somehow knowing that it was one of my parents and they would want to talk about everything again. Would they blame me for Chester too?

"Yeah, see you then," Alex stated before pulling the phone away from his ear and holding it out to me. "Dad for you."

Groaning inwardly, I took the phone and waited for my brother to leave before I put the phone to my ear. "Hi." I winced, waiting for the frantic scolding because we hadn't called them earlier.

"Hi, sweetheart. How are you holding up?" Dad asked. The familiar sound of his voice made my eyes prickle with tears. I didn't realise until now just how much I missed him and my mom being here.

"I'm fine," I lied.

"Alex told me what's been happening. I'm not going to get into the whole *'you should have told me as soon as everything started happening'* thing, because I don't think that's going to help the situation at all."

I smiled gratefully and looked up at my ceiling, willing my tears not to fall. I was already sick of crying over this. "Thanks, I appreciate that," I muttered.

"I need you to promise to be careful. Don't go to places on your own, take Alex or Luke with you, alright?"

Luke? So he's forgiving Luke now? "I will," I promised, nodding. Now that I knew it wasn't Sandy the seriousness of the situation weighed down on me. It could have just as easily been me or Alex that had been poisoned, if the person had sprinkled that rat poison onto something in the fridge then maybe we would have unknowingly eaten it. It wasn't as if they didn't have access to the house and our food, they'd let themselves into my house for goodness sake. I knew I needed to be careful.

"How's Grandad?" I asked, wanting to change the subject.

"He's... he's okay," Dad answered, not seeming too sure about it.

A lump formed in my throat. "No he's not."

Dad sighed deeply, his breath crackling down the line. "He's in a bad way, but he'll be fine. He's through the worst of it now," he assured me. "So, I'd better go and tell Mom everything that's been going on. I'll be home tomorrow when you get home from school though so I'll see you then."

I closed my eyes; the nerves in my stomach seemed to settle as I thought about getting one of my dad's hugs. They always made everything seem better. "You don't have to come home. Stay with Grandad," I protested, trying to make my voice sound like I wasn't desperate for him to come home. "We're fine here. You don't need to come back."

"Yeah I do, sweetheart. No arguing, I'm coming home. End of conversation."

I smiled to myself at the finality of his tone. "Okay. I'll see you tomorrow."

"Love you." His words made a warm fuzzy feeling settle over me. There was no denying I was a daddy's girl.

"Love you too, Dad."

After speaking to my dad and the knowledge that he was coming home tomorrow kind of made my mind settle a little and the worry recede marginally. Finally, after another hour of working on my assignments, I drifted to sleep listening to the rhythmic sounds of Alex hitting the punch bag down the garage below my bedroom.

• • •

WHEN MY ALARM buzzed next to my bed in the morning I groaned loudly. I'd had a restless night sleep, my dreams plagued with a faceless person chasing me, every single time I'd ran into a room only to find it filled with lilies. Each time I'd woken, startled and sweating, only to go back to sleep and have the same dream over again. My whole body now ached from exhaustion. I really didn't need another day at school today, especially if it was going to be a day like yesterday where everyone was whispering about me. And on top of that I had to face Sandy, now knowing that it wasn't her that was sending me all of those nasty things. Did I have to apologise to her today for accusing her? Deep down I knew I should, but the thought of saying sorry to that boyfriend stealing hoe almost made me sick to my stomach.

After laying there for as long as I could without making myself and Alex late, I finally threw off the bed covers and headed for a quick shower. Alex was already dressed and ready by the time I made my way downstairs. He smiled sympathetically, silently pushing an empty bowl and a box of cereal towards me. I waved it off, turning my nose up at the thought of eating. My appetite was as non-existent as my will to apologise to Sandy.

"I'm not hungry. Shall we just go?" I mumbled tiredly.

"Yeah if you want. By the way, I called the animal hospital already and the guy said that Chester can definitely be collected today." He slid his cell phone into his jeans pocket and picked up his keys.

I smiled at the news. At least one thing was going well today then. "Is he better today?"

Alex nodded, biting off another piece of the banana he was holding. "Apparently he's good this morning. I could hear him barking in the background," he answered.

"That's great news." I blew out a breath, letting out some of the stress that was pent up inside me. At least that was one less thing for me to worry about.

On the way to school Alex seemed like he was doing everything to try and keep my mind off the police and the stalker I seemed to have gained. He sung badly to the music, told terrible jokes and was generally just his usual goofy self. It felt nice to just be normal after everything that had gone on recently.

By the time we pulled into the parking lot though, the normality seemed to evaporate immediately. I frowned as I looked around. People were crowding outside, huddled together in groups; some were hugging and seemed to be crying. Alex could barely get his car rough the gates of the parking lot because everyone was standing around.

"What the hell's this?" Alex muttered, blasting his horn to get a couple of freshmen to move out of his way so he could pull in.

"No idea," I muttered, shaking my head in confusion. People were normally inside by now, chatting in the hallways before classes, but instead it seemed that half of the school was standing or sitting in the parking lot. Across the sea of faces, some looked rather excitable, some were just standing there silently, their faces pale, but some were clutching Kleenex, hugging and shaking their heads in apparent horror.

As we both got out of the car some people turned to look at us. A hushed silence settled over the people closest to us as I swung my bag up onto my shoulder and weaved through the crowd with Alex at my side. Then, just like yesterday, the excited whispering started as I walked past. I rolled my eyes; silently wishing the ground would open up and swallow me. I fought the urge to turn and run back to the car just because people were turning to stare at me as I walked up to where I was hoping my friends would be waiting for me.

Charlotte and Beth were standing in the same place as yesterday. "Hey. What's everyone standing around for?" I asked, stepping to their sides and waving my hand around at the crowd.

Charlotte's mouth dropped open with an audible pop. "You haven't heard?" she gasped. I raised one eyebrow in question, waiting for her to continue. "It's been all over the news this morning," she said, her hand reaching out and clutching at my forearm.

My confusion built. "What's been on the news?" Alex interjected, looking at Charlotte quizzically, obviously as lost as I was. News wasn't something that usually graced our TV in the morning; Alex usually opted for sports channel or SpongeBob SquarePants.

Charlotte's grip tightened on my arm as her eyes widened even more. "It's Sandy. She was murdered last night."

chapter twenty-one

My breath seemed to catch in my throat, forming a lump that I had to swallow down before it choked me. *Murdered. Sandy has been murdered? How, who, why, when?* All of those questions sprang to my mind as I stood there, gaping at Charlotte like an idiot.

"What the actual fuck? Is that a joke?" Alex gasped, shaking his head in disbelief.

Charlotte's grip tightened to the point of pain on my arm as she shook her head. "No, seriously. It's been all over the news. The cops arrived a little while ago and are in speaking with Principal Bennett right now," she said, nodding off to my right.

I gulped and looked in that direction, indeed seeing two squad cars parked there. They were partially obscured by the swarm of students converging around. A lot of people were leaning down, trying to get a look into the cars, probably to satisfy some sort of sick, morbid intrigue.

"I can't believe this," I muttered, shaking my head in disbelief.

"Have they arrested the person that did it?" Alex asked Charlotte.

She shrugged. "Don't think so. The news said that she'd been stabbed and that she was found by a passer-by. She was stabbed and left in an alleyway. They're ruling out a mugging because she still had her purse and cell phone," Charlotte answered.

Even though I hated her, I still felt a pang of sorrow that she'd died. No one deserved that, and now her parents were going to have to deal with the loss of a child. "That's so sad," I croaked. "Her poor parents." I imagined my parents and what they would be like if I'd been killed, they'd be in pieces. I couldn't bear to think about what Sandy's parents would be going through at this moment. I looked around again, seeing the cheerleaders, Sandy's minions, all standing in a group off to the side. They were upset and most of them had even cried off their make-up, leaving black trails down their cheeks.

"I heard that the police are going to be interviewing her friends at school today so that they can try and ascertain who saw her last and piece together her last moments," Beth chimed in.

I looked at her curiously. "How do you know that?"

She smiled guiltily. "I was talking to the receptionist earlier. You know how she likes to gossip. She was complaining that she had to clear Principal Bennett's schedule so she could sit in on the meetings today."

Gossipy receptionist, she never had been able to keep her opinions to herself. As we stood there talking about Sandy, a hand touched my arm. "Baby, I need to talk to you." I turned looked up into Luke's face. "It's important, can we talk right now?"

I nodded, bemused as to what this would be about. He looked a little concerned as he glanced around before nodding at the front doors of the school, shifting awkwardly on his feet. His hand closed over mine, leading me in that direction before I even had a chance to ask him what was so urgent. Once we got into the hallway I noticed that the place was deserted. It seemed that the entire student body was outside still, talking about the events of last night. Luke pulled open the door to the old geology classroom that was now out of use. Once we were in the classroom he closed the door tightly behind me before taking my face in his hands. His eyes were blazing anguish as he looked down at me.

"Where were you last night?" he asked.

I frowned, taken aback by his question. "At home, why?"

He gulped, bending so that our faces were on the same level. "With Alex? Did he see you there?"

What the heck is this about! "Of course he saw me. What on earth are you asking that for?" I chuckled, pulling my face out of his hands, studying his face to see if he had actually gone insane.

"Maisie, Sandy was murdered last night. You remember the last thing you said to her yesterday morning?" he asked. I thought back but couldn't really remember. We were fighting and screaming at each other, I could have said anything in the heat of the moment. "You said you'd kill her," Luke said when I didn't speak.

My mouth popped open in shock. "What the... I didn't mean it! Jeez, are you asking me if it was me? Are you crazy?" I gasped, suddenly getting angry because maybe he didn't know me at all. I glowered at him and shoved on his chest, trying to get him away from me, but he didn't budge.

"No! Christ! I was just checking to make sure you had an alibi for last night.

If someone tells the police that you said that then they're going to have to look into it, they won't be able to dismiss it as an offhand comment, they'll have to look into it," he explained, wrapping his arm around my waist and holding me in place as his words sank in.

A cold shiver worked over my body giving me goosebumps. I chaffed my hand on my arm, trying to warm myself up as all of a sudden the temperature in the room seemed to plummet. "I didn't! I swear I didn't. They won't think it's me, surely," I muttered, shaking my head in disbelief.

"Baby, I know you wouldn't have, I don't think that," Luke assured me, touching my cheek lightly. "You were at home with Alex, you spent the night with him downstairs, right?" he checked.

I chewed on my lip. I hadn't really seen Alex that much last night. I'd stayed up in my room all night long, the only time I saw him was when he brought me the sandwich and phone. He'd gone into the garage after that, working out with the punch bag, I'd heard the familiar sounds of it vibrating as he hit it. "I didn't really see him much. I was in my room studying, and he was working out in the garage," I answered.

Luke closed his eyes, his arm tightening on my waist. "So the police could argue that you could have left the house without Alex knowing."

"I hardly think they're going to suggest that!" I scoffed, waving my hand dismissively.

"But they could. And you would have no way of proving otherwise, do you?" he inquired.

"Well… no," I replied, looking away from his worry filled eyes. "But they won't ask that anyway. If they ask anything at all it'll be where I was, and I was at home, end of conversation."

"I'll give you an alibi just in case," he muttered, pulling me against his chest. "Tell people that I snuck into your house like we used to sometimes. Say that Alex didn't even know I was there. We could say that I came over about eight and we snuck straight up to your room, and I left at about six o'clock before Alex even woke up."

I snorted in disbelief. "Luke, I'm not lying. Besides, there's no point because they won't think it's me anyway," I muttered. But in the back of my mind his words were making sense. DI Neeson knew that I had a problem with Sandy; she knew that I'd accused her of poisoning Chester and that we had a fight at school. A couple of quick questions to some of the students would confirm that I'd uttered those words, and then she'd be duty bound to treat me as a suspect. I shivered. Was Luke right, would they view my alibi as weak and question if I could have gotten out of the house without my brother noticing? Was that why people stopped talking as I walked past them earlier and then whispered behind my back? Were people assuming that it was me because I'd said the wrong thing in the heat of the moment?

I pulled back and looked up at Luke. He looked extremely worried as he cupped my face in his hands and planted a soft kiss on my forehead. "I don't want to see you in trouble," he whispered, begging me with his eyes.

I shook my head quickly, pushing off his hands. "Thank you for the offer, that's really sweet of you, but honestly I'll be fine. There's no need to worry. They won't think it's me." I forced a smile.

He nodded despondently, letting his arms drop down to his sides. "Yeah, you're probably right. But if you change your mind then I'm happy to say I was with you all night last night."

Gratitude for him being so sweet, made me go up on tiptoes and press my lips to the corner of his mouth, kissing gently. His body stiffened as he moaned quietly in the back of his throat. His breath blew down my neck and I didn't want to move, I just wanted to stay in this empty classroom with him forever.

"Thank you. But honestly, you're being silly," I assured him, forcing myself to step back away from his body. When I was that close to Luke my resolve faded and all I wanted was to turn back time and have him back again, for him to be mine and no one else's.

His gaze slid over my face as he reached out and touched the spot just below my right eye. "You look tired, baby," he whispered, frowning. I nodded in confirmation and turned my face into his hand more, closing my eyes at the softness and warmth of it pressed against my cheek. "Has anything else happened? More calls, anything? Have the police said anything else?" he asked.

I reached up and took his hand, interlacing my fingers with his. I needed to get out of this classroom and start moving around because I literally felt like a zombie just going through the motions right now. "No, no news and nothing new. Don't stress," I pleaded, seeing how concerned he was about me.

He blew out a big breath and ran his free hand through his hair, making it stick up everywhere. "Don't stress? Someone wants to hurt my girlfriend, and you think I'm not going to stress?"

"I'm not your girlfriend." The words left my lips before I could stop them.

His face fell; his pain filled expression was enough to make my heart ache. "I know that. Fuck. Don't you think I don't know that? I think about it every second of every day. You're not the only one having trouble sleeping you know," he retorted. His grip loosened on mine, attempting to drop my hand but I held fast not wanting to break the connection.

"Luke, we're trying to be friends," I muttered, shaking my head, knowing that it was useless. No matter how many times I said the word 'friends' I knew it would never apply to us. We would always be more than friends, I just had to find it in my heart to let his indiscretion go and try to move on.

He sighed. "Friends, yeah, I remember."

I opened my mouth to speak, but nothing came out. I had no clue what to say. Luckily for me the bell sounded above my head, signalling a five minute warning for the start of first lesson. "We'd better get ready for class," I mumbled, hating the sad expression on his face. He nodded and reached for the door, yanking it open and waving for me to go through first.

I stopped abruptly as we stepped into the hallway. It seemed as though everyone that was outside had entered all at once, so the hallway was rammed with people hurriedly trying to get their books from their lockers before classes started. People turned to look at me as I took a tentative step into the crowd. I frowned, looking down at the floor, my face flaming with both embarrassment and anger as the gossiping started.

"Do you really think it was her?"

"She said she was going to."

"I bet they class it as a crime of passion."

"Don't they say that nine out of ten victims know their murderer?"

"Who would have thought that someone so quiet could do something like that. It's sick."

I gritted my teeth, glaring the nearest person to me who was watching me with a mixture of fascination and fear. The girl looked away quickly, giggling with her friends that I'd just given her a death glare.

"Stabbed repeatedly apparently. Blood everywhere. A friend of my mom's was the one that found her, said she looked like she'd been gutted," a freshman muttered to his friend off to one side. Vomit rose in my throat as images of Sandy strewn out in some dark alleyway with knife wounds swam before my eyes.

"I spoke to Maisie once, she seemed nice, I didn't every think that she would go crazy like this."

Tears of indignation stung my eyes as I looked over my shoulder at Luke. I begged him silently with my eyes to say something, to stop them talking about me like that. They'd listen to him, he was popular and everyone hung on his every word because of that.

He lifted his chin, looking out over the people that were standing around watching us carefully. "What the hell are you all thinking it's Maisie for? It wasn't her so just stop with the gossip and go to class!" he ordered. No one moved so he scowled around at the crowd. "She was with me last night anyway, so go find some other innocent person to pin it on because you're all behaving like a bunch of moronic children right now."

I gulped, trying not to act surprised at his revelations. I'd just told him that I didn't want to lie and say he was with me, but with everyone looking at me like that, accusing me with their eyes, I was actually immensely grateful that he had lied for me. At least now people would have to look elsewhere for who had done it. Hopefully that would quash the ridiculous accusations towards me before it reached the police officers, and I was incorrectly arrested for something I hadn't done.

Luke threw his arm around my shoulder, using his other arm to push his way through the crowd towards my locker. I pressed myself against him, gripping his shirt tightly in my fist as the whispering continued - but now it was different, people were asking who it was if it wasn't me, they were speculating that it could have been anyone. By the time I had my books and Luke had weaved us through to where my first class was, peoples' suggestions were getting wilder and wilder, I even heard one guy joke that maybe Sandy was a whore and was murdered by her pimp.

Luke stopped outside my classroom, looking at me apologetically. "I'm sorry I said that. I know we just agreed that we wouldn't, but I couldn't just let people look at you like that. I'm sorry," he whispered, wincing as if he was waiting for me to scold him.

"Thank you," I whispered, pressing my face into the side of his neck. His smell filled my lungs and my knees went a little weak, probably from the lack of food and the shock of what I'd heard.

He chuckled making the sound vibrate through his chest. His hand closed around my ponytail, pulling gently but firmly, forcing my head to tilt up. "There was me thinking I was going to get a mouthful of those awesome cuss words," he teased, grinning down at me wickedly.

I smiled despite the fact that inside I felt like crying. "Some other time, I'm too exhausted to cuss you out today."

"See you at lunch," he said as the second bell went, signalling he was now late for his class which was half way around the building from here. I nodded, waving a goodbye as he turned and ran off. I took a few deep breaths, steeling myself because I knew I was going to see people now and had no Luke to lean on and hide behind.

What I'd forgotten though when I'd hardened myself against what I was going to encounter in my first class, was that Sandy shared this class with me.

As I pushed the door open I saw that most people were sitting down already, the teacher was sat at her desk, seeming a little bemused as to what to do. Sandy's empty desk caught my attention immediately. A cold shiver seemed to tickle down my spine as I hunched my shoulders, pulling the strap of my backpack further up as if I could somehow hide behind the thin strip of nylon. The room had an eerie silence, so a few people looked up at me as I stepped into the room. Thankfully I wasn't the only one late though as a couple of others breezed in behind me. Twenty-five sets of eyes seemed to pierce into me as I shuffled into the desk that I usually occupied in this class. I dropped my gaze to the table, shifting uncomfortably in my seat praying for the end of the day already.

Fortunately for me, one of Sandy's close friends had this class too so she took the attention off me as soon as she walked in the door. She came in, still crying - not the quiet sobbing kind, but full on wailing, snot on the face, red puffy eyes crying. The teacher jumped up from her seat, rushing over and immediately wrapping a supportive arm around Rochelle's shoulder.

"I'm g-going to m-miss her s-so much!" Rochelle croaked, blowing her nose loudly on a hankie that Mrs Walters seemed to materialise out of thin air. "She was s-so p-perfect, and now she's g-gone! Who would d-do such a horrible th-thing?"

I closed my eyes, resting my head down on my arms trying not to let my imagination run wild. If this was what Sandy's friends were like, what on earth must her parents be like today? How were they coping? I didn't want to think about it, but I couldn't stop myself. Even though I never liked the girl, my eyes glazed over hearing how much she was going to be missed. Though, somewhere in the back of my mind, I wondered just how much of Rochelle's wailing was an act so that people would feel sorry for her. The whole of the cheer squad were fake and bitched behind the other's backs so it wouldn't surprise me if I learnt that Rochelle didn't even like Sandy that much.

They placated her with kind words and hugs. The teacher abandoned the lesson plan for today. After a while there was a knock at the door and the receptionist poked her head in. "Hi, I need a few moments with Rochelle Levine and Maisie Preston," she said, reading our names off a piece of paper.

I frowned, looking at her quizzically. *What does she want me for?* Mrs Walters walked over to me, tapping on my desk. "Off you go, Maisie," she instructed, nodding at the door. I gulped, standing quickly and gripping my backpack that I hadn't even opened yet. Rochelle was glowering at me hatefully as she swiped at her nose again with the hankie. I sidestepped around her, following the receptionist out into the hall. A group of about ten students stood there too, all looking bemused and bored at the same time. Most of them were from the cheer squad, some of them from the football team and also a couple of stragglers from my year that I knew by face only. When Rochelle stepped out she was immediately greeted by cooing words and hugs, which of course started the tears all over again.

"Come with me, please," the receptionist requested, marching off up the hallway. I walked behind her, somewhat taken aback by how quickly she walked. She was getting on in years, I would guess in her late fifties, but she marched along the hallway like a spring chicken.

I jogged to catch up with her, setting my pace alongside hers. "Where are we going?" I asked, looking back at the group who were idling along behind us.

She glanced at me from the corner of her eye. "Police just want a word with you students first. They'll be talking to most of your year about the murder, but they're doing it in stages. Just routine so I've been told," she answered somewhat excitedly.

I gulped. So why was I getting questioned first? I looked back at the group. They were all close to Sandy one way or another, but I wasn't... had someone told the police about what I'd said when we were fighting? I was silently thankful to Luke for helping me and giving me an extra alibi. I hadn't done anything wrong, but I suddenly felt as if I was about to face the firing squad.

chapter twenty-two

The receptionist led us to the south side of the building and to a row of chairs that had been set out along the side of the hallway. A police man in full uniform stood outside a classroom door, regarding us with intrigued eyes as we all filed down towards him.

"Take a seat. You'll be called in one by one to answer a few questions. Hopefully we won't keep you long," he instructed, waving a hand at the chairs.

I sat, setting my backpack on my lap and hugging it to my chest. Practically as soon as we were all seated, the classroom door opened and another uniformed officer, this one female, stuck her head out. "Alright, who's first?" she asked, looking down at her clipboard. "Terence Fuller, please," she added, looking up at us.

Terrence stood, shoving his hands into his pockets as he trudged past me, not seeming intimidated by this in the least. When the door closed shutting Terence off in there with the police, I looked around at the other faces that were here with me. Everyone seemed a little apprehensive; some of them still had puffy eyes where they'd been crying. I hugged my bag tighter, pleased that it wasn't just me that seemed to be nervous about what I was going to be asked.

Terence was in and out within five minutes, disappearing down the hallway without another word. The next person was called in and still I sat there, my stomach churning with anticipation. Finally, after four other people had been in and left already, I was called in.

I gulped as I stood. My legs felt weak as I took the few steps towards where the female officer was standing with the clipboard, waiting for me. I lifted my chin, trying not to show I was nervous. I had nothing to be nervous about anyway but I was always a worrier with things like this. When I got to the police lady she stepped back, waving me into the room.

An ageing plain clothes police officer sat there with a notepad and coffee set on the desk in front of him. He swept a hand through his short salt and pepper hair and regarded me with hard, steely grey eyes that made me squirm on my feet. Principal Bennett sat in the corner of the room and smiled kindly at me as I sat in the chair that had obviously been set out for me.

"Good morning. My name is Detective Inspector Bartrum; I'm with the homicide division. You are Maisie Preston, correct?" he asked, raising one eyebrow.

I nodded, willing my voice to work when I spoke. "Yes," I confirmed.

"Okay, Maisie, I just want to ask you a few questions to help with our investigation. Because we're conducting these questions on school premises, Principal Bennett is sitting in on them too, it's just standard practice," he muttered, picking up his mug and taking a loud slurp of his coffee.

"Okay." I nodded in understanding, wanting this over with already.

He nodded, looking down at his notepad and flipping over a page before looking up at me. "Did you know Sandy Watson well?" he asked.

"Um, not really. We weren't friends or anything," I answered.

He sucked his teeth with his tongue, just looking at me without speaking. The silence stretched on and on, and I cringed under his intense gaze. "I've been informed of an incident between you and the deceased that happened yesterday morning. Would you please tell me about that?" he asked finally.

I groaned inwardly. "We had a fight in the hallway. She said something that upset me and I reacted badly. I'm sorry about that, I shouldn't have done it," I admitted, looking at my feet, suddenly ashamed of myself. I'd jumped the gun yesterday and assumed that it was her that had sent me those things and poisoned Chester when I now knew that it wasn't even her.

He picked up his pen and wrote something that wasn't even legible; he would probably have trouble reading his notes again later. "What was the argument about?" he asked.

I sighed, closing my eyes, hoping he wasn't going to ask this information. "Lately I've been getting these weird phone calls, threatening notes, that kind of thing. Then, two days ago, someone broke into my house and poisoned my dog. I've reported it to the police; DI Neeson is the lead officer on my case. I thought it was Sandy that was doing it, so I confronted her about it and we ended up fighting. But I later learned that it wasn't her anyway because she was somewhere else when my dog was poisoned."

Principal Bennett sat forward in her chair, her eyes concerned. "Oh, Maisie, why didn't you come to me and tell me?"

The inspector held up his hand and shook his head, signalling for Principal

Bennett to be quiet. "DI Neeson you say?" he asked, scribbling her name on his pad. I nodded in confirmation. "I have witnesses to the fight that say you actually told Miss Watson that you'd kill her if she came near you again. Did you say those words?"

I tightened my jaw, nodding guiltily. "I think so. It was all so fired up and stuff. I can't remember my exact words. I didn't mean it though; it's just something that came out. I'd never hurt anyone, ever," I replied quickly, begging him with my eyes to believe me.

"So why would you say it?"

I shrugged, not having an answer. "I don't know. It just came out. I was angry, we were both screaming stuff at each other. I don't really remember everything that I said."

He nodded, picking up his coffee and regarding me over the rim as he took a deliberately slow slurp. When he put the mug down he cocked his head to the side. "This is just routine questioning at this time, Miss Preston. I'm just talking to everyone that had direct contact with Sandy yesterday, trying to piece together her last day." His eyes bore into mine, seeming like he was trying to drag any lies out without me even speaking. I was incredibly intimidated by the way he looked at me; it didn't feel like these were just routine questions.

I chaffed my hand up my arm, flicking my eyes up to the clock on the wall. I'd already been in here for almost ten minutes; everyone else had been out within five so far. Was that a bad sign?

"Where were you between the hours of nine and eleven last night?" he asked suddenly.

"At home," I answered quickly.

He nodded. "And people were there with you? Parents, siblings?" he asked, leaning back in his chair.

I nodded. "My brother was downstairs, and also my, um, boyfriend, well, kind of ex-boyfriend, he came over last night," I stumbled over my words, not quite knowing what to class Luke as anymore.

Inspector Bartrum raised both eyebrows at that. "What time did your boyfriend, kind of ex-boyfriend, come over?" he asked.

"About eight," I lied. "I snuck him into my room, and he spent the night." There, it was done; the lie was told. Now I should be allowed to leave and he would stop looking at me with those scary, challenging eyes.

A smile pulled at the corners of his mouth. "Spent the night? I'm guessing that the parents don't know that they boyfriend slash ex stayed over?" he inquired.

I shook my head quickly. "My parents are out of town, but my brother doesn't know, he'd go crazy if he did." I winced, thinking of how annoyed Alex would be if he found out this news, and I wouldn't be able to tell him it was a lie either because then the police could find out.

A disapproving click of the tongue came from the corner of the room, and I felt my face flame with embarrassment because Principal Bennett now believed that Luke had slept in my room.

"And what is the boyfriend slash ex-boyfriend's name?" the inspector asked, his pen poised above the paper ready to write.

"Luke Hannigan," I answered, watching as he scribbled it on the pad.

"He's at this school?" he asked. I nodded in answer, and he looked up at the female officer that was holding the clipboard and standing by the door. "Can we get Luke Hannigan in for the next round of students?" he requested. She nodded, writing on the clipboard too. Inspector Bartrum looked back to me. "Do you know of any reason why someone would want to hurt Miss Watson?" he asked.

Despite the fact that she's a spiteful, nasty witch? was my first thought, but, "No," was what I answered instead.

He sucked on his teeth, just watching me silently again for a few seconds before he spoke, "Okay, I think that's all for now. I'll put in a call to DI Neeson and speak to her about your case and let her know that Miss Watson has been a victim of homicide," he said, waving his hand at the door. "You're free to go. Please don't talk to the other students sat outside, just go straight back to class."

I nodded quickly, relived that it was over. "Okay, thanks." I picked up my bag and practically ran from the room, ignoring how the remaining students on the chairs watched me as I walked past. I tried not to wonder what they thought about the fact that I'd been in there three times as long as everyone else. Would they see that as something else to gossip about, and another factor to add to my guilt? I hoped not.

• • •

IN EVERY SINGLE CLASS I went to after that, the receptionist popped her head in and pulled out at least one student, in my last class of the morning she actually removed five students. As the time passed people seemed to be looking at me less and less. News seemed to be spreading of the fact that Luke snuck into my house last night, I was secretly dreading lunchtime when I would see Alex, and he would ask about it. I was going to have to lie right to my brother's face and wasn't looking forward to it in the slightest.

When the bell sounded I hung back in my class, deliberately wasting time and procrastinating before deciding that I would forgo the confrontation all together. Instead, I decided that I would spend my lunchtime in the library. I sent a quick text to Charlotte informing her of my plans and that I had an essay to finish and then snuck out of the class in the direction of the library.

The volunteer librarian looked up as I walked in but because I came in here a lot all she did was a casual wave as I strutted past and into the back where they had the comfy reading chairs. I didn't have any work to do, so on the way past I nabbed a romance novel with a decidedly sickly cover of a couple embracing on a beach. When I got to the chairs I settled down in the seat to read it for an hour.

My plans were ruined when a bag dropped down next to me ten minutes later though. I cringed and looked up expecting Alex to come and give me the third degree. I was pleasantly surprised to see Luke standing there instead. "Hey," he greeted somewhat cheerfully.

Hmm, I guess Alex hasn't caught up with him yet! "Hey. How did you know I was here?" I asked. I hadn't told Charlotte where I was going, just that I had work to finish off and wasn't going to lunch with them.

"You weren't at lunch, so I thought to myself, where would Maisie be? Then it hit me, comfy chairs at the back of the library," he mused, plopping down in the chair opposite mine and ripping open his black backpack. "Hungry?" he asked, pulling out a sandwich carton and bottle of Pepsi.

I nodded, taking it eagerly as my stomach gave an angry growl. I hadn't realised how hungry I was until then. "Thanks, Luke."

He smiled, taking out another sandwich and sitting back in his chair. "What you hiding in here for? Are people still saying things? Who is it? I'll talk to them," he suggested, looking at me curiously.

I sighed and ripped open the packet, lifting out half of the cheese sandwich. "No it's fine. I'm just kind of trying to avoid Alex. He's gonna go mad when he hears that you stayed over last night," I explained, wincing.

Luke cringed and nodded. "Hadn't thought of that. Hiding in the library is a good plan. Think we could stay here forever so I don't get my ass beat?" he joked. His eyes twinkled with amusement, and I couldn't help but chuckle.

"You should probably move towns," I teased, winking at him playfully. "My dad's back this afternoon too so you'll have two Preston males out for your blood." I bit into the sandwich greedily, not even bothering to savour it. I hadn't eaten anything all day so now I was actually ravenous.

Luke waved his hand dismissively. "I can handle them. You're worth it," he replied, smirking at me. "How'd your interview go? All as planned, right? You said what we agreed?" he asked, lowering his voice and leaning forward in the chair.

I nodded, looking around quickly, but there was no one near us at all. It was only us and the volunteer librarian in the room, and she was standing on the other side of the room at the counter. "Yeah, I said what you told me to," I confirmed.

He smiled, and his shoulders seemed to relax. "That's good then. I had mine too this morning so I said the same thing. You should be in the clear now.

They won't question it. The policeman was one of my dad's old golfing buddies, he recognised me when I walked in. I could have told him anything and he wouldn't have questioned it," he boasted, shrugging easily.

"Thanks for doing that, Luke. Even though you're now gonna be in trouble with Alex for it probably." I smiled gratefully. My eyes drifted down to his mouth as he ate, I watched his lips as he licked off a crumb from the corner of his mouth. I'd never wanted to kiss him more than in that moment. How I was restraining myself from getting out of my chair and closing the short distance I didn't know.

"You don't need to keep thanking me." He shoved in his last mouthful of food and opened his drink. "Beth had her interview too already. She went at the same time as me. I reckon they'll be doing them interviews for a couple of days. Depends on if they're doing our whole year or just people who knew her." We sat there for the rest of lunch, speculating about who would get called and when and what the police would learn from talking to students. I didn't get any of the book read, but if I was honest I would much rather spend the time talking to Luke anyway.

The afternoon passed differently to the morning. Instead of subjecting us to lessons, they made everyone do a kind of study hall, quiet time. Luckily for me I'd had the forethought to borrow the book I'd started at lunchtime, so I sat there in silence reading that while other students around me put their heads on their desks and slept, started assignments for the following day or just doodled in their notebooks.

Thankfully, with the whole silence is golden thing, I had managed to avoid speaking to Alex all afternoon. During sixth period a balled up piece of paper sailed across the room and hit me in the arm, bouncing onto the floor and making me squeak with fright because I was so engrossed in my book. I looked up, shocked, to see Zach chuckling behind his hand. I scowled at him but just got a smirk in return before he pointed down at the paper discreetly.

I sighed, closing my book and marking my page before dropping my pencil and then bending down to scoop it back up along with the paper. The teacher looked up, raising one eyebrow in question. I stuffed the note up my sleeve before holding up my pencil in explanation, smiling apologetically. With a bored expression she turned away, obviously satisfied that I wasn't up to anything sinister. When I was confident that she wasn't going to look, I pulled out the note and unscrewed it, flattening it out and seeing Zach's messy handwriting on there.

STILL STUDYING AT MINE AFTER SCHOOL?

I looked over at him to see him watching me curiously. I nodded, screwing the note back up and shoving it into my pocket. He smiled, settling back into his seat. "What you reading?" he mouthed, pointing at my book. I held it up so he could see the cover, watching as he crinkled his nose distastefully and rolled his eyes at me. I chuckled and opened my page, reading again for the rest of the lesson.

When the final bell went I sent a quick text to Alex, reminding him that I was going home with Zach tonight. He replied that he was going training anyway but that I was in trouble when I got home. I winced, shoving my phone into my back pocket, now not wanting to go home at all. Hopefully he wouldn't tell my dad otherwise I would probably be grounded forever. Mind you, after someone sending me all that stuff and what happened to Chester, I wouldn't have been surprised if I wasn't grounded forever anyway as a safety precaution!

Zach slinked over to my desk, skilfully jumping a chair on the way instead of walking around it. "Studying time then," he groaned as we walked out of the classroom.

I smiled at his dejected tone and opened my mouth to answer when I saw Luke leaning against the wall outside the door. "Hey, what are you doing here?" I asked, confused.

"Hey, baby," he greeted. "Came to give you a ride home. Alex told me earlier that he was training tonight," he said, already reaching to take my bag from my shoulder.

I twisted my shoulder away so his fingers grasped thin air. "I'm tutoring tonight so I'll be going home with Zach," I answered, willing him not to freak out and start ordering me around like he did last time he saw me going home with Zach.

His posture tightened, his teeth snapped together with an audible click as his eyes flicked behind me to Zach who I could feel practically pressed against my back. "Oh," he grunted.

My bag was slid off my shoulder, and I looked around quickly to see that it was Zach that had taken it. "I got it from here, quarterback," he said smugly.

Luke's eyes narrowed as he stepped closer. Panic built up instantly because the annoyance and anger was plain to see on Luke's face as he glowered just over my right shoulder. "Make sure you take care of her," he ordered. "Don't let her out of your sight."

Zach grinned and did a mock salute, clicking his heels together to thoroughly complete the action. I rolled my eyes and gripped Zach's arm, giving him a little tug in the direction of the parking lot. "I'll be fine, Luke. Please stop worrying about me," I begged. "I'll see you tomorrow," I muttered, before turning to Zach. "Come on, let's just go," I suggested. I couldn't wait to be out of this place and away from prying eyes.

Zach let me lead him along and out of the front doors as he dug in his pocket, pulling out his bike keys. "So, had a good day?" he asked casually, as if just making conversation and didn't know what a horrible day I'd actually had.

I sighed and nodded as we marched across the parking lot. "Brilliant. You?" I replied sarcastically.

He chuckled at my annoyance. "Tomorrow will be better," he said confidently. "The gossip will have moved on to something else tomorrow. I don't know why the idiots thought it was you anyway, I mean jeez, you couldn't stab anyone, you can barely even get the straw into a Capri-Sun," he joked, barging me with his shoulder making me stumble sideways a step.

I burst out laughing as I slapped his shoulder. "Shut up you. How the heck do you come up with this stuff?"

He chuckled, his eyes glittering with amusement. "Saw it on a Facebook status once, been dying to use it ever since," he replied, winking at me playfully. "Anyway, let's change the subject, what shall we have for dinner tonight?" he asked as we made our way over to the side of the parking lot where he usually parked his motorcycle.

I shrugged easily. "Whatever, I eat anything I'm not fussy," I replied.

We reached his bike then so Zach swung his leg over the seat, holding out the helmet that was fast becoming familiar to me.

"Zachary Anderson?" We both looked back to see DI Neeson standing there, dressed in a brown pant suit and cream shirt. She was accompanied by the same uniformed officer that had the clipboard when I'd given my statement this morning.

"Yeah?" Zach muttered, frowning.

"I'm Detective Inspector Neeson. I'd like a few minutes of your time please," she answered. Her voice wasn't friendly like it always was when she spoke to me.

I frowned, confused. Surely they could wait until tomorrow to take his statement that they'd been obtaining from the students. "Can't he do his statement tomorrow?" I asked hopefully. I really wanted to leave this place already, not sit around waiting for him to give his statement.

DI Neeson shook her head. "No. I'd like to speak to Zachary now."

Zach made a scoffing sound and shook his head, turning back to face the front and shoving the key into the ignition. "I'll do it tomorrow. We have somewhere to be. It's not convenient right now," he snapped.

He twisted the key making the bike roar to life with a loud growl. DI Neeson and the uniformed officer that she was standing with both took a step forward. "Mr Anderson, if you're not prepared to answer questions willingly then I'm afraid you leave us with no choice."

I frowned, stepping forward too. *Surely they can cut him a little slack. What difference does it make when he answers those stupid questions?* "Aww come on, we need to go so we can study. Can't you just ask him your questions tomorrow?

What difference will a few hours make?" I bargained.

"Get on the bike, Maisie," Zach ordered, shifting forward in his seat to make room for me behind him.

DI Neeson took another step, her hand coming up in a halting gesture, so I stood fast, shocked by her stern expression. "I can't allow you to leave with him, Maisie," she said, before turning to Zach again. "Are you going to come with me willingly?" she asked him.

A cocky smile slipped onto his face. "Maisie, get on the bike, we're leaving. I'll talk to these lovely people tomorrow," he said, smiling politely.

The officers moved before I could. The one in uniform stepped to the other side of the bike as DI Neeson reached out, planting her hand on Zach's shoulder. "Zachary Anderson, I'm arresting you on suspicion of harassment, threatening behaviour, breaking and entering, and cruelty to animals," she stated, shoving on Zach's shoulder as the other officer grabbed Zach's arm, twisting it behind his back while they continued with the arresting spiel that I'd only ever heard on TV.

I stood there watching with wide eyes, just dumbfounded as the words sank in. This wasn't about Sandy... it was them wanting to question Zach about my case instead. "What? You don't think... he's..." I stuttered, unsure what I wanted to say as I watched Zach's jaw tighten as he leant forward over the bike, not resisting arrest. *No. He wouldn't have...*

The officer helped Zach off the bike, holding him to her side as she cut the engine and shoved Zach's keys into her pocket. I frowned, looking at Zach, confused. He hadn't said anything, but his eyes locked onto mine. As he stood there with his hands cuffed behind his back, his expression was resigned, relaxed even, like he'd been through this a hundred times and was just one of those things.

"I don't understand. What are you arresting him for?" I asked desperately.

DI Neeson stepped to my side, placing a reassuring hand on my elbow, squeezing gently to get my attention off Zach who was still just looking at me with that same bored expression. I gulped and looked up into the kind green eyes of the police officer that I'd met the other day, not the one with the stern expression from moments before.

"We have the fingerprint reports back in full. We're just conducting our investigation based on some new evidence. I'll call you when I know more," she said. Movement from behind her caught my attention and I looked up in time to see Zach being led away towards a waiting squad car.

"You think it's Zach that was sending me that stuff?" I asked. My eyes prickled with tears as I hugged myself against the chilly breeze that blew across the parking lot.

"At this time I'm not at liberty to discuss it. I'll call you once we've conducted more investigations." She squeezed my elbow one more time before turning on her heel and marching over to the squad car, sliding into the open passenger side.

I couldn't move. Zach turned in the seat, looking out of the window, his gaze locking on mine. In that moment I was totally lost. I had no idea what to think. Was it really Zach that was doing it all? What possible reason could he have for wanting to hurt me? I could think of none. Luke's words rang in my ears again, *'how much do you really know about him?'* Apparently I didn't know him at all based on DI Neeson's assessment of his character.

chapter twenty-three

I watched as the squad car pulled out of the parking lot. My feet seemed to be welded to the floor, my eyes wide and my brain scrambled. Had that really just happened? 'New evidence' she'd said – what kind of new evidence would make them arrest Zach like that?

A cold wind blew across the parking lot; ruffling my hair and making my skin break out in goosebumps. I didn't know what to do or think. Was it really Zach that poisoned Chester? DI Neeson seemed to think so. There had to be some evidence linking him to it in order for them to arrest him. My stomach churned with worry and nerves. I'd trusted him. I'd defended him when Luke had suggested him, and now this? I felt a little betrayed. But at the same time part of my brain just refused to believe it. He seemed like such a nice guy, and he'd had plenty of opportunities to hurt me if he wanted to, but he hadn't raised a finger. I felt guilty for even considering the possibility that it was him. I had always believed in innocent until proven guilty. I just tried not to believe that him being arrested wasn't solid proof that he'd done it, after all, mistakes were made all of the time. And she hadn't actually wanted to arrest him in the first place, just speak to him, but because he refused to talk to her she had no choice. My mind was whirling so fast it was practically spinning out of control.

I swallowed loudly and looked around the rapidly emptying parking lot. Some people were standing around, watching me; their faces wore excited expressions so I knew that they'd just seen Zach get led off into a cop car too. It would be all around school by tomorrow lunchtime.

I needed to leave. I reached into my pocket, trying to ignore the fact that my hands were shaking as I pulled out my cell phone. The first person I thought of, as always, was Luke. Struggling with my trembling fingers on my screen, I finally got his number up and pressed call. He answered after a couple of rings; I could hear his car radio playing in the background, so he was obviously on his way home.

"Luke, is there any chance you can come back to the school and get me?" I croaked, my voice barely working because my mouth was so dry.

"Come and get you? I thought you were tutoring," he replied.

I closed my eyes, turning and perching on the seat of Zach's bike. "I was but... please? Can you come back here and take me home? I'll explain when you get here," I mumbled.

There was barely even a second of decision time before he answered. "I'll just be a couple of minutes."

I smiled and ended the call, slipping my phone back into my pocket and ignoring the stares that were directed at me. A couple of minutes later Luke's Jeep rolled into the parking lot, stopping in front of me. Luke's concerned face peered through the windscreen as he popped his seatbelt and moved to climb out. I waved a hand and quickly jogged to the passenger side, climbing in.

"Thank you," I gushed, settling into the familiar seat and closing my eyes.

"What happened to Zach?" he inquired. "Thought you were tutoring?" His eyes flicked to Zach's bike still parked there, and he frowned in confusion.

I groaned and turned in my seat to face him. *He's going to go crazy when he finds out!* "The police just arrested him," I replied, wincing and waiting for his reaction.

A smug grin crossed his face. "I knew that dude was no good. What did they arrest him for?" he asked, obviously happy that someone who he saw as a rival for my affections was now in trouble.

I licked my dry lips before answering. "For the notes and stuff that I've been sent, and for poisoning Chester," I told him.

His eyes widened in shock before his teeth snapped together with an audible click. "What the hell? It was him?" he growled, tightening his hands into fists.

I shook my head quickly. "It might not be. They only wanted to talk to him, that's all," I countered.

He made a half scoff, half growling sound in the back of his throat. "They don't arrest people for nothing, baby. Son of a bitch! I can't believe it was him the whole time!" he ranted.

I frowned at that, still not wanting to believe it. I always liked to see the good in people. "Luke, they're just conducting their investigation. He might be innocent."

He shook his head, scrunching his nose up angrily. "Doubt it. I told you it was him, didn't I?"

"Can you drive me home? My dad's home and he was picking up Chester this afternoon, I really just want to go home," I asked, wanting to change the subject. By the sound of it, Luke didn't believe in innocent until proven guilty and I didn't want to sit here debating it with him.

"Yeah," he sighed, twisting the key to start the engine.

The ride home was practically silent as I became trapped in my thoughts again, trying to link up Zach to all the things that had happened recently. He had the time and the ability, but I couldn't think of a motive at all. It didn't make sense.

By the time I got home my brain hurt from thinking about it so much. When we pulled up Luke moved to get out but I shook my head and leant over the middle of the seats, planting a kiss on his cheek. "Thank you for the ride, but I don't think you should come in. My dad's still pretty angry with you and I just can't deal with anymore arguments or distasteful looks right now," I said, willing him to understand. "You know he takes a long time to forgive people."

Luke nodded in agreement. "Yeah, I guess."

I sighed and looked up at him gratefully. "Thank you for the ride home. You're always there when I need you. I don't know what I'd do without you," I cooed. The honesty of the words rang in my voice. I really didn't know what I would do without him.

He smiled, his eyes soft and tender. "Good thing you'll never have to find out, huh?"

I chuckled, straightening up and grabbing my schoolbag from where I'd stored it at my feet. "I'll see you tomorrow. Thanks again for the ride." I hopped out; waving at him as I practically ran to the front door in a bid to get in quicker.

As I slid my key into the lock, the familiar barking sounded from inside the house. An excited giggle slipped out of my lips as I shoved the door open, stepping in and dropping my bag as Chester came strutting up the hallway. He didn't run like he used to, but just the fact that he was here made my heart ache. I dropped to my knees and took his face in my hands, laughing and stroking him excitedly.

"He's been waiting for you."

I looked up, seeing my dad standing there in the kitchen doorway, arms folded, lazy grin on his face as he watched me. My breath came out in one big gust at the sight of him. I didn't realise until that point just how much I'd missed my dad and how much I obviously leant on him while he was here. Before I knew it, a sob rose in my throat. I pushed myself up from the floor, crossed the hallway and threw myself at him as I burst into tears, letting all the stress, worry, confusion and fear leave my body at once.

• • •

IT TOOK A COUPLE of hours for me to go through everything with him, to tell him all that had happened since the start of it all. Of course this time I got the lecture that I should have told them the first time I got a silent phone call and that I was to tell him everything in the future. It felt nice to offload to him actually.

When I'd told him about Zach being arrested at school he'd gone quiet and thoughtful. I'd told him that I didn't think it was Zach, and that the police must have made a mistake, and he hadn't had any answers for me about it. After we'd finished talking, he'd tried to call DI Neeson but she was busy and hadn't returned his call. That was why we were now sat in one of the small, dull and empty rooms at the police station. Dad had driven us down here a little while ago so that we could try and get an update on what was going on with the case and Zach. We were now just waiting for DI Neeson to come down and meet with us.

Just after nine thirty the door to the room opened. I looked up quickly as she walked in, folder in hand, smile on her face that seemed a little forced. She probably didn't like being dragged away from whatever she was doing to come down and update us, but my dad had been insistent to the receptionist, who finally agreed to put in a call to her.

"Maisie," she greeted before turning to my dad. "And you must be Mr Preston, Maisie's father. I'm Detective Inspector Neeson." She extended her hand, shaking his firmly.

He nodded. "Nice to meet you."

She motioned for the chairs that were placed around the table in the centre of the room. "Shall we sit? I'll do a quick update meeting but then I need to get back," she suggested, her tone brisk and slightly annoyed. I sat down, looking at her expectantly, as did my dad. She placed her file down, clasping her hands together on top of it. "We've arrested someone in connection to your case."

I nodded, my mouth dry. "Zach."

She gave a curt nod. "That's right. As you know, we were waiting for the recognition department to finish their report on the fingerprints that I took from your house," she explained, raising one eyebrow. I nodded, waiting for her to continue. "Well, we found Mr Anderson's prints on your bedroom door handle, and we also ran your dog's collar for prints, and found a partial print on there too."

I swallowed, waiting for her to continue, but she didn't. *That's it? That's all they arrested him for?* "And that's it?" I asked, my tone coloured with disbelief. "He's been to my house. We went into my bedroom, he petted my dog. Is it not possible that the prints could have gotten there then? That seems kind of weak evidence for you to arrest him for! This is all just silly. You should let him out and start looking for the real person who sent it," I ranted as anger built up inside me.

Lines formed between her eyes as she frowned at me. "Mr Anderson has previous history with the police. I asked him for a few minutes of his time, but he refused," she countered, her tone belittling and harsh.

Whoa, wait, Zach has a police record? I didn't know that...

My dad sat forward in his seat and placed a hand on my arm, a silent warning to tell me to calm down. "I'm sure you can appreciate the delicacy of the situation. Maisie is frustrated because Zach is a friend of hers and she feels like this may be a mistake on your part."

Hmm, he worded it better than me as usual.

"I assure you, we're looking into everything thoroughly. I'm aware that it may be frustrating for Maisie if they're friends, but I'm sure she would rather us treat her case seriously than gloss over leads and not investigate them," DI Neeson rebutted.

"Of course. We appreciate you doing your job to the best of your ability." Dad nodded, flashing his charming smile at her. Instantly, she shifted in her seat, looking away from him and fiddling with the file. I tried not to cringe because I knew in that moment she was thinking about him naked. I guess my dad was considered good-looking to some, my friends certainly thought so, but seeing a policewoman flustered by a smile made me cringe in my seat. "The thing is, I thought Zach was a pretty decent kid. I mean, yes, he's a little troubled, and he has a *very* weird idea of what classes as a sport, but other than that I genuinely liked him. It's a little hard for me to believe that he's involved in this," Dad continued.

DI Neeson looked up then. "There are things you aren't aware of, Mr Preston. I'm sure you've heard from Maisie that one of her fellow students was murdered last night," she asked, raising one eyebrow. Dad nodded in confirmation, and I frowned instantly wondering where she was going with this. "Well, we have reason to believe that the person behind the incidents involving Maisie, is also the person who murdered Miss Watson."

I almost choked on air. The same person? The person who was harassing me had killed Sandy too? "What? Why do you think that?" I gasped.

She turned her eyes to me. "A call was made to Miss Watson's cell phone an hour before the estimated time of death. It's from the same number that made the calls to your cell phone. Miss Watson wasn't at home when she was found. We think that the person called her and lured her out with the intention of killing her."

"Oh God," I muttered. Anguish and worry built up in my stomach. If the person who was sending me that stuff had killed someone then what was to stop them from killing me? Maybe they'd even been harassing Sandy too before she died! Maybe I was next. Maybe I was in danger right now, and someone was going to stab me so many times that it looked like I'd been gutted, just like the witness said that Sandy had. I had to get out of here. I had to leave and...

"Maisie, sit down and breathe!" A hand closed over mine, pulling me back to my seat. Until then I hadn't even realised that I had moved. I looked up into the concerned green eyes of my dad. "Just calm down. Everything's fine, I promise," he cooed, squeezing my hand gently. He turned back to the police officer. "So you're now treating Maisie's case as a possible murder case too?"

DI Neeson thumbed the file on the table. "At this time we're still conducting investigations, but from here on out I'll be sharing information with the lead officer from our homicide department."

I blinked a couple of times at that information. DI Neeson was now obviously working with the officer I had spoken to this morning, the one with the intimidating eyes.

Dad nodded, giving my hand another reassuring squeeze. "And you believe this person is Zach? Have the phone records confirmed that?" he asked curiously.

I looked at DI Neeson. That was a really good question and I was incredibly glad that my dad was here with me. He always seemed to have the right things to say in these situations. A muscle in her temple twitched as she sat there, seeming to be choosing her words carefully. "His phone records show nothing out of the ordinary. I have officers conducting a search of Mr Anderson's house right now; we believe that the calls are from a different phone and number. Once we find the phone we'll have more to go on."

I cringed, thinking of poor Olivia having to watch as people searched her house for the phone. No doubt Zach's uncle Alan would be ranting in the background about what a deadbeat kid he was. I felt a pang of guilt. Zach would probably be in for a rough time when he got home because of all of this.

Dad cocked his head to the side. "But at this time all you have to go on are the fact that Zach's prints were on my daughter's bedroom door and the collar of the dog?" he asked. DI Neeson gave a curt nod of confirmation. "What was he arrested for before? You said he has previous history with the police."

DI Neeson cleared her throat and stood up. "I'm afraid I'm not at liberty to discuss that information. Now, if you'll excuse me, I have just under nineteen hours left to question Mr Anderson before I'm forced to release him. I'll call you with any news." Her tone was final as she stuck out her hand towards my father. "It was nice to meet you, Mr Preston."

"You too. Thank you for taking the time to talk to us," he replied politely. She marched out of the room, closing the door firmly behind her and my dad turned to me and smiled teasingly. "You need to work on your people skills. You can't just go off ranting at these people and then expect them to help you. You have to know the right way to handle it. Politeness and reasoning usually works best."

I rolled my eyes. "And you've had a lot of dealings with the police have you?" I joked.

A sad smile twitched at the corners of his mouth. "Let's get you home. We're obviously not going to learn anything else here. Sounds to me like they're clutching at straws and hoping that it's Zach. She knows it too. She doesn't believe it's him any more than I do, but they have to go through the motions, especially now that the same person apparently called Sandy's phone. They'll release Zach tomorrow without charge," he assured me, before frowning and adding, "Well, unless they find something at his house."

I gulped, not even wanting to think about it. I refused to believe that someone I was close to would be capable of something like that.

• • •

I SKIPPED SCHOOL the following day, mainly because I didn't want everyone looking at me again, and also because I didn't want people asking me why Zach was led off in shackles the previous day. The only bad thing about skipping school was that I was then home with my dad who still had time off work because they thought he was still off taking care of my grandad. It wasn't that I minded hanging out with my dad – on a normal day I would actually love it. But it was just that he was smothering me. I hadn't really had a minute to myself all day long because he was doing his overprotective caveman bit. It got even worse when Alex came home from school because then I had two of them following me around like little puppies asking if I was alright and if I needed anything.

Because my dad didn't want me wallowing and thinking about it all the time, he insisted that I stay downstairs and hang out with them rather than be alone in my room. I knew they were only doing it because they cared and were worried about me, but by dinnertime I was about ready to scream. I felt trapped, and I needed a change of scenery before I went insane.

I excused myself from watching some car chase programme that they were both engrossed in, and headed into the bathroom. As I closed the door behind me, I leant against it and blew out a big breath. I needed air. It felt like I was slowly suffocating, choking on the overprotective fumes that filled my house. I needed out for a little while.

I looked around hopelessly, knowing that as soon as I said I was leaving the house my dad and brother would insist that one of them came with me. I fruitlessly tried to think of a plan that would give me a few minutes on my own. All I could come up with was leaving without telling anyone, but I wasn't that desperate, or stupid. People in horror movies always did stupid stuff like leaving without telling people where they were going so it took ages for them to be missed. No, I wasn't stupid enough for that. But I needed to get out of the house.

Charlotte. A visit to Charlotte's would calm my nerves; we could talk about unimportant things and then maybe this nervous tension would leave my body for a while. I grinned as I pulled my phone from my pocket, dialling her number.

She answered on the fifth ring. "Hey," she chirped.

"Hi. Are you home? I need to get out of the house and just do something normal. Want to hang out and watch a movie or something? I'll bring something sickeningly romantic," I suggested hopefully.

She chuckled. "Sure. I'm home, come on over."

I smiled gratefully. "Okay, see you in a bit."

After disconnecting the call, I flushed the toilet to keep up with the act that I'd needed to go, then silently slipped out of the bathroom and headed to the hallway closet, pulling on my jacket and grabbing my purse. Once I said the words to my dad I knew I'd need to make a swift exit before he changed his mind and refused to let me go. I stepped into the lounge, seeing him and Alex sitting there still watching the same car chase programme.

"Dad, I'm going to Charlotte's for a while." I smiled sweetly, hoping he wouldn't refuse.

His head snapped up in my direction, his eyes narrowing disapprovingly. "What, now?"

I nodded. "I've just called her. We're going to watch a movie. I just need to get out of here for a while and do something normal," I persuaded.

He nodded, pushing himself up and throwing the TV remote control to Alex. "Okay. Let me just find my shoes," he muttered, picking up his coffee mug and downing the contents.

I shook my head, looking at him pleadingly. "Dad, I'll just drive. I'll go straight there. No stopping. I'll even call you when I arrive," I suggested. "I just need a few minutes alone. I'm going insane with all this protective caveman stuff that you two have been subjecting me to lately," I whined, begging him with my eyes and sticking out my lip. "Please?"

He sighed, not looking happy about it in the slightest. "You go straight there. No stopping at all, understand?" he instructed sternly. I nodded, grinning now. "And you call me the minute you get there. It's about a ten minute drive. If you haven't called me within fifteen minutes then I'm coming looking for you and I'll lock you in your room until they find the guy who's behind all of this." His green eyes bore into mine and I could see the seriousness of this now. If I didn't call he would have no qualms in locking me up forever, that much was obvious from his expression.

"Deal," I agreed, stepping forward and going up on tiptoes to kiss his cheek. "Can I borrow Mom's car?" He grunted in agreement, nodding towards the car keys that hung in the hallway on the key rack. "Thanks. I'll call you as soon as I get there," I promised as I practically skipped out of the room and grabbed the keys to my mom's little red Rover.

As soon as I stepped out of the front door I sighed as the fresh air hit me all at once. Seeing as it was already dark outside, I tilted my head up, taking in the starry sky in all of its glory. Looking up at the stars brought on a round of nostalgia as images of camping with Luke came flooding back. I sighed sadly wondering if we would ever get back to that point again where we would do that. Depressingly, I wasn't sure of the answer still.

Knowing I was short on time and that if I stood there for too long my dad would come out and insist that I not go at all; I quickly headed to my mom's car. Her remote central locking wasn't working again it seemed as I pressed the unlock button on the key. I smiled to myself as I shoved the key in the lock instead, twisting and unlocking my door. I slid in, cranking up the heater to full blast as I started the engine and pulled out, heading down the road quickly.

By the time I got half way to Charlotte's I remembered that, in my haste to leave the house, I hadn't picked up a movie like I said I would. I groaned in frustration, hitting my hand on the steering wheel. Then a thought occurred to me. Dad said that Charlotte's house was a ten minute drive, but he was wrong, she only lived five minutes' drive. It was Beth who lived ten minutes away. That would give me an extra five minutes before he was expecting a call. That would give me time to stop at the movie rental store that was around the corner from Charlotte's. Pleased with my plan, I indicated off the main street and headed to the rental store.

By the time I got there I still had ten minutes before I had to put in a call to my dad. Locking the car, I darted out into the store heading for the rom com section at the back. Choosing the first Matthew McConaughey movie I came across, I headed to the checkout to pay.

The bored looking cashier was just scanning my membership card when my cell phone buzzed in my pocket announcing a new message. I frowned and pulled it out. *Dad's obviously jumping the gun*, I thought as I shook my head, grinning as I opened the text message that had come through. Only it wasn't from him. It was from an unknown number.

'What are you doing out all alone?'

It felt like someone ran an icy finger down my spine as I twisted, whipping my head from left to right, trying to see if some deranged killer was there. All I saw though was an empty video store and rows and rows of DVD cases. My heart was slamming in my chest as panic made my ears ring.

"Miss, that'll be four bucks," the assistant announced.

My phone buzzed again, another message. I gulped, looking down at it with wide eyes as I tried to regulate my breathing.

'I see you. Do you see me?'

My feet were moving before I could even comprehend what I was doing. I streaked across the store as fast as my legs would carry me, ignoring the assistant shouting me. In my haste I practically ran into the door, fighting with it for a second as I tried to push it even though it was a pull. My whole body was shaking by the time I came to my senses enough to pull the door.

As I stumbled out onto the street I bumped straight into someone who was going into the store, almost knocking us both over. "Hey, slow down!" he cried angrily. I screamed as his arms closed around me. My panic was at an all-time high, my pulse drumming in my ears as I thrashed and screamed, shoving myself away from him. "Whoa, careful! What's wrong with you, girl?" the guy snapped, shaking his head at me and glaring as he righted himself. "Aren't you even going to apologise for almost knocking me on my ass?"

I was hyperventilating now, my tears made everything blurry as all I could think about was getting away, running, finding help. My hand was still clutched my phone so tightly my knuckles were hurting. I whimpered, shoving my hand in my pocket and looking for my keys as I turned and ran towards where I'd parked my car about two hundred yards away.

Get in the car. You'll be fine in the car. The car, salvation, was getting closer and closer, my target seemed achievable and just within reach. *It's just fifty yards now, Maisie. Just get in the car.* I chanted the instructions over and over in my head as I yanked my keys out of my pocket. The car was about twenty steps away now, but my hand was shaking so badly that the keys slid out of my hand. Where I was running they hit my foot, skidding into the road and straight under the car parked three cars away from mine.

"Damn it!" I hissed.

"Maisie?"

The sound of my name being shouted made my muscles tighten all over my body. My head whipped up, seeing a guy a couple of hundred yards away. His face was hidden because of the angle of the street lights beating down on him.

I gasped, immediately ducking between the cars that were parked along the edge of the street. I dropped to my knees, crawling around to the other side. I leant down quickly, seeing my keys just behind the tyre at the back of the car next to the one I was crouched behind. Footsteps sounded, getting closer. I held my breath, willing my heart to quieten because the sound of it hammering in my chest was sure to give away my whereabouts.

The footsteps were closer now. My eyes widened as I crawled quickly to the next car, leaning down and reaching behind the tyre, but I couldn't find my keys. My hand slapped at the ground under the car, my fingers finally grazing the cool metal of a key. "Oh God, come on, please?" I whispered, fumbling again, touching the tip of the ring with my finger.

The footsteps were the other side of the car now. I looked down under the car, seeing sneakered feet walk past the other side of the car to me, heading to the spot a few cars up where I'd darted between them. I knew I needed to move. The taste of my own blood filled my mouth as I bit the inside of my cheek, frozen, wondering if I could even move if I tried. Some burst of energy seemed to come from nowhere as he took another step towards the other end of the car from where I was.

By sheer luck, my finger caught the loop of my keys and I shoved myself to my feet. My heart sank as I suddenly realised that I wouldn't be able to get to my car now anyway because it was too close to where the guy was. I swallowed awkwardly where my mouth had gone dry, and decided that my best chance was to get back to the movie store, lock myself in and demand that they call the police.

My feet were on the move again as I turned on my heel and ran as fast as I could towards the store. But because I was shaking so badly I somehow managed to roll my ankle to the side. I yelped at the pain, stumbled, and lost my balance. I slammed into the concrete floor, throwing my hands out to protect my face from hitting the floor. My hands and knees scraped across the pavement as I fell. My phone skidded along the floor, my purse opened spilling the contents everywhere, but I didn't care. I whimpered, getting up on to all fours, ignoring the burning pain on my hands. My gaze was firmly focused on the door to the store that was illuminated merely two hundred yards away from me. I had to make it.

Quick footsteps behind me sounded, and before I even had the chance to panic and push myself back to my feet again, hands clamped around my upper arms. My natural reaction was a piercing scream that echoed off the cars and walls of the buildings, cutting through the night and making a bird take flight into a nearby tree.

chapter twenty-four

"Maisie, Maisie, Jesus, what's wrong with you? Stop screaming! What have you hurt? Have you broken something?"

"Get off me!" I screamed, trashing, trying to wriggle out of the vice like grip that was wrapped around my arms. "Get the heck off me, you psycho!"

Almost instantly the hands disappeared. "I was only trying to help you up," the voice snapped behind me. "Stop shouting and screaming, people are gonna think I'm hurting you or something. I'll end up arrested again if you don't stop!"

Arrested again? What does that mean? I blinked a couple of times, looking over my shoulder, trying to get my emotions under control. Zach scowled down at me as he took a step back, holding up his hands innocently. His eyes were concerned as he regarded me worriedly.

I gulped, pushing myself up to sitting, keeping my eyes on him in case anything happened. Was it just coincidence that those texts were received saying someone could see me and then Zach was there? I didn't know the answer. But just the fact that he was standing there was surely a sign of his innocence. The police had let him go, which meant they hadn't found anything in his house that connected him to the phone calls.

"Are you okay? What were you running like that for? You looked like you were going to shit a brick," he muttered, lowering his hands, moving slowly as if he was trying not to startle me or anything.

"I was frightened. I..." I gulped, my voice barely above a whisper. "I need to go. There's someone watching me. I need to get home!" I awkwardly tried to push myself up but as soon as I got half way an agonising pain shot through my ankle making me drop down to the floor again and yelp.

My eyes glazed over as I clenched my jaw, trying to think of anything else.

Zach squatted down in front of me, his hands instantly going to my ankle. "Stay still. Let me see," he cooed.

"I need to go home," I croaked, looking longingly at my car before glancing up and down the street, waiting for some knife wielding maniac to jump out and hack me to pieces. My whole body was trembling now. Cold seemed to seep into my very veins, turning my blood into ice. My teeth knocked together loudly, so I clenched my jaw, trying to keep myself focussed by watching what Zach was doing.

Zach shook his head, carefully unlacing my sneaker and easing it off along with my sock. "Let me just take a look and make sure it's not broken before we move you," he instructed. I closed my eyes as he felt and prodded at my ankle causing more pain to erupt in little bursts. "This isn't broken. I think it's just sprained," he said finally.

All of a sudden my emotions got the better of me and I burst into tears, covering my face with scratched hands and pulling my good leg up to my chest.

"Maisie, shh, it's alright. Are you okay?" Zach's voice was soft as one of his hands stroked the back of my head and the other rubbed on my shin.

I peeked through my fingers, seeing that he was looking at me with worried eyes. "I'm okay. It's just my ankle really," I croaked.

He groaned, leaning forward and pressing his forehead to my temple. "Let me see these," he cooed, taking hold of my wrists and pulling my hands away from my face. I looked down at my hands too, seeing lots of tiny scrapes and grazes with blood oozing out in parts. "These don't look too bad. We should get the dirt out though." He pulled the bottom of his sweatshirt up, wiping my hands gently, brushing off the dirt and little stones that were there before blotting the blood away. "I suppose you think I'm the one that killed Sandy too, huh? That's why you were running from me," he observed, his voice sad as he kept his gaze firmly locked on my hands.

I gulped. Did I think it was him? I was just frightened in the heat of the moment; I didn't know that the guy who shouted my name was Zach. Would I have run if I did? I didn't think so. Now that I knew it was him, my heart rate had started to slow down, the fear had started to ebb away, and I was actually incredibly glad that he was here. I wasn't frightened of him in the slightest as he crouched there tending to my wounds.

"I didn't know it was you that shouted me," I explained. "I was already frightened and then I saw a shadowy figure in the street shouting my name, and I freaked out even more." I hissed through my teeth as he turned his attention to my knees, rolling up my jeans so he could see the scratches there too. "And I don't think you killed Sandy," I added confidently. I didn't know why I was so sure that it wasn't him, I barely even knew him, but what I did know about him told me that he wouldn't knowingly hurt a girl. A guy, yes, but a girl, no.

His lips parted as he turned his head, his gaze meeting mine. His eyes shone with gratitude in the darkness as his fingers deftly worked to roll my jeans up over my sore knees. "Well you and Olivia are the only ones that seem to believe that," he muttered somewhat angrily. "Why were you frightened in the first place?" he asked, frowning.

I gulped. Zach didn't know much about the harassment that had been going on. Other than family, I'd only told Charlotte, Beth and Luke. All Zach knew was that Chester had been poisoned because I told him at school the other day. "Some things have been going on recently. Someone's been harassing me. I've been getting threatening letters and phone calls."

His head snapped up at that. "Seriously? Wait, phone calls? Is that why the police kept asking me if I had another phone? They think I'm the one that's harassing you?" he asked, shaking his head in disbelief.

I shrugged, looking away from him because I actually felt terrible that he'd been arrested for it. "I guess so. The person broke into my house and poisoned Chester, which is why they were asking you about fingerprints in my house and on his collar," I explained.

He sucked in a deep breath through his teeth, nodding slowly as if everything was now dropping into place and he understood what was going on. "That makes sense now. They just kept asking and asking how I explained my prints being on the collar and in your house. It's so stupid. Of course I touched your dog, it was hard not to when he's jumping around your feet asking to be petted," he muttered. "And then they were asking about a phone, where I put it, where I bought it, that kind of thing, but I didn't really know what they were talking about. Now it makes sense."

I nodded, tentatively touching one of the cuts on my knee and wincing when it burned. "Apparently the number that keeps calling and messaging me, called Sandy an hour before she was murdered," I added, my voice wavering as the trembling in my body seemed to double.

His eyes widened as his grip on my hands tightened. "The person who killed Sandy is contacting you too? No freaking wonder why they were busting my ass in there. They were relentless. Now everything makes sense." He stood up, looking up the street. "There's a café open up there. Let's get you off the cold floor and in there in the warm. I'll get you some ice for that foot before it swells too badly. I'll take you home in a little while," he suggested, before bending down and picking up my purse for me, collecting all of the contents and shoving it back inside.

He grabbed my shoe and sock, slipping it under his armpit before standing up and holding down both hands to me. I smiled gratefully and placed my hands in his, letting him pull me to my feet, trying not to wince as the little scratches ached on my hands. "Keep that foot off the floor," he instructed, looping my arm over his shoulder and wrapping his other arm around my waist, taking most of my weight. I nodded in agreement, not planning to put it on the floor anyway because the ache was already bad enough and I didn't want to make it any worse.

He looked down, frowning before reaching down and brushing his hand over my butt a couple of times, obviously wiping something from there. I gasped, shocked by his hands on my body. "Shouldn't you a-ask before you start f-feeling me up in the middle of the s-street?" I joked weakly, stuttering as the shivering started to get worse.

His eyes widened and he whipped his hand away quickly, a subtle blush forming on his cheekbones as he looked away and up the street. "Sorry. You have mud and dirt all over you, I didn't mean..." He shook his head, tightening his jaw.

I couldn't help but chuckle at how uncomfortable he was. "I was k-kidding," I muttered, giggling at his horrified expression. I hadn't taken Zach for the innocent type; he was always so cocky and self-assured. Why was he so embarrassed to have touched my behind? It was obvious that it was an innocent move.

He sighed deeply. "Maisie, you're shaking. I'm not sure if you're going into shock," he muttered.

I shook my head at that, tightening my arm around his neck as I shifted my weight on my good foot. "I-I'm f-fine. Just c-cold," I stuttered as another shiver racked my body.

His eyes tightened. "Come on. Let's get you in there so you can sit," he said, nodding at the café again.

Awkwardly, we hobbled and hopped up the street to the café with Zach taking most of my weight as we went. As he pushed open the door and helped me inside, the smell of coffee hit me in the face making me moan in appreciation. The warmth of the place was a little overwhelming on my skin, but it was like my insides had frozen solid. The place was deserted.

The waiter looked up as we walked in, a startled expression on his face. "Is she alright?" he asked, coming over to us quickly.

Zach nodded, letting the door swing shut behind us. "She just fell. I think she might be going into shock though. Can you make some tea with lots of sugar, and then get some ice for her ankle?" he asked, leading me over to the nearest table and helping me into one of the metal chairs. The waiter disappeared. Zach smiled down at me as he pulled off his black hoodie and then crouched down in front of me. "Put this on," he ordered, already pushing it down over my head.

"You're so b-bossy," I griped. He chuckled, and I leant forward in the chair, letting him help me put my arms into the oversized material.

The waiter came back then, setting down a mug of watery brown liquid in front of me and a jug of milk. "Sugar is there," he said, motioning to a glass pot with a spout on the table. "I'll just get some ice," he added before stalking off again.

Zach stood up, grabbing the sugar pot and tipping it into the tea. I cringed and shook my head. "I don't t-take s-sugar," I mumbled almost incoherently as I tried to reach for his hand to stop him putting in more.

He shook his head, taking my hand in his and tipping the pot up another three times. "Today you do." I watched, disgusted as he added a generous slosh of milk and then stirred it all up before pushing it towards me. "Drink it," he ordered, guiding my hand towards the cup. I cringed again, wrapping my hands around the mug, letting the warmth seep into my fingers to get the blood going again. I had no plans to drink it though.

"I don't l-like tea with s-sugar," I protested, trying not to spill the contents of the mug because of my shaking hands.

He sighed deeply. "Drink it, Maisie. It'll help you," he insisted, wrapping his hands around mine and lifting the cup, guiding it towards my mouth. As I opened my mouth to protest he forced the cup up, tipping some of the sickly sweet warm liquid into my mouth. I groaned, swallowing it quickly just to get rid of it as he tipped the cup up again sloshing more into my mouth. After the third mouthful the waiter came back, so Zach took the cup away from my mouth, helping me set it down on the table.

"Ugh, that's gross!" I whined, shuddering at the lingering taste in my mouth.

"Is this okay?" the waiter asked, holding out a bowl of ice and a small, thin, blue towel.

Zach nodded, smiling gratefully. "Perfect, thanks." I watched as he laid out the towel before scooping out a handful of ice into the middle then wrapping it up into a thick bandage shape. "Let's get this on then," he mused, reaching down and taking hold of my calf, carefully guiding my foot up and into his lap. I looked down at it and turned my nose up, seeing a lump on the outside of my ankle. A small, surprised yelp left my lips as Zach laid the extremely cold towel containing the ice onto my ankle. "Alright?" Zach asked, nodding down at the makeshift icepack. I nodded, smiling gratefully. "Drink your tea," he added, motioning towards my cup again. I pouted but reluctantly raised it to my lips, wincing as some of it spilled over the edge, dripping into my lap and down my chin. When I put the cup down he took my hand, picking up a napkin and dipping it into the ice bowl, wetting it a little before using it to clean up the cuts on my hands.

"So, why were you running? You said you were frightened, what spooked you?" Zach asked, cocking his head to the side and watching me curiously as he worked.

I sighed, reaching for my purse that he'd dropped onto the table when we came in. I pulled out my cell phone, noticing scratches on my screen and a little chip at the edge, but at least it wasn't smashed beyond repair. "I got another couple of m-messages from the private number, and I f-freaked out. I was just trying to get back to my car so I could go home and then you shouted but I didn't know it was you. I assumed it was the p-person who sent the messages. Want to s-see?" I offered, holding out my phone to him, noticing that the shaking was easing up slightly now.

He nodded, taking the phone from my hand and fiddling with it for a few seconds. I watched his face as he read them. "What the hell?" he growled. His head snapped up, looking around quickly, before fixing his eyes on the café window, squinting, obviously trying to check the street for the perpetrator. "Someone was watching you? Why the hell are you out on your own with all of this going on, Maisie? That's stupid!" he berated. "You need to call the police, show them these. Did you see anyone else hanging around the street other than me?" he asked.

I shook my head quickly, drinking the last of my tea. "No, I was too busy fleeing for my life," I joked. The sugar was obviously kicking in now, my brain was slowly returning to normal, and I could focus again.

Zach didn't laugh. Instead, he put the phone down on the table and slid it across to me. "Why the hell has your brother let you out on your own? Does he know all what's going on, that someone's calling you and stuff? He shouldn't let you out on your own, I thought better of him than that," he ranted, shaking his head in disbelief.

I frowned at his anger. It was kind of sweet, I knew he was only angry because he obviously didn't want to see me hurt, but I still didn't like him complaining about my brother – or inadvertently about my dad. "I was going to Charlotte's. I was supposed to go straight there and call when I got there. But I forgot the DVD so I stopped at the rental place. I thought it would be fine. I didn't think," I muttered. Suddenly, what I'd said registered in my head. I was supposed to call home. My dad was expecting a call any minute to tell me I'd got to Charlotte's safely. I winced, knowing he was going to be even angrier with me than Zach was when he found out that I'd stopped to get a movie.

Zach made a scoffing noise in the back of his throat. "If you were my sister I'd never let you hear the end of this," he muttered.

"Do you have a sister?" I asked, suddenly aware that I didn't know much about him at all.

He shook his head quickly, still looking angry with me for being out on my own. "No. I'm an only child."

I stored that little titbit of information for another day but tried to get back to the matter at hand. "Zach, will you do me a massive favour?" I asked, smiling what I hoped was a persuasive smile. He nodded in agreement, so I continued. "Will you call my dad and tell him what happened? Tell him where I am and that I'm fine, but ask him to come and get me?" I asked.

He raised one eyebrow. "So you can prolong the asskicking you're going to get for not going straight to Charlotte's house?" he teased.

"Yeah. Please?" I begged. I just needed another few minutes before I was subjected to that scolding. Hopefully by the time my dad arrived here he would have calmed down slightly before I had to deal with him.

Zach sighed, picking up my phone and finding my home phone number on there. "You owe me," he muttered as he put the phone to his ear. I watched as Zach explained that he was with me and that I'd gotten frightened by a text and fallen over. He told my dad where we were, offered to drive me home and was obviously subject to a verbal lashing because he winced a lot and opened his mouth to speak but then was obviously cut off. The whole time he was on the phone, Zach's fingers were tracing a pattern on my shin. I didn't think he was even aware he was doing it. It was extremely distracting but nice in a strange, unfamiliar way. No one had really touched me like that other than Luke, and it wasn't that it was sexual at all, but it was just intimate in a comforting way. I liked it.

When he disconnected the call he smirked over at me. "You're in deep trouble, missy. Your dad asked me to pass that message on," he gloated smugly. I groaned helplessly, not even bothering to protest. No doubt I would be grounded for as long as I lived when my dad arrived. Zach lifted the towel off my foot, refilling it with ice. "This looks a lot better now," he commented, placing the freshly made icepack back over my ankle.

"Where did you learn first aid anyway?" I asked. He'd not even been fazed by me hurting myself at all. I would have been a mess if someone had fallen and then gone into shock in front of me.

He shrugged. "You pick up a lot of stuff as you go along. I see a lot of injuries while I'm training," he answered. "So, do you have any idea who's sending you those messages?" he asked, motioning towards my phone.

I shrugged noncommittally. "I thought it was Sandy, but..."

Understanding crossed his face. "Ahh, now I get the reason behind the fight the other day. You said something about her poisoning your dog," he muttered. "Did you really think it was her?"

"Yep," I answered. "So now I have no clue. The police obviously have no leads either because they arrested you," I added, rolling my eyes.

A smile twitched at the corners of his mouth. "I've never really had anyone believe in me before. Only ever Olivia," he mused, seeming a little taken aback by it. "The police were going on and on. They didn't really want to let me go I don't think, but they're just trying to pin it on someone. I guess someone like me fits the bill pretty nicely." His tone was harsh, hurt, and full of annoyance.

I chewed on my lip, trying to read his expression to see whether I should say this or not or if he would be angry with me for bringing it up. I decided just to go for it, I could always apologise if I upset him. "They said you had previous history..." I trailed off, wincing because I was prying into something that was clearly none of my business and he was perfectly within his rights to tell me to butt out of it.

His eyes flicked up to meet mine before dropping back down to the table. "Yeah I do." I held my breath, hoping he would continue. He sighed, massaging the back of his neck roughly. "I used to be... different. Before I discovered parkour I was a mess. You see, I have ADHD which basically means that I have too much energy and no concentration span. I get bored really easily, especially when structure is involved, so school is kind of hard for me. Because I was acting up in class I got myself a bit of a reputation, and because of that I fell in with a bad crowd. One thing led to another, and I did a lot of stuff that I'm not proud of. I can't ever get rid of that past unfortunately, so I guess they see a kid with a bad rap sheet with his fingerprints in the scene of a crime and automatically I'm guilty."

I gulped, taken aback by all of that information. "You have ADHD?" That explained a lot actually.

He nodded. "Yeah. I'm on medication for it and stuff, but sometimes I get a little... over the top. That's why I run and exercise a lot. It seems to calm me down. My condition is also why I have to graduate this year so I can prove to the film producers that I can stay on track and be committed to something," he explained. "Oh, and apparently I have an attitude problem and dislike authority too, but that's common with ADHD sufferers."

I gulped, unsure what to say. "Oh."

A grin split his face. "Yeah, I only ever told one person, and that was his reaction too," he mused.

"I just don't know much about the condition so..." I trailed off, looking at him apologetically.

He shrugged. "It's a genetic thing. My dad actually had it too. He was worse than me though because he refused to stay on his tablets."

I looked at him curiously, wondering how to word this next question. "Why do you always talk about your dad in the past tense? Is he," I winced, "has he died?"

Zach frowned, nodding and looking down at my ankle again, adjusting the cold compress probably just for something to do. "Yeah. He killed himself a couple of years ago," he confirmed. Inwardly I groaned at that information, overcome by a wave of compassion. "My mom didn't cope too well when he died, so she turned to drink. I guess me being trouble all the time made that worse too. When I was seventeen she told me to leave. I was still going through a bad phase then, but Olivia took me in and saw something in me that no one else saw. I owe her a lot."

All of these revelations made me understand Zach and his attitude just that little bit more. His condition and his parents abandoning him one way or another was probably the reason that he put on that cocky, rude act in a bid to try and keep everyone else away from him. Maybe it was why he'd once told me that he didn't date. The words slipped out of my mouth before I could stop them.

"Is that why you said that you wouldn't want a girl to fall in love with you?" I asked.

His eyes flicked up to meet mine, a bewildered, shocked expression on his face as if he hadn't expected me to remember that he'd said that once when we were sat in my bedroom. "Yeah, I guess. I mean, I wouldn't want to inflict this disease on someone else. My mom went through hell every time my dad refused to take his tablets and stuff. I saw what it did to her when he'd lose his job all the time because he'd lashed out at his co-workers or just didn't show up because he'd forgotten or gotten distracted. He sank into depression and dragged her down with him too. And then he left her in the end, left her with a kid that he'd infected with the same poison." His hand tightened into a fist on the table as he looked out of the café window. "It's best if I just stay single, that way I won't put anyone through what my mom went through. Plus, the genetic line will end with me then. No baby Anderson's to fuck up anyone else's lives then."

I watched him, shocked by the passion that went into his words. He truly meant it. "So you'll never date a girl, ever?" I clarified.

He shook his head, adjusting the towel on my ankle again. "Nope."

"Have you ever dated?" I asked, suddenly wondering now about his past. Was that why he was so embarrassed when I joked about him touching my ass outside earlier? He shook his head, frowning down at his hands as his finger started tracing a pattern on my shin again. "Wow. I think that's..." I struggled for the right word to finish that sentence.

"Honourable?" he offered, looking up at me then.

I shook my head. "No, not honourable," I disagreed. "Freaking stupid!" I finished, frowning at him.

His mouth popped open in shock, his hand stilled on my leg. "Stupid? How is that stupid?"

I made a scoffing noise and waved my hand at him in example. "Look at you," I cried.

He rolled his eyes. "Because of the way I look I should date people? I'm depriving the girls of my six pack, is that what you're getting at?" he asked angrily.

"It has nothing to do with what you look like. It's how you behave. Look at yourself right now, Zach," I instructed, shaking my head and pointing at my ankle. "You've been taking care of me for the last ten minutes. You're worried about me. You're kind, thoughtful and generous. You're funny, smart, loyal and considerate. Surely you can see what a special person you are. Why do you have such a negative image of yourself?" I asked. As I spoke his expression was turning more and more bewildered, as if he'd never had anyone see good in him before.

"I've seen what it does to someone when episodes of ADHD start. You think I'm all great now, but that's because I'm on the tablets. What happens if one day I start acting like him and think I don't need them? What if I fall back in with that bad crowd? What if I turn out to be exactly like him?" he countered, shaking his head angrily.

"But what if you don't?" I argued.

He didn't have any words for that. His mouth opened and then snapped shut again as his eyes locked onto mine. There was a fierce intensity there. I had a feeling that no one had ever challenged his idea of the disease before.

I carried on challenging his ideals. "What if you continue to work hard on your parkour and become an awesome traceur that kids look up to and have posters of on their walls? What if you never stop taking your tablets and never stop being this kind person that you always are to me? Some girl would fall madly in love with you and you could make her happy for the rest of her life. You don't deserve to shut yourself off from things, Zach. You deserve to be happy too. Just because you have ADHD doesn't mean that you can't live your life and be happy. And some girl deserves to have you treat her like a princess every day, just like you always do me. So get over it and this negative image you have of yourself."

He swallowed loudly, looking away from me as his fingers started the pattern again on my leg. "I don't treat you like a princess," he muttered after a minute of awkward silence. His words were barely discernible, but I made them out somehow.

"All girls wish for a guy that is interested in what they have to say, that thinks they're funny and appreciates the small things that they do. They want a guy to give them their jacket because it's cold, and someone that looks out for them and worries about their safety. That's what I class being treated like a princess. Girls like that stuff. You don't do that for me?" I asked, wrapping the string of his hoodie around my finger and raising one eyebrow challengingly.

He frowned, digesting my words. Finally, he spoke, and a small smirk slipped onto his face. "I'm only interested in what you have to say because you're helping me graduate."

I smiled knowingly. He was a nice guy; he just wasn't ready to admit it yet. I turned my head, looking out of the window of the café. "Whatever you say, Zachary."

From the corner of my eye I saw him watching me. A smile played at the edge of his mouth. We were silent then for a few minutes, and then a car skidded to a halt outside the café, two doors slammed and I closed my eyes, knowing I was about to get it in the neck from both of the Preston men. I tried to mentally prepare myself for the long, sleepless night ahead.

chapter twenty-five

To say that I was in trouble for stopping at the video store would be an understatement. I not only got it in the neck from my dad and brother, but also from Luke. By the time I'd gotten home from the café that I went to with Zach, my ears were hurting probably more than my ankle form the verbal bashing my dad gave me all the way home.

We'd called the police again and done a report over the phone. They'd told me not to delete the messages and that they'd lift them off my phone the following day. I'd assured my dad that my ankle was fine and that all I needed was rest. Zach had backed me up on that front, telling my dad that it was a sprain and that I should just take it easy and keep an eye on it to make the swelling didn't get worse.

I had barely slept that night. Once I was alone in my bedroom, my mind wandered to the fact that someone had followed me from my house and to the rental store. They must have been camped outside my house somewhere, hidden in the shadows, watching and waiting. When my dad had gone to bed that night, an eerie silence crept over the house which made my stomach ache. With the house so quiet it seemed to magnify the sounds of everything else outside. The trees rustling in the wind, a cat meowing, a car driving up the street, all of it was somehow now frightening as I imagined the guy out there in the street, watching the house and just waiting for me to leave on my own again. That wouldn't be happening though. Not only had my dad strictly forbidden me to be so stupid again, I actually didn't want to go out alone again.

I hadn't been able to get myself warm for hours, no matter how many sheets and blankets I piled up on top of myself. Loneliness and fear had kept me awake until the early hours of the morning. I longed for Luke. I longed for his arms and his smell and his warmth. By the time morning came around I gave up trying to put on a brave face and just called him, asking him if he'd come over and hang out for a few hours.

Once he'd finished giving me the lecture about how silly it was that I'd gone out on my own when anything could have happened, Luke and I spent all day up in my room watching the movies that he'd brought around with him. It was nice, and just like the old Saturdays before we'd broken up. A couple of times I'd even completely forgotten that we'd broken up and cuddled up against him, enjoying his comfort and the safety that he emitted.

He came over again on Sunday, but that wasn't as easy as the day before, because Zach turned up unannounced while he was there. He'd come to see how I was and if I needed anything. Luke had sat there with a scowl on his face, obviously biting his tongue so he didn't say anything about it. I appreciated that he was working hard on not being jealous, though I could still see it in his posture for the ten minutes that Zach had sat on the edge of my bed for. It was kind of a relief when he left if I was honest.

By the time Monday came around my ankle was a lot better and I could walk on it for a short time before it started to ache again. Luke begged me to let him pick me up for school, and since I'd leant on him all weekend I couldn't really refuse. It was so weird seeing his little sports car parked in my driveway when he came to collect me.

I frowned at it distastefully. The last time I'd been in that car was when I was speeding it away from Ricky's party after I'd caught Luke cheating. Luke seemed to be driving his Jeep more lately. In a way I kind of wished he'd brought the other one today, I didn't really need more to deal with on top of the memories of him with someone else.

"Morning, baby," he chirped, jogging up to meet me as I hobbled up the path.

"Hey," I greeted, handing him my bag because I knew he'd take it off my shoulder anyway. He smiled, looping his arm around my waist and helping me to the passenger side of the car.

"I brought this one so you don't have to stretch to climb in. I know you were a lot better yesterday but figured every little helps," he explained, opening the door for me and looking down at my ankle worriedly.

Oh. Well then I guess I can't exactly complain if he's actually put thought into bringing this car for me! That's sweet. "Thanks, Luke." I slid in, swinging my legs and smiling gratefully. I secured my seatbelt while he headed around to the driver's side.

"So, how'd you sleep in the end?" he asked as he started the engine.

I smiled tiredly. I hadn't slept well again last night, as he well knew because

I'd called him up at midnight and asked him to talk to me a little until I fell asleep. Of course he'd offered to come over and keep me company, but I'd been strong and refused. Instead, I'd listened to him reading Jules Verne down the phone to me for an hour before my eyelids had started getting heavy.

"Fine," I lied. I couldn't tell him the truth that my dreams last night had been filled with faceless people chasing me with a bloodied knife while I ran and ran but never seemed to get anywhere. "Thank you for last night."

He reached out, tugging on the end of my ponytail playfully. "Anytime."

• • •

BY THE TIME WE got to school, Charlotte and Beth were waiting for me in the parking lot and skipped over to the car, wrenching open the car door before Luke even got the parking brake on. "Are you okay?" Beth asked worriedly.

I nodded in confirmation. I'd spoken to them both over the weekend and explained everything. Charlotte already knew that something had happened because my brother had called her Friday night and told her that I wasn't going to make it to hers. "Yeah, I'm fine," I answered, swinging my legs out of the car and gripping the door frame, awkwardly pulling myself up to standing.

Charlotte gripped my elbow, steadying me as I wobbled a little. "What did the police say about it? Did they do anything? Arrest anyone? Was there CCTV on the street? You said the guy said he could see you, well if he could then maybe he was caught on CCTV or something," she suggested, raising one eyebrow hopefully.

I shrugged. "They were going to look into it. To be honest, Char, they don't tell me much about it. I hate not knowing, I just wish they had some idea of who's doing it."

I looked around the parking lot as I closed the car door. Last time I came here in the morning, the parking lot was full of grieving students, now the place was just as normal. You wouldn't think that anything untoward had happened at all judging by the people standing around chatting about their weekends and exchanging stories. It was like Sandy hadn't even existed. The cheerleaders were all sitting around, giggling and flirting with the football team, applying make-up and fluffing their hair. As I stood there I had a strong feeling of being out of place because nothing was normal in my life at the moment, and I wasn't sure it ever would be again.

Charlotte looped her arm through mine, waving her hand dismissively at Luke who stepped to my side to help me. "I've got her now," she stated smugly. It was very apparent that Charlotte still hadn't forgiven Luke for his indiscretion. Luke frowned but nodded, falling into step behind us. I smiled at him apologetically and got a beautiful smile in return which made my heart pick up double time.

"What about the phone that you keep getting the calls and texts from, can't they trace that?" Charlotte asked, her voice showing her frustration.

I shook my head, wincing as we started to make our way slowly up the steps at the front of the school. "Don't think so. DI Neeson said that the phone isn't on contract and is always turned off. Don't think they can do much with it," I admitted. She pursed her lips as her eyes flashed with something that made me a little nervous. She only ever got that glint when she was up to no good, or planning to be up to no good at least. "What are you looking like that for? What are you scheming?" I asked, cringing.

She raised one eyebrow, faking innocence. "Me? Absolutely nothing. I definitely wasn't thinking that I could hack into your phone company and find the number of the person that's been calling you," she said, shaking her head but grinning at the same time.

I groaned. "I don't think that's a good idea," I protested weakly.

She pulled me to a stop, looking at me intently as she leant in conspiratorially. "I could get the number, and you could have Alex or Luke send it a butt load of angry messages and stuff telling them to leave you alone or else," she countered.

I shook my head forcefully. "Just let the police handle it. Don't get involved. You could end up causing more trouble or something," I warned. "If this is the same person that killed Sandy then I don't want Alex or Luke getting themselves involved with anything. It could make matters worse. Just let the police do their jobs," I said the words firmly, looking her right in the eyes so she knew I was serious.

She sighed dejectedly, letting her shoulders slump. "Fine. I'll stay out of it," she grumbled.

I smiled gratefully, giving her arm a little squeeze. "Thank you for the offer though."

Her face brightened, some of the defeated expression disappeared. "I'm always available if you change your mind."

When the bell sounded overhead they both disappeared off to their respective classes, leaving me with Luke who walked me to my first period and kissed my forehead gently at the door. "I'll see you at lunch?" he questioned. I nodded in agreement. "Call me if you need me."

"I will. Thanks." That statement was true. Luke always seemed to be the first one I called on for help and the first one that sprang to mind when I needed a shoulder to lean on. As he jogged off up the hallway, I turned and limped to my desk, plopping down and pulling out my books that I'd need.

A chair scraped beside me so I looked up to see a girl from my class sitting herself down next to me. She smiled at me happily as she dropped her bag onto the desk. I tried not to react to the fact that this girl had never once sat next to me or attempted to talk to me before today. She was one of the mid-popular girls from our year, but she was well known for being the gossip queen. She even wrote a gossip type column in our school paper.

"Hi. How are you?" she chirped, turning in her seat and beaming at me.

My mouth popped open, but nothing came out. I flicked my eyes to the front of the classroom, seeing that the teacher hadn't arrived yet. "Um... I'm fine thanks," I muttered awkwardly, picking up my notebook and thumbing through the pages just for a distraction. The way she was looking at me so intently made me shift in my seat self-consciously.

She propped her chin on her hand and leant in closer to me, smiling as if we'd been best friends all our lives and were swapping intimate secrets. "So, what was Zach Anderson arrested for on Thursday? Neither of you were in on Friday. Everyone was going crazy. Was he arrested for Sandy's murder? Did he get charged? Is he in jail right now?" she asked, looking at me with wide, excited eyes.

I narrowed my eyes angrily. *So that's what she's sitting there for? Gossip!* "Look, just go away. Zach didn't do anything wrong so just stop all this gossipy talk," I scolded.

She seemed a little taken aback by my outburst as she pushed her glasses up her nose. "Well everyone was only wondering because of what happened with him and Sandy on Wednesday when you were fighting. That would explain his reason for killing her. To, you know, keep her quiet," she muttered, nodding along with herself as she spoke.

I frowned, confused. "What do you mean by that?"

She sighed, rolling her eyes as if I was asking something stupid. "Sandy said she knew stuff about him from his other school, stuff that he wouldn't want common knowledge. He killed her to keep his secrets safe." Her voice was so matter-of-fact, so preachy, that I stared at her in disbelief.

How can one person be so deluded? What is wrong with society today? "Seriously? Zach didn't kill Sandy! Jeez, you lot that stand there gossiping are pathetic. Let the police do their jobs and leave innocent people alone. Last Thursday morning people were looking at me like I'd done it because of what I said to her. Just get your facts straight before you go around accusing innocent people, you can ruin lives that way you know," I snapped. "And you can quote me on that if you want," I added acidly. I shouldered my bag, deliberately swinging it so that it bumped her as I stood up. I grabbed the couple of books that I'd already gotten out and moved to a spare desk that was off to the side. I kept my head held high, refusing to look in her direction as I sat down and slammed my bag onto the table noisily.

I'm sick of this place and the rumour mill of immature, bored people. I can't wait to leave and go to college. Just three weeks and then school is done. That thought made me feel a little better as I sat there, waiting for the teacher to arrive, staring at the blackboard, ignoring people that were obviously trying to catch my attention and ask me if I knew what was going on.

I willed the end of the day to come quickly. If my day was already this bad, I dreaded to think what Zach's would be like. People would be staring and gossiping about him all day no doubt. I silently wished I hadn't skipped school on Friday. If I had come to school then I could have quashed the rumours and told people that Zach was innocent. That news would have sunken in over the weekend and then he wouldn't be facing this kind of thing today. I made a mental note to find him at lunchtime and show my support.

• • •

BY THE TIME LUNCH came around I was in the worst mood I had ever been in. Everything made me angry, even the smallest thing like breaking the lead on my pencil made me growl in frustration. It was all because everyone was asking me about Zach. It seemed that everyone was eager to tear strips off him and assume things about him. It was so unfair that even my jaw was hurting because I'd been grinding my teeth trying to keep calm.

I hadn't seen Zach at all, so I didn't know how he was coping. I'd tried to call him during the break between classes, but he had rejected my call. Luke met me outside my last morning class. His face fell as he looked at me; obviously I wasn't hiding my angry expression very well. "You okay? Has something happened?" he asked, reaching for my hand.

I shook my head, blowing out a big breath, willing myself to calm down. "I'm fine. Have you seen Zach?" I asked, looking down the hallway in the hopes that I'd catch a glimpse of him.

Luke made a distasteful scoffing noise in the back of his throat and shook his head. "I don't have any classes with him," he muttered, somewhat angrily.

I squeezed his hand reassuringly. I didn't want him feeling jealous of Zach all the time. There was nothing between us other than friendship; there was no need for him to worry about that. I still loved Luke dearly, everyday I was starting to realise that more and more. "I know I said I'd eat with you but I really need to find him and make sure he's okay." I willed him with my eyes to understand and not somehow think that I was choosing Zach over him. It wasn't like that at all.

He clicked his tongue and nodded. "Figured you'd say that. Everyone's been talking about him all morning. I guessed you'd be worried about how he's coping," he muttered. "You're too nice for your own good sometimes," he added.

I smiled, stepping closer to him and letting my side brush against his. "Do you think you could give me a ride home tonight? Alex is training, he was going to drive me home first, but I'd rather you do it," I asked, knowing that would put him in a better mood. I wasn't just playing him; I was genuinely planning on asking him for a ride before I cancelled our lunch plans.

He grinned at me then, nodding eagerly. "Sure! Is your dad home or is he back to work?"

"He's working," I confirmed.

Luke's eyes lit up at that. "Maybe I should stay at yours for a little while tonight then, just so you're not in the house on your own," he suggested, grinning slyly.

I chuckled and nodded. "I'd like that." Now I definitely couldn't wait for the end of the day to get here. Another reason to look forward to the end of the school day!

"I'll help you find, Zach," Luke suggested, stepping to the side so I could start walking.

"I know where he'll be." *At least, I think I do anyway.* "I just want to grab a sandwich first," I added, leading us towards the lunchroom.

After buying a sandwich for both me and Zach, Luke followed me out to the school field. Just as I thought he would be, Zach was running laps. Not just jogging this time though, he seemed to sprint for a hundred yards then jog again. He obviously had a lot of stress and issues to run away today. Maybe his ADHD was playing up because of everything that was going on this morning.

I stepped onto the field and saw Zach's head turn in my direction. He didn't stop though, just carried on right past me with his little jogging/sprinting task. I turned back to Luke and smiled sweetly. "Thanks for making sure I got here okay. I'll be fine now. I'll meet you at the end of school."

He frowned, looking up at Zach again for a few seconds before he nodded and walked off. I sat down on the grass, sighing contentedly as I straightened my legs, finally taking the weight off my ankle. It felt as though it was swollen again because I'd been walking too much on it.

When Zach didn't stop next to me a second time I cleared my throat dramatically. "Are you ignoring me? Kinda rude don't you think?" I called to his back as he streaked past. He slowed down, looking at me over his shoulder, his brows furrowed. I smiled and held up the sandwich that I'd bought for him. "You know you want to sit with me really," I called teasingly.

A smile tugged at the corner of his mouth as he slowed down again before coming to a stop, turning and taking lazy steps towards me, his breathing ragged. A bead of seat ran down the side of his face and he swiped it away quickly as he got to me, looking down at me with confused, inquisitive eyes. I tilted my head up, squinting because the sun was just over his shoulder and was shining in my eyes.

"Why do you never take the hint and leave me alone? Seriously, you shouldn't talk to me, especially not with everyone looking at me like I'm the devil incarnate," he huffed.

I chuckled and patted the grass beside me. "Maybe I'm not too good at taking hints. Or maybe I know you're not the devil incarnate and want to be your friend," I suggested.

He just stared at me for a few seconds, seeming unsure and confused. I guessed then that he wasn't used to having friends because he didn't seem to understand that I just wanted to hang out with him for no other reason than to see if he was alright. Finally, he sat down next to me.

I held out the sandwich carton and bumped his shoulder with mine. "Stressed?" I asked.

He snorted and nodded, taking the packet and tearing it open. "Hard day, yeah," he confirmed, taking a humongous bite of his food. "How about you?" he asked. "How's the ankle now?"

I wriggled it a little, testing it, and winced. "Sore. It's alright though," I answered. "Want to talk about your morning?"

He blew out a big breath and shook his head, his shoulders slumped in defeat. "I'll deal with it in my own way," he muttered, looking out across the school field again as he took another bite.

"By running?" I asked. He nodded in confirmation, and we fell into silence. I didn't really know what to say, he obviously didn't want to talk about it, and I didn't want to make it worse by forcing the issue. I was hoping that just by being here I was showing support. I hoped he took it that way at least.

After we'd finished eating in silence, he pulled one leg up, leaning over and stretching out his thigh and back. "I got a show this weekend," he said suddenly.

A *show?* "Yeah? A freerunning show?"

He grinned then, his body seeming to loosen and be more like the free and easy Zach that I was fast becoming used to. "Well it's hardly going to be a strip show, is it?" he teased.

I giggled, chewing on my lip as I hit him on the arm. "Shut up," I scolded. "So am I invited?"

"Er..." He seemed a little shocked by my question. "If you want to go, sure, I guess."

I grinned excitedly, clasping my hands together as I nodded eagerly. "Heck yeah I want to! Where is it? Do I need to buy tickets?" I asked, already planning to ask Charlotte and Beth to come with me so that I wasn't alone. I figured that my dad would insist that Alex come along too, but I didn't mind that actually.

Zach grinned, his whole face lighting up as if he hadn't expected me to want to watch him perform. "It's at the fairground. You know they sometimes book acts to perform at the back arena, well this Saturday afternoon that's me and my team," he boasted proudly.

The fairground, this sounded even better by the second! I knew the place he was talking about too. They often booked live bands or demonstrations and stuff to entertain the crowds. If it was a fairground then I could probably get a group of people to go and watch Zach too. Everyone loved to go there and we hadn't been for ages.

"I'm definitely coming!" I chirped excitedly. "I can't wait to see you actually perform properly."

Zach grinned, pulling up a few strands of grass and launching into a spiel about their routine and what they were trying to include in it. When the bell rang half an hour later his face fell. The easy smile that was there seconds before, was now gone, replaced by a resigned frown.

I gripped his knee, squeezing gently. "Just ignore everyone and what they're saying. I know you didn't do anything wrong, and they'll all feel stupid when they catch the murderer and have to apologise for doubting you. Rise above it. Don't give them a reaction, because that's what they're looking for," I advised, looking at him sympathetically.

He sighed and nodded, pushing himself up and then holding down both hands to help me up. "You're full of this kind of encouraging crap, huh? Don't you ever think that it would just be easier for you to ignore me and not draw attention to yourself like this?" he asked curiously.

I shrugged, placing my hands in his. "Sure. But then I'd miss your sparkling wit and dumbass teasing comments," I joked, laughing and letting him pull me to my feet. He burst out laughing, shaking his head in amusement.

chapter twenty-six

By the time the day of the fair came around, I was more than excited to see Zach perform. I hadn't seen him do his thing since the last time I went to watch him with his group. A whole load of us were going to the fair, watching his performance, and then spending a little time on the rides before I was heading back to Charlotte's place for sleepover. It was going to be a fantastic day, and made even better because of the fact that this was the first time I had been allowed out of the house without having either my dad or brother escort me. Though, of course, I was with Luke, so he was in sole charge of protecting me and delivering me to Charlotte's place in one piece. I actually liked the fact that my dad had started trusting Luke again.

In the last week Luke and I had grown closer again. Several times over the last few days I was close to just throwing my arms around him and letting everything else disappear. The tension between us had been hotting up everyday. I wasn't used to hanging around with him and not kissing him and cuddling him. I missed him so much that it hurt.

We'd been at the fair for almost two hours already, just wandering around and going on the odd ride. Luke had already won me a stuffed crocodile from one of the stalls and a cheap plastic beaded necklace that he insisted that I wear because he'd tried so hard to win it for me. When the loudspeaker announced that the traceur spectacular would be starting in ten minutes, Beth looped her arm through mine. "Let's go get a spot near the front," she suggested, guiding us towards the back of the fairground where they said it would take place.

The grassy performance area was huge. It was cordoned off by a little red ribbon that ran around the whole place so that people could sit all the way around and still have a clear view. Beth walked us right up to the front, stepping over people and ignoring them as they complained. She waved her hand dismissively, telling them that we were friends with the performers, so we had priority. That hadn't really gone down too well, but we didn't stick around to hear the rest of the complaint as we weaved through the waiting people, getting closer and closer to the performance zone.

When we got right to the barrier, Beth smiled with satisfaction and sat down on the grass just behind the ribbon that signalled the line we weren't allowed to cross. I sat down next to her, ducking my head and trying to ignore the people whining behind us that they now couldn't see very well and were going to have to move.

I flicked my eyes around, looking for Zach, but there was no sign of him. Instead though, staff were helping put the finishing touches to the area by bringing in cars that they parked on the grass, and checking the bolts on the large pieces of scaffolding that were dotted around. The staging area looked fantastic already, and I was excited to see what Zach and his boys would do with the ropes that hung from the trees and the massive trampoline was off to one side. Just as I expected, there were no safety mats or equipment.

"So what kind of thing do they do then?" Beth asked, looking around at the crowd that was starting to form around us as people took their places ready for their performance. Charlotte sat down next to me, frowning distastefully at having to sit on the grass.

I shrugged in answer to Beth's question. "I have no idea how to describe what Zach does. You'll just have to watch it and see." Luke and a couple of his friends sat down behind us. He tapped me on the shoulder, and when I turned around he held out a bottle of soda. "Thanks," I smiled gratefully and got a beautiful, straight teethed smile in return.

We made small talk then; all of us listing the rides that we wanted to go on. The boys were whining that they were hungry already. After a few minutes a guy with a microphone walked out into the middle of the arena and smiled at the crowd.

"Ladies and gentlemen, prepare to be entertained by this next act. I first saw them perform a year ago, and they blew my mind. I'm so excited to introduce this team of guys to you today. I know you're going to love this and will be talking about this for days. Please put your hands together for Equilibrium." He waved his hand to the side, and Zach and his team emerged from a large green marquee that I hadn't even noticed.

People clapped, but not very enthusiastically. Most of them, like Beth, probably didn't even know what they were going to witness today. I clapped loudly, putting both my hands above my head, not caring that people cast weird glances at me. Zach's gaze roamed in my direction, and he gave me a slight nod of the head as a little smile pulled the corners of his mouth. I hadn't seen him all morning, but I had sent him a quick message this morning wishing him good luck and telling him that I'd meet up with him after.

I grinned, dropping my hands down as they all stood in a semicircle in the middle of the arena. They were all dressed the same today and actually looked quite smart. They donned black sweatpants and a black vest that bore the name Equilibrium across the chest.

Reggie took the microphone from the announcer guy and smiled out over the crowd. "Okay guys. I hope you enjoy the show that we're about to put on for you. As you can see, we perform without safety mats. Some of the stunts are very dangerous, so please ensure that you stay behind the ribbon at all times, that's for your safety mostly, as well as ours. I just wanted to say, please don't try any of these stunts at home. We train for hours every week, and still some of these stunts are dangerous even for us," he stated confidently, as if he'd given this speech a lot of times and knew it word for word. "Anyway, I hope you enjoy it." He handed the microphone back to the announcer guy who slapped him on the shoulder and ran out of the arena with an excited smile on his face.

Zach smiled at me one last time before walking over to the edge of the arena, the other boys doing the same to different, obviously predetermined spaces. One by one they all seemed to crouch down onto one knee and give a thumbs up signal to show they were ready. When the last guy had given his signal, the music started and then it began.

Just like the last time I saw it, the freerunning was mesmerising. I sat there, transfixed, as did everyone else. The routine was polished, daring, inventive, exhilarating and frightening all rolled into one. People around me gasped, clapped, held their breath and, on more than on occasion, shrieked. The pride that swelled inside me was enough to make me feel like I would explode with it.

My heart was in my throat the whole time, my eyes glued to one person. Zach. He looked so happy, so free. I loved the passionate look on his face and his smile of enjoyment. I watched the way he moved, so fluid and easy. I found myself noticing the rise and fall of his chest and the flex of muscles in his tanned forearms. I gulped as a wave of something seriously inappropriate washed over me. I had never been attracted to any guy other than Luke, so the feeling was incredibly alien to me. I didn't quite know how to deal with it.

For the big finale they all did something different. Zach and Jase did some huge synchronised gymnastics style floor routine that involved so many somersaults, backflips and spins that I could barely keep up. By the time they were done I was breathless with excitement and on my feet whooping and shouting excitedly.

When they all joined hands and did a bow at the end, Zach looked out over the crowd, catching my eye and sending me one of his cocky little smiles.

I chewed on my lip, watching him in awe, before he gave me a little wave and disappeared off with his group through to the performers' tent at the back.

Once he was out of sight again I swallowed loudly, trying to get a grip of myself. When I watched him perform he kind of put me in a trance, making me feel and want things from him that I shouldn't even think about. But I couldn't help it. There was some kind of attraction there for Zach, I couldn't deny it – but I couldn't quite understand it either because I knew I was still in love with Luke.

A hand closed over my arm. "That was seriously hot!" Charlotte hissed in my ear. "Who knew that guys jumping off stuff and doing stunts could be such a turn on?! Seriously, that was incredible, and it's made me look at Zach in a new light."

Me too. I didn't say those words though, just nodded because, for some reason that I couldn't understand, I didn't like the fact that Charlotte was attracted to Zach. I also didn't really like the fact that lots of young girls were now hanging around the entrance to the performers' tent, giggling and obviously waiting for them to come out.

I shook my head, trying to clear it. *Seriously, what's wrong with me?*

Luke stepped to my side then, smiling his dazzling smile down at me, and I felt my face flood with heat because my insides were still quivering, and for once it wasn't him that had caused it. "Hey, we're gonna go hit the refreshment stand and get a burger or something. Coming?" he asked, nodding over his shoulder at his friends who were already making their way to the line for the burger van. Charlotte nodded eagerly and trotted off after them.

I was conflicted. Part of me wanted to go with Luke, but part of me wanted to go and congratulate Zach on his performance. I didn't know what to do. "Um..." I chewed on my lip, looking back at the tent, seeing that the crowd of teenage girls was growing larger by the second. I knew I should probably stay away from Zach for a while so that I could let this feeling disperse, but I longed to run there and see him right this very second.

My mouth made the decision that my brain and heart were struggling with. "I'm not that hungry. I'm gonna go tell Zach well done."

Luke frowned, but nodded. "Alright. Don't go anywhere on your own though," he instructed.

I nodded, waving a dismissive hand. "I'm only going into the tent and then Zach will be there."

He squared his shoulders, taking a step back. "Go on then. I'll watch and make sure you get in there okay before I go get my food," he replied.

I sighed, loving how sweet that was. "See you in a bit."

I turned and made my way over to the tent, hobbling a little on my ankle because I'd been standing too long on it today and it was now starting to ache again. When I got to the mouth of the tent I had to squeeze past the excited gaggle of fangirls that were standing around. I pulled back the rough material and went to step inside, but a guy with a black security t-shirt put his arm out to block my way.

"I'm sorry. Performers only. Wait outside with the others," he grunted, nodding back at the other girls.

I smiled and shook my head. "I'm friends with them. I just want to talk to Zach," I replied, peeking in to the tent and seeing them all standing around, chatting and grinning as they drank from bottles of water.

The security guy turned to look in too, waving me forward a step. "Guys, this one with you?" he called.

Newt and Zach looked up. A smile crossed Zach's face as he nodded. "Yep. That's mine," he chirped. I couldn't help the scoffing noise that escaped my throat at his words.

The security guy nodded, stepping to the side and pulling the cloth doorway back further and waving me in. I ignored the grumbling and whining from the girls behind me as I walked in.

"That's mine?" I repeated distastefully as I made my way over to where Zach was standing. He grinned, shrugging nonchalantly as he chugged some more water. "You're a pig," I scolded, but I couldn't help but smile at the same time.

"So, what'd you think? Like the routine? I saw you screaming like a fangirl out there. I'm surprised you didn't throw me your panties with your number written on the back," he joked.

I chuckled, feeling a blush creep up my neck. I had been shouting, so that was true. "If you didn't already have my number then I might have done," I joked. *Wait, am I flirting right now? Stop it, Maisie!* I decided to change the subject and hopefully that would stop my insides from squirming. "You did great. I loved it. It scared me a little in places, but it was awesome," I gushed, looking at him in awe. "You were incredible."

A huge proud smile stretched across his face as he dropped his eyes to the floor, almost seeming embarrassed by my praise. "Thanks," he muttered. He turned and took hold of the back of the white plastic chair that was beside him, pulling it out. "Here, sit down. You're limping again." He took my hand, giving me a gentle little tug in the direction of the chair, so I sat obediently, smiling gratefully. He definitely did treat me like a princess, even if he didn't want to admit it. He would make someone a fantastic boyfriend - if only he'd let go of his fear about his condition. "I'm just gonna change then we're out of here. I'll buy you a cotton candy, how about that?" he offered, already yanking his vest over his head.

I averted my eyes, looking at the side of the tent, but I hadn't done it quickly enough so that I didn't catch a glimpse of his tight, sculpted abs. Another wave of that unfamiliar attraction washed over me again, and I shifted in my seat, swallowing and fighting the urge to just turn and watch him dress.

"Sure," I agreed, my voice barely above a whisper. At my side I could hear him fumbling around, the sounds of clothes rustling and a zipper being fastened, but I didn't allow myself to turn around.

After a minute a hand was placed on my shoulder. "I'm done. You ready?" Zach asked. He tossed a carrier bag across the tent towards where their other gear was stacked. "Guys, I'll see you in the week. Someone collect the money from the organiser guy before you leave. I'm now off," he informed his teammates as he held down a hand to help me up from the chair.

As I put my hand into his, the other boys all bid their goodbyes, congratulating each other on a job well done and agreed who was going to go and collect the fee from the person that booked them. "I'm not an invalid you know," I muttered, allowing Zach to pull me to my feet.

He smiled sweetly, dropping my hand. "I know. Just being my usual helpful self," he replied. "So, how are you with fairground rides? Scaredy-cat I bet," he mused, taking a couple of backwards steps towards the entrance to the tent while he smirked at me cockily.

I raised one eyebrow at the challenge in his voice. "Actually, I like them. Bet you scream like a little girl though," I joked.

He grinned. "Let's go see. You up for it?" I nodded in agreement, following him out of the tent. "Okay to walk? I could give you a piggyback if you want," he offered, looking down at my ankle worriedly.

"I'm fine. I might take you up on it later though," I agreed, knowing that it would only feel worse and not better the longer I walked on it. He smiled, and we slowly wove through the crowd, heading towards where they had a waltzer ride set up at the end. There was a small line waiting for the ride so we joined the end and I perched precariously on the metal fence that cordoned the ride off at a safe distance, lifting my foot off the floor for a while. We would be waiting for a few minutes anyway.

"I bet you're tired after all that running around, huh?" I asked, looking up at Zach's happy, smiling face.

He shook his head in response. "Takes a lot more than that to wear me out."

A group of pretty, giggling girls walked past, accidentally bumping him as they did, smiling flirtatious smiles. "Oh I'm so sorry," the one at the front gushed, chewing on her bottom lip and looking at him through her long fake eyelashes.

He smiled and shook his head, barely even looking at her or her chest that was obviously being given a helping hand by a padded bra. "No worries."

"Hey, aren't you one of the guys that just did the freerunning presentation?" the same girl asked, faking shock as if she hadn't just followed him over here and bumped him on purpose just for an excuse to talk to him.

"Yeah," he agreed, smiling awkwardly.

She stepped closer to him, putting her hand on his arm and placing her other hand over her heart. "I have to tell you, it was incredible. The stunts you did were great. Do you perform a lot? Where can I see you next?" The suggestion in her voice was blatantly obvious; she didn't mean that because of his freerunning, she meant when can she see *him* next.

Zach missed it though. Grinning and digging in his pocket, he pulled out a flier for the village fair that was happening in a couple of weeks. "We're performing here in a few weeks. You should come along. Our routine will be different there because there's less space there than here," he replied, handing her the flier and turning back to me. I grinned as the girl frowned, seeming thoroughly confused at his knock-back. Zach cocked his head to the side. "You hungry? Want to get something to eat while we wait for the ride?" he asked me.

"I'm fine," I refused, chuckling because the girl and her friends were still standing there waiting to be acknowledged some more and he hadn't even really noticed. "Maybe you should do the girls an autograph?" I suggested, chuckling wickedly as she shot me a dark look.

Zach looked at me like I was crazy and the girls turned on their heels, marching off, probably whining about me. "I don't think they were after an autograph," he muttered, shaking his head and laughing under his breath.

"Oh you did notice then?" I joked, rolling my eyes.

He shrugged. "I noticed. I'm just not interested. Blondes don't do anything for me," he said, faking sadness. The line moved then so we inched up a little further towards the entrance of the ride before stopping again. Suddenly Zach's cell phone started ringing in his pocket. He pulled it out, answering quickly. "What's up, Newt?" His eyes tightened as he listened for a few seconds. "Yeah? That's great news. Yeah tell him we'll do it for the same fee as today. Why can't you deal with it? You have our bookings calendar there in that stuff. I'm in line for a ride; we're almost at the front. Seriously, Newt, you just book it. You'll see what days we're already busy. Why does he want to talk to me?" He sighed deeply, closing his eyes. "Seriously? This sucks! Yeah fine I'll be there in a minute." He disconnected the call, looking up at me with apologetic eyes. "I need to go back to the tent. Apparently the guy who booked us today wants to book us for a series of six shows too."

I gasped excitedly. "That's fantastic," I chirped proudly. "Congrats!"

He smiled and nodded. "Thanks. But apparently the guy wants to talk to me and for me to book it seeing as I was the one that dealt with him last time. I have to go back and meet him now." He nodded over his shoulder back the way he came. "I'll only be a few minutes and then we can come right back here and go on this." His voice was slightly annoyed as he spoke, obviously not happy with having to lose our place in the line.

I looked back over his shoulder, seeing the tent about two hundred yards away. I groaned thinking about walking all the way over there again on my now aching ankle. "You go. I'll wait for you here and then we can go on," I suggested.

He didn't look like he was going for it though. "No way. I'm not leaving you here on your own," he protested.

I pouted, really not wanting to walk again. "Zach, I'll be fine. I'll wait right here for you until you get back. I'm surrounded by people; nothing's going to happen to me. I seriously can't walk all the way there and back again. I'll wait here. Go, hurry up," I insisted, waving my hand at the tent.

"Maisie," he whined, his expression pained.

Placing my hand on his shoulder, I gave him a little push away from me. "Go talk to the guy. I'll be right here. I promise I'll be fine."

He groaned, looking down at my ankle before he nodded and stepped closer to me, his eyes fierce and warning. "Stay right here. Don't move," he huffed.

I smiled and nodded. "You're so bossy," I joked, turning my nose up at him playfully. He chuckled and turned, running off quickly towards the tent. I watched him until he was out of sight, and then adjusted my weight on the fence to get more comfortable. I busied myself by looking around at the crowd. My friends were probably around here somewhere, but I couldn't see anyone I knew. The line moved again, so I waved the people behind me on, telling them I was waiting for someone. The noise and laughter circulated around me; the smell of popcorn and hot doughnuts made my mouth water as I sat there, just enjoying the atmosphere.

After a couple of minutes my cell phone vibrated in my pocket. I pulled it out, grinning down at it, expecting to see a text from Zach asking if I was alright. Instead, the screen announced that I had a message from an unknown number. My eyes widened before I even opened it. My skin prickled as the hair on the nape of my neck stood on end.

Not again, please!

I barely had the nerve to open the message. For a few seconds I just looked down at the notification, wondering if I didn't open it whether that would somehow make it disappear. In the end my fingers got the better of me and I opened it, holding my breath as I read the words.

'Comfortable, sitting there all alone? Want some company?'

The words weren't sinister, but for some reason my heart plummeted down towards my toes. They could see me again. Had they followed me here, were they watching me all the time? I jumped to my feet, almost falling when my ankle gave way, making me lurch forward into a tall guy who swore and grabbed hold of me in a bid to keep himself upright. I gasped, looking up into a pair of angry eyes as he frowned down at me.

"Sorry. Sorry," I muttered, shoving myself away from him. My eyes darted around quickly, seeing if anyone was watching me or paying too much interest in me or something. Was the person who sent it hidden in the crowd, laughing at my clumsiness?

My cell phone vibrated again in my hand, and I looked down at it in horror. I swiped my thumb over the message tab and up popped another one from the unknown number.

'If I were you, I'd run'

Run. The word echoed in my head. Run. Run. Run. I didn't think twice, I took off in the direction of the tent, knowing Zach was there, silently scolding myself for suggesting that nothing could happen because I was surrounded by people. Wrong again it seemed.

Tears built in my eyes as I did my best to dodge around people, wincing with every step because my ankle was burning and almost giving out with each movement. People scolded me and griped as I narrowly avoided bumping into them as I stumbled past. The tent was getting closer and closer, and I could feel my hope building up. Zach was in there; once I got in there everything would be fine again.

But as I burst through the door at full speed, I was greeted by nothing but the empty chairs and a few empty water bottles. My eyes widened. *Where the hell is he?* "Zach?" I shouted, spinning on the spot, hoping he'd materialise from somewhere, but no such luck.

My cell phone started ringing in my hand then. A little squeak left my lips as I dropped my phone onto the floor in my surprise. I clamped my hand over my mouth as I stood there, staring at it, seeing that it was a private number calling me. There was no way I was answering it. I didn't know what to do, the phone seemed to be deafening as it continued to ring and ring.

My thoughts shot to Luke. I wanted Luke – no, that wasn't quite right, I *needed* him. My need for Luke suddenly made things clearer for me. I needed to call him and get to somewhere where he could find me. I shouldn't be standing on my own in a marquee where anyone could come in and no one would be any the wiser.

I bent and snatched the phone from the floor, instantly rejecting the call as I bolted back out of the door and into the middle of the crowd, not stopping until I was right in the centre of the attractions where it was busiest. I knew that if the guy was watching me that he'd be able to see me right now, but at least he wouldn't be able to do anything while I was surrounded by people. I kept darting my eyes around for anything suspicious as I hit speed dial one and called

Luke's number. As the line connected my phone battery beeped, signalling it was about to die soon. I whimpered, praying it would hold out enough until I spoke to Luke.

Thankfully he answered after a couple of rings. "Hey, baby. Where are you?"

The sound of his voice brought a lump to my throat. "Luke, oh God, the phone, a message, please," I rambled.

"Message? From the person that's harassing you? Damn it! Where are you? Tell me where you are and I'll meet you there. Stay with Zach!" he barked angrily.

My chin trembled as I looked around quickly, trying to find something I could describe to him so he'd know where I was. "The shooting stall next to where you won my crocodile," I muttered, not having the will to explain that I was on my own.

"Okay, I'll be there as quick as I can." He disconnected the call. I let my hand drop to my side as I walked further into the crowd and just stopped in the middle of the walkway, not even apologising when people walked into me or bumped me because I was in the way. The crowd made me feel slightly safer, but not as safe as I knew Luke's arms would make me feel.

• • •

AN HOUR AND A half later I'd given a full report to DI Neeson. Luke had called them after he'd finally managed to calm me down. He'd also called Zach, laying into him down the phone about leaving me alone and how he was lucky I was alright and hadn't been hurt. The happy atmosphere had died out almost straight away; the fun had been sucked out of the night. Luke and I had left the others at the fairground to continue with the merriment, while Luke drove me to a McDonalds close by so I could give my statement to the police. He'd arranged with Charlotte that I was just going to stay at his place tonight instead of going to hers. I was actually extremely grateful for that. Being in Luke's arms tonight was just what I needed. I hadn't informed my dad of the change of plans. He would probably say no and insist that I go home, but I couldn't be alone right now. Staying at Luke's was what I desperately wanted.

I swallowed the last of my coffee, looking up at him now. His expression was a mask of concern as he looked back at me with those big brown eyes that I fell in love with so deeply. He reached out, taking my hand across the table and interlacing our fingers. DI Neeson had not long left and we'd just been sat in silence for the last few minutes. I didn't even know what to say. I longed for life to go back to normal, for us to be normal and together, for me to stop being terrified all the time. I hated everything about my life at that moment.

"Come on, let's go. I'll run you a nice hot bath when we get to mine and you can soak and relax," he suggested, helping me up from the seat.

I sighed dreamily at how nice that sounded. "Thanks." We hobbled out across the practically deserted parking lot and over to his Jeep that was parked in the corner. When we got to it I leant against the side of the car, watching as he dug in his pocket for his keys. "I can't wait to graduate and leave for college," I mumbled, shaking my head tiredly. "Think all this will stop when we go away to college?" I asked hopefully.

His eyes searched mine as he nodded. "Yeah," he confirmed. "Have you... have you decided on college then?" he asked, dropping his eyes to the floor and playing with his keys in his hand.

Decided on college? What is he asking me that for? "I thought we'd decided on that months ago."

He looked up, confusion clear across his face. "Yeah but, you know, things changed since then. I screwed up. So I assumed you'd be looking at colleges closer to your family instead."

I shrugged. "Why would I do that?" I questioned. We'd talked and talked about colleges before, we'd decided on one that offered us both great opportunities.

His mouth dropped open in shock. "Are you saying that maybe we could still go to Oregon together?" he asked. The hopeful tone to his voice made my heart stutter.

Standing in the cool night, illuminated by a streetlight a little way away, it hit me just how much I loved him. All of this stuff that had happened recently just proved to me how much I needed him in my life. He was the one for me. He was my first thought when I was scared, the one I wanted to comfort me when I cried, and the one I wanted to share everything with. He had always been that person for me, I'd just been too clouded by hurt to see that us being together was inevitable.

All of this stuff, this being in danger stuff, had all served to show me how precious each day was. I shouldn't be wasting time being sad and lonely, when the thing I wanted more than anything, wanted me too. I was just doing myself an injustice by denying myself something that made me incredibly happy all the time.

"When we leave school I think everything will be better. Right now every time I look around I get reminded of what you did, the people all know so I feel like they're laughing at me. I think once school is over and we're at college then we can start afresh," I suggested. Starting afresh sounded like bliss to me.

His eyes widened as he stepped closer to me, so close that his body was merely inches away and his toes actually touched mine. "Start afresh. Please tell me you're saying what I think you're saying," he begged. His voice broke as he looked at me so intently that it made my stomach flutter.

"Well, do you think I'm saying that I just can't be without you anymore?"

I asked, reaching out one hand and placing it over his heart. I could feel the steady drumming under my palm, and I smiled at how precious it felt to me.

"That's what I pray you're saying, baby," he whispered, leaning in closer to me and touching my cheek, brushing his fingers there softly. He leant forward, placing his forehead against mine as his breathing became more ragged. His other hand gripped my side tightly. "Please. Please, Maisie," he begged.

Emotion was threatening to boil over as happiness hit me in waves. I knew then that this was the right thing to do. Screw everything and everyone else. Luke Hannigan made me happy, and I just couldn't *not* be with him anymore.

"Tell me you love me." I slid my hands up to his neck, pushing one into the back of his hair and weaving my fingers into the soft silky strands.

He gulped loudly. His eyes danced with excitement, his whole body seemed to go rigid. "I lov-" I crashed my lips to his before he could finish saying it. I didn't need him to say it. I already knew.

As soon as his lips were on mine, everything else seemed to evaporate and all that was important was him and me and that his lips belonged on mine. He made a small startled moan in the back of his throat but kissed me back immediately, pushing against me, trapping me between the hardness of his body and the cool metal of his car. The passion that went into the kiss almost knocked me sideways as his tongue met mine. His taste exploded against my taste buds as I fisted my hand into his hair, squeezing myself to him tighter, wanting to melt inside him and never get out again.

Everything about the way he kissed me, the feel of his hands as they gripped my waist, the way he pinned me tightly against the car as he kissed me like I had never been kissed before in my life, all of it was beautiful. It was familiar, incredible, passionate, but most importantly, it was right. My whole body seemed to come alive with a hunger that he always seemed to evoke in me. I pulled my mouth away from his, desperate for air, gasping as my knees went weak with longing. My love for him was overwhelming, almost too much to cope with as everything built inside me like a raging inferno. I needed to release this passion before it made me explode. I fumbled behind me, grabbing the back door handle, pushing him away from me for a second so I could move to the side and force the door open.

When I looked up at him I knew that he felt exactly the same as me in that moment - desperate and needy. My skin seemed to prickle all over as I whimpered. Grabbing his shirt and yanking him towards me, I sat on the back seat, hooking my legs either side of his and trapping him against me. "Luke," I whined, not having the words to describe what I needed from him.

He flicked his eyes behind him, a little bewildered as he gasped for breath too. "Here? Seriously?" he croaked, his voice all husky and thick with lust.

I didn't answer, just leant forward and pressed my mouth to his again, capturing his bottom lip between my teeth and biting roughly. He grunted, and that seemed to be all the encouragement he needed as he moved forward, forcing me onto my back as he leant on top of me, wriggling and fumbling behind him, slamming the door closed, trapping us in the back of his car. Almost instantly the temperature in the car seemed to spike as he looked down at me with eyes that were so ecstatic that it made my heart ache.

Reaching out, I snagged his hoodie and t-shirt, yanking them both over his head in one easy movement. His phone slid out of his pocket and thumped to the floor, but neither of us paid any attention as he leant down, brushing his lips against mine softly, just once. My fingers dug into the bare skin of his back, just marvelling over the weight of his body on top of me again.

"Tell me you love me," he whispered, tracing my nose with his.

My legs moved, wrapping around his waist, pinning him to me. "I love y-" but just like I hadn't let him finish, he didn't let me finish. I felt him smile against my lips as I wrapped my arms tightly around his neck, happier than I had been in weeks. While I was with Luke like this, everything was right in the world and nothing else mattered.

chapter twenty-seven

As sleep ebbed away, the first thing I noticed was how comfortable I was. The soft sheets were pulled up to my chin, and the hard, warm thing I was cuddled up to felt like luxurious satin against my bare skin. A lazy pattern was being drawn on the small of my back with a fingertip. My first thought was: heaven. Blissful, beautiful heaven I was waking up in. I already knew what I would see when I opened my eyes.

Blinking against the sunlight that was filtering in through the blood red drapes, I looked up into Luke's warm brown eyes. He was already awake, just lying there silently, watching me sleep as he traced his fingers over my back. His other arm was wrapped loosely around me, holding me against his chest.

Happiness seemed to radiate through every cell in my body at once, warming my skin and making my heart stutter. I raised a hand, tracing the line of his jaw, just wanting to check to make sure he was definitely here, and that this was definitely happening. It almost felt like a dream. It had been so long since I'd woken up with him like this, like part of a couple, that it didn't feel real. His night's growth of hair scratched against my fingertip and I let out a little contented sigh.

A smile twitched at the corners of his mouth, his eyes glittered with elation as his arm tightened around me. "Hi," he whispered.

I chewed on my lip, fighting with my hormones that were currently raging and would soon burn everything in their wake. "Hi," I croaked, hating that my voice was thick with sleep and not in the sexy way that some girls had.

His boyish smile grew into an outright grin as I snuggled closer to him, wanting to feel every part of his skin on mine. As I moved, I realised that my body ached in delicious ways that it hadn't ached for in weeks. My muscles felt tight and overused because of what we'd gotten up to last night in the back of his car, and after in the front hallway downstairs, and then again in his bed. My body was out of practice with all this physical exertion, but I would get used to it again pretty quickly, that much I was sure of.

"How are you this morning?" he asked, his eyes searching my face, almost as if he was trying to ascertain the answer without me even speaking.

I felt the heat flood my face. Silly little girl in love Maisie was back again. "My body aches. I think I have sex muscle syndrome," I answered, giggling and looping my arm around his neck.

He laughed at my answer and rolled gently so I was half under him. "You do? Want me to give you a massage?" he offered, bending his head and tracing his nose across my cheek before breathing in lungful's of my hair as his hand instantly started massaging my outer thigh.

I closed my eyes, overcome by sensation as my fingers dug into his shoulders. "No," I croaked. "How about we just stretch them out again?" I offered, gasping as he kissed the sensitive spot on side of my neck, just below my ear.

He didn't immediately jump on me like I was expecting. Instead, he pulled back, his eyes tight, seeming slightly worried. "Baby, this isn't just a sex thing is it? This thing that's happened, this is us getting back together again, right? Not just us sleeping together." His eyes searched mine and his hand stilled on my thigh as he seemed to hold his breath in anticipation.

My heart melted because he just looked so hopeful and so pleading. He wanted me back so badly that it made my insides tremble. In that moment, my love for him was overwhelming, and I knew that he felt the same as me, that we belonged together. Even after everything that had happened, I was destined to be with Luke Hannigan forever, I knew it deep down in my heart.

"This is us getting back together again," I confirmed, fisting my hand into the back of his hair.

His whole body seemed to relax as he closed his eyes and gulped. "Thank you," he whispered. His eyes opened, glistening in the dim light of his bedroom as he smiled down at me. "Thank you. I promise I won't ever do that again, not ever. You're my life, Maisie, and I almost lost you. I won't ever do anything to jeopardise that again. I'm so sorry." His voice was earnest and full of emotion as he spoke.

I nodded. "I know you are." That was the truth, I knew he was sorry, and I knew how important I was to him.

"I'll spend my life making it up to you, I promise." He bent and kissed my cheek, and I felt everything fall back into place, just like it was before all of this happened.

"How about you start right now?" I suggested, raising one eyebrow suggestively as I hitched my leg over his hip and pulled his body closer to mine.

He sucked in a breath through his teeth and let it out as a low groan as his mouth headed towards mine. I smiled against his lips and melted into his embrace, giving myself over entirely, body, mind and spirit.

• • •

TWO HOURS LATER and we had only just dragged ourselves out of his bed. For ages I'd just laid there in his arms while we talked about random stuff, with the TV showing nothing in particular in the background. In my eyes, it couldn't get any more perfect than that. I'd wanted to stay in that moment forever, never moving forward or back, just frozen in time with him. Unfortunately, being an eating machine, his body had something else to say about my staying in bed forever plan.

"There's nothing much in here," I muttered, frowning into his half empty fridge. I picked up the remaining two eggs and the packet of suspicious looking ham. "I guess we could make a ham omelette?" I offered, turning my nose up at the prospect. The ham looked like it had been open for a while, the edges curling in a stomach wrenching way.

His arms wrapped around me, his bare chest pressing against my back as he pulled me away from the fridge gently. "I have a great idea," he said into my ear before kissing the back of my neck softly and playing with the edge of his t-shirt that I was wearing.

I tipped my head to the side, smiling now. "I thought you were hungry," I teased.

He chuckled, taking the eggs and ham out of my hands and placing them onto the counter top. "I am hungry. Which is why I was going to suggest that we get dressed and take a drive over to that little café that you like, the one that makes those muffins with the cranberries?"

I gasped, my eyes widening with excitement as I turned in his arms and grinned up at him. "Yeah?" I chirped. "I love that idea!" The café he was talking about was a quaint little old fashioned tea room that we had found once when we were camping. It was about an hour drive from here, but the muffins and pastries were to die for. Luke and I had made a point at stopping there whenever we went that way to camp.

He grinned, tracing my lips with his index finger. "I thought you might. Come on then, let's get dressed and go. It'll be like a date."

I grinned ecstatically. If he was going to be making this much of an effort to make it up to me then I was a seriously lucky girl. "Race ya," I joked, shoving myself out of his arms and dashing for the stairs. He chuckled darkly, and I heard his heavy footsteps behind me. He caught up with me before I even made it half way up the stairs. I gasped as he swept my legs out from under me, pulling me into his arms and crashing his lips down to mine. I giggled against his lips, wrapping my arms around his neck and kissing him back instantly. Of course I'd known that the running away from him action would bring out his playful side, so no doubt the trip to the café would be put on hold, at least for a while anyway.

• • •

THE CAFÉ WAS JUST as lovely and romantic as I remembered. We had been the only ones in there, sitting in the corner, feeding each other iced pastries and muffins while the early afternoon sunshine shone in through the window. The lady even recognised us and gave us a free refill on our coffees. It had been perfect; every single second of the day with him had been spectacular, and I didn't want it to end. I didn't want to have to share him with other people again when we went back to school.

"I can't wait to go to college," I mused as he threw money down on the table to cover our meal.

He looked up at me and grinned. "Me either, it's going to be great. Just me and you, away from everyone and everything that's happened here. It'll be like a fresh start for both of us," he replied, holding out his hand to me.

I placed my hand in his, letting him help me out of the booth. I smiled at his words. That was exactly what I felt too. With us going away to college together and moving to another town hours away, there would be nothing there to remind either of us of the bad things that had occurred recently. "Sounds great." His arm slipped around my shoulder as he guided me out of the little café, both of us waving to the owner on the way out. I climbed in his Jeep, watching as he walked around to the driver's side. The little smile on his face made my heart melt.

As he got in and started the engine I suddenly realised I didn't actually want to go home. I liked being out here with him, with no one to bother us, and no need to worry about some psycho that wanted to hurt me. A sigh of disappointment left my lips as I scooted down into the seat, trying not to let my feelings show on my face. I didn't want to ruin this happy day, but I couldn't get my mind off the fact that everything would be different once we got home.

"What's up, baby?" Luke asked as he backed the car out and headed in the direction of home.

I shrugged, not really knowing how to explain that I was just fed up with feeling frightened all the time; that I was fed up with looking over my shoulder and not knowing what was going to happen next. "I just don't really want to go home. You know, the police thing and stuff," I explained. "I just wish it was me and you all the time and that all that other stuff would just disappear."

"Hmm," he mused, nodding in agreement. "Why don't we just go away for a bit? Just pack up and leave together for a while or something?" he suggested casually, as if that was just something that could happen.

I laughed at the hopefulness in his voice. "Luke, we can't." I shook my head at how silly he was being. *Maybe he's had too much sugar from all those muffins!*

"Why not? I'm being serious. Let's just pack up and leave, screw everything else, just me and you together." He glanced over at me, keeping one eye on the road as he continued, "I can protect you. All this stuff will stop, the phone calls, the flowers, all of it will just go away and then it'll just be us. We'll travel for a while, see some sights, and do some of the things you've always wanted to do. It'll be perfect."

It sounded so nice, and I unconsciously started playing that out in my head. Us waking up together every day, falling asleep in his arms, no pressure, no more being frightened. Everything sounded so great, but I knew that was impossible, at least for the next few weeks it was impossible anyway. "We have our finals, we can't just up and leave," I protested. A frown lined his forehead as he looked back to the road and sighed deeply. I chewed on my lip and reached out, taking his hand and pulling it onto my lap as I stroked his knuckles with my thumb. "Luke, it sounds great, and if we didn't have finals then I'd be saying heck yeah let's go right now, but we have responsibilities, we have to graduate in order to get our places in college. We can't let something like this ruin everything we've worked so hard for," I persuaded.

His grip tightened on my hand as he nodded dejectedly. "Yeah I guess."

"There's just three more weeks left of school now, let's just get those out of the way and then we'll think about it, alright?" I bargained, wanting to take the sad expression from his face. We hadn't made any plans for the summer, and travelling for a month or so would certainly be fun.

He sighed and nodded, bringing my hand up to his mouth, planting a soft kiss against my palm. "Okay."

I smiled and settled down into my seat, watching the road stretch out ahead of us. Everything seemed chilled and relaxed when I was with Luke; nothing seemed to faze me because I knew that whatever happened he would look after me, just like he always promised he would. I looked over at him from the corner of my eye, feeling a little smile tug at the corners of my mouth. I couldn't wait for those three weeks to be over with so that we could live out his plans. He was right, it would be perfect and I couldn't wait. He caught me looking and smiled over at me. His brown eyes were soft and tender as they caught mine. "I love you, Maisie."

My heart stuttered as I nodded in confirmation, I didn't need him to say the words, I already knew it, I always had done. "I love you too." He grinned that dazzling smile and turned back to the road, turning up the radio a little more so the soft tones of The Script filled the car.

After a while I remembered that I needed to charge my cell phone. "You have your phone charger in the car?" I asked, digging my cell out of my purse.

He nodded, reaching out and pulling his in-car charger from the dashboard, plugging it in for me and holding out the end. I smiled gratefully and plugged it in, waiting a few seconds before attempting to turn it on and then fitting it into the little drinks holder in his car. A couple of minutes later my cell beeped. I picked it up, looking down at the screen to see that I had a new text message from Charlotte that had been received when my phone was off. I smiled and opened it, still singing along to the music. The words died on my lips as I read the message.

'I know you said not to, but... I just got the phone number from the cell phone company database. Here it is. Seriously, let one of the boys call it and frighten the crap out of the guy!'

Then there was a cell phone number after it. I gulped, reading the message again with wide eyes. Seeing it there, glowing in the fading daylight, made everything come to a head. It seemed to make everything more real somehow. Now that I had the number I wasn't sure what to do with it. I shouldn't do anything with it; the police had the number but couldn't trace it because it was a pay as you go with no contract or fixed address. I shouldn't get involved. Just like I told Charlotte in the first place, I should just let the police do their jobs and wait for them to contact me again so that they could trace the call like they wanted to.

But seeing it there was just too tempting. Maybe I could call it. Maybe the guy would answer and then... what? What would I do then? I frowned down at it, confused and a little afraid of it. I wanted to call the number. Curiosity was getting the better of me. I started thinking that maybe I'd recognise the voice of the person and then I could tell the police who to look into. Maybe it would be that easy and then it would be over. My mind was whirling, dreaming up and dismissing scenarios so quickly that it made my head spin.

Without thinking anymore about it, I clicked on the number, bringing it up on my screen. My thumb hovered over the green call button as I fought with myself, trying to debate if I was going to do any damage by actually calling the person. The chances are it would be switched off, like it always was when the police tried to call it. But what if they actually answered? What would I say then?

"Everything okay?" Luke asked, looking over at me with one eyebrow raised. I cleared my throat and nodded, still undecided. "Who was that from? Not that Zach guy again." His voice was practically a growl as he said Zach's name.

I shook my head slowly, unsure how I was going to tell him that Charlotte had illegally hacked the phone company and found the number of the guy that was calling me. I gulped, knowing he would be mad at me for getting involved. "No. Charlotte found the phone number of the person that's been calling me. She's just text it to me," I mumbled, my words all mashing together as I spoke. He obviously understood though.

He straightened in his seat, his hands gripping the wheel so tightly that his knuckles went white. "She what? How? What the fuck, Maisie?" he ranted, reaching to grab my phone from my hand.

I shook my head and quickly moved it out of his reach. "I could call it. Maybe then I'll recognise the voice and everything will be over, I can tell the police, and they can investigate and arrest them. It'll be over," I countered, looking at him for his opinion.

His opinion was clear across his face though, I could see it clearly enough. He was horrified, totally against the idea by the look of it. Again my finger hovered over the call button. "Don't, Maisie, for Christ sake don't," he cried, reaching for the phone again.

I pushed his hand away quickly as he slammed on the brakes of the car, screeching us to a halt just as we were about to cross a bridge over the river. I was thrown forward against my seatbelt from the force of the stop, my ribs and chest instantly burning and aching from the pressure. "Damn it, Luke! What the hell are you doing?" I shouted, pulling at my seatbelt to try and get it to loosen but it was no good; the quick stopping motion had made it too tight across my chest and lap.

"Give me the phone!" he barked, holding out his hand for it.

Car horns blasted behind us where we were blocking our side of the road. "Luke, people can't get past," I observed, nodding my head at the traffic that was queuing up behind us pretty quickly.

He shook his hand in front of me again. "Give me the phone," he repeated.

I gulped and pressed the call button, knowing that as soon as he took my phone off me he would delete the number so I couldn't call it. His eyes went wide as I put the phone to my ear, hearing the little tinkle where the phone connected to the line. Almost immediately a bell like sound came from behind me. I frowned, looking over the back of the seat to the footwell behind me. The sound seemed to be coming from there. I flicked my gaze up to Luke only to see he had his eyes closed, his head hung dejectedly as the bell sound continued in the background, muffled by the song on the radio.

I frowned, confused. "What's that?" I asked, looking around for the source of the noise. I twisted awkwardly in my seat, reaching behind me and batting the other junk out of the way. My hand touched cool, vibrating plastic, so I gripped it and pulled it into the front. It was the cell phone that had fallen out of Luke's pocket last night when we were making out in the back of the car. But looking at it again now in the daylight, I realised that it wasn't actually Luke's cell phone. It was one that I had never seen before, a cheap Nokia one and not something like Luke would buy at all.

What puzzled me the most is that my number was flashing on the screen as it continued to vibrate in my hand. "Who's is this?" I muttered, shaking my head in confusion. Luke's gaze lifted to mine. An apologetic, pained expression covered his face as realisation hit me like a bucket of cold water. The number that Charlotte had found for me, was calling Luke? My heart sank as my blood seemed to turn to ice in my veins. "Oh God, no," I mumbled as everything seemed to hit me at once.

Luke.

It was Luke.

He gulped, his mouth opening as he seemed to struggle with his words as the phone rang and rang in the background. "Maisie..." he croaked, shaking his head slowly, his eyes not leaving mine.

No. No. No. No!

It felt as if a knife pierced into my heart, twisting, killing me slowly.

"It was you? But why?" I whispered, horrified, mortified, hurt, and crushed because not for one second had I ever suspected that the person I loved would do this to me.

chapter twenty-eight

"Why?" I repeated, pulling at my seatbelt as my heart dropped down into my stomach. I'd never felt so let down or disappointed in all my life. But I just couldn't understand it, I couldn't take it in. Why would Luke want to do that to me? Did he not love me at all? Why would he be trying to hurt me?

He groaned, closing his eyes as he raised his elbow and pressed down his door lock, locking us both into the car. Before he did that I hadn't even thought about exiting the car, but now that I knew I was locked in my mind was instantly wondering why he would want to keep me in the car. Would he actually want to hurt me, like the notes had suggested?

"I love you so much," he croaked, turning in his seat to look at me as he unclipped his seatbelt and scooted closer to me.

My eyes filled with tears as everything flashed up in my mind, the notes, how scared I'd been, how he'd held me and told me that he would never let anyone hurt me. When my thoughts turned to Chester I felt my heart break even more. He couldn't have done that, surely. He knew how much I loved my dog; he wouldn't have hurt him, would he?

A strangled noise came out of my mouth as I struggled to comprehend everything. All of it, everything that had happened in the last few weeks, it had all been the love of my life? "No," I groaned, shaking my head, begging him with my eyes for some other explanation, that he'd found the phone somewhere, that he was holding it for someone else, anything.

He nodded sadly, resting his head back against the seat. "I did it because I love you. I never meant for it to go this far. I just meant to show you that you needed me, I didn't mean to take it this far," he whispered, fisting his hands in his hair.

I whimpered, my mouth agape, just staring at him, waiting for him to tell me this was some sick joke. I paid no attention to the cars that were struggling to drive around us, blasting their horns and shouting abuse out of their windows.

Luke turned to me then, his eyes so sorrowful that it made my stomach ache. “I was desperate. I could see I’d lost you after what I did with Sandy at the party, and I just needed to get you back. I need you, Maisie; I need you in my life. I have nothing without you. You’re the only one that ever really saw me for me, and I couldn’t lose you over a stupid mistake.” He gulped, running a hand through his hair. I noticed with some level of gratitude that he hadn’t moved to touch me at all; he was just begging me with his eyes to understand and listen.

“So you decided the best way to win me back was to send me death threats? Poison my dog?” A sob rose in my throat as he winced when I said about Chester. “Please tell me you didn’t do that, that someone else did that, please tell me that,” I begged.

He shook his head slowly. “I didn’t mean to make him that sick,” he croaked. “I gave him the meat, and I thought he’d be sick a few times. I know you can’t deal well with sick, so I figured you’d call me up to help you. I didn’t realise it’d be that bad, I never meant for that to happen.”

Anger took over then. Looking at him as he apologised just drove me to the edge. I twisted in my seat and slapped his shoulder and chest as hard as I could, over and over. “You sick, sick bastard! How could you do that? He didn’t deserve to go through that! You’re demented, Luke. What kind of sicko does that to a dog just to get some attention from his girlfriend?” I screamed, slapping him again for emphasis.

He grabbed my wrists, clenching his jaw tightly as he restrained me, pinning my hands down into my lap effortlessly. “Maisie, please. I did it all because I love you.”

I glared at him, struggling against his hold. “You can’t love me! That’s not love, that’s obsession!” I scoffed.

He scowled at me and let go of my hands, moving back into his chair again. “Don’t ever think that I don’t love you,” he snapped. I opened my mouth to make another angry retort, but he carried on speaking, cutting me off. “I got the idea that day at school when you saw that frog and you jumped on me. I knew then that you needed me, you just didn’t realise it.”

The frog. When I’d screamed and jumped on him. He somehow connected me being scared with me needing him? That’s where he came up with this twisted idea? I pressed back into the door, wanting to get as far away from him as possible. “So you just decided that frightening me would be okay, did you?” I spat angrily.

He shrugged and nodded. “I didn’t mean to take it this far. I just meant to send you a few notes, the flowers and stuff. But the more frightened you got, the more you came to me. The further I pushed it, the closer I got to getting you back," he explained casually, as if this was the most normal conversation in the world.

"And that makes it okay? The fact that you didn't mean any harm by it makes it okay in your head does it?" How could he be so casual? How could he think his actions were justified just because it showed me that I needed him by frightening the life out of me and poisoning my dog.

He shook his head quickly, his eyes meeting mine as his shoulders slumped. "No, it's not okay, I know that. I didn't mean to hurt you; I just meant to frighten you a little."

"So you could swoop in like a knight in shining armour?" I snapped, glaring at him.

He nodded. "Kinda, yeah." He gulped, nodded down at the cell phone in my hand that had finally stopped ringing because it had been trying to connect for so long. "I bought that and just meant to call you a couple of times, but things got out of hand, I lost the plot a little, I know that."

Lost the plot a little? Try a lot! Suddenly Sandy crossed my mind and my eyes widened as another thought occurred to me. The police said that there was a possibility that whoever was harassing me was the same person that had killed her. *Oh God.* "Sandy," I croaked. He wouldn't have gone that far, surely.

His teeth snapped together with an audible click as he wrinkled his nose distastefully. "She fucking deserved it. All of this was her fault in the first place. The little dirty whore was going to ruin everything!" he growled. His hands clenched into fists as he ground his teeth.

Horror settled in the pit of my stomach. He'd killed someone. Luke was a murderer. I was sitting in the car with a murderer. The guy I was hopelessly in love with was a cold blooded killer.

He shook his head as if thinking about something that made him angry. "The little tramp was blackmailing me, trying to get me to date her. She saw me buying the meat and put two and two together. She guessed that it was me that poisoned Chester. She threatened to tell you if I didn't do as she said."

I swallowed the lump in my throat and swiped at the tears that now spilled over and fell down my face. "So you killed her?" I squeaked, praying he would say no. I almost wanted him to be angry with me for even suggesting something so absurd.

"Yeah." He nodded, closing his eyes in obvious remorse. "I didn't mean to. I didn't plan it or anything, it just happened. I called her to meet up and just went to talk to her, to tell her to back off and that I wasn't going to go along with her plans. I only had the knife to threaten her, nothing else. But she just kept going on and on about you. The things she was saying," he gulped, "she's nasty piece of work. I just lost it, I grabbed the knife and… and…" He looked down at his hands as if expecting the knife to still be there or something.

My heart was slamming in my chest. I didn't know what to say.

He looked up at me then with wide eyes, his chin trembled. "Please don't hate me," he whispered. "I didn't mean for any of this to happen. I just wanted you back, and then things got out of control. I'm so sorry. I never would have hurt you; I just wanted you to think that someone wanted you hurt so that I could protect you."

I looked at him, completely and utterly shell shocked. I didn't know what to do or say. In the deep recesses of my mind I could actually understand why he had done it. Luke had never really had anyone else in his life, his family all but abandoned him all the time, and his friends were more like leeches just after his popularity or talent. No one really understood Luke like I did, we had a special connection, I knew that. I knew that he loved me. I'd just never realised how distorted his idea of love was, or how far he would take things to hold on to me. But I could kind of understand it all because I loved him probably just as much - though I would never resort to drastic measures like he had.

"There's something really wrong with you, Luke," I muttered, shaking my head, pulling again at my seatbelt. I needed to get out of the car. The air seemed to be getting thicker, making it harder to breathe. I needed to get away from him so that I could think clearly.

His hand reached out, stroking the side of my face with one finger. I cringed away from his hand, instantly thinking of him holding a knife and plunging it into Sandy's body. He was a killer. Even though I still loved him, I now viewed him differently. He wasn't the person that I thought he was, he wasn't sweet, loving Luke that would do anything for me. He was sick, twisted Luke that would do anything to keep me. He scared me as he looked at me so pleadingly.

"Don't touch me," I hissed, pushing his hand away from my face.

He groaned. Tears glistened in his eyes as his shoulders slumped in defeat. "Please forgive me, Maisie. I'm nothing without you," he rasped.

"Forgive you? What… how… Luke, I can't even look at you right now!" I gasped, shaking my head as I fumbled with my seatbelt again, but my hands were shaking too badly so I couldn't depress the button properly.

He made a strangled gargle and shook his head. "Don't say that. I love you; I did all of this because I love you! Everything was for you. All of it."

I gulped as my mind raced and whirled with thoughts. *He's going to be in so much trouble. The police will arrest him and he'll be charged with murder, he'll go to jail for years.* I hated the fact that the thought of him being punished for his crimes actually made my heart ache. He was sick in the head, but I still loved him, even after all he'd done to me this last couple of weeks.

"Luke, we need to go to the police. You need to tell them what you did," I whispered.

He shook his head adamantly, his eyes widening in apparent horror. "No. Maisie, no, please?" he begged. "Can't we just forget this happened? I promise I'll stop now; I won't ever do anything like this again, please?" His eyes were going to be my undoing, so frightened looking, so pleading and desperate. I turned away from his expression. It wasn't just about what he'd done to me; it was about the fact that he'd killed someone. We couldn't just pretend like that didn't happen, he needed to be held accountable and get the help that he clearly needed.

"We can't." I shook my head, wiping a shaky hand over my face. I needed fresh air, I felt too hot. I couldn't deal with all of this right now. I looked back at him and whimpered at the sad and devastated expression that I saw on his face.

He looked back out the windshield, a tear slid down his face slowly. "I can't see you make a life with someone else. I can't lose you, baby," he mumbled. "I love you more than anything, more than life itself. I have no life without you, nothing worth living for." His sad tone actually made my insides tremble; I could almost feel the pain and torture in his words. "I'm never going to get you back after this, am I?"

I gulped as he turned his head to look at me. His brown eyes that I loved so much looked desperate, dejected, and resigned. His sorrowful expression made me feel nauseous as the hair on the back of my neck prickled. "I don't think so," I admitted. Nothing would ever be the same after this. I couldn't just forgive him for everything. He'd killed someone; he wasn't the person who I thought he was.

He nodded, his hands tightening on the wheel. "I can't see you with someone else. You're mine, forever, just like we always said," he whispered. "I love you, baby."

Before I could answer, or even think about what he meant by that, he released the parking brake and shoved his foot down on the accelerator, narrowly avoiding a collision with a car that was in the process of pulling around us. I gasped as the force of the take-off threw me back into the seat. Suddenly the tyres squealed as he twisted the wheel quickly. My eyes flicked up, shocked, only to see that we were now heading towards the metal barrier of the bridge.

"Luke! What the hell are you doing?" I screamed. But my words were lost in the blast of noise as the car hit the metal barrier with a deafening crack. I gripped the edges of my seat, watching with wide, frightened eyes as the protective side of the bridge just crumpled under the force of the crash, part of it splintering up and hitting the windscreen hard enough to shatter it. Small lumps of glass spattered across my lap, stinging my exposed skin. Everything seemed to happen too fast for me to comprehend. First the glass smashed, and then the car hurtled off the side of the bridge, heading for the dark, watery depths that I knew were below.

chapter twenty-nine

My stomach lurched up to my throat as we seemed suspended in the air for a second before we were plummeting down the thirty or so feet towards the river below. The sounds of Luke still gunning the engine were all I could hear as the car tipped forward slightly so I could see the water as it rushed up towards me. I couldn't even scream. It felt like I was paralysed as every muscle in my body seemed to go stiff with fear. I watched in horror as the water got closer and closer, filling my vision in a swirling mass of light brown.

The front of the car broke the surface first. A loud crunch, a twisting of metal and a deafening roar of water filled my ears. My seatbelt pinned me back into my chair, seeming to cut off my breathing as pain exploded everywhere at once, so much pain that I couldn't even distinguish where it hurt the most. From the corner of my eye I saw Luke's body being thrown forward from the force of the crash. He put his arms up to protect himself, but it was no use, the momentum of falling and hitting the water made him defenceless. His head collided with the steering wheel, and his body went limp almost instantly.

That was when the brown, murky, icy cold water started gushing in through the windshield so fast that it made a loud roaring sound as it pooled around my legs, getting higher and higher with each passing second. It was so piercingly cold that it felt like I was being stabbed with a thousand tiny needles everywhere it touched. For a couple of seconds I didn't know what to do. I just sat there, watching as death flowed in a relentless stream, filling the car quicker than I thought possible. I was numb. My brain just wouldn't work; my mind was blank as the shock of what had happened took over. Luke had just driven us both off the bridge because he couldn't bear the thought of being without me.

As soon as my thoughts turned to Luke I seemed to wake up out of the trance I'd somehow slipped into. Whipping my head around I saw him slumped forward over the wheel. Water gushed down on the top of his head, plastering his hair to his face. I screamed, thrashing, trying to unbuckle my seatbelt, but it was stuck. I reached out and grabbed his shoulder, squeezing hard as the water reached my stomach.

"Luke! Are you okay? Luke?" I screamed, shaking him. He didn't answer; his head just rolled lifelessly on his neck as blood tricked down the side of his face, diluted by the constant stream of water that flooded in.

The car was still moving, slower now as we sunk deeper under the water. Panic took over completely as I screamed and screamed for help, pulling Luke's body towards me as the water started to rise up to my chest. I tilted his head back, praying he was just unconscious instead of dead. I fought desperately against my seatbelt, wriggling, trying to get free. The dark, murky water swirled around me, now up to my chin as I fumbled with my belt, fruitlessly pressing the release button over and over so I could get out and drag myself and Luke to safety.

"Help us!" I screamed hysterically. "Someone help us!" I couldn't get my seatbelt loose, I was trapped, and Luke was no help at all. I shook him roughly, trying to wake him up. "Luke! Wake up, please wake up, please!"

The water rose higher, it seemed to be filling the car so quickly that it was almost impossible. The car was completely submerged now. I twisted in my seat, looking out the back window, seeing the daylight fading as we sank lower and lower into the river that seemed bottomless.

"Luke, wake up! We need to get out quickly!"

I had no idea what to do as my body was pinned into my seat. The water rose higher, so high that I had to tilt my head right back to keep my mouth above the surface. Luke's body was floating lifelessly next to me, his arms weightless as his clothes billowed out around him. I whimpered as the water went into my mouth, and I knew that my air was fast running out. Pretty soon the water would rise so far that it would go over my mouth. I gulped in lungful's of air, thumping my hand down on my seatbelt release, trying in vain to get it off, but it was no use.

A couple of drops of water trickled into my mouth, so I strained my neck, pushing up against the restraining belt as hard as I could. I screamed for help again, choking as water flooded my mouth. I whimpered and took one last deep breath just as the water rose over my lips. Panic surged over me now that I was submerged and trapped. I straightened my arm, keeping Luke on the surface of the water for as long as possible in case help came, but the water was almost touching the roof now, so I knew he would be out of time too.

Almost instantly the icy cold made my whole body ache as my arms and legs took on a weightless sensation. The only thing keeping me in place was the strip of nylon that was designed to save my life but was actually now sentencing me to death. I squinted through the dirty water, looking around frantically for anything that could help me get free.

My lungs were hurting. I needed to breathe. My body seemed to react immediately and without my conscious permission. I sucked in a breath, immediately choking as water flowed in. Swallowing, I clamped my lips together as my panicked tears mingled with the cold river water. I was going to die. The water was everywhere, there was no escape. This was it. Seconds passed, maybe minutes, I had no idea of time, no awareness of anything other than the fact that I was surrounded by freezing cold and that the light was slowly fading around me where we continued to sink.

Help us, please help us! I screamed the words over and over in my head, but no help came.

I had to breathe again. I couldn't hold it anymore; I had no other choice as my lungs actually ached from the lack of oxygen. As I choked in another round of water I could literally feel it in my lungs. I could feel it filling me up. It felt like I was being crushed from the inside out, my chest felt full to bursting point.

I squeezed my eyes shut. My body had obviously taken more than it could and I was sick, expelling some of the water again. Even that wasn't a relief though, because as I panicked, I sucked it straight back in again. The dim light from the back of the car was life, it was air, it was home. It was so close, so painstakingly close, but I could do nothing to get to it. I stopped struggling; I stopped fighting and thrashing because I knew it then. I was going to die. I accepted it. In a way I almost welcomed it because the cold water inside me was more painful than anything I'd felt before in my life. It was so cold it felt almost as if it was burning me, which was a strange sensation. This was it, this was how it ended. At eighteen years old I hadn't even really had a chance to live, yet it was over. I was going to drown, and there was nothing I could do about it.

A sense of foreboding settled over me as I forced my eyes open again, seeing that Luke's lifeless body had floated away from me a little. I reached out for him, stretching, gritting my teeth in frustration as my fingertips brushed his shirt. My body felt weak and heavy, but with one last herculean effort I pushed that extra inch against my belt and managed to snag his sleeve enough to pull him over to me. His body twisted in the water, his face coming into view. He looked so peaceful, so beautiful as he floated there, eyes closed, almost as if he was asleep. I envied him, not having to go through this pain and fear. Silently I wished that I'd hit my head too and not worn my seatbelt because my lungs felt like they were on fire as I fought desperately against the urge to breathe in any more of the dirty water.

His blood from the cut on his head was slowly mixing with the water, floating there for a split second, almost looking like strands of fine red hair before they dispersed and more took its place. I gripped Luke's hand tightly in mine, not wanting to be alone as I became so disorientated that I wasn't even sure which way was up anymore. All I could see was darkness and shadows. As I sat there, holding his hand, waiting for it to be over, I thought of my parents, my brother, and my friends. I squeezed my eyes shut as emotional agony joined that pain that ruled my whole body. They would be devastated when they learnt of my death; my mom would be a wreck, I could practically see it. And Alex, my stupid twin brother, I didn't even know how he would cope at all; if our roles were reversed I would feel like a piece of me had died if he did. I choked on a sob, heaving again against the water that seemed to fill every available space in my body.

Everything seemed to be fading out now; my picture of them in my head was becoming less clear. I couldn't be certain of anything other than three things: the blinding pain in my lungs, the seatbelt restraining me, and Luke's hand in mine. I looked at him now, not even blaming him for putting me through this. I looked at his face that I loved so much and I was kind of glad that we'd gone together like this; it was almost poetic in a horrifying, twisted, mortifying way. I blinked once, twice, three times, but when I tried to open my eyes after the third time I just couldn't.

chapter thirty

An incessant beeping was the first thing I noticed, not loud, but just loud enough to catch my attention. My eyelids felt like ton weights as I registered another sound - soft snoring. I swallowed and then instantly wished I hadn't because my throat was so dry that it actually hurt. My tongue felt too big for my mouth as I tried to lick my dry, cracked lips. My whole body felt heavy, like my limbs had suddenly turned into lumps of concrete. As I turned my head towards the snoring sound, pain zipped like lightening down across my shoulder and chest.

I groaned and squeezed my eyes shut tighter, fighting against the urge to cry. Confusion built up as I cracked my eyes open, blinking against the fogginess that seemed to have settled over me. Above me was a foam tiled ceiling. I frowned at it, trying to work out where I was. My hand moved, fingering the scratchy cotton blankets across my body. I swallowed painfully again, and ignored the pain in my neck this time as I turned my head to the side.

Immediately my gaze settled on Alex. He was slumped awkwardly in a chair, his head resting on his hand as he snored quietly. He looked a mess, his clothes were rumpled, his hair sticking up at all angles, and dark shadows resided under his eyes. I tore my gaze away from my twin, flicking my eyes around the room, taking in the white walls and the blue curtain that hung on a rail around my bed, separating off the room. I had a sudden feeling that I was in a hospital, but I had no idea why. I wracked my brains, thinking of anything that would cause my body to feel like I'd been hit by a train.

All at once it came back to me. The bridge, the water, the cold. I gasped and tried to sit up as my thoughts turned to Luke. A yelp left my lips as I fell helplessly back down to the pillows as pain burned through my chest, seeming to make my lungs constrict. The feeling of drowning washed over me as visions of the rising water filled my brain. A deep terror set in that was like reliving a nightmare as I fought against myself to get my breathing under control.

"Maisie?" Alex croaked sleepily.

I squeezed my eyes shut as my lungs burned with the memory of being filled with the murky, freezing water. It was all rushing over me again, like a flashback, little bits stabbing at my mind. Visions of the water rising, the light slowly fading out, the blood trickling down Luke's forehead as he slumped over the steering wheel, his clothes floating around him as the water got too high, all of it filled my mind, almost making me lose grip on reality as if I was back there again.

I was vaguely aware of a loud moaning sound. It sounded like death, like someone was dying slowly and painfully. There was a pressure on my shoulders that made my neck ache as I was shaken gently. My name was being repeated over and over in a voice I recognised, but I was trapped, still trapped in that car with Luke. I knew the moaning sound was coming from me, but I just couldn't stop it.

"Maisie, for goodness sake calm down!" Alex ordered, pulling me roughly so that my back rose off the bed. His arms slipped around me as he crushed me against his body. One of his hands gripped the back of my head as I tried to fight the drowning memories. The pain that burned through my ribs as I moved was enough to jerk me out of the car and drop me back into the hospital bed.

I still couldn't open my eyes as my twin's warmth flooded my system, warming my cold and shocked body. His breathing was also laboured, as if he was struggling to remain in control too. My arms were like ton weights, but somehow I managed to get them up and wrap around his shoulders as the shock slowly sank in and relief built up inside me. I didn't think I would ever see him again, but here he was, clinging to me like his life depended on it. I was alive. Somehow I hadn't died in the car. I'd never been more grateful for life than in that moment. No more would I ever take anything for granted, because that experience just proved that it could all be taken away from you in a matter of seconds.

I pulled back slightly and kissed his cheek, seeing that he was close to tears as his blue eyes seemed to be memorising every inch of my face. "You frightened the shit out of me. Don't ever do that to me again," he grunted, shaking his head as he stroked my hair back softly.

I nodded, instantly groaning because it hurt to move even an inch. "What happened?" I choked out, my voice hoarse and barely above a whisper.

"Here, let's lay you back down," he murmured. Frown lines covered his forehead as he gently helped me lay back into the firm pillows. Once I was settled, he sat on the edge of my bed, taking my hand and holding it too tightly for comfort, but I was too grateful that he was here to complain about it. He didn't look at me as he spoke, "Luke's car went over the side of the bridge. You nearly died. Actually, you did die for a while, but some people saw it happen so they climbed down the verge and dived in after you. They pulled you out, and luckily one of them knew basic CPR so he got you breathing again," he said quietly. He swallowed loudly as his eyes met mine. "You were lucky. The doctors said that if you'd been without oxygen for any longer then you wouldn't have been able to be revived, or if you were revived then you might have had brain damage." He shifted on the bed gently, making the pain more prominent in my ribs as the mattress dipped. Alex winced apologetically. "You have broken ribs and bruising across your stomach from the seatbelt. You have whiplash too," he explained.

My injuries were the last thing I was thinking about now though. Alex words were slowly filtering through my brain. Someone dived in and saved us? Gratitude made my eyes prickle as I realised that I would never be able to repay this person who risked their own life to dive into the depths of the dirty water to save us. The word hero didn't really seem enough to describe this faceless, nameless person. Luke and I would be in their debt for ever.

As soon as I thought about Luke, my eyes flitted to the side, looking around the room that was empty other than me and my brother. Luke must have his own room.

"Where's Luke?"

Alex shifted again, getting to his feet, his eyes leaving mine. "I'll go get Mom and Dad and tell them you're awake, they're getting coffee," he mumbled.

As he turned to leave I grabbed his hand, needing to know. "Alex, where's Luke?" I whispered. Dread was already settling in the pit of my stomach. I think deep down I already knew, but I needed to hear the words anyway.

Alex's face contorted in pain as he turned back to me, his hand tightening on mine to the point of my fingers feeling about ready to snap from the pressure. "He didn't make it, Maze-daze," he croaked, shaking his head, his voice filled with pain.

My breath left my body in one big gust as my heart seemed to shatter into a million pieces. He'd died. He'd left me here to pick up the pieces and live without him. In a way I hated him for it, but another part of me loved him so much that it was like someone had stabbed me in the stomach. The grief was crushing as Alex bent over and wrapped an arm around my shoulders awkwardly, pulling me into another hug as he gripped my shoulder tightly.

I didn't know what to say as I cried helplessly, clinging to Alex as if he could somehow make it better and take away the pain, to fill the gaping hole that resided where my heart used to be. Alex mumbled soothing words as he stroked my back, telling me how sorry he was, but I could barely hear him. My heartbeat was banging in my ears, echoed by shrill beeping from the machine I was attached too.

Luke's face swam before me, haunting me, terrorising me, but most of all, ripping my heart into a million pieces. He was my everything, and now he was gone. I'd only just got him back, we'd made plans for our combined future, and now he was gone. He'd left me, and now I was going to have to be without him.

I could barely cope as in the back of my mind I registered being forced back into the pillows as I thrashed and cried, gasping for breath, wishing for death because the emotional pain was too much for me to deal with. I barely registered that there were people around me, holding me down, shouting words to one another, words like sedative, IV line, oxygen and cardiac arrest.

I saw the flash of a syringe before the person holding it pushed it into the drip that was hanging next to me. I choked on my sob, swatting away the plastic mask that someone was attempting to put over my face. My dad's worried face, my mom crying, Alex looking at me with wide, horrified eyes; those were the things I saw as my eyes started to get heavy. My efforts to fight them off became less and less violent as my body started to get heavy. I gave in, hoping that whatever they'd given me would just kill me so I wouldn't have to deal with this grief.

Unfortunately, the sedative seemed to turn off my body, but not my brain. It paralysed me, trapping me in a sleep which I didn't want to be in. A sleep where Luke floated in front of me, gasping for breath, clutching at his throat as the cut on his head slowly turned the water around me into blood. His eyes were terrified, fearful, and hopeless. They were the eyes I'd seen just before he told me he couldn't live without me and then drove us off the bridge. In the dream I screamed and screamed for help that never came, so I watched him drown before me while I clutched at his hand, my lungs burning as I tried not to drown in his blood too. I was trapped in a never-ending nightmare, replaying the whole thing over and over. It was like hell, and I actually wondered if maybe that stranger hadn't saved me after all, maybe I died in that crash and this was hell that I was doomed to watch my boyfriend die over and over while I could do nothing about it.

• • •

FOR TOO LONG I drifted in and out of my nightmares. Just as some semblance of the world came back to me again I was pulled back under, crushed by the onslaught of both memories and dreams. By the time I could fully open my eyes and blink without being dragged back into sleep, it was dark outside. The glow of the halogen strip lighting was too bright as I squinted up at the ceiling. My whole body hurt, but mostly my chest which felt like someone had hollowed me out with some rusty, blunt instrument, leaving just an empty shell behind. The grief felt like it had torn me apart inside, took all my hope, dreams and happiness and separated them from me completely so that I could barely even remember what it felt like not to feel like I'd been hit by a train at full speed.

I closed my eyes again, swallowing as another wave of sadness rushed over me. The pain was so bad that I wanted to double up, wail and scream - but none of that happened. Instead, a silent tear rolled down my cheek, tickling as it fell down to the pillow. I didn't even have the energy to wipe it.

"Maisie? Sweetheart, are you awake for real this time?"

My dad's voice used to be so comforting to me, the very essence of home, but I felt nothing as he spoke. Numbness and sadness were the only things that registered. I closed my eyes, hoping that if I faked sleep everything would just disappear. I couldn't speak to anyone right now; if I did I wasn't sure what would come out of my mouth. Maybe it would just be a banshee like scream that lasted forever.

A hand stroked the hair back from my forehead. "Are you okay?" Dad asked, his voice cracking either through emotion or worry.

The devastation of losing Luke, of finding out all of those awful things about him before that, all of it had just left me broken. My vision swam before my eyes as more tears pooled there. I felt like I was stuck in some sort of snowstorm, unable to see the end of this turmoil. Again, I had that notion of free falling, like I was hurtling towards the earth with no control and nothing to grab on to. Luke was my thing that I could always hold on to, but now he was gone. So this time I was going to hit the ground – actually, it felt as if I already had. It felt like I'd crashed down to earth at full speed, smashing everything in my wake, a fall that was sure to kill me. Only it hadn't. And I hated that I was alive. I hated that Luke was gone and that I was going to have to deal with this all alone. For so long I'd had him to lean on, I wasn't sure I could cope without him. I hated that my dad was trying to comfort me. I hated that all I wanted to do was scream, but I seemed to have lost the ability to do so.

"Mom's outside getting some air. You want me to get Mom?" Dad asked, stroking my hair again. I turned my head, looking up at him properly for the first time. Worry lined his forehead and made crinkles around his concerned green eyes. He looked like he'd aged ten years since I last saw him. He smiled sympathetically as his thumb rhythmically brushed across my forehead like he always used to when he was trying to get me to go to sleep when I was a small child. "What can I do? Are you in pain? Want a doctor?" he asked. His voice was so stressed that before this happened I would have felt awful for putting him through this, but now that Luke was gone I couldn't feel anything.

Using the all of my strength I twisted, rolling over so that my back was to him. I ignored the pain in my ribs and the tugging sensation in the back of my hand from the drip that I had inserted. I honestly couldn't care less if it came free or not. I pulled the sheets up to my chin and laid there staring at the black sky out of the window as I cried silently, soaking my pillow within seconds.

Dad sat on the bed behind me, stroking the top of my head, gripping my shoulder too tightly for comfort. "I'm so sorry, Maisie. I wish I could stop this, I wish I could help you, but I just don't know how," he muttered. "Luke was a good guy. I know you loved him. I'm sorry he died, I'm so sorry. It may not feel like it now, but you'll get through this, I promise. We're all here for you."

My thoughts wandered to the last conversation Luke and I had. My memories of him were now tarnished, now a little dirty and ruined because I'd found out the real him, the one that did all those horrible things, the one that had actually committed murder. The pain seemed to double in my chest because I couldn't even grieve properly for my boyfriend because all that I could think about was the fact that he wasn't the person I thought he was. I hated him for that, for ruining my memories and painting them with something dirty and unimaginable. But still I grieved for the future with him that I'd lost.

Somewhere in the back of my mind my dad's words registered. Luke was a good guy? Did he really say that? Did he not know that Luke had driven us off the bridge on purpose, that he had killed Sandy because she was threatening to tell me that Luke was the one behind all the strange things that had happened?

In a way I envied my dad. I wished I didn't know about this part of Luke either. I wished that I still thought he was a good guy instead of the new things I'd learnt about him. Everyone was going to know what happened soon enough too. And I was the one that was going to have to deliver the blow. I was the one that was going to have to tell everyone what Luke was really like. It was me that was going to devastate his parents and friends by telling them the sweet and kind Luke didn't actually exist. I was going to have to tell his mom that her son was a murderer. I had no idea how I was supposed to do that. How could I shatter the illusions of everyone and make them think ill of the dead?

My dad sighed and bent down, kissing my cheek softly before wiping away my tears. "I'm so sorry," he croaked.

I swallowed loudly, closing my eyes. "Do his parents know that he... he..." I swallowed, unable to say the words. "Luke's housekeeper will know how to get hold of them if they're not in the country," I muttered, not wanting to talk but knowing that I needed to.

"Yeah. They flew in yesterday morning. They came by to see you earlier but you were still unconscious."

They flew in yesterday morning? The crash only happened last night. Or did it? "How long was I asleep for?" I asked, confused.

"Two and a half days. We were worried that you'd never wake up. Your mom's been a mess; I swear I've never seen her like this at all. She's usually so strong in hospitals but not this time. And Alex, even the nurses couldn't get him to leave. He sat by your bed the whole time, even slept here. He said it was a twin loyalty thing." His tone was light, as if he was trying to make me feel better. It didn't work though. "Mrs Hannigan left you some stuff for when you woke up." He shifted on the bed and my ears perked up at that. I turned my head, pushing myself up carefully as my dad offered me a lumpy brown bag.

My chin trembled as I fought the urge to break down. I didn't want to be sedated again in case the nightmares started again. I looked down it, unsure if I was strong enough to see what was inside. Dad sat back down next to me and draped his arm across my shoulder supportively as he leant in and pressed his forehead to my temple. "You don't have to look now if you don't want to. Mrs Hannigan just wanted you to have these because she knew how close you two were," he said soothingly.

I nodded, trying to breathe normally as my heart constricted. My hands were shaking as I reached into the bag, pulling out three things. The first was his football lettered jacket. He didn't wear it very often; I had probably worn it more times than he had if I was honest. It still smelt like him though, and a strangled whimper left my lips as I held the soft material up to my nose and inhaled deeply. I knew then and there that I would never get over him. There would always be a part of me missing inside, a broken part that would never heal.

A sparkle of light caught my eye on my lap, so I moved the jacket, seeing that one of the other items was a silver photo frame, I recognised it immediately. I could barely make out the picture through the blurriness of my eyes where they were filled with tears, but I didn't need to look to know it was the photo of us at the dance. It was Luke's favourite picture and the one he had by his bed. He even had a smaller version of it in his wallet.

I hugged the photo to my chest as I picked up the last item. It was a small envelope with purple flowers in one corner. My name was written on the front in handwriting I didn't recognise. I looked up at my dad, not wanting to open it in front of him. For some reason I needed to do this in private, but I couldn't even explain why. My dad hadn't moved the whole time that'd I'd opened the things. He smiled down at me now, brushing my matted hair over my shoulder.

"Think I can have some privacy to open this?" I asked, hoping he wouldn't put up a fight. He didn't. He just nodded, kissed my forehead and stood up, strutting out of the room and letting the door swing shut behind him.

I turned my attention back to the envelope. The writing was pretty, curly, and definitely female. I gulped as I slid in one finger, ripping it open and pulling out the single sheet of matching paper. I held my breath as I read the words.

Maisie,
I hope this letter finds you well. We did try to visit, but you were sleeping.

I've given you a couple of Luke's things. He loved you so very much, and I know he would have wanted you to have them.

I missed so much of Luke's life, I was barely around for him, and even when I was here I was too busy to spend time with him. I barely even knew him and what he liked and disliked. Had I known that the time with my son would be limited, I would have done things differently and spent more time with him. But it is too late now.

I never got the chance to tell him how proud I am of him. I never got to watch him play football, and I never got to see him dressed up in a tux to take you to the dance in this photo. I was too busy to do those things, and for that I will never forgive myself. I was a terrible mother to him, as you probably noticed, but I loved him dearly.

I wanted to thank you for making Luke so happy. If there was one thing I was sure of with Luke, it was that he was desperately in love with you. He told me several times that you were the one and that you two would be together forever. Had this terrible accident not happened I have no doubt in my mind that he would have been a fine man, and that you two would have gone off to college, gotten married, and then made me a grandmother several times over. I wish with all of my heart that could still happen.

I know I wasn't there for Luke in his life, but if you let me, I would very much like to be there for you. I know you must be in agony right now, so if you need to talk or even want to come and sort through Luke's possessions then you're very welcome to come to the house any time. Perhaps, in time, I can get to know my son through you and your memories of him. I know this is a lot to ask of you, and I do not deserve it, but if you could find it in your heart, I would be most grateful.

In a strange way this has all taught me a valuable lesson, all be it too late now. Words of advice from a stupid old lady, Maisie, never take your family for granted. Make the most of every day with them and never be too busy to spend time with a loved one, because one day all you'll be left with are your memories, and sometimes, like me, maybe not even those.

Take care,
Judith Hannigan

I read the note twice, my heart in my throat. Although the note was fairly formal, I could feel her guilt and pain behind the words. She had barely known her son, and now he was gone so she would never have the chance. Again, I hated him for what he'd done and for the fact that his mother was going to find out all of those horrible things about him. How was she going to feel then? How was she going to deal with the horror of it on top of her grief and guilt for not being there?

I closed my eyes and tipped my head back. "I hate you, Luke," I whispered. I didn't though, that wasn't true. I didn't think I could ever truly hate him, I just hated being in this situation, and he was the one that put me here.

Suddenly a thought occurred to me. Did I really have to tell the truth? No one but me and Luke knew that it was him. The police investigation had brought up nothing conclusive. There was never anything to link Luke to the things he sent to me, or to Sandy's murder. Did I really have to break the hearts of so many people? I thought about my memories of Luke. With every part of my being I wished I didn't know this information. It was so hard to deal with the loss and the knowledge together. If I could erase the knowledge from my memory I would do it in an instant. So why was I about to make other people hurt this much? Why was I planning on telling his mother all these things, when there was nothing they could do about it now anyway? What good could come of me telling people the truth? I could see no good in anything anymore, and the more I thought about it, the more confused I got.

I read Luke's mom's note one more time, but this time with a fresh perspective. She was so proud of him, she'd said so herself, but if she knew the truth would that take that away from her pride? Luke was dead, he had already been punished, and nothing else could come of people knowing that he was behind it all. However, deep down I knew that if the thoughts that were formulating in my mind were to come into practice then I'd have to lie to every single person I loved, just to save the memory of the man I loved. I wasn't sure what to do for the best.

"Knock, knock?"

I looked up quickly, seeing Alex peeking in through the door, obviously waiting for permission to enter.

Seeing his face seemed to snap me out of the self-pitying horror that I'd seeped into. A smile twitched at the corner of my mouth as I waved him in. As he pushed the door open I saw my mom in full sob mode behind him. She practically pushed my twin out of the way as she ran for the bed, engulfing me in a hug that I so desperately needed. I wrapped my arms around her, put my head in the crook of her neck and felt myself relax into her as fresh tears started to fall.

• • •

DOCTORS CAME AND went fairly regularly. No one really spoke about Luke or the car. Mostly Alex blabbered about random stuff, made jokes about hospital food and how nice and quiet it was at home without me. I almost believed him when he said that he didn't want me home, until I realised that he hadn't let go of my hand for almost an hour.

Just as I started to get tired there was a knock at the door and a doctor peered in. Everyone looked up but he caught my dad's attention and motioned with his head for him to go outside. Dad stood up. "Maybe I have to settle the bill?" he joked, shrugging and winking at me as he walked out of the door.

"What's that about?" Alex asked, watching over his shoulder as if he could somehow hear the conversation if he focussed enough.

Mom shrugged. "Probably arranging a time when we can get your sister home. Maybe they need the bed for someone else?" she suggested.

A minute later and the door opened again. Dad stepped back in, closing the door softly behind him. He looked a little apprehensive, his eyes were tight. He didn't look too happy about whatever had gone on. "Maisie, the police are here to ask you a few questions about the crash. Do you feel up to it or should I ask them to come back tomorrow?" Dad asked, cocking his head to the side and regarding me worriedly.

I gulped. This was it. Now I had to decide, and I still wasn't sure what to do.

"Um... I'm fine," I answered. My palms started to sweat almost instantly so I dropped Alex's hand and wiped them on the sheets as I shifted awkwardly on the bed, trying to get comfortable.

Dad nodded and turned back to the door, pulling it open and motioning someone inside. DI Neeson stepped into the room and my back instantly straightened from the shock of seeing her here, causing pain to zap across my rips. I let out a little involuntary yelp and gritted my teeth as my mom sprang out of her chair and gripped my arm with wide eyes.

"I'm fine. Just moved too quickly," I croaked through gritted teeth. The pain slowly receded again and I breathed a sigh of relief. Mom nodded, still watching me with frightened eyes as she let go of my arm and stepped away from the bed. I looked back to DI Neeson, unsure why I was so shocked to see her here. She probably got assigned this case because she was the lead investigator for the harassment and murder case, and it was me, yet again, that was involved in something. "Hi," I muttered.

She smiled sadly. "Hi, Maisie, how are you doing?"

I shrugged but then wished I hadn't as another bout of pain swiftly followed the movement. "Okay I guess." That was the best I could come up with.

She nodded, coming over to the side of the bed and pulling out her notepad and pen. "I need to get your statement about what happened on the day of the crash." She looked almost apologetic, as if she didn't really want to be here harassing me after everything that I'd been through. "I know it's probably hard for you to talk about, but I need to get your statement."

I gulped, looking around at the faces of my family. They were all standing there, watching me, waiting for me to say the words. This was it. Truth or lie time. Truth and I crush people's memories irrevocably, lie and people get to keep their opinions of Luke untarnished.

I looked back to DI Neeson. "What happened?" she asked, her pen poised over a fresh sheet of paper in her notebook.

I looked up into her inquisitive eyes and fought with myself. I had a choice; did anyone really have to know? What difference did it make now that he was dead? What was the point in leaving people with sour feelings for Luke? How were his parents supposed to grieve? Would they blame themselves for leaving him so much? No good could come from telling the truth, surely.

"Maisie, can you tell me what happened on the bridge?" DI Neeson repeated her question and I made up my mind.

"Luke lost control of the car. It was an accident." As soon as I said the words I knew I'd made the right choice. I wouldn't have to look his parents and friends in the eye and see that hurt and devastation there. This knowledge and pain was my cross to bear, no one else's.

chapter thirty-one

I stood in the centre of my room, looking around at the emptiness of it. I'd never seen it this bare before. This had been my room ever since I was a baby so seeing it like this now was a little weird. The room seemed smaller somehow without my stuff lying around. I turned in a small circle, looking at the naked window because even my drapes had been removed. The walls were dotted with marks where I'd had posters and photos stuck up there. My parents would have to redecorate by the look of it.

Six weeks had passed since the incident with the bridge. The time had taken forever to pass. Every day felt like an age, small things were so much effort as I struggled not to fall into depression. Luke's funeral had just about killed me inside. It was the hardest thing I had ever done - saying goodbye to the person I thought I would have forever. The service had been lovely, with people saying beautiful things about him and how much he would be missed. I hadn't spoken. I'd just sat there, dying inside as they lowered his body into the ground. After, I'd sat at his grave for almost an hour, going over and over things, memories, promises, things he'd said to me, plans we'd made. It had torn me apart inside all over again. When it had started to get dark, my brother had ended up carrying me away from his grave because I didn't want to leave Luke on his own.

I'd only been to his grave once since then. I'd given him a bunch of daisies, and sat down with him apologising over and over for not noticing how insecure he was and how starved he was for attention. His clinging to me after we'd broken up was an act of desperation, I saw that now, and I hated that I'd not just forgiven him earlier so that he hadn't felt the need to resort to those things. Maybe if I'd forgiven him earlier then he'd still be alive right now and we'd be leaving together. Those thoughts haunted me when I was both awake and asleep. In a way, I'd kind of killed him by not forgiving him earlier.

Of course, after going through all of that, school was the last thing on my mind, so I didn't make an effort in the final three weeks. I'd barely passed my finals and graduated, but somehow I managed it. That feat was mostly down to Zach, who refused to let me succumb to depression and forced me to study with him every day. He claimed that he needed help graduating, but deep down I think it was more for my benefit than his.

The depression had almost gotten me. I'd almost given in. The whole situation with Luke, and the fact that I was the only one that knew, weighed heavier on me than I thought possible. The police were still looking for the person who sent me all those things, and Sandy's murder investigation was still open, but they didn't suspect Luke at all. They had believed my story of what happened on the bridge entirely. I'd told them that Luke and I were arguing, that we pulled up and got into a fight, but when he started driving again he'd lost control and drove into the barrier. The witnesses confirmed our story. The only ones that had left statements, told what they believed to be the truth - that they saw us stop the car, and then when the car started again it drove over the edge. No one except me knew that it was deliberate, and that knowledge would go with me to the grave. I refused to let Luke's legacy be diminished like that. It would do no good for anyone in the long run and would just cause more damage for others.

The calls and gifts stopped, obviously, but no one pieced it together correctly. I'd heard my parents speculating once when they thought I was in bed. They seemed to be under the impression that whoever was sending that stuff to me, thought I'd been through enough and was stopping the hate campaign. My dad and brother still worried about me like crazy. It was only recently that they let me out on my own without a bodyguard.

Six weeks of grieving and barely sleeping had passed me by. Everything had changed since then, but most of those changes had happened inside me. I'd realised that life was short and that you shouldn't waste it. It was actually Luke's mom that made me have that epiphany. She'd come around to see me in the previous week and she'd sat there for an hour just talking about all the wrong choices that she'd made in life. Her words had struck me deeply, and I realised that I couldn't be here anymore. Everyone knew what had happened, everyone had a sympathetic glint in their eye as they looked at me, everyone felt sorry for me here because I'd lost my boyfriend and almost died myself. All that sympathy did was serve as a reminder that my life had turned upside down and would never be the same again.

So I'd made a decision to leave. Luke and I were planning to move away to college so that it was just the two of us, so I made my mind up that I would stick to that. I would get a fresh start with new people and not be reminded of it every day and in every little thing that I saw. I needed a fresh start, I needed to let go and start living again.

I'd put in a few calls, asked Principal Bennett for a favour, and I'd somehow, despite my grades not being as perfect as they should be, managed to land myself a summer school teaching assistant job. The job was about ten minutes away from the college I would attend in the fall, so I was to move there early and help teach high school kids in summer school. It sounded like a great opportunity for me to get my foot on the teaching ladder which had always been my chosen profession. But it meant moving away from my family three months earlier than planned. And that had taken a heck of a lot of convincing on my part, but they finally understood that I needed to get away and put the past behind me.

I sat on the edge of my bed – the only thing I wasn't taking with me. I chewed on my lip as I replayed some of the great times I'd had in here, sleepovers, movie nights, laughing with the girls, sneaking Luke into my bed, studying, dancing like a moron with my headphones on. I smiled but stood up quickly when I could feel my eyes prickling with tears. I didn't want to cry. I'd done too much of that recently, and I refused to cry anymore.

As I stepped out of my room, Chester came lolloping over to me, wagging his tail as he looked up at me with his big brown eyes. I smiled and bent down, petting his head before nuzzling my face into the side of his. I sighed, knowing I needed to get going. I was already an hour later than I said I wanted to leave. I had a long drive ahead, and if I wanted to make it there before nightfall I needed to get a wriggle on and go.

Heading down the stairs, I purposefully tried not to listen to the snivelling that was coming from the lounge. I knew I was going to be missed. "Guys, I'm ready. I'm just taking the last bag out now if you want to come and see me off," I called, picking up my backpack that was packed full of sandwiches, drinks and candy bars. The big bulky furniture had already been sent ahead and was waiting for me in my student accommodation that I would be sharing with three others. All I had was my clothes and small possessions left to take with me in the car.

I didn't wait for them to follow me, just turned and headed out of the front door. I'd already done my last tour of the house, now I was eager to leave and get a new start.

When I got to my mom's cherry red Rover I popped the trunk, throwing the last bag in and then struggling to close it again after. I was borrowing my mom's car for now, until I could afford to buy one of my own and then they would take it back apparently.

Zach was the first to reach me, followed by my parents and brother. I'd already said my goodbyes to Charlotte and Beth last night when we had a girlie night. I was kind of grateful that they weren't here now; both of them had been a mess last night so their crying today probably would have started me off all over again.

Zach stopped at my side and chewed on his lip. "You're really going?" A frown made crinkles around his eyes.

I nodded in confirmation. "Yep."

He sighed and shook his head. "But I didn't get a chance to make my move on you. I was building up to it and everything. You never know, in another couple of weeks I might have worked up the nerve to ask you out," he said, raising one eyebrow teasingly.

I chuckled, knowing he was only joking. "You should start dating, Zach. Don't keep thinking that you're not good enough because of your ADHD. You'll make someone a great boyfriend," I replied, slapping his shoulder in encouragement.

A gave me a sad smile. "Well that's all well and good, but you're now moving halfway across the country for four years," he replied cockily.

I couldn't help but roll my eyes. He never did give up teasing me, but I had actually come to like it. I would probably miss his teasing when I was alone with no friends and no one to talk to. "Shut up, Zachary." I stepped forward, wrapping my arms around him and hugging him tightly. "Look after my brother for me, huh? He's gonna play the big macho kickboxer routine, but I know he's gonna miss me more than he's letting on," I whispered.

He nodded, his hand stroking my back softly. "I will. Promise." He kissed my cheek gently before I pulled away and smiled. "I'm going to miss you, little rebel. We'll keep in touch though, right?"

I grinned and nodded. "Right," I confirmed. I took a deep breath, steeling myself for the next goodbye as I turned to my dad. My mom was still sobbing up a storm, blowing her nose loudly into a Kleenex so I wanted to leave her for another minute to sort herself out. "Bye, Daddy." His arms wrapped around me tightly, too tightly, and for too long. It was almost as if he couldn't let me go, but then he groaned and released me all at once, stepping back and shoving his hands into his pockets and looking at the floor.

I turned to my mom and smiled, chuckling to myself. "You're coming to visit me next weekend," I reminded her, shaking my head.

She blew out a big breath and looked up at the blue sky. "I know, I know. I just all of a sudden developed empty nest syndrome. Maybe I should have listened when your father tried to talk me into having more kids a few years ago," she replied, chuckling too as she swiped at her nose again.

"I'm still up for the idea," Dad said behind her.

I cringed, as did Alex. "Seriously. No," I begged. "Save that conversation for once I've left, okay?" I joked, wrapping an arm around my mom's shoulders and planting a kiss on her wet cheek.

"And once I've left home too. I *do not* want to hear that kind of thing," Alex chimed in, dramatically shuddering.

I giggled, loosening my grip on my mom and stepping back so she was at arm's length. I gripped her shoulders, looking into her blue eyes that I'd inherited. "I'll see you in a week. I love you," I told her honestly.

She sniffed loudly and lifted her chin. "I love you, too."

And then it was Alex's turn, which was probably going to be the hardest one of all. We'd never really been apart before. Although he drove me crazy, we were still very close so it was hard knowing that I wasn't going to see him for a while.

He kicked at the ground, his shoulders hunched as he frowned down at the floor as if it had offended him somehow. "Gonna miss me?" I asked, cocking my head to the side, willing myself to be strong and not cry. I didn't want to have a watery goodbye, so I'd promised myself that I'd be strong for this.

"No," he scoffed, shaking his head dismissively. "You gonna miss me?"

A smile twitched at the corners of my mouth. "No."

He chewed on his lip and kicked at the floor a couple more times before looking up at me with sad eyes. "Make sure you tell everyone that you have a brother that's a kickboxing champion and that he'll happily beat the shit out of every single guy that looks in your direction." His tone wasn't even a little bit joking which made me laugh.

"I will don't worry." I crossed my heart with one finger, grinning up at him.

He sighed and reached out, yanking open the driver's door for me. "Drive carefully. Keep your chin up. And don't let those summer school kids walk all over you," he instructed. "I'm at the end of a phone, and I can be there in six hours if you need me."

"It's a nine hour drive," I teased smugly.

He shrugged. "I could make it in six if I needed to," he joked. Suddenly he sighed, looking away from me and up at the horizon. "I don't want to say bye, so just go. I'll see you soon." He was gnawing on his lip furiously, and I was sure he was going to hurt himself soon, but that was his way of coping. He didn't really like to show a weakness. It was probably down to his training for his fights, he was always taught not to show weakness because it can so easily be used against you.

"I'll see you soon," I replied. I looked back to see that my dad was hugging my mom who was all out bawling now and was sure to be leaving a gross trail all over his shirt, but he didn't look like he cared. His eyes met mine and in those few seconds his eyes told me everything I needed to know. He didn't need to say the words for me to understand how much he was going to miss me and how worried he was that I was going off alone after everything that I'd been through recently.

I smiled reassuringly before catching Zach's eye and giving him a small wave.

I didn't wait for anymore goodbyes; I just climbed into the car and buckled my seatbelt, letting Alex slam the door behind me. His hand gripped at the open window frame, his knuckles going white before he let go, turned and stalked back into the house without another word.

I swallowed the lump in my throat, but I didn't doubt that I was doing the right thing for myself in leaving. I needed this. I was suffocating here, and I needed to escape the memories that taunted me on a daily basis. As I started the engine I noticed that Zach had followed Alex into the house. I smiled to myself because I knew that he'd keep good on his promise and would make sure that my brother was okay.

I pulled out of the drive, determined not to look back. The car rolled down the road and as I got about three houses away I suddenly started to panic. My foot came off the gas and hovered above the brake. I hesitated for a second, looking in my rear-view mirror, seeing my parents standing there still, watching me go. My resolve faltered, my courage disappeared in an instant, and I suddenly doubted that I was strong enough be alone and start over.

Just as I was about to depress the brake and turn the car around so I could stay, my dad raised his hand, waving goodbye before turning my mom away and leading her inside.

My eyes glazed over as I turned my attention back to the road ahead. That one little move from him gave me my confidence back. He hadn't stood there expecting my return, he'd waved goodbye and then gone back inside. He had more faith in me than I did and had no doubt in his mind that I was leaving and that this was it. He obviously hadn't seen my foot hovering as my mind wavered. My dad's small wave goodbye gave me one last boost in confidence, so I pressed my foot down on the gas and rolled down the road again.

As the street disappeared behind me, so did my nerves. I was going to make it, I knew I was. Sure it would be hard, but I would get there, eventually. Maybe one day my heart would stop hurting and I'd be able to think of Luke without it crushing me inside. Maybe I'd even be happy again one day. Who knows?

epilogue

The necklace dangled where it had been hung for the last year or so – over the post of my bed. Every now and again the light would catch it in a certain way, making the diamond on the front sparkle. Then it would draw my attention and the memories would flood back at once. That was usually one of the nights that I cried myself to sleep. It didn't happen very often now though; for the most part I'd moved on. I used the words 'moved on' in a very liberal sense because only parts of my life had progressed beyond eating ice-cream and sitting around in my pyjamas. I knew I would never be over it completely.

In some ways though I had managed to regain some semblance of the old Maisie. I had just started in my second year at college; I had a new bunch of friends, and a job that I worked at the weekends selling electrical appliances. My new friends didn't know much of what went on, just that my boyfriend had died in an accident, nothing else. One of my roommates was even doing the same course as me, so we had become pretty close.

Today was a hard day. Today was Valentine's Day, and of course I didn't have a date. Not that I wanted one, because I didn't date at all, not since Luke. But today was a day for love, for kissing and cuddling, and for telling your partner that you loved them entirely. And I was alone.

I sighed now and reached for the locket, easing it up off the bedpost. The metal was smooth and cold to the touch as I ran my finger over the swirly pattern on the front. When I got to the side of it, I popped the catch and looked down at the photo. I hadn't changed it from the one that Luke had put in there when he gave it to me. I smiled down at the badly cropped photo of us that he'd managed to get inside there. My smile in the photo was a genuine one, and I longed to be able to smile that easily again. Happiness came so easy back then, but now I had to work hard for it. Being 'normal' was hard work for me, but I still had hope that one day I'd get there.

I didn't read the words on the back of the locket, they always upset me and made me feel miserable for the whole day, so instead I just closed it and hung it back into its place on my bed. I forced myself to get to my feet. *Maybe college will give me a distraction and stop me feeling sorry for myself.* Grabbing my backpack, I slipped on my converse and trudged across my room to my door. I was in halls, so I had my own room but shared a bathroom, kitchen and lounge with three other, what can only be described as, animals. I cringed as I stepped out into the messy hallway, almost stumbling over a pair of shoes that had been abandoned casually in the middle of the walkway. I sighed and kicked them over to the side, shouldering my bag as I stepped into the kitchen.

Georgia was sitting at the counter, munching Cheerios straight from the box, watching Jerry Springer and chewing loudly. She stopped, a handful of Cheerios half way to her mouth. "What the? He's not the dad? Well be grateful, sister, because bad teeth are genetic," she jeered, chuckling to herself before throwing in another mouthful of cereal, dropping some down her shirt in the process. I smiled. Georgia, my best friend at college, was a talk show freak, and had to have her fill of drama before college every day.

"Morning," I greeted, dropping my bag on the counter, narrowly avoiding knocking over a dirty bowl that looked to have contained cereal once.

She didn't take her eyes off the TV as she offered me the box of cereal she was eating. "DNA tests reveal that he's not the father of her child even though she told him she didn't sleep with anyone else while they were married. Apparently he has his suspicions that she slept with his brother though," she explained without greeting me.

I stuffed my hand into the box, grabbing a handful out too. "Sounds like it's just getting interesting," I replied, pulling up a stool and watching too, just for something to do.

Georgia glanced at me from the corner of her eye. "You okay today?"

"Peachy," I lied, nodding and willing her to drop the subject.

She snorted, putting down the box and turning off the TV as she twisted in her chair so she was facing me. "Know what we're going to do tonight?" I raised one eyebrow in prompt, shrugging. "Drunkeness. Total fall on your face, flash your underwear, and throw up in the street drunkenness," she answered, crossing her arms over her chest. Her expression was stern, challenging even, almost as if she was daring me to oppose her.

I laughed and let out a little groan. When she turned off Springer I knew she was serious. She never turned off Springer for anything, she was a total fangirl. If she wanted drunkenness tonight, then drunkenness would be had whether I wanted it or not. Georgia, being the great friend that she was, had rejected the date with her boyfriend, Ste, tonight because she knew that I would be alone. She was a great friend even though I had only known her for a year and a bit.

"Sounds great. I'll remember to put on nice underwear then," I joked, rolling my eyes.

She grinned. "I'm going to wear Bridget Jones pants and make sure that Ste gets a peek, you know he loves those big pants, the freaky boy."

I laughed and shook my head; she was always like this, crude, loud and in your face. But it was nice because she seemed to bring out the best of me too. "Are we ready for class?" I asked hopefully.

She nodded, throwing in one last handful of cereal. "Mmm rebby," she mumbled with her mouth full.

The walk to college was short because we lived just outside the campus. Georgia linked her arm through mine as we walked; telling me about the bars that we would visit tonight and which ones we had to avoid because they'd already rumbled our fake IDs.

When we finally arrived and started making our way up the steps into the main building, someone called my name behind me. I turned, automatically plastering on a fake smile because I knew that was to be expected of me.

As I turned I saw a guy with light brown hair that fell over his forehead and curled at the nape of his neck, and a shaggy, messy beard covered his face. His blue eyes met mine and crinkled around the edges as he smiled broadly. I frowned, a little bemused. I didn't recognise the guy at all, so had no idea how he would know my name.

"Hi," I greeted politely.

He laughed, and the sound struck a chord somewhere deep down inside me, but I had no idea why. "Don't you recognise me?" he asked, holding his hands out to the side and looking down at himself. I raked my eyes over him too. Taking in his cowboy boots, fitted jeans, his white button down shirt, and brown suit jacket that that he wore over the top. He held a single red rose in one hand. I looked back up at his face. His nose and lips looked a little familiar, but other than that, nothing.

"Should I?" I asked, raising one eyebrow in question.

He took a step closer to me and Georgia's hand wrapped around my forearm, pulling me closer to her. The guy noticed and grinned, shaking his head. "I won't hurt her, don't worry."

His voice. There was something about the way his words sounded and flowed, how his amusement coloured his tone. It was extremely familiar to me, but I couldn't place it.

"Still not recognise me? That hurts, little rebel," he teased.

My heart leapt into my throat at the nickname. "Zach?" I gasped, looking him over again and shaking my head in disbelief. He looked so different it was no wonder I hadn't known who he was.

A grin split his face. "The one and only," he confirmed cockily.

Before I could stop myself I'd taken the three steps and closed the distance between us, throwing my arms around him and hugging him tightly. Tears pooled in my eyes as he hugged me back, lifting me clean off my feet and crushing me against his chest. His smell filled my lungs as his familiarity washed over me, calming my senses and relaxing my muscles. I laughed, letting some of the stress leave my body. I'd missed him something chronic.

We still kept in touch regularly, emailing, texting and skyping, but I had only seen him in person once since I left home because his schedule was full and we couldn't ever get time to meet up. When I skyped with him two weeks ago he hadn't told me he was coming here – and he definitely didn't have long hair and a scruffy looking beard!

"What are you doing here? Why didn't you tell me you were coming, and what on earth is up with the big homeless person beard?" I cried, squeezing him tightly.

He laughed and set me back down on my feet, keeping one arm around my waist. "I'm working. I wanted to surprise you. And the beard is for the shoot," he answered my questions in turn, grinning from ear to ear.

My mouth dropped open in shock. They were filming a movie in and around our college at the moment and had been for the last couple of months. Apparently it was about a college professor who gets into trouble when he witnesses a murder of one of the students. They'd paid our college a lot of money to use the campus, and a lot of us even had roles as extras as we roamed the halls.

I looked around quickly now. Cameras, both handheld and mounted, were strewn everywhere. People sat around in wooden chairs eating and drinking food from the static caravan thing that was parked there. When they first arrived there had been a huge buzz about it all, but the novelty had worn off it now, so it was more of an inconvenience to the students because it meant we couldn't just cut across the middle of town to get to college, we had to take a longer route, and we had to be quiet all the time while the cameras were rolling. Apparently they were scheduled to do another month of shooting here at least before they moved off to another location. The film crew had been on campus for the past two months, and in that time we'd been fortunate enough to meet both Hugh Jackman and Charlize Theron. That had made Georgia's year.

"You're working? Here? On this movie?" I gasped, looking at him proudly. He hadn't mentioned anything about this at all. He'd told me he was trying desperately to get a part that he wanted, but he didn't say it was for this one.

He nodded. "Yep. You're looking at Hugh's body double and the lead stuntman for the movie," he boasted, smirking at me.

I let out a little squeal as I jumped on the spot. So far in his career he'd never been lead stuntman, only part of a team of them. "Zach, that's great!" I chirped, throwing myself at him for another hug. His beard scratched my cheek as I squeezed him tightly. "Though I'm not too sure about the hair and make-up," I added, fingering the back of his hair as I pulled back slightly. The hair felt weird, wiry, and I realised then that it was a wig.

He chuckled and nodded, rubbing along his jawline and turning his nose up. "I look like an old man, huh?" he mused.

"And you're wearing contacts," I observed, seeing that his eyes were blue instead of the usual chocolate brown. I preferred the brown if I was honest. Zach had lovely warm eyes and the contacts masked that.

"Yeah. They irritate like a son of a bitch," he muttered, blinking a couple of times.

I grinned, turning to look at Georgia as she touched my back. "It's nice to see you in person, Zach," she greeted. She'd spoken to him a couple of times when she'd been in my room when we'd skyped, but they'd never officially met. She turned to me and smiled apologetically. "We should get to class."

I frowned, turning back to Zach. I didn't want to go to class; I wanted to catch up with him. "Maybe I could skip and we could hang out?" I offered.

"Are you asking me out, Maisie?" he gasped, faking shock and putting his hand over his heart.

I laughed, feeling heat flood my face as I slapped his shoulder. "No!" I protested. "And you don't date anyway, so what's the point?" I added smugly. Zach still hadn't been out with anyone since I moved away. My talk with him on the day I left had obviously had no effect at all. He was just as single as I was.

He shrugged casually. "The only reason I haven't dated anyone for the last year and a half is because the only girl I've ever been interested in doesn't look at me in that way. I got friend zoned to the max. It doesn't help that she moved halfway across the country so I barely get to see her. Plus, she's not ready to date anyone yet after all the shit she went through," he replied. His head cocked to the side as he looked at me through the coloured contacts.

I shifted on my feet uncomfortably, dropping my eyes to the floor, not knowing what to say to the revelations. *Zach likes me, for real? Or is he joking?* I gulped and forced my eyes up to meet his. "I… I…" I stuttered, shaking my head. I wasn't really sure how to feel about my newfound knowledge. On the one hand, dating wasn't something I had ever considered, especially not dating Zach. But now that he'd said the words the idea of having someone there for me, of being part of something special, I missed that. And it wasn't as if I wasn't attracted to Zach, because I was, of course I was. He was handsome, funny, witty and thoughtful. But I wasn't sure I was ready for anything more, with anyone, let alone a friend that I held dear to me.

He smiled sadly. "You should go to class. I have a scene to shoot anyway. Maybe we could meet up for coffee after you're done? Catch up? By then I'll have this ridiculous get up off," he suggested, scratching up under the side of his wig and tugging on the lapel of his jacket. "Can't do anything about the facial hair though for a while, that's mine unfortunately and I have to keep it until they finish shooting," he added.

I chuckled awkwardly. "I actually don't mind the facial hair. In a weird way it kind of suits you," I admitted, smiling. I wasn't a beard kind of girl, but he actually pulled it off. "And I'd love to catch up." It was weird seeing him again in person. He was taller than I remembered, broader across the shoulders, like he'd maybe built a lot of muscle for the part or something. "How long do I have you for?" I asked, silently praying he wasn't going to disappear out of my life too quickly.

He raised a teasing eyebrow as a smirk slipped onto his face. "How long do you want me for?" he answered. I rolled my eyes and pushed on his shoulder playfully. He chuckled. "A month. I'm here for a month."

My heart leapt at that knowledge. A whole month of hanging out with Zach. It sounded fantastic. "Yeah? That's great!" I chirped, grinning from ear to ear. "I've missed you," I admitted, dragging my eyes over his features that I recognised, his straight nose and his full pink lips.

A smile tugged at the corners of his mouth. "I've missed you too," he replied. He brought his hand up, holding out the single red rose that I'd noticed earlier but not paid any attention to. "Happy valentine's day," he said softly, bending and planting a lingering kiss on my cheek.

His lips felt oddly beautiful on my skin. I closed my eyes, turning my head an inch towards his as my arm snaked up around his neck, clamping him to me. The hardness of his chest pressed against mine made my heart start to flutter and the hair on my scalp prickle with sensation. My breath caught in my throat as something I hadn't felt for a long time settled in the pit of my stomach. He pulled his mouth away from my cheek. His breath blew down my neck, and I suppressed a little shiver at the sensations that were invading my system.

More confused than I had been in a long time, I pulled back, looking into his now blue eyes. "Thanks for the rose," I whispered, chewing on my lip.

"You're welcome." He stepped back, letting his arms drop from my waist as he nodded over his shoulder. "I'd better get back, the crew will be wondering where I am. I'll meet you here at what time?" he asked.

"Three?" I suggested, shrugging.

He nodded, smiling that cocky smile that I remembered so well. "It's a date," he confirmed. Before I could protest and say anything about it not really being a date, he turned and jogged across the campus, effortlessly leaping the wooden barrier that cordoned off the film set, and was out of sight within seconds. I stood there, unable to move as I watched the last place that I'd seen Zachary Anderson. Suddenly I realised what that feeling was that I'd felt when he'd kissed my cheek. The feeling was so alien after so long that I hadn't recognised it at first, but now I knew, and I wasn't sure how to deal with that knowledge. The feeling had been longing, need, happiness and contentment.

I could feel a blush forming, creeping up my neck and slowly filling my whole face as I looked down at the rose that I held in my hand. My lips twitched with a smile as I brought it to my nose, inhaling the sweet aroma. A month was a long time but, seeing him now, it didn't seem nearly long enough.

The End

Made in the USA
Monee, IL
12 September 2020

42260045R00166